THE
WEATHER
WOMAN

THE
WEATHER
WOMAN

SALLY GARDNER

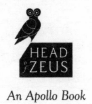

An Apollo Book

First published in the UK in 2022 by Head of Zeus Ltd,
part of Bloomsbury Publishing Plc

9 7 5 3 1 2 4 6 8

A catalogue record for this book is available from
the British Library.

ISBN (HB): 9781786695253
ISBN (XTPB): 9781838931698
ISBN (E): 9781786695246

Typeset by Divaddict Publishing Solutions

Printed and bound in Great Britain by
CPI Group (UK) Ltd, Croydon CR0 4YY

Head of Zeus Ltd
5–8 Hardwick Street
London EC1R 4RG

WWW.HEADOFZEUS.COM

For Becky Congreve.

For my darling Aunt Jo.

The silver Thames was frozen O'er
No difference Twixt the stream and shore
The likes no man had seen before
Except he lived in days of yore.

Printed on the ice at the printing office, opposite
St Catherine's Stairs, in the severe frost of January 1789

Saturday 17.– The captain of a vessel lying off
Rotherhithe, the better to secure the ships cables, made
an agreement with a publican for fastening a cable to
his premises; in consequence, a small anchor was carried
on shore and deposited in the cellar, while another cable
was fastened round a beam in another part of the house.
In the night the ship veered about, and the cables holding
fast, carried away the beam and levelled the house with
the ground; by which accident five persons asleep in
their beds were killed.

Famous Frosts and Frost Fairs in Great Britain
William Andrews, F.R.H.S.
Printed in London in 1887
400 copies were printed

Part One

Dear Courteous Reader,

On the 25th of November last year a frost set in which lasted seven weeks. It was recorded that the thermometer stood at 11 degrees below freezing point in the very midst of the city. The Thames was frozen at London Bridge and the ice on the river assumed all the appearances of a frost fair.

I

Thursday, 15th January 1789

This January Jack Frost has sunk his freezing fingers into the Thames and the river below London Bridge is silenced by ice. The watermen, quick to make money, begin to charge a toll to help tentative visitors climb down onto the glassy surface, the stage for an improvised frost fair. Here, for two weeks, all sorts of entertainments are on display: dancing bears, jugglers, puppet shows, exhibitions of wild beasts. A tented street built of rowing boats and canvas springs up, selling gifts. There are booths with gingerbread and alcohol aplenty. One ferryman has the bright idea to make a paper boat to pull his customers across the frozen surface. The fair folk are masters of the entertainments and London is transformed into a land of winter merriment. Such jollity makes people reluctant to leave, and even though they know the frost never holds a permanent footing, it does not stop the crowds of visitors.

Amid the bustle one small child crouches and listens intently to the ice and the unearthly sound it's making. She tries to mimic what she hears. She thinks about the fish frozen stiff beneath the feet of the crowd.

Her father calls.

'Neva!' He picks up his little daughter. 'We have a show to do. I told you to stay in the tent.'

She sings the song of melting ice to him as he walks with purpose towards a red and white striped tent.

Mr Cutter, known as the Bosun though retired from the sea, does a roaring business when the river freezes, letting booths to fair folk. He is waiting by the entrance of a tent where a sign reads *The Unbeaten Chess-Playing Bear*. He has still to be paid for the rental of this one.

The Russian and his wife are notorious for their rows. He has heard they have a child.

'Is this your daughter, Mr Tarshin?' asks Mr Cutter. 'A pretty little thing – such black eyes and hair.'

Her father nods. Mr Cutter holds back until the oil lamp is lit and then follows him inside the tent.

There, emerging from the darkness into the light, stands the chess-playing bear. It casts an inky black shadow over the back of the tent. The child knows that when no one is looking the bear moves around, hungrily sniffing out her mother, waiting to gobble her up.

'Not a word from you and no singing,' says her father, putting Neva behind a straw bale. 'Did you hear me, girl? Not a word.'

He speaks to Mr Cutter, assuring him he will have his money tomorrow. Or, if he wishes, he can take the pretty child instead, at a bargain price of course. Mr Cutter laughs but Neva knows her father means it. When he's drunk, he often argues with her mother, saying they should leave her in a church for the parish to look after, or give her away to someone who would want her. He says it would be for the best. These arguments usually end with another bottle until they no longer remember what they were arguing over.

Years later, when Neva thinks back to this time in her life, some things appear brighter in her memory even as other images fade. How much she has pieced together with the wisdom of age, she cannot tell. For these events will be recounted to her by Mr Cutter who remembers Andre Tarshin, the arm-wrestling champion from Russia, his petite wife Olga, and, of course, the chess-playing bear.

Colours, Neva feels, are more reliable for the truth of her emotions. Her mother was red, orange, a flash of lightning yellow. Her father, ice-blue steel and greyish black. They were two weather fronts that collided to make a storm. She was born into the tempest of them, with no way of escaping from the eye of their fury or her mother's hard hands. The terror of being washed away in one of her parents' rages will forever haunt her.

This afternoon Neva stays forgotten in her hiding place. She is scared of the chess-playing bear, with its lopsided snout and staring glass eyes that open and shut. Every day the bear eats a little bit more of her mother.

For what will be the last time, she watches Olga climb into the bear's belly. Andre's giant hands make sure she is sewn in tight. Then he moves the automaton and connects it with the cabinet on which the chessboard sits. The magnets on the bases of the chess pieces show Olga her opponent's moves while she works the bear's paw with a series of levers that grasp the pieces, lifting them into position. On a small table sits a candelabrum. Finally, a large mirror is placed behind the bear so the audience can see its moves.

The reputation of the chess-playing bear has spread well beyond the frozen river and this evening two elegantly dressed gentlemen walk to the front of the queue. The drunker of the two boasts he can beat the old fleabag and wagers twenty guineas.

'Let me see your money first, sir,' says Andre.

'Here,' the man replies, taking the coins from his purse.

Andre tries not to show his desperation. The sum of money on offer is a king's ransom and would mean he would be able to pay the clockmaker to redesign the automaton.

Mr Cutter is there. At least here's a chance he'll be paid but he can see Mr Tarshin hesitate.

'Go on, Mr Tarshin,' he urges quietly.

'The bear always plays black,' says Andre to the gentleman.

All Neva can hear is the ice groaning under the weight of the people. Why can't anyone else hear the song it's singing? She feels it in her belly, an unearthly sound, angels calling out a warning.

The drunken gentleman sits with his back to the audience. 'Be prepared to pay up, Russian,' he says, making his opening move.

The tilted mirror shows the game being played. When the bear lifts a chess piece it is accompanied by a mechanical, clockwork noise.

'This scrawny old fleabag will never win against me,' says the young gentleman.

In fewer than ten moves he has lost.

He turns to his companion. 'Well! I'll be damned,' he says.

'My dear friend, I'll win it back for you.'

'That's another twenty guineas, sir,' says Andre.

The tent is full of people, standing rather than sitting on the straw bales to better see the game. The second young dandy sits languidly in the chair, one arm stretched out, his hand resting on the silver top of his ebony cane. As he rocks it back and forth Neva catches a glimpse of his ring glittering in the dark. She watches his demeanour change from nonchalance to intense concentration. In less than half an hour he too is beaten and his gloved hand knocks the chess pieces to the ground.

'It's a trick,' he snaps, rising to his feet. 'A cheat.'

Andre, who has been expecting this reaction, moves forward, as does Mr Cutter, and Mr Cutter, having the better English, says, 'You chose to bet, sir. You lost, you pay. Now leave.'

Knowing he is outmatched, the dandy says, 'I would like to meet the man who's inside there.' He pokes his cane into the bear's fur.

Mr Cutter holds Neva's father back.

When they are all gone and Mr Cutter has received his money, Andre closes the tent flap to make sure there are no prying eyes before he goes behind the bear and removes the stitches.

'I am unbeatable,' says Olga.

'Nevertheless,' says Andre, pulling her, hot and sweaty, out of the bear's belly, 'we have to pack up and go.'

'Why? I could beat Catherine the Great,' she protests.

'But no one beats the ice,' says Andre. 'We are leaving, don't make me say it again.'

'Why? Why?'

'Because the ice is going soft. The child thinks it's—'

'You are soft – in the head,' snaps Olga. 'She is three and thinks nothing, you superstitious old fool.'

Andre takes no notice, packs up the cabinet and the bear and loads the handcart. It's just before dusk when they start for the shore on the Surrey side of the river. Andre takes his daughter's hand and Olga follows, pushing the cart, grumbling loudly. Neva listens to the high-pitched notes of the ice singing its farewell song.

Suddenly behind them is a frantic rush of people. Andre quickly lifts Neva onto his shoulders and tells her to hold tight. Grabbing the bear with both hands he shouts to Olga to run. People push past them but Andre strides toward the shore where he leaves Neva on the bank with the bear.

'Hold onto him,' he orders.

She clutches the bear as her father rushes back to help Olga. Neva sees him lift the cart, hears Mama scream.

'Andre, don't leave me!'

He reaches out his hand for her. She hesitates. Amid the mayhem, the ice is on the move.

'Olga!' he yells as he puts the cart down.

She leaps. He catches her and they slip down onto the riverbank. He pulls her to her feet, puts Neva on his shoulders again and lifts up the bear. Olga drags the cart up the shore and only when safely away from the river do they look back to see the scene they've left behind. It is one of chaos, everything in motion. The ice has cracked and broken free. People on the shore frantically call out for those still on the ice to jump to safety. The Tarshins watch in horror as those unable to save themselves are carried away down the river, their shouts for help disappearing into the night.

'I hope those two buffoons drown,' says Olga.

Neva has her hands over her eyes. She peeps through her fingers as the Punch and Judy man screams.

'The devil! Do something!'

The river answers as only a river can and he sinks beneath its freezing silver waters.

The next day their wagon is fully packed and they set off towards Kent. On the way her father stops to visit the clockmaker, Victor Friezland, who is well known for making automatons. He had said he could help Andre refine the chess-playing bear.

The housekeeper answers the door. Her master has gone to Kent, but he is expected back tomorrow.

'Who shall I say called?'

'Andre Tarshin.'

'We should stay in Southwark,' says Olga.

'No, we must go further. It's too costly,' replies Andre.

'It's thanks to me, you pig-headed, salty man, that we have money enough to stay in a decent inn and amuse ourselves with the sights.'

Every word Olga speaks goads Neva's father and the bitter easterly wind howls their frosty words back and forth as they make their slow, argumentative way towards Rotherhithe.

Neva sits huddled in the covered wagon next to the overworked chess-playing bear. It stands upright and is held fast with ropes. The wind finds its way through the metal structure so the creature sounds as if it's gently moaning.

'Why didn't they know?' she asks.

'Know what?' says her mama.

'That the ice was melting.'

'Ridiculous child. What are you talking about? No one could have known that. You see?' she turns to Andre. 'Look what you've done with all the nonsense you talk. Stuffed the child's head full of damp straw.'

'But I knew,' says Neva, more to the bear than to Olga.

They stop at a riverside inn, her parents leaving her in the wagon with only the bear for company. Its prickly fur is frozen stiff. After several such stops, Mama and Father are fighting drunk. By the time the light begins to fade, Neva is cold, hungry and miserable. She has no words for the sick feeling in her head. When she closes her eyes, she sees the screaming puppet man. While there is still a little light she tries not to look at the river but concentrates on the clouds as she curls into herself. Her eyes close and she slips into sleep.

She wakes in a blizzard to find the chess-playing bear gone. For a terrifying moment that yawns into forever, she thinks her parents have finally abandoned her. She pushes back the canvas flaps of the wagon, stands up and screams, feeling the words rise raw in her throat. 'Mama! Father!'

Nothing. Just the ice cracking in the river and the whistling of the rigging of tall ships frozen in the water.

Neva has all but given up crying for help when she sees, coming towards her, a lantern waving in the snow. The innkeeper, muttering curses, scoops her up, calling for his wife. It takes her a while to realise he is not furious with her but with her parents.

'She should never have been left out in the wagon on such an atrocious night as this,' he says, handing her to his wife's warm embrace. 'Why, the little mite's half-frozen.'

The inn is full of sailors, drunkenly singing sea shanties. Neva, who is well used to crowds, isn't frightened by the raucous rhythm of the songs.

'Drunken idiots – shouldn't be allowed to have children.'

Neva doesn't know if the innkeeper's wife means the sailors or her parents. She will never forget the meal they give her, the potatoes, soft and fluffy, with steak and kidney pie. She enjoys feeling full. She must have fallen asleep because she wakes with a start to find a group of sailors, all swaying as if the waves are still beneath them, carrying a small anchor.

'Where's the cellar?' they shout, and the innkeeper shows them.

Neva can hear the ice arguing with the thaw; it makes a taut, high-pitched sound which she supposes drunken ears can't hear.

The innkeeper's wife takes her upstairs to her parents' room and knocks hard on the door.

There is no answer, so she lifts the latch and says to Neva, 'They must be sleeping. Go in quietly. See you in the morning.'

Neva can just make out her father's shape and her mother's thin form in the dark. They seem to be tangled round each other in the bed. There is no room for her. The bear, its glass eyes wide open, stands sentinel over their belongings. She stumbles near the bed and her father puts out his hand, not to embrace his little daughter but to push her away.

Her mother says sleepily, 'Quiet.'

There is nothing else to do. Exhausted, Neva covers herself as best she can with the clothes lying on the floor. Something familiar presses hard into her. She finds it and holds it tight in her hand. She can still hear the ice moving in the river.

She wakes with a start, not sure if she's dreaming. As the shutter swings open and the moon shines in, a picture falls to the floor and the chamber pot and chairs dance across the room. She looks up to see that the bear, shimmering and shaking, has come to life. It wobbles, topples and falls forward, banging her hard on the head as it pins her down. For a moment there is nothing. Then she comes to and in the mouth of thunder a floorboard snaps. The room is being pulled apart. Beams come crashing to the floor, plaster explodes in a fog of dust, walls pulsate, and ceilings fall on top of the chess-playing bear that now holds Neva safe in its steely embrace.

She hears muffled cries and groans around her, but when she calls out for her parents, they don't answer her. They have left her for good. The destruction slows down and then all is eerily quiet.

The stillness that surrounds her after the inn has come tumbling down holds an unfathomable peace. In this hush comes a feeling of detachment, of floating high among the clouds in a lullaby.

She thinks someone asks her, 'What do you want, little one?'

She replies in a whisper, 'Home.'

2

January 1789

Victor Friezland, the clockmaker, has hired a coach so he might deliver a carriage clock to a client in Kent and having done so he is on his way home to Southwark. The confounded carriage is freezing, his boots are in a straw box and the blanket wrapped round him smells of horse. His bones ache with cold, his fingers numb, and he feels the blue dog descending on him as it often does. It matters little, he tells himself, it's because of the weather, nothing more. Still the familiar feeling of failure haunts him. He thinks back to his marriage, if you could call it that. A farce. He hasn't seen the boy since he was three months old. Victor's good fortune has been to find an excellent housekeeper. In his experience, they are as rare as hen's teeth. Lord knows how he would manage without her. He remembers when he was a young man; he had such hopes and dreams: a big family, a happy home, but that was another life, not to be his.

'How long?' he asks the driver.

'We're coming to Rotherhithe, sir. Not far now to Southwark and it's always easy to find your house.'

That's true. He'd built his home from materials he'd found at ship salvage yards – doors, balustrades, staircases, planking, a captain's galley, even a balcony or two that in early summer are wreathed in wisteria and jasmine. It is an original home, unlike any other. He has an orchard at the back, a vegetable garden and lawns that slope down to the banks of the Thames where he keeps a boat.

He thinks that this spring he will plant asparagus. But you only plant asparagus if you have children, it takes so long to grow. No, he'll do turnips as usual. Thoughts of vegetables run through his mind, which is better than dwelling on the past.

Suddenly the carriage jolts and Victor flies off his seat as the coach comes to an unnatural stop.

'Sorry, sir,' says the coachman, quickly climbing down to inspect the damage. He swears softly. 'It's the wheel rim.'

Victor joins him to have a look but it's no good, the coachman hasn't the right tools.

'The George isn't far,' says the driver, naming a coaching inn.

Neither is my house, Victor thinks miserably and wonders if he shouldn't perhaps walk the distance. If it wasn't snowing, he would be tempted. A funeral procession couldn't go slower than the carriage as it limps along until it collapses into the yard of the George. Victor Friezland climbs out, promising himself that if he ever is such a fool as to set out in inhospitable weather again, he will first buy a proper greatcoat and a warm muffler, and hire a decent, well-maintained carriage.

The inn is busy and he enquires if they are serving food. He stands near the fire, warming himself while a waiter prepares a table for him. He glances in the mirror above the fireplace and sees a ghost girl reflected in the smoky glass. He turns but finds no one there. This day, he says to himself, would have been better if I hadn't risen until Sunday.

'Your table's ready, sir,' says the waiter and shows him to the coffee room. To Victor's surprise he is the only diner there.

'No one else eating?' he asks.

'No, sir. There's been a dreadful accident not far away at one of the riverside inns. The magistrate and the constable were called and they brought the survivors here.'

Victor doesn't register the tragedy. Perhaps his mind is so cold it's no longer functioning. At last food and a hot toddy warm his bones and he feels sufficiently human to take in his surroundings and ask what happened at the riverside inn.

The waiter says, 'It's terrible and it could have been avoided. A ship was frozen in the ice and the captain, unable to drop anchor on account of it, thought instead to secure the ship to the inn. The crew put the small anchor in the cellar and tied the ropes to the beams. The ice and the ship moved in the night and brought the whole inn down. Five persons are believed dead.'

Victor has paid his bill and been informed that the carriage wheel is mended when the waiter says, 'But a child survived. That gives you hope. The little mite was found curled up under a chess-playing bear.'

Victor asks the waiter to repeat what he'd said.

Three weeks previously he had met an arm-wrestling champion from Russia named Andre Tarshin, who was the owner of a chess-playing bear. It had been a great sensation at the fairs because the bear hadn't lost a single game. It was a crudely made automaton and the Russian wanted the workings of the bear to be more sophisticated. Victor had offered to help next time the Russian was in London. Thinking about him now, he can't imagine that hard-drinking furnace of a man was married, let alone the father of a child.

He is about to leave when the door to the coffee room opens, and there stands the same small ghost girl he saw in the mirror. She is covered in a film of white dust and has a bandage wrapped round her head. She studies Victor, and then, as if she has made up her mind, walks purposefully towards him.

A woman runs up behind the child and takes her arm. 'No, no, no! We told you, you're to stay seated, you're not allowed in the coffee room.'

The little ghost girl pulls her arm away. Victor is impressed by her determination to speak to him.

'You will have to learn to do as you're told,' says the woman.

'Madam, where will she go?' asks Victor.

'I don't know as yet. It's being decided by the magistrate. I can tell you this, our parish doesn't need any more orphans, especially not ones talking gibberish and born with no manners or respect for their elders.'

'That's a harsh judgement to make,' says Victor. 'Especially as you haven't understood a word the little girl is saying.'

'A heathen, that's what she is! I can always tell a heathen.'

'Let the child speak for herself.'

'Speak?' snorts the woman. 'I wouldn't call it speaking.'

Victor bends down to the child's height. The woman straightens herself, indignantly dusting the dirt off her gloves.

The child says, 'Do you have a home?'

'Yes, I have a home,' Victor replies.

'I've been waiting for you,' says the ghost girl. 'I knew you would come.'

Victor feels her little hand in his and a shiver goes up his spine. As if in a dream, he hears himself saying, 'Perhaps I have been waiting for you too. I just didn't know it.'

He looks into the child's dark eyes that have a flash of lightning about them.

'You understand all that?' asks the woman, quite taken aback.

'Yes,' says Victor Friezland. 'She is speaking Russian.'

'And you speak Russian?'

'I do.'

What he doesn't say is Russian is his mother tongue. He feels the child's grasp of his fingers stronger now. He bends down again to ask the ghost girl her name.

'Neva.'

'It's a lovely name,' says Victor. He's surprised at himself for usually he is such a ditherer. But in this moment, he is resolute. 'I must see the magistrate. I knew this little girl's father and I would like to relieve your parish of the onerous duty of having to care for her a moment longer than necessary.'

Elise Gibbs has been with Victor for ten years, ever since his wife left him. He was barely twenty then, not much more than a boy. She manages his house as if it is a museum. The cupboards are meticulously organised, the sheets carefully starched and the utensils always shining. She takes great pride in her work. A meal has been prepared and the fires lit in the long drawing room, yet there is no sign of Victor. News has reached her about the accident at the inn. It's all anyone in the neighbourhood is talking about, although the details are hazy. Some say five died, some say more. A terrible thought comes to her. But no, the master wouldn't have changed his plans and spent the night there. Then again, he can be quite absent-minded at times, particularly when he's working on a design for a clock or an automaton. There's something very childlike and endearing about her master, and yet there's a profound sadness in him too.

A sense of dread comes over her. She sees him attacked by highwaymen or thrown from that rickety old carriage he hired. Now having thoroughly scared herself she waits anxiously by the front door, imagining the very worst.

It's still snowing when she hears the carriage pull up outside the gate. Taking the lantern with her, she goes out to

greet Victor and for a moment she can't make out what it is
he's carrying. He calls out for a link boy and now Mrs Gibbs
is truly worried.

'Are you all right, sir?'

'I want the lad to fetch a doctor,' he says by way of
explanation, which explains nothing at all to Mrs Gibbs.

'Sir,' she says, 'are you hurt?'

'No, but the child is.'

Child? What child? She lifts the lantern closer and sees the
face of a small girl, covered in dust and blood, with a filthy
bandage round her head.

'Lord in heaven,' she says.

'There's been an accident,' he says.

'So I heard. Let's get her inside.'

The child hasn't said a word, not one word, since they got
in the carriage. In the drawing room Mrs Gibbs fetches a
bowl of hot water, and in front of the fire she gently washes
Neva. Still she is quiet. By the time the doctor arrives she's
clean and dressed in one of Victor's nightshirts and propped
up in an armchair. Wordlessly she clings to Mrs Gibbs when
the doctor examines her. After he's gone Mrs Gibbs makes
up a bed in the room next to hers and Victor carries Neva
upstairs.

Only then does the child speak. '*Mogu ya ostat'sya zdes?*'
she says.

'*Da,*' says Victor.

'What does that mean?' asks Mrs Gibbs.

'"Can I stay here?"' says Victor.

'What language is it?'

'Russian.'

'And you understand Russian?'

'Yes, I myself am from Russia.'

Mrs Gibbs is unsure what to say. She knew her master
wasn't born in England, but that was all.

They look at Neva, who is fast asleep.

'Would you join me for a drink?' asks Victor. 'I don't know about you, but I certainly need one.'

'What about your supper?'

'Nothing to eat, thank you, Mrs Gibbs. Just a strong drink.'

In the long drawing room, Victor stands in front of the fire, a brandy in his hand.

'The woman looking after the child called her a heathen. I remember when I first arrived in London, I couldn't speak English and I was called that – and worse.'

'Where in Russia are you from, sir?' asks Mrs Gibbs, trying not to appear too nosy.

Victor seems lost in his own thoughts and for a moment she thinks he hasn't heard her. 'I came from Saint Petersburg when I was about ten years old,' he says at last. 'I was an orphan and was sent to live with a distant relative, a cruel bastard, if you'll forgive my language, but at least he taught me a trade.' He pauses for a moment. 'But that is by the by. I'm not sure I can be a good father to this child. Look what happened with Aubrey.'

'If you don't mind my saying so, sir, I believe your wife was in love with another man.'

'Yes, indeed. And I, like a fool, still married her. But she always hated this house, thought it a disgrace, and so off she ran, baby and all, to the redheaded lieutenant.'

Mrs Gibbs has heard that Aubrey has the same colour hair as the lieutenant but she doesn't mention it. Instead she says, 'You're a good man, an honourable man. You have tried and tried to see the boy.'

'Thank you, Mrs Gibbs.' He thinks for a moment. 'I'm not expecting you to take on any more work. I'll hire a nurse and a governess.'

'But, sir—'

'Please – Elise,' interrupts Victor, 'we have known each

other long enough, perhaps it's time to do away with formalities. Call me Victor.'

'There's something about the child that made you bring her home – Victor – and I don't think it was just the language. I don't need any extra help and, as for a governess, surely you would make a far better teacher.'

'Do you really think so? When her hand found mine, I knew I couldn't leave her. Perhaps you're right, together we might be able to do this.'

'I believe we can, Victor.'

'When I was small, I was completely lost, like the child,' Victor says quietly, staring into the heart of the fire. 'I would tell myself there was a ladder to the moon in someone's attic, in some house, somewhere, in this vast, lonely city and it was just a matter of knowing where it was. I used to think if I could find that ladder, well, perhaps all the other impossible things might become possible.'

Elise smiles and says, 'Perhaps today you found that ladder.'

3

At the clockmaker's house, the child hardly dares breathe in case the enchantment is broken, for the bed is soft, the nightshirt crisp and food is plentiful. Victor and Mrs Gibbs are kind, there's nothing harsh about them, no jagged edges and no hard, unforgiving hands. They are two clouds from a sunset, soft pinks and pale purples, they blend together.

Before the mattress holds the shape of Neva, only the doctor is a grey fog. He comes many times and the child is fearful that he's going to take her away and everything will start moving once more. She lies in her bed, looking through the porthole window at the sky and singing the rain. Neva can make the sound without opening her mouth.

The doctor is concerned but Mrs Gibbs says, 'She often sings like that. I think it's beautiful.'

'By my reckoning the child is about three,' he tells Victor. 'But she may well have suffered a more severe head injury than I first thought and it might affect her ability to learn.'

Neva wonders why the doctor hasn't had the foresight to bring an umbrella with him for it's going to rain. When he leaves she goes back to looking at the sky, following every cloud, for each one tells her the story of the weather to come.

At night, she fears going to sleep because when the bedchamber door is closed, the chess-playing bear's mangled remains creep into her room and stand at the end of her bed, waiting.

She wakes screaming, the sheets are wet and she daren't move. Mrs Gibbs picks her up and hugs her until the bear leaves her chamber followed by the Punch and Judy man. Mrs Gibbs cheerfully changes the bed and once more she is tucked up. Neva calls Mrs Gibbs 'Auntie' and Victor 'Papa'.

One night she wakes, the bed isn't wet and, instead of screaming, she walks straight past Mr Punch who shouts out:

'Catch her, Judy, and give her a whack,

For not wanting her parents back.'

The bear is waiting by the stairs and she hears his belly rumble, just where her mother used to be. Neva doesn't run, although her heart is in her mouth; instead she lets herself into Papa's bedchamber, where she is sure the bear and Mr Punch can't follow.

Inside there is a candle on the night table illuminating the four-poster bed. The curtain isn't closed and Victor is lying with a nightcap on his head and Auntie asleep in his arms. Neva climbs in unnoticed and sleeps without dreams. She is too young to understand she has inadvertently given a blessing to what Victor calls his great love. Elise blushingly calls Victor her 'dear fool'.

Here is the family Victor has always wished for. According to Elise, it was on this night Neva finally uncurled her fist and revealed the carved, black, wooden knight from the chess-playing bear.

'Perhaps,' says Auntie, 'the bear only comes to this house because he's looking for the missing chess piece. If we leave it outside your bedchamber door, I'm sure he'll not bother you again.'

Neva thinks, but what about Mr Punch?

The doctor is partly right. Neva is not like other children, but then Victor is not like other men. He is intrigued by his little daughter's way of seeing the sky; how it seems as if she is always singing the weather. He has never heard anyone do that before. For the first time he thinks of the weather as the music of the heavens. As for Neva, she is still little enough to believe that everyone can do what she can.

For his part, Victor wishes he could agree with her. Instead he tells her no man has the skill to know what the weather has in store.

Neva looks at him, full of doubt, before asking, 'But are you sure?'

He tries to explain that the sky is the realm of the Lord Almighty and between the sky and the stars there is Heaven.

The tide changes, time passes, and Neva follows her papa every day to his workshop with a skip and a hop. Three hops to be precise and exactly one clap of her hands as she reaches the door, just so the spiders might know she's coming. There is a precise order to their day, which starts with lighting the stove and the lamps. The roof of the workshop is the upturned keel of a boat that looks to Neva like the ribs of a whale. Here, in its belly, she feels safe among Victor's clocks and automatons – singing birds chirping in cages and dancing ballerinas. Amid this theatre of clockwork and half-made things, she has no desire to be anywhere else.

Sometimes he asks her, 'Aren't you bored? You can always go indoors and help Auntie.'

She has recently decided she is not going to answer foolish questions. How can she be bored? She is fascinated by the clocks Papa makes. If there were no clocks, she wonders, would that mean there was no time?

But it is the stories she tells herself that keep her the most entertained. In her imagination she has made up a whole kingdom of palaces, castles, dragons, princes and princesses; a place where there are no chess-playing bears. It is in this inner world she discovers a cloud walker; he is a little older than she and his name is Eugene Jonas. He will only come down to earth when she needs him. He, too, likes Victor's workshop. He likes the whole house, which is more galleon than house, and Neva wonders if the timbers miss the oceans and what the portholes once looked out on. Books, she thinks, would have the answers, so Eugene Jonas teaches her to read from a manual on grandfather clocks. Unlike Papa, Master Jonas has a London accent and refuses to speak Russian; he tells her she must learn English. It doesn't take her long to master the words in the manual.

She asks Papa, 'Do you have any books someone my age might like to read?'

Victor looks up from his work and says, 'I'll teach you to read when you're a little older.'

'Oh, there's no need. Master Eugene Jonas has already done that.'

'And who is Eugene Jonas?' asks Victor, amused.

'A friend who comes and goes,' she says.

'A friend?'

'Don't worry, Papa. He's only a made-up friend. I don't think I want any other kind. What I would like is more books and so would Master Jonas.'

Victor puts down the timepiece he is working on and, picking up a book from his desk, asks, 'Can you read these words?'

'Yes,' she says, and she reads to him. He laughs. 'Why am I funny?'

He hugs her. 'You are very clever, Neva, just like your mother. She was a chess master, I believe.'

'Will you teach me to play chess?'

Victor has read the works of many of the women thinkers of the day in France and in England. He found he agreed with the importance of young women having a breadth of knowledge and, unlike many fathers who see the education of girls as unnecessary, he takes enormous pleasure in educating his daughter. He teaches her French, which she thirstily drinks in. Soon he finds he is unable to beat her at chess. She learns Mathematics, Geography, History and English, subjects she is not particularly interested in, until Victor finds a way of relating them to the weather. He buys the almanack for the year and now he has Neva's full attention. She is fascinated by the astrological predictions and the meteorological observations.

She says to Victor, 'You see there are people who can predict the weather.'

'No,' says Victor, 'the almanack is compiled for the year that's just passed.'

Neva is crestfallen.

He reads her Aristotle's *Meteorology*, which she declares to be a fairy tale. He buys her a barometer, which she names 'The Cheating Wizard'.

'It can't really predict the weather,' she says. 'It merely pretends to and what use is there in that?'

The older she becomes, the more she reads the sky. In good weather she sits for hours on the whale back of the workshop roof and here she stays, looking out over London, and dreaming of different skies in different worlds.

One May afternoon, while hanging upside down amid the blossom of an apple tree, she sees a face she hasn't forgotten.

Mr Cutter the Bosun has come from the river into the orchard. Looking at him this way, he has a sad, upside-down face.

'Hallo,' he says, smiling. 'What does the world look like to you up there?'

It's a good question and Neva is fond of those. 'Different,' she says. 'You look sad. And sadder still when you smile.'

'What if I do this?' says Mr Cutter and he stands on his head.

And that way they talk about the river and Neva tells him she wishes to learn to row.

'If you row, you must be able to swim,' says Mr Cutter. 'A sailor who can't swim is as good as a drowned man to his captain.'

Victor comes out of his workshop and the sight that greets him is so ridiculous he bursts out laughing. Neva giggles and Mr Cutter, embarrassed, springs nimbly to his feet. He picks up his hat and brushes grass from his hands.

'Sir,' he says, 'I...'

'Most impressive,' says Victor.

'Mr Friezland,' says Mr Cutter, 'I had hoped to introduce myself in a more dignified manner.'

'Papa,' says Neva, jumping down from the tree, 'Mr Cutter and I have been talking and we have an idea.'

It seems to Neva when she thinks back to the rosy days of her childhood that the fulfilment of the idea was simple, though she supposes it couldn't have been, knowing how anxious Papa would become over anything he deemed dangerous. She imagines there must have been many conversations between him and Auntie and exhaustive enquiries made regarding the character of Mr Cutter.

There is no escaping the fact that Neva is never destined to be a little girl who sits demurely at her needlework. As she says to Elise, she has springs in her slippers. Elise is more concerned with the immodesty of a girl hanging out of a tree with her skirts tucked in her pantaloons and now proposing to learn to row.

Neva has never liked the notion of leaving the house and its gardens. She is fearful that if she does, it will all vanish, the enchantment broken, and she might never be allowed back here again.

Elise and Victor try to take her out but it causes her such distress and ends with her saying, 'I would like to go home, please. Now, please.'

But Auntie is right. 'If you're going to learn to row, you'll have to leave the house,' she says.

'Of course,' says Neva. But the conflict is too great and there is only one way to comfort herself. She finds a piece of loose skin on her index finger and works at it. It's painless to start with but the deeper she goes, the more intense the agony. When the flap of skin is off, she feels a surge of relief, and her fear subsides in that moment.

'Neva!' says Auntie, too late. She takes Neva's hands, applies the balm she keeps by for such an injury then wraps the finger in a cloth. She sits Neva down. 'It follows that you will need boy's clothes,' says Elise. 'And I can't buy them on my own.'

'What if I can never, ever leave this house? What happens then?' says Neva. She tries to fiddle with her fingers, desperate to find another piece of skin that will give her as much satisfaction.

'No, no,' says Auntie, holding her hands tight. 'That's not the right question. The question I want to ask you is: what do you think will happen if you do leave the house?'

'It will melt away and Death will know where to find us.'

'Death is what we're born with, Neva. It's the only certainty in our lives.'

Neva feels a lump of rage in her throat. Torn skin. To be torn away from here. 'It's no good. I won't be able to learn to row,' she says, trying not to cry.

'I don't like leaving this house either, but for another reason.'

'You don't? What do you think will happen?'

'I'm afraid someone – someone I know – might find me. I'm not telling you more. But what if we try this together? Remember we have Eugene Jonas with us.'

'Yes, he'll help us. And if...'

'And if not, we'll come home.'

Neva hardly sleeps. Auntie suggests she write down everything that she's frightened of, then roll up the paper, put it in a bottle and let the tide take away her fears.

Neva watches the bottle float away as the sun rises in golds and reds on a new day. That morning, Papa makes sure the hackney carriage comes to the gate and once Auntie and Neva are inside and the wheels begin to move Neva waits for panic to engulf her. When it doesn't, she starts to laugh.

'What is it?' asks Auntie, anxiously.

'I think,' says Neva, 'I'm excited to be going out.'

They spend the day in Cheapside, looking in the shop windows. They stop to watch soldiers in their blue coats march down the street to the beating of a drum, with a little lad skipping behind blowing a tin whistle. Eventually they find a small tailor's shop that keeps items customers haven't collected.

'You'll be as tall as me soon,' Elise whispers to Neva as they pick out a pair of boy's breeches, shirt, waistcoat and short jacket.

Neva is thrilled with their purchases. Elise hires a waterman to take them home. In the boat, Neva says, 'I think I will be able to leave the house, now.'

'I never doubted it,' says Auntie.

When it comes to her first rowing lesson she tells Victor not to worry: she won't be going on the river.

'No?' he says.

'No, I'm leaving Neva in my bedchamber. Mr Cutter will teach Eugene Jonas how to row.'

The freedom she finds in wearing breeches is a revelation. If gentlemen were drowning in fabric, she thinks, cities would never be built and wars never fought. Under her cap she makes a respectable lad but Mr Cutter warns her not to speak as her voice would give her away.

It doesn't take her long to master the oars and learn the ebbs and flows of the river. Mr Cutter's pupil, Master Jonas, becomes known along the riverbank. And here among the ferry boats and the bargemen, she begins to see how vital to them knowledge of the weather is. But she's puzzled. Why can't they see when the weather is changing? Why do ships' captains set sail into storms? And on land, why do builders start work on a roof in a high wind? Even Mr Cutter doesn't know. She is forever telling him which days are good for her rowing lessons. He admits she has a knack for predicting the weather conditions but adds that only the Lord himself knows what mysteries the skies hold.

Neva thinks that can't be right. She starts to keep beautifully illustrated weather diaries. Victor, while most impressed with her drawings, doesn't take much notice of the daily predictions recorded there. Neither does he realise they are for days yet to come. If he had done so, it would not have taken him so long to find out she had a gift, an extraordinary ability accurately to foretell the weather.

★★★

At night Eugene Jonas stands at the end of her bed. She asks him quietly to never leave her, even though she knows she's probably too old now to have a made-up friend. He promises he won't. It is because of Master Jonas that her nightmares don't come often, but the bear still waits in the shadows. Sometimes in the darkness she sees its eyes glinting.

4

Spring 1801

Time, which seems to young Neva to unroll in a never-ending road, has brought her to fifteen years this spring. She can now row as well as any ferryman, and Victor – always a nervous passenger – and Elise enjoy their outings on the Thames with Master Jonas, who takes them upriver to Vauxhall Gardens. From the river they see the coloured lights illuminate the dusk and listen to the music as it drifts over the water. They hear the giggling visitors and catch glimpses of society moths as they are ferried in, attracted to the lights.

'One day,' says Elise, 'you'll go there with a fine gentleman.'

Neva doesn't think so. At fifteen she has already decided she has no wish to be chain-stitched to a dull marriage, to be worn thin by childbirth, an embroidery sample of a bright life lost in the needlework of a thousand faded threads. She thinks she's been born into the wrong time, not necessarily the wrong sex. As for her mind, that belongs to a different world altogether.

She rows Papa and Auntie home down the river.

'Good evening to you, Master Jonas,' calls a ferryman. 'What say you to the weather?'

Neva has been perfecting the art of lowering her voice.

'A high tide, and a strong wind tomorrow, Mr Bates.'

'Do you know everyone on the water?' asks Auntie.

It is a rare week when she does not tell Auntie which day is best to hang out the laundry, or when Papa should take an umbrella or wear a thicker waistcoat. Perhaps because her predictions have not been fully noted, no one is aware she is always right. Until, that is, she is given a ship in a bottle.

George Cutter is, by then, a regular visitor to the Friezland house. Having established he is of good character, Elise is always pleased to see him. Victor has taken to calling him the Sports Master, which Mr Cutter likes for such familiarity shows he is a part of their family, lifting a little the sadness in his heart. He once was married, his wife as pretty as a plump plum, her greengage eyes shining from her cheerful, round face. And she loved him, oh, how she loved him. Kissing his wife and baby son goodbye, he set sail, returning a year later with a wooden horse for the boy and a gold necklace for his love. He found the house inhabited only by mice, his sweet cherry-plum wife and son removed to the churchyard. His soul was shipwrecked.

Without knowing it, Neva helped to refloat George Cutter. He feels he has a family of sorts, even though it is a borrowed one. Mr Cutter had explained to Victor that he had never forgotten the little Russian girl, and, on hearing she'd been adopted by the clockmaker, had been anxious to see that she was happy.

He often stays for dinner and is questioned mercilessly by Neva about his seafaring days. He tells her stories of faraway places but never has he spoken of his wife or son. It's his tales of the weather – winds and gales and tempests – that fuel Neva's imagination. If a bottle of rum is on the table, he will entertain them with sea shanties, keeping the beat with the drum of his feet. Recently he has started a business in a warehouse close to Tooley Street, a school for teaching boxing, wrestling and fencing to young gentlemen.

Victor, always concerned for the safety of his unconventional daughter in these uncertain times, suggests to Mr Cutter that perhaps Neva should learn to defend herself.

'Nothing too strenuous, Mr Cutter, nothing dangerous, but something...' Here Victor trails off and ends by saying, 'You're the Sports Master, you'll know best what's... er... *appropriate*.'

'Of course,' says his friend.

Far from disapproving, Elise says as they walk home from the first lesson, 'I wish I'd been taught how to protect myself.'

'Would it have been a help?' asks Neva.

'Yes,' says Elise. 'Oh yes.'

Neva says, 'Mr Cutter is always so cheerful but I think he's sad. A deep sort of sadness.'

'I think he is too,' says Elise. She has heard the story of the death of his family, but she doesn't tell Neva.

This Wednesday – a word that, as far as Neva is concerned, has a superfluous letter 'e' – Mr Cutter brings her a present, a ship in a bottle made by a sea captain called Hurricane Joe.

Neva stares into the bottle, mesmerised. 'But how did he get the ship in there, with all its rigging and its sails billowing?'

'He slides the ship inside the bottle with the sails down,' says Mr Cutter, 'and then it's a matter of pulling the threads to make the sails stand up. It's very fiddly work, Neva.'

Still examining the ship she asks, 'Why is he called Hurricane Joe?'

'Because he has a knack of finding storms.'

Victor, tempted out of his workshop by the smell of roast chicken, comes into the kitchen. Unaware they have a visitor and only having eyes for Elise, he gives her a hug and a kiss on the neck.

'Sir,' says Mrs Gibbs, 'what will Mr Cutter think?'

'Oh,' says Victor, looking up. 'Very good to see you, Mr Cutter.'

'And you, sir,' says Mr Cutter, smiling. 'What do we think, Neva, about Mr Friezland and Mrs Gibbs?'

'I think they love one another, and because they do, they love me too.'

'You see?' says Victor. 'That's how it is.'

Elise blushes.

'When is Hurricane Joe setting sail again?' asks Neva.

'Tomorrow, as it happens,' replies Mr Cutter.

When he's about to leave Neva says, 'Tell Mr Joe not to sail tomorrow morning, for although the day will start sunny with the wind fair and the river calm, later there will be a strong wind playing north-easterly weather. I think it would be better if he were to leave the following day. The skies will be overcast in the morning but once he is out at sea, there will be a breeze in his favour with four days of good weather.'

'Neva – weather is beyond the wit of men,' says Victor.

'But I do not believe it is beyond the wit of Neva,' says Mr Cutter. His usual jovial expression turns serious. 'As you know, sir, I met Neva when she was just three, in the company of her parents, Andre and Olga Tarshin. Her father told me she had a knack of knowing what the weather will be. That day, 15th January 1789, a day I won't forget, Neva knew the ice on the river was melting. Several people died who wouldn't have if they'd listened to this little girl.'

It is the first time Neva can remember her gift being acknowledged. But no one has fully understood her predictions are never wrong.

★ ★ ★

A week later, Victor takes Neva to the Summer Exhibition at Somerset House. It's an outing Neva has been looking forward to. She has a new tea gown and a bonnet, although she is not so fond of the bonnet.

'No young lady goes out without one,' says Auntie firmly.

'I look nearly grown up,' Neva says, catching a glimpse of herself in the mirror.

'You look a picture,' says Victor.

The people in the gallery don't seem interested in the paintings. They are here to be seen for the fashions of the day, for the rise and fall in the women's waistlines, the thinness of their muslin gowns and the sweetness of their figures. These impossibly well-turned-out gentlemen and ladies are far grander than any of the numerous paintings on display, housed though they are in elaborate frames, stacked all the way to the ceiling. To Neva the ladies seem like flightless birds in wingless gowns.

Neva and Victor look intently at paintings of sunsets, of ships tossed at sea, of frosty landscapes and foggy London. She is foxed by the insipid renditions of the elements and concludes they must be badly painted.

'Is this how you see the clouds?' she asks her papa.

'Yes,' says Victor. 'Don't you?'

She thinks about this and, genuinely puzzled, asks, 'Do you think this is how most people see the sky?'

'Well, a painting is open to interpretation, but on the whole, yes.'

'If they only see clouds like this, it explains why people never seem to know what the coming weather will be.'

'Does it?' asks her father.

'Yes, because if these paintings are anything to go by, most people are blind to what the sky is telling them.'

Her father laughs. 'That's a little strong, Neva. No one can tell what next week will bring, let alone the weather.'

'When I look up to the heavens I see patterns and intense colours there, none of which are depicted in these paintings,' says Neva. 'Some clouds are crosshatched and others patchworked; all of them tell a story of what the weather has in mind. Even in a blue sky. Don't you see that too?'

It takes Victor a few minutes to realise this is no invention on Neva's part; she means it with all her heart.

Neva wonders if she isn't from another realm. The look on Papa's face suggests she is perhaps a changeling child. There among the paintings and fashionable people, she imagines flying above them, a red kite in a blue, cloudless sky. She tries to comprehend the idea that no one else understands the clouds the way she does. In heavy slippers that were light only hours ago, she slips her arm through Victor's and they walk down the Strand to have tea.

Over French pastries, Victor says, 'To see things differently is a gift, Neva. It makes you unique.'

'You don't think it makes me odd?' she asks.

He laughs. 'To be a little odd is, I think, a very good thing. Do you really wish to be like all these sheep gathered in this coffee house, worrying about what they look like, how they're dressed and who they know? You, my little love, are by far the most interesting young lady in the room.'

'Why do you think I see the sky differently?'

He thinks for a while and says, 'Perhaps it goes back to when you were small and the accident at the inn. Although I'm sure you don't remember.'

'I remember the bear and the sound of the ice cracking.'

'Your mother too was extraordinary. She would be proud of you, of that I'm sure.'

The following day when Mr Cutter knocks on the door of Victor's workshop, he has a shilling for Neva for she was right about the weather. Hurricane Joe has asked if she might do her trick again for him.

'That is,' says Mr Cutter, 'if your papa has no objection.'

'I think we should put Neva's talent to a test,' says Victor.

'Most wise, sir,' says Mr Cutter. 'Most wise indeed. But after you have done that could I then ask Neva for a few more predictions?'

Victor Friezland has finally to acknowledge that Neva's talent is unlike anything he's seen before and doubts he will ever see again. Having been slow to understand her gift he now is keen to know how she does it.

'When you look at the sky to predict the weather, is it like a mathematical equation, something you have to work out in your head?'

'No, it's not something I'm calculating. It's very hard to explain, except to say it's more something I'm *being*.' She pauses. 'I suppose it's as much of a mystery to me that you don't see the sky as I do.'

'That's a fair point,' says Victor.

'Does the "how" of it really matter? Surely what's important is that I can help the many tradespeople in the neighbourhood whose work relies on the weather? My weather predictions can be of service; what harm can come from that?'

Dear Lord, what harm, thinks Victor, who can see nothing but danger in the whole enterprise. He asks himself what would happen if it was ever known that his beloved daughter possessed this extraordinary ability. The answer frightens him. After all, this is Southwark and in recent years it has changed. When first he came, there was a community of craftsmen and like-minded folk. There were open spaces and gardens, but slowly, over time, like the silt from the river, it has washed up the dregs of humanity. These streets are now home to the Borough Boys, river pirates, highwaymen, drunks, prostitutes and vagabonds. In short, all the best that London has to offer now appear in and around Tooley Street. It is a neighbourhood that delivers a constant supply of criminals for trial at the Old Bailey, to enrich the lawyers and to dance to the hangman's rope. If it becomes known that Neva can precisely predict the coming weather, she could be kidnapped or much worse. Some superstitious people may even believe she is in league with the devil.

He struggles to find an answer when Neva, for the hundredth time, asks him, 'But *why* can't I tell people my weather predictions?'

'First,' he says, 'we should do an experiment to find out just how accurate your predictions are.'

5

Victor buys a ledger, some rather fine-nibbed pens and a pot of black ink. These he lays out on a desk before Neva. He is determined that there must be a practical way of proving the accuracy of her forecasts. She is bemused to find each page already meticulously dated.

'This is for you,' he says. 'Today we are going to do an experiment.'

'What kind of experiment?'

'I am going to observe you writing down your weather predictions and in a separate notebook I'm going to write down my observations – how you go about your calculations and the time it takes you to make your predictions.'

'Why only a week's worth?' she asks, looking at the ledger.

Victor, slightly baffled, replies, 'I would have thought a week is as far as anyone can see into the future.'

Neva has never seen her gift as being that of a clairvoyant. 'I can only see what the weather will be,' she says, almost apologetically. 'I can't tell you what Napoleon is going to do next.'

'I know,' says Victor.

'When I was small I could only see a few days' weather at a time, but now I am able to see much further.'

'How much further?' asks Victor.

'Well, I know the coming winter will be very cold and the winter after that even colder.'

It's on the tip of Victor's tongue to say, 'Don't be ridiculous,' but he swallows the words. Instead he says, 'This ledger is a way of proving that you are correct, that your predictions are indeed—'

She interrupts him, saying, 'I'll write out the weather for the coming month, that way you will be able to check the day's weather daily against my predictions. But there are variables.'

Victor is beginning to feel decidedly out of his depth. 'What variables? Remember, I haven't studied the skies like you. Mainly because, foolishly it seems, I believed weather belonged to the God of Chaos. That is, until I met you.'

Smiling, Neva says, 'I am talking about the amount of smoke that rises up into the sky from all the chimney pots of London and the factories. I think perhaps the vapours produced by the industries of men can change the colours in the sky. Sometimes I see this greyness rising and when it reaches the clouds it seems to dull them somehow, their colours becoming less bright. It's only a theory.'

'I see,' he says, 'and you believe the vapours have a bearing on the conditions?'

She looks at him with her most quizzical expression and says, 'Are you sure you really can't see it too?'

'No, Neva, I can't. To be honest, I don't know if there is anyone else who can. Of course, there's the astronomer from Sam Johnson's *Rasselas*, who believed he had sole charge of the weather – but he was a character from a book.'

It occurs to Neva that her ability is not the same as embroidery or harmless paintings of flowers, activities that trouble no one, that don't compete with men's intellect or ambition. Her gift, she thinks, outdoes rational thought, making her an island utterly disconnected from others. At night she sometimes overhears the worried conversations that Papa and Auntie have about her. More than once she's heard Victor say, 'It would be very easy for someone to think she was insane.'

Seeing Papa look so anxious, she says, 'Perhaps I'll grow out of it.'

Victor secretly hopes she will, although he wouldn't dream of saying so.

'I will watch you fill out your predictions in the ledger and you must then leave the book with me. I must be present every time you write them down.'

That makes her smile. 'Is it because you think there's a fairy underneath my chair who tells me all the answers? Perhaps that's who gave me this gift. What else is there to bestow after beauty, wealth and charm?'

'Try to be serious, Neva,' says Victor, although he is himself laughing.

'I am trying.'

'This experiment must be as scientific as it can be.'

With a cheeky grin on her face she asks, 'But we do stop for meals?'

It's a cold day in April and Victor sits in his workshop, watching Neva as she lifts her pen. She starts at the beginning and works her way through the days. She doesn't talk and for long periods she simply sits, staring up at the sky. All of these observations he too writes down. By teatime her work is finished, and she leaves the book on the desk.

With a sigh she says, 'There must be other people interested in the weather and how to predict it.'

Victor has already looked into this. He has joined a dinner club which includes many eccentric gentlemen, other clockmakers and gentlemen who are fascinated by machines and the sciences. They meet once a month to discuss their experiments and designs over dinner. Victor is more than aware that such gentlemen, for all their imagination, would never permit a girl into their inner circle. They would, he suspects, be humiliated that she can do with ease what many of them are striving to comprehend: meteorological science.

Every day for the following month Victor checks Neva's predictions and every day she is correct down to the hour.

'Can I do my weather forecasts now?' she asks.

'No,' replies Victor, still trying to grasp how it is that she is so precise and seems to be able to do what no other human can do.

'For the umpteenth time,' she says, 'there is simply no way of explaining it. It's a language without full stops and commas.'

'What does that mean?' asks Victor.

'It doesn't possess grammar, it's instinctual and wordless, it lies in the earth of my soul.'

Victor sighs. 'It's very hard for me to understand.'

'And in the meantime,' says Neva, 'ships are lost at sea and the people whose work depends on the weather have no idea when is best for putting on a new roof or mending a road. Perhaps we should do another practical experiment and see how many people are in need of accurate weather predictions. We could charge a penny, and no one need know it's me.'

'I don't want anyone coming to the house asking for weather predictions,' says Victor, firmly.

Elise has the solution. 'If Mr Cutter is amenable, he could collect the dates the seafaring folk are enquiring about and bring them to Neva. She could write out individual predictions.

That way no one will know it's Neva and, better still, no one would ever need to come here.'

A philosophical experiment, thinks Victor. It would be an opportunity to see if anyone is interested in such an unusual thing as weather forecasting. Reluctantly he agrees.

So it begins. One request leads to another, and then another. Word is passed from the seafarers to the tradespeople and then to the fair folk. Rumours turn to fact. There is someone in Southwark who knows the secrets of the weather and, most extraordinarily, is never wrong.

Suspicion first falls on Mr Cutter as it's he who is making the enquiries. But it's noticed that he goes again and again to the clockmaker's house and the neighbourhood decides it's all Mr Friezland's doing. He isn't from round here, he's a foreigner and furthermore Mrs Gibbs is thought to be more than his housekeeper. And there's that girl of his.

'Didn't your daughter used to go and play with her?'

'My girl said she was trying to conjure spells to make it rain when she was just seven.'

Half-truths and fabrications make up this particular cloth.

The tittle-tattlers agree there's alchemy and black arts going on at the clockmaker's house.

The proprietor of the gin shop sums up the feelings of his neighbours when he tells his wife, 'It's not godly nor Christian and all this talk of the weather is affecting my bones.'

Victor puts an end to the experiment. The conclusion is simple: there are many people whose livelihoods depend on knowing what the weather will be.

He thinks of Neva's mother who also had a gift, one she kept concealed from the world inside the chess-playing automaton. He thinks about his clocks that squeeze the infinity of time into something as simple as the swing of a pendulum. Would people question Neva's weather predictions if they believed they came from a machine? Could he build an automaton like no other, one which appeared impossibly complicated so that the mechanisations themselves would steal people's attention? Surely men would be more likely to believe a machine capable of such predictions than a girl?

Could Neva's genius, like her mother's, find refuge behind the mundanity of wheels and cogs? He resolves to concentrate on designing a machine – an automaton that looks capable of doing what Neva can do in secret.

And here lies his quandary. Neva has worked and learned alongside him since she was a child. She is clever, she is curious, she wants to know more. What, he asks himself, is he supposed to do? Shut her out of the workshop, tell her that she must stay with Elise and learn how to be a young lady? Maybe he should forget about the automaton and concentrate on his orders.

He doesn't. Instead, he justifies his actions by telling himself that such a talent as Neva's cannot be limited by her sex. There is a magic in Neva that needs expression.

'Don't you think we should put an end to Eugene Jonas?' says Elise. 'Neva is nearly grown up. It was one thing to play a boy when she was a child – but now?'

The question hangs there, a bell waiting to ring out a warning.

But Victor can't and doesn't want to let go of Eugene Jonas. He is becoming vital to his work.

'Only for a little while longer,' he says.

'Nothing is without its consequences,' says Elise. She doesn't like to go out much, she says there are too many questions – from the market stallholders, the shopkeepers, neighbours – about the young man.

'Such as?' asks Victor.

'Does he live here? How old is he? Is he English? And on and on.'

To clarify the situation Victor puts up a sign above the gate. It reads:

FRIEZLAND AND JONAS
MAKERS OF CLOCKS AND AUTOMATONS

It's the only way that Victor can think to acknowledge Neva's role in the creation of the automaton. All it does is raise more questions.

'What will become of Neva?' Elise asks Victor.

'I don't understand,' he says.

'My love, you do. What chance does she have of finding a husband when she is playing the part of a man?'

Victor looks crestfallen. 'Without Eugene Jonas there will be no automaton,' he says.

'That's not the answer to my question,' says Elise.

The months roll into a year and Neva is now sixteen. Together she and Victor have made several prototypes and none of them are convincing. The question of how Neva can make her predictions without giving herself away remains unanswered.

These days Victor's thoughts are concerned with money because to build such a machine as he has in mind will cost a substantial sum and his savings are running low. Victor has never been a gambling man but for the first time in his life he contemplates placing a wager, one he is certain he will win.

It's at the dinner club that he hears of Mr Karavino's Mysterious Cabinet. Mr Karavino is performing at the Lyceum Theatre but such is the popularity of his performance there is not a ticket to be had.

'It's a pity,' he tells Elise as she climbs into bed one night.

'I would like to have seen that cabinet. I think it might have helped us.'

'And would Eugene Jonas see it with us or Neva Friezland?' says Elise.

'Come here,' says Victor and wraps his arms round her. 'Don't worry; once the automaton is made everything will go back to how it should be.'

But he lies in bed, unable to sleep. Now he has let the genie out of the bottle, how will he ever coax it back in again?

6

In April Elise receives a letter from Mrs Cora Dent, a name
from her past. She writes that she wants to see Mrs Gibbs
on a matter of some urgency. She hopes it is convenient, and
she will send a carriage tomorrow morning to pick her up.

'Ten o'clock in the morning,' says Victor, 'is a very
unfashionable hour to be expected to visit anybody.'

Nevertheless, at ten o'clock the next cold and overcast
morning, Elise is waiting in the elegant and beautifully
furnished drawing room of No. 10 Harley Street. She and
Mrs Dent had lived in rented accommodation in Soho, well
before Mrs Dent met Lord Sutton. Now sitting there with just
a ticking clock for company, Elise can almost make out the
ghost of the young woman she once was. How broken she
had been by the grief of losing her baby, filled with an aching
melancholy, terrified to even stand straight. She lived in dread
that her violent husband would find her and carry out his
threat to beat her to a pulp. She smiles a little to herself now.
Well, Elise, you never thought you would meet Victor, did
you? Or have Neva in your life. Look at you, sitting here,
with your head held high.

'There you are, my girl,' says Mrs Dent, coming into the

drawing room. She is a small, over-dressed woman with a loud voice and a strong cockney accent. An image of a chandelier comes to Elise, for Mrs Dent is draped in gems, none of them fake and all of them shining with the iridescent energy of eternal youth, sending flickers of light over the woman's painted face.

'What a fine lady you are,' says Mrs Dent as she sits down opposite Elise.

They begin to talk about the past, finding footholds in the mountain of time that has kept them apart, until finally they reach the summit of the present.

'I was so sorry to read of Lord Sutton's death, Cora,' says Elise.

'He's been gone eighteen months, three days and twelve hours. And there's not one of those days or one of those hours that I haven't missed him. We had a great deal of fun and we both made the very best of the life we had. He bought this house before it was even built.'

'And a lovely house it is,' says Elise.

'My solicitor told me that most houses in London end up, by default, being owned by women. My Lord Sutton left me well provided for. I have enough money to rescue ill-treated servants and those born into slavery, which I enjoy making the rich pay for. Now, tell me – do you still live in dread of that husband of yours finding you? Because it's part of the reason I asked you here today. I've received a letter from a vicar in Lewisham who took on one of my girls. Here – you read it. It's topped and tailed with all the usual politeness and salutations but the meat of it's in the middle.'

The meat is indeed the best part. Elise reads aloud: '"Robert C. Gibbs was wounded in a duel on 6th December 1789 and died three days later. It is said that he was too drunk to hold his pistol straight and was unable to fire his weapon."' She reads it to herself three more times to make sure the words haven't rearranged themselves into something altogether more frightening. It takes her a moment and, no, they still read *he's dead* and she feels a lightness come over her. The day is brighter and she no longer needs to be frightened of the shadows.

'All this time I've been thinking he's most likely alive when I've actually been a widow,' says Elise. And the word *widow* tastes delicious in her mouth.

'Now you can make yourself respectable again,' says her friend, 'and marry Mr Friezland, if you so wish.'

Elise is about to say something when Mrs Dent continues, 'But, as I said, this letter is only half the reason I wanted to see you. The other half is more complicated. I hope you know that you're under no obligation but I thought you might supply the solution to a particular problem.'

Mrs Dent rings a bell on the table next to her and the butler appears. 'Could you kindly ask Miss Lamb to join us? And some refreshment wouldn't go amiss. Hot chocolate if you will, there's a love.'

When the butler has left she says, 'All my staff are rescued from one appalling household or another and this young lady I want you to meet is looking for a position. She's a hard-worker and bright as a gem.'

Mrs Gibbs looks up as a shy girl, head bowed, enters the room.

'It's all right, love,' says Mrs Dent. 'Come, sit down. You're among friends.'

She'd be as pretty as a spring day if she wasn't so overcast, thinks Elise.

'Mrs Gibbs,' says Mrs Dent, 'may I introduce Miss Cassandra Lamb. Cassie, Mrs Gibbs was once one of my girls. Will you tell her what's happened to you?'

'It doesn't matter who tells it,' says Cassie. 'It can't make it any better or any worse.' She is silent for a long while and

Elise is beginning to wonder if she will say any more when, with a deep breath, she begins.

'I was born in Lambeth, the eldest of thirteen, and I helped bring up my half-brothers and sisters. I was fourteen years old when Mother found me a position in a grand house in Pall Mall as a scullery maid.'

Mrs Dent clears her throat and says, 'Cassie, being very quick to learn, worked her way up and became lady's maid to her mistress, who was, I believe, most fond of her.'

Cassie continues, 'I started to notice the master watching me and that's when the trouble began. My mother may have had thirteen children, but she never taught me anything. I knew little of how the world spins and certainly nothing of what goes on below the waistline of a man's breeches. The housekeeper, having been with the family for some years and having an inkling of what might be in store, gave me Mrs Dent's address in case I should need it. One night I woke up and the master was there. He told me to be quiet and I leapt out of bed. He tried to grab me but I was too fast for him. I started screaming at the top of my lungs. I called him all kinds of names. I made such a hullabaloo I woke up the whole house, including the mistress. But his high and mightiness told her it was all my doing and she had me thrown onto the streets at three o'clock in the morning. There I was, with no money and just one address.'

'Bravo, dear,' says Elise. 'There's no need to look so downcast – you escaped. I thought it was going to be far worse.'

'That's it, there's more,' says Mrs Dent. 'The master is a gambler through and through and he had bet some duke or other one hundred guineas that he would bed Cassie before the year was out, so he's been searching for her ever since.'

'One hundred guineas!' says Elise. 'Why, that's a king's ransom.'

'And one I fear he's unwilling to part with,' says Mrs Dent. 'This means Cassie has to be kept hidden, at least until the end of the year.'

'We'd better make sure he doesn't discover her,' says Elise. 'Well, Cassie, Victor Friezland is not comfortable with the term "servant", so if you do decide to come you would live as part of the family.'

'Is it just the two of you?' asks Cassie.

'There's Neva too.' Elise wonders how best to describe her. 'She's sixteen years old and Mr Friezland's adopted daughter.'

Elise thinks it wisest to leave it at that and let Cassie come to her own conclusions about Neva. It's agreed she will come to Mr Friezland's house that afternoon.

As Elise is leaving, Mrs Dent says, 'My barouche will take you home. And thank you, my dear, I knew you could be relied upon.'

Elise sits in the luxurious, red velvet interior of Mrs Dent's carriage, confident Victor and Neva will be thrilled with the three tickets Mrs Dent has given them for her Magical Soiree next Thursday. Elise doesn't think about Cassie, not now, not at this moment, but says over and over again, 'I am a *widow*,' until she feels the words are hers to own. The monster lurking in the darkness is dead. As the carriage crosses London Bridge, the sun comes through the clouds. A new day, she tells herself, a brand-new day.

'These are the most sought-after tickets in all of London,' Neva says, as if Auntie is unaware of this, which of course she isn't. 'We'll see Mr Karavino's amazing Mysterious Cabinet. It's one of the wonders of London this season and this is his very last performance.'

Still Auntie seems remarkably unimpressed. 'I'm glad you're pleased, Neva,' is all she says.

'Pleased?' says Neva. 'I'll jump over the moon for joy!'

'I have other news,' says Elise and carefully gives her an abridged version of what befell Miss Cassie Lamb.

Neva picks at her fingers. 'What will you tell her about my weather predictions? And about Eugene Jonas?' she asks.

'Leave it to me,' says Auntie. 'And stop picking, you will have eaten them all by the time you're eighteen if you're not careful.'

She knows Neva is right; the idea of having someone else in the house is perhaps more problematic than she had initially thought.

'If you feel that it's right for Cassie Lamb to come here,' says Victor, 'then I'm sure it is.'

Elise is anxious. It won't take Cassie long to work out that she and Victor live together as husband and wife and neither will it take her long to realise Neva predicts the weather.

Elise is relieved that Neva and Victor are out when Cassie Lamb arrives. She's now convinced herself the arrangement could go very badly indeed. Cassie is solemn and hardly says a word. After showing her the house and her room, Elise gives her a few minutes to settle in and goes down to the kitchen to put on the kettle. What is it, she thinks, about putting on a kettle that always makes her feel calmer, as if a cup of tea will make everything better?

'You keep the house beautiful,' says Cassie, coming into the kitchen. 'Do you have any help?'

'No,' says Mrs Gibbs. 'Neva helps me occasionally, but on the whole it's just me.'

Cassie looks awkward and says, 'There's something I have to say, Mrs Gibbs.'

Mrs Gibbs braces herself and wonders what it could be, expecting Cassie to say she doesn't like the oddness of the house and would prefer to go back to Mrs Dent's.

Cassie Lamb stands upright.

'Don't stand on ceremony,' says Elise, 'let's hear it.' She thinks she says it too sharply.

Cassie is on the brink of tears. 'I don't know what to do with the words I've got inside me, Mrs Gibbs,' she says, 'except I've got to say them out loud and when I've done that, I'll feel better.'

'Why don't you sit down,' says Elise, softening, 'and have a cup of tea.'

'If you don't mind, I'll stay standing. I think my words come out better when I'm standing.'

Mrs Gibbs thinks she needn't have made such a big fish pie.

Cassie takes a deep breath. 'I know you said your master don't like the word "servant", but I grew up believing the Lord above made some of us rich and others poor. Some masters and others servants. And all men, even the king, are servants unto the Lord so it's not for me to question the Almighty's judgment in these matters. I can't sit about doing nothing, that wasn't what the Lord had in mind when he sent me here.'

Elise feels like laughing and thinks Cassie Lamb could go on the stage. But she checks herself.

'In that case,' says Elise, 'I could do with some help. What are you good at?'

Cassie thinks for a moment. 'I liked being a lady's maid and I love using my needle and thread.'

An idea comes to Elise. 'You could try to take Neva in hand. Her clothes are in a state and she hasn't anything to wear for Mrs Dent's Magical Soiree next Thursday. I can of course buy—'

'Yes – I can be a maid of all sorts,' interrupts Cassie. 'Oh, I don't think I said that right.'

Elise smiles and says, 'In that case we'll pay you ten guineas a year. Does that seem reasonable?'

'Ten guineas,' says Cassie, her face lighting up. 'Yes, Mrs Gibbs.'

Elise opens the box containing the housekeeping money and counts out five guineas. 'The rest at the end of the year. I take it you weren't paid what was owing when you left your last position.' Cassie shook her head. 'All I ask, Cassie,' says Elise seriously, 'and this is most important, dear, is that you don't gossip about us – not to anyone.'

'Never,' says Cassie with real passion. 'Never, I promise.'

7

Neva likes routine. On Thursdays there will be chicken pie and on Friday there will be fish. She is not good with change and it's a delicate balance she must keep. The idea that there will be someone else living in the house she finds extraordinarily worrying. It has put her off doing her predictions and most of the afternoon she spends staring at the sky, dreaming. It is in this hinterland between conscious and unconscious thought that Neva feels certain the tide has changed. Not the tide of the river or the sky but something deeper is shifting. She puts it down to variables and it's just dawning on her: life is full of those.

When Neva was younger Elise had often invited children to play with her but it always ended in disaster. The children called her names, called her soft-boiled. The girls were worse in their cruelty than the boys. And now here is Cassie Lamb and the only person who seems pleased about this is Auntie. Neva picks at her fingers. There is satisfaction in the sharp pain caused by pulling off the skin. It stops her mind from spinning, distracts her from the fear that, like the children she had tried to play with, Cassie Lamb will think her peculiar.

That evening Neva has finished lighting the candles in the

long drawing room when the door opens and there is Cassie.
It's a relief to see she is different from Neva in every way.
Perhaps two years older, and where Neva is thin, some might
say too thin, Cassie Lamb appears to be full, like a vase of
voluptuous curves.

Neva says straight away, 'What do you think of the house?'

Auntie follows Cassie into the drawing room. 'Neva,' she
says calmly, 'this is Miss Cassie Lamb.'

Neva immediately feels stupid. Of course she should have
waited and asked the question after they'd been introduced.
She is less awkward when Victor enters the room.

'Ah, here you all are,' he says. 'I'm very pleased to meet
you, Miss Lamb, I'm Victor Friezland.'

Cassie bobs a little curtsey.

'Tonight, you are my guest,' says Victor. He goes to the
end of the long drawing room and opens the doors leading
into the dining room beyond. Elise has already laid the round
table with the prettiest china.

Cassie, letting out a little gasp of surprise, is drawn to the
large lattice windows looking out over the Thames.

'This whole room,' says Victor, 'was built from a galleon.
This part was the captain's cabin.'

Victor pulls out a chair for her to sit on.

'Please, sir, can't I help?' she says as Victor pours the wine.

'No, just sit and enjoy the evening.'

Over Auntie's delicious fish pie, Neva asks her question
again.

'Miss Lamb, what were your first impressions of this house,
when you saw it? There aren't many like this.'

Cassie thinks for a moment. 'I thought it looked like a ship
run ashore with a whale.' And hastily adds, 'I didn't mean
that rudely. It's a compliment. I think the house is magical.'

Victor laughs. 'We can make a sea shanty of that – a ship
run ashore with a whale.'

Neva smiles. It's the answer Eugene Jonas approves of.

Cassie, feeling a little bolder, says, 'I hope it doesn't ever get pulled down. There're so many wharves going up round here.'

'That's the trouble,' says Victor. 'A house like this won't be remembered in the history books. Only the bricks and mortar of rich men's dwellings leave a stain there.'

For the first time since she arrived, Cassie smiles and Neva thinks she looks like winter walking into spring.

Cassie quietly asks her, 'Do you ever sit here and think to yourself of all the faraway places the captain's cabin would have seen before it came to this harbour?'

'Yes,' says Neva. 'I used to think about it all the time and I made up lots of stories.' She stops, worried that she is sounding childish.

'I used to make up stories too,' says Cassie.

'What were your stories about?' asks Neva.

'You will think them silly.'

'I won't, I promise.'

'I thought I would become a pirate and have my own ship. I used to imagine the lands I would visit. But then I thought I would be seasick and so instead I told myself stories about finding a knight or a duke to marry.'

'I don't ever want to get married,' says Neva. 'I'm more than content to live a life without the consequences of falling in love. Let fools and jesters believe in such notions, not me.'

Everyone at the table laughs.

'When you fall in love, you will have to think again,' says Auntie, glancing fondly at Victor.

By Monday it feels as if Cassie has been with them as long as anyone can remember. Luck was something Cassie had believed belonged to other people. She had been brought up by the Old Testament; not having it read to her but being beaten with it. Such beatings were her daily bread. She never spoke of her dreams about escaping from the drudgery of caring for so many children.

Cassie's mother was born lazy and her father died of drink. Her stepfather, hoping to become a preacher, bought a ticket to America for his new family shortly after Cassie started work at the house in Pall Mall.

But luck hasn't forsaken her. Here in Southwark, away from the outside world, she has her own room with a cabin window looking out over the river, a fire with a full coal bucket and money in her trunk. She feels as rich as any queen, perhaps richer.

For the first time in her life, Cassie is happy and feels safe. She has no desire to get married. Here at Victor Friezland's house, she thinks she has the happiest of endings. Elise says she is to call her Auntie, and Victor, Uncle. This is her new family – a kinder family than she has ever known.

If she could alter one thing, it would be that Neva was more approachable.

Quietly, Auntie tells her a little – not all – about Neva's background.

'She's very far away,' says Cassie. 'I never seem to catch her when she comes back.'

'Just be yourself,' says Elise.

Neva is simply a revelation. Cassie is more than a little intimidated by how clever she is and fascinated by the way she sees things and talks in colours when she can't think of the right words for an emotion. Auntie has told her she can also sing the weather.

On a grey, overcast day, Neva is reading and Cassie, busy

sewing by the window, looks up and says, 'Do you really sing the weather?'

'Yes,' says Neva and goes back to her book.

After a minute or two Cassie says, 'Do you hear that? It sounds like it's raining but there's no rain.'

Neva smiles. 'No, it's me.'

'How do you do that?'

Neva shrugs. 'It's going to rain in ten minutes and then it will clear up.'

'You can't know that.'

'But I do. When I was younger I thought everyone could and the only reason they didn't was because telling the weather was beneath them.'

'I thought everyone died on a Thursday,' says Cassie.

'Then I'm not the only one who's odd,' says Neva.

'I also believed there was art in heaven,' says Cassie. Neva looks quizzically at her. 'You know, the Lord's Prayer. "Which art in heaven." I was so disappointed when I found out it didn't mean that. Especially as I'd never seen any art on earth.'

Neva laughs and Cassie thinks the sun comes out when she looks like that. She gently takes Neva's hands to stop her picking her fingers.

Neva says abruptly, 'I predict the weather, that's what I do. Now you know my secret.'

It's this conversation that starts a friendship.

All Neva can think about is Mrs Dent's Magical Soiree. It seems to her that time has slowed down and the days have their boots stuck in the mud of the week, refusing to move as fast as they should. She hasn't given much thought to what she will wear; neither does she think to ask what Cassie might be making with her busy needle and thread.

Finally, the day arrives and Victor stops work early at four. So that they might all look presentable he's ordered a carriage to take them to Harley Street at six o'clock.

Neva goes to get dressed for the evening and realises she has only the tea gown that she wore to Somerset House. It will have to do, she thinks, climbing the stairs to her bedchamber. She finds Cassie sitting on the top step.

'I've been waiting for you. Come on.'

'I don't need any help, I know what I'm going to wear,' says Neva.

'But I have a surprise for you,' says Cassie. Surprises, like change, disturb Neva, though she doesn't say so. 'Don't look like that,' says Cassie.

Neva thinks today Cassie is a blue sky that no cloud would dare darken.

Cassie says, 'Do you know, I thought this bit would be easy.'

'What bit?' asks Neva.

'You and clothes. Any other young lady would be in a pickle to think they were going to Mrs Dent's soiree in a tea gown.'

Neva has to admit that she's never thought much about clothes, except when they're uncomfortable, and she's very pleased not to wear a full corset.

'Tonight, my lady,' says Cassie, 'I'm dressing you.'

She says this in such a cheerful manner that Neva resigns herself to whatever the surprise might be. She sits in the chair while Cassie brushes out her long, dark, curly hair.

'Why have you covered the mirror?' asks Neva.

'I thought it best if you don't see yourself until I'm finished,' says Cassie.

Confused, Neva searches for something to say.

'Are your parents still alive?' she says at last, then regrets it in case the question seems impolite.

But Cassie isn't in the least offended. 'My mother is. My father died of the drink. Mother married again and I was the eldest of thirteen and I did nothing but look after my half-brothers and sisters until I was fourteen. Then Mother sent me out to find a job.'

Neva is silenced by this glimpse of a life so unlike her own. Meanwhile Cassie is plaiting her hair and pinning it high on her head.

'Now close your eyes and don't look until I've got you into the dress.'

'What dress?'

Only when Cassie is satisfied does she say, 'You may open your eyes.'

With a flourish she removes the shawl that she'd hung over the mirror.

Neva gasps when she sees her reflection. She is looking at a stranger, no longer a girl but a young lady in a muslin gown embroidered with stars and moons. Small stars glint in her hair.

'What do you think?' asks Cassie.

Neva says quietly, 'I've never owned anything as fine as this. When did Auntie buy it?'

'She didn't, I made it.'

'You made this?' asks Neva, feeling it almost incomprehensible that Cassie could have made such a dress in so little time.

'You do like it?' asks Cassie anxiously.

Neva, who hasn't any interest in clothes except in how they inconvenience her, now sees how a well-made dress can alter everything.

'You're an artist,' she says. 'And it fits me perfectly.'

She stares at the young woman looking back at her from the mirror and moves to make sure the reflection is really hers. She experiences a strange sensation as if the image she once had of herself and the one in the mirror are beginning to merge.

'You've made me look beautiful.'

'That's because you are,' says Cassie.

'Oh my,' says Auntie when she sees Neva.

'Enchanting, completely enchanting,' says Papa and he turns away to wipe a tear from his eye.

Neva will never forget this day, the day she wore a dress embroidered with the moon and stars.

8

Every room of No. 10 Harley Street is this evening lit by candles and the vases are filled with more cherry blossom than is borne by all the trees in Vauxhall Gardens. The doors at the farthest end of the drawing room are thrown open to reveal the room beyond and here is a makeshift stage, in front of which is a collection of spindly, golden chairs waiting to take the weight of the audience.

Mrs Dent is dressed in the latest fashion from Paris; on her head is a bejewelled turban, with a feather that sticks up like a pole.

'I am pleased to see you have all come, Elise.' She turns to Neva. 'And this is Miss Neva Friezland? My word, what a rare beauty you are.'

Not for the first time this evening, Neva is conscious of people staring at her. This particular exchange is being watched with great interest by the many guests who want to know who the young lady is.

'Thank you for inviting us, Mrs Dent,' says Neva, giving a curtsey.

'A pleasure,' replies Mrs Dent. 'She's a credit to you, Elise,

and to you, Mr Friezland. I'm delighted you're here.' Turning
to Elise, she says quietly, 'Is Cassie all right?'

Elise nods.

'When is it starting?' asks Neva.

'Some might say, my dear, it's already begun,' replies Mrs
Dent and she goes to welcome more guests.

By now the drawing room is full and, refreshments having
been taken, there is an impatience for the show to begin. Mrs
Dent is holding a little bell which she is about to ring when
a fashionable gentleman makes his entrance accompanied by
his wife and two daughters.

The fashionable gentleman stands with his gloved hand
resting on his silver topped cane which he gently rocks back
and forth. He is a brooding thundercloud, thinks Neva,
that seems to absorb all the candlelight in the room. The
atmosphere, which had been jovial, has become overcast.
Mrs Dent greets him. 'Welcome, my lord. We are about to
start the entertainment.'

'You know Sir Richard Palmore?' says the lord, indicating
a gentleman who has come with his party.

'A pleasure,' says Mrs Dent.

The fashionable lord takes off his gloves and heedlessly
drops them. They are caught by a footman before they reach
the floor.

'This is most interesting,' he declares. 'I have been thinking
of investing in one of these little houses. Now, Mrs Dent,
you must show me your many modern conveniences. I'm
sure I don't speak only for myself – everyone here would be
delighted to be given a tour.' He waves a languid hand in the
general direction of the other guests.

Mrs Dent has no choice and so it is that the whole party
follows her, Papa and Auntie among them. Neva is not keen
on sheep or people behaving like sheep, so she stays exactly

where she is. It is only when the flock has left that she notices a young gentleman in the corner of the room. In his hand he is holding something which he moves between his fingers with great speed. She thinks he is older than she and that he looks somewhat awkward. As he moves out of the corner she realises he's not awkward at all, he's angry.

'Are you not interested in seeing the house?' she asks.

He stares into the distance, not looking at her, and only when she questions him again does he reply simply, 'No.'

There is something about his movement, the way he walks, that has a natural grace to it. Now she rather wishes she hadn't spoken. She looks down at her slippers which are new and pretty with ribbons that lace up around her ankles. Neva was hoping that by staying behind she would have a moment on her own. She determines not to say anything more. But does it really matter what she says to him? He isn't listening. She can see the colours in him are bright, yet anger is fogging his soul.

'I think perhaps you don't much want to be here,' she says.

For the first time he turns to look at her and Neva feels a shiver go up her spine.

Stumbling on her words she says, 'Your anger takes away all the colours that make you unique.'

He laughs then, a genuine laugh. 'People don't usually say things like that.'

Neva blushes. 'I do. I'm really not very good in society.'

He looks at her, his expression serious. 'No, I think it's fascinating. Do you see everything in colour?'

'Sometimes – people's emotions, I mean. But your colours make me think you are very angry. Sorry, I don't know your name.'

'My name is Henri Dênou. At your service, *mam'zelle*.' He bows.

She hasn't noticed until now that he's French. An émigré, she thinks. '*Je m'appelle Neva Friezland, m'sieur.*'

'They'll be coming down soon,' he says.

She wishes she wasn't wearing gloves; at least she could pick at her fingers.

She wonders if she has said that out loud because Henri turns to her and says, 'I have a pebble.'

He shows her a perfect, oblong, black pebble and puts it in her hand. It is smooth, well worn by the sea and then by the lonely hands of a small boy.

'Where did you get it?' she asks.

'On a beach in Normandy when I was nine. It was just before I was sent to England.'

There is so much more she wants to ask him. He's the most interesting person she has ever met. Now the guests are on the stairs and they're coming down.

'Here he is now,' says Henri. 'A man whose soul might be lodged in a nutshell without inconveniencing the maggot who lives in it.'

Neva giggles. A voice calls out for Henri. She finds she is still holding his pebble, but he is gone. This little treasure is warm in her gloved hand, and as they take their chairs, she wonders how she might give it back to its owner.

The weather inside people interests Neva as much as their colours. The audience that evening are little white skittish clouds. But not the fashionable lord. To Neva he is a man of thunderous resentment. Having already delayed the beginning of the show, he is now being particular about where he and his party should sit. Eventually they are seated in front of Neva, Auntie and Victor. He shows no concern about his wife, a dull bird compared to the peacock that is her husband. His two daughters look like worried wrens perched delicately on the spindly chairs.

Neva observes this while holding tight to the stone as if

it might bring back its owner. She turns, trying to see if Mr Dênou is there, but he is not. When everyone is seated and the footlights have been lit, Mrs Dent walks onto the stage to applause. She thanks the audience for their patience and informs them the performance will consist of three acts and afterwards a light supper will be served.

'Magic,' she says, 'demands silence and so, without another word, let us begin.'

Neva looks round the room again.

Elise whispers, 'Who are you searching for?'

Neva opens her hand. 'The owner of this stone.'

A violinist steps up to the stage. All eyes turn to him as he takes his seat. He is followed by a gentleman in evening dress, white gloves and an elaborately embroidered waistcoat who wheels a painted cabinet. This is Mr Karavino. He bows to the audience.

'My lords, ladies and gentlemen,' he says, 'tonight for your entertainment I will...'

The fashionable lord has already talked through Mrs Dent's introduction and is now speaking louder still about a wager he has made with the Duke of Trafford. He is telling the story as if he wants the whole room to appreciate his wit. Mr Karavino, on stage, stands completely still, staring at him. Neva can see the noble lord has no intention of being quiet. Mrs Dent is now on her feet looking uncertain.

Neva is appalled and, without quite meaning to, finds herself saying loudly to the green-frock-coated lord in front of her, 'Who are you, sir?'

'He's Lord Wardell,' Elise hisses. 'Do be quiet.'

Elise receives no support from Victor, who appears not to be listening. Lord Wardell doesn't pay any attention. But then Neva asks him again, only louder. When he continues talking, Neva, to Elise's complete horror, taps him on the back. Now she has his full attention. He turns to Neva, a look of disdain changing to one of incredulity.

'Who are you, sir? Are *you* a magician? Because we all came here to see a magician, not to be taken on a tour of the house or to listen to a story about the joys of wasting money.'

The silence is as dense as one of Auntie's fruitcakes. A stifled giggle is heard at the back of the room.

Lord Wardell swivels in his chair and stares at Victor, his teeth curling into a snarl. 'You, sir, should teach your daughter manners.'

Victor replies with a charming smile. 'You, sir, should have the manners to be quiet, as our hostess requested.'

'How dare you speak to me like that! Who are you?' says Lord Wardell.

'Sir, that was my daughter's question to you, but you chose not to answer. I claim the same privilege.'

Lord Wardell stands abruptly, the spindly chair falling backwards onto Neva. He looks around the room for support. Elise, crimson with embarrassment, sees that all eyes are on the floor, the walls, the ceiling, anywhere but on Lord Wardell. He takes out his handkerchief and waves it, as if words could be easily dismissed.

Neva notices Mrs Dent doesn't rush to beg him to stay although Lord Wardell pauses, waiting for her to do so.

'You're leaving us before you've seen the first act?' she says at last.

'I was only interested in seeing this small house and what it had to offer,' he says as he leaves. 'I can't imagine this part of London becoming fashionable.'

Neva can clearly see that Lord Wardell's true colour is mouldy green. His wife and daughters, crestfallen, follow in his wake. With every step he makes more disparaging remarks about the house and about the hostess. In the hall he stops and shouts, 'Palmore, are you coming?'

Reluctantly, the baronet rises and joins Lord Wardell.

Neva wonders if Mrs Dent will ask her to leave but Papa smiles at her reassuringly as Mrs Dent steps onto the stage.

'Shall we start from the beginning?' she says.

The violinist lifts his instrument and starts to play as the magician bows to the audience, and although Neva doesn't notice, Elise sees him direct a bow to her.

'It's all right,' says Victor quietly.

'I didn't mean to say it out loud,' whispers Neva. 'Well, not to begin with anyway.'

All is forgotten as the magician takes out a key and unlocks the cabinet door which concertinas to one side showing the inside is empty. He turns the cabinet fully around and, sliding the back open, moves his entire hand and arm through the cabinet. Then he chooses a member of the audience, a gentleman, to lock the doors and take the key with him to his seat. Mr Karavino is silent as he rotates the cabinet three times and taps it with his wand before calling the gentleman back to unlock and open the cabinet. There is a gasp from the audience for inside is a white rabbit, calmly eating a carrot. The whole sequence is repeated again, but this time when the cabinet doors are opened, inside is a woman. A rabbit? Perhaps. But a woman? This is nothing short of impossible. There is great applause and the magician bows.

'What about the rabbit?' shouts a member of the audience and the magician produces it from his coat, along with the carrot.

'Wonderful! Bravo! Again!' call the audience.

Victor is transfixed by the feat.

The next two acts are not as spectacular as the first. A

ventriloquist comes onto the stage holding a doll and the doll starts to talk. Neva is not giving it her full attention; it is the magic cabinet that fascinates her. She thinks she might know how the illusion is done. Something about it reminds her of the chess-playing bear. She has no doubt there is someone in the cabinet who doesn't mind small spaces.

The final act is a fortune-teller whose predictions are said to be excellent. People shout out questions and she gives them her answers.

As she is coming to the end of her piece, she says, 'I believe someone here has a very special gift... it is to do with the weather.'

Neva is on the edge of her seat. But there is silence and to Neva's great relief the fortune-teller takes another question. When the entertainment is over the audience give a rapturous round of applause and begin to go downstairs to supper.

'Perhaps' says Elise, 'we should leave and not...' but Mrs Dent approaches them.

'I want to thank you, Neva,' she says quietly, 'for ridding us of one of the biggest bores in London. Aren't you staying?'

'No, no,' says Victor. 'A wonderful evening, Mrs Dent, truly inspirational.'

Neva asks, 'Mrs Dent, do you know a young gentleman by the name of Henri Dênou who was here tonight?'

'You mean Lord Wardell's nephew.'

'Nephew?' says Neva.

'That's right, although he treats the lad more as if he's a servant.'

In the carriage, Neva is surprised to find she's not thinking about the magical cabinet but about Henri Dênou, and why Lord Wardell would treat him so badly.

'What are you thinking?' asks Victor.

Not wanting to say what's really on her mind, she says,

'You are right about L-shapes. That's the only way you would be able to get a woman into the cabinet.'

'Yes,' says Victor. 'That's why the doors open to one side – they hide the fact you need more space.'

'Apart from pulling the magical cabinet to pieces,' says Elise, 'did you enjoy yourselves?'

9

May 1802

There is now a sense of urgency in what Victor is planning. He is certain he can build a machine in which to conceal Neva.

'Cogs and wheels are all fine and well,' says Elise, 'but it needs a centre to it. Perhaps a woman. After all, even a clock has a face and hands.'

Victor draws up his idea of what Neva calls the Weather Woman. Yes, thinks Victor, a little lady about the size of a three year old who sits on top of the cabinet with her feet hanging down. He could make her head turn from left to right as if listening and he could make her eyes open and close. The mouth would need to be worked from within. He estimates the cost of building such a machine and thinks it far out of his reach.

He is not a man given to gambling which he considers a disease. But he is faced with a dilemma: to make the Weather Woman and keep the house running will need a substantial sum. His answer is to take a gamble on a weather phenomenon, a weather event that is out of the ordinary, unusual enough for someone to place a wager on it. The answer comes to him on a Sunday evening in May. Victor and

Neva are in the captain's cabin looking over his drawings for the automaton.

Neva glances out of the window at the sky. Full of excitement she says, 'Papa, this coming Thursday there will be a hailstorm with hailstones the size of marbles.'

'Are you sure of this?' he asks.

Neva replies, 'Yes, I wouldn't mention it if I didn't know it would happen.'

'In the afternoon or morning?' he asks.

'The afternoon.'

The lines from *Julius Caesar* come to Victor: 'There is a tide in the affairs of men... we must take the current when it serves or lose our ventures.' If ever there's a time for the tide to turn in his favour, it is now.

He reads the newspapers to find any articles to do with gambling and the huge sums that are lost nightly on cards and dice. Wagers made by foppish young men for whom the closest any will come to a battlefield is the nightly gambits they play at the tables. He suspects gambling in this day and age may be one of the only ways available to redistribute the wealth that the inbred and foolish rich have hoarded for themselves.

Sir James Copely bets Lord Primrose twenty guineas to ten that Sir Sydney Seabright is returned for Herts in preference to Lord Primrose.

Sir Henry Mildmay bets Mr Brodick one hundred guineas to ten that Bonaparte returns to Paris as Emperor.

'"There is a tide",' Victor repeats to himself again and again. But does he have the courage to sail on it?

He has on his finest clothes and is at the door putting on his coat when Elise asks him where he is going.

'To see a client,' he says.

He doesn't tell her what he is about to do. Elise is no fool. She knows perfectly well he's up to something and she watches as he walks to the bottom of the garden where a waterman is waiting with Victor's boat. Victor never usually hires a waterman to row his boat.

Victor has a feeling good fortune is more likely to come if you are generous. Lady Luck is a fickle creature who may well avoid those with miserly dispositions. Without a glitter of silver or a sparkle of gold, how else is he to catch her attention?

They roll out past the tall ships with the tide in their favour and before they run the rapids of London Bridge, he wonders whether it would be wiser to ask the waterman to turn the boat round.

When he was a boy, Victor had sworn he would never be a gambler for he had been born into a wealthy family in Saint Petersburg and his father had gambled away the entire estate, leaving a pistol and a single bullet with which he blew his brains out. Victor's mother, who had never done a thing for herself, overdosed on laudanum, and within a week Victor found himself an orphan. There was a feeling among his relatives that young Victor was cursed and he was put on a ship bound for England where his uncle who had long since immigrated was in need of an apprentice.

Victor is, as always, relieved when he has passed under London Bridge. Today the sky is clear blue with a promise of summer but the air is cold and still holding onto the tails of winter. London is magnificent in the midday light. Only when boating up the Thames do you see the full majesty of this city, he thinks. If you enter London in a carriage or on horseback, you never appreciate the true splendour of the old lady.

From the Temple Steps it is a pleasant walk through the Lincoln's Inn gardens to Mr Gutteridge's chambers. The solicitor is fascinated by well-made clocks and Victor has supplied him with three. Having no appointment, he is told by the clerk to wait and he does for a full hour before Mr Gutteridge is ready to see him.

The lawyer's chambers have a smell of well-thumbed briefs and desiccated legal documents, which to Victor's way of thinking sums up the perfume of human misery. Still uncertain of the wisdom of his plan, he takes the seat offered to him. Mr Gutteridge is a tall man though he rarely stands straight. He is genuinely pleased to see the clockmaker and listens with great interest to what Victor has to say.

'To summarise: you want to gamble on the weather?'

'Yes, Mr Gutteridge,' says Victor. 'I need a player who is prepared to put up a large enough sum.'

Mr Gutteridge reflects for a moment and then enquires after the clockmaker's health.

'I am perfectly well, thank you, sir. Why do you ask?' says Victor.

'Simply because this is the most madcap scheme I have heard in a long while. If I hear you right, Mr Friezland, you wish to gamble that there will be a hailstorm this coming Thursday. Are you able to be more specific, sir?'

Victor says, 'There will be a hailstorm in the afternoon.'

The lawyer writes this down. 'Define afternoon.'

'Between midday and five o'clock.'

'A satisfactory answer,' says Mr Gutteridge. 'And where will this hailstorm happen?'

'In London and the hailstones will be the size of marbles.'

Victor, realising that what he is saying is not being taken seriously, adds, 'I will give you five per cent of any winnings if you can guarantee me a gentleman with means who will take up my wager.'

Mr Gutteridge gets up from the table and looks out of the window thoughtfully. 'There is of course Lord Wardell, for it's true to say he very much enjoys gambling on oddities. But the minimum he will put on the table is one hundred guineas. I know him well and I must tell you he is clever and rarely loses any of his wagers.'

'Two hundred guineas,' says Victor.

'Before I could even suggest this idea to him, I would need a guarantee that the debt can be covered if you were to lose. A banker's draft would be sufficient.'

The solicitor concludes the interview with wise words. 'Don't do it, Mr Friezland.'

Victor feels his heart skip a beat as he says, 'I assure you I will get such a note to you by the end of the day.'

This is a lie for in truth he has no idea if he can. The one person who may be able to help him is his brother-in-law, the moneylender Mr Ratchet. There is no one else of his acquaintance who has access to this amount of money. They used to be neighbours, but Victor fastidiously avoided him, fearing whatever he did and wherever he went would be reported to his absent wife. But it has been twenty-three years since Victor last saw Mary and he doesn't even know if she's still alive.

The boat takes him to the Old Swan Stairs and again he tells the waterman he will not be long.

Mr Ratchet has done well for himself, moving from Tooley Street to a good address in Cheapside. But the windows are filthy and the door is guarded by Mr Ratchet's notorious dog, Old Bones. Somehow the moneylender knows who's outside before they've had time to ring the bell.

His office is a confusion of papers and boxes rising uncertainly and towering about him. On top of them are all kinds of strange objects: a bizarre skeleton, a taxidermy bird and some children's toys. Again, Victor finds himself thinking back to his childhood and to a world long ago lost to him.

Mr Ratchet has a customer. Victor wonders if he should come back later but fears if he was to leave so would his courage. He lingers in a shadowy corner of the shop. He can't see the moneylender who is hidden behind piles of papers but he has a good view of the angular, angry man who is doing the talking. The military redcoat he's wearing is a size too big for him.

'I don't believe you've been in battle once,' says Mr Ratchet. He has concluded the redcoat is stolen. The dog growls. 'Old Bones knows a lie when he hears one.'

'I've done my bit for King and Country,' says the angry man. 'I fought with the Duke of York at the battle of Bergen. It's due to this injury I got on the battlefield that I can't fire a rifle. Uncle, all I ask is a little loan to get me back on my feet.'

Uncle? Victor stares intently at the man. Can it be Aubrey? Red hair tied in a pigtail, a pronounced Adam's apple. Good-looking in a cruel way.

Old Bones is still growling.

'Shut it, shut it,' says the man.

'Get out now,' says Mr Ratchet. 'No one speaks to Old Bones like that.'

It's said he rescued his dog from a bear fight, when he walked into the arena, picked up the dog and walked out again. He tended Old Bones for nearly three months until the dog recovered and now his devotion to his master is boundless.

'Go and sell your coat. I've nothing more to say to you.'

'Fuck you and fuck your dog.'

He turns and walks out. The door rattles shut behind him and a pile of paper cascades to the floor.

The papers are still fluttering when Mr Ratchet, who

Victor thinks hasn't seen him, says, 'Now, Mr Friezland, to what do I owe this visit?'

Victor's brother-in-law is of stocky build and it's hard to define how old he is. Victor thinks he's must be older than Mary, but he wonders if Mr Ratchet hasn't looked the same since he was ten. One leg is noticeably longer than the other and a hefty boot redresses the difference.

'After all these years with you residing but a stone's throw over the water, never once have you come my way. I hope you're in good health?'

'Yes, thank you, Mr Ratchet. But was that—'

'Aubrey. Yes, it was and if you ask me it would be better if he'd never been born.'

'That's harsh, sir.'

'It is, Mr Friezland.'

'I wonder... Mary... is she...?'

'I don't know if she is still with us or has found a grave to rest in. Neither does Aubrey, or so he says. But I suspect you're not here to find out if your wife is living or dead.'

'I want to borrow two hundred guineas. I will repay you on Friday.' Victor realises he said this with his eyes closed.

The sum of money is vast. The amount, and the man asking for it, surprises the moneylender.

'How would you repay me, if I were to lend you this money?'

'If needs be, I would sell everything.'

'My nose tells me you are gambling. So what are you gambling on?'

'I am placing a wager that there will be a hailstorm, with hailstones the size of marbles, on Thursday afternoon.'

'Unless you have God's ear, sir, I strongly advise you against this,' says Mr Ratchet. He stands up and for a moment Victor thinks he is about to refuse but he locks the street door. 'Shall we go upstairs and sign the documents in peace?'

Nervously, Victor follows him while fearing he doesn't have the measure of this man. The staircase is narrow and, much to his surprise, leads to a set of spotlessly clean, well-organised rooms. Here everything is harmonious and Victor thinks it is always a bad idea to make judgements on others without seeing the whole picture. Mr Ratchet has some fine possessions.

The moneylender brings out a bottle of sherry and two glasses. He looks Victor straight in the eye and says, 'I have always liked you and I think Old Bones likes you too. I feel my sister treated you badly.'

'I was a fool to wed her,' says Victor.

'She was a fool to leave you,' says Mr Ratchet. 'I haven't seen her in more than a decade. Still, I hear you're much happier now and have a family of sorts.'

Victor says nothing.

'I have an instinct,' says Mr Ratchet, tapping his nose, 'that is second to none. I suspect you are an honourable man.'

'I believe I am,' says Victor.

'Foolish men keep me well stocked.' Mr Ratchet pushes a glass of sherry towards him. 'These are my terms and conditions: I lend at five per cent, rising to ten if the money isn't repaid within the month.'

'You'll have it within the week,' says Victor.

'That seals the deal. Drink on it then. Chin-chin.'

Victor drinks and to his surprise the sherry is remarkably good.

The following day a note arrives from Mr Gutteridge to say that Lord Wardell accepts his wager. Victor feels his heart pulsing in his ears as he writes a note of agreement to send to Mr Gutteridge. He has all of Tuesday, all of Wednesday and the whole of Thursday morning to contemplate the folly of what he has done. He is terrified to ask Neva again about the hailstorm, in case this time she says something different.

Thursday arrives as bright and as sunny as any Thursday in May could. Elise is increasingly concerned about Victor and isn't sure that taking Neva out for the day and leaving him alone is a good idea. Victor does his best to be jovial but his face remains grey.

Before they leave Elise says, 'You're up to something, Victor Friezland. Don't lie to me, I know you are.'

He kisses her and says, with more confidence than he feels, 'All will be well.'

After they leave he tries to work, and the hours drag painfully into the afternoon. The sky is resolutely blue and shows no sign of clouding over and no sign of rain, let alone hail. By three o'clock he regrets with such a passion that he has done this incredibly foolish thing. No, luck doesn't favour the brave. By four o'clock the sky is as blue as it was in the morning. Now he is in no doubt that he is a pitiful fool.

I am mad, he thinks to himself, how could any sane man believe Neva is capable of such a thing, to be able to see into the future, to predict the weather? How will I ever tell Neva? She would never forgive her own mistake. And how will I ever tell Elise? And what about Cassie? I've made them all homeless.

Once more he remembers the lonely voyage to London after his parents died and the dreadful place where he lived in Whitechapel with his uncle; the clawing poverty of it.

By half-past four he can barely bring himself to look at the clock. He's utterly exhausted by worry and ice cold with fear. He buries his head in his arms. Everything becomes black and in his mind an army is marching on him.

He sits up with a start as he hears Neva coming into the workshop. 'I told you the hailstones would be the size of marbles,' she says.

He looks out of the window, wondering if he is dreaming. The hail is crashing down, peppering the garden and dancing on the river.

In Mr Ratchet's office in Cheapside, the moneylender smiles to himself, over his glass of port.

At White's, Lord Wardell looks up from his newspaper with a sinking heart. Another damn wager lost.

That night Victor, a new man, lies in his chamber, waiting for Elise to come to bed. He remembers when they first became lovers. He was chasing little Neva around the kitchen.

'Look at you two!' Elise had said, and laughing, Victor replied, 'It's the warmest room and I'm in the best company.'

A giddy Neva had wrapped her small arms round his legs and he danced with her on his feet. That night, after the child was in bed, Victor had asked Elise to join him for a drink in the long drawing room, and there he confessed his love for her.

All she could think to say was, 'Sir – Victor – what's come over you?'

He had looked at her and said, 'Don't worry, Elise. I won't pester you again. I shouldn't have said anything in the first place.'

He smiles to think that it was she who took his hand and led him to her bed that night.

'Thank goodness, you're looking better,' says Elise, coming into the bedchamber.

'Will you take off your nightgown and let me see you naked?' he asks.

'Don't be a silly old fool, I'm too fat, with a stomach no one needs to look at unless I'm lying down.'

'Please.'

'And it's freezing cold,' she says.

'Please.'

He watches her move the candles and she stands before him naked. 'You are beautiful and I think you become more so, not less. Now leave your nightgown off and come to bed.'

In the passion of their love-making, he tells her bit by blissful bit what he has done that day and just as they are both reaching their peak he tells her how much he has won.

The following Tuesday, Victor Friezland pays a visit to the solicitor, this time in a hackney carriage.

The money has been neatly divided and Mr Gutteridge, taking his five per cent with a most cheerful smile, says, 'Lord Wardell is not happy. He wants to know how the hell you predicted the weather. He even accused me of some skulduggery. I assured him there was none. You really ruffled his feathers and for that alone, sir, I have much admiration. But make sure he never stumbles across your name again, for he is a man of wealth and grudges.'

Part Two

Part VI

IO

October 1804

After much discussion, Victor and Neva decide against concealing her inside a device in the manner of Mr Karavino's Mysterious Cabinet. Victor is making a grandfather clock when he has the idea of how the Weather Woman might work, and he refines his design.

This is the curious machine that Victor and Neva demonstrate on the evening of 2nd October 1804 to a select audience consisting of Mr Ratchet, Mr Gutteridge, Mrs Dent and Mr Cutter, who are all uncertain as to what awaits them. The invitation simply says: *You are invited to the unveiling of the Weather Woman, followed by a light supper.*

Mr Gutteridge is no stranger to the long drawing room at the house in the lane off Tooley Street since for the past year he has become a regular Monday evening visitor. Victor believes it's the solicitor's auspicious presence, combined with the acquisition of a business partner, Eugene Jonas, that gives him an air of respectability.

Mr Gutteridge has pursued a friendship with the older man. Fascinated as he is by clocks, his other great passion is chess. After a year of delightful Monday evenings, the solicitor still has no idea how his friend was able to predict the hailstorm. Neither has he once been able to beat Neva at chess. He is completely bewildered by her skill.

'Why didn't I see that?' he says after every loss.

Neva uses the games to winkle out of the lawyer information about Lord Wardell's nephew. All Mr Gutteridge will say is that he was appointed by Henri's father to be his legal guardian jointly with his mother's brother, Lord Wardell. Henri's father was French and both his parents were guillotined in the Terror. Only the boy was saved and he has been at Lord Wardell's beck and call ever since.

But the main topic of conversation is always Napoleon Bonaparte and the two hundred thousand soldiers amassed on the Calais coast who are awaiting his orders to invade England.

'One wonders where this will end,' says Mr Gutteridge lugubriously.

Victor tries to lighten his friend's pessimistic nature with a more humorous point of view.

'I read,' he says, 'Bonaparte has a plan to dig a tunnel under the Channel from Calais so his army can invade England at their leisure without fear of seasickness, while the generals float above in balloons on the hot air of their success.'

Not a trace of a smile crosses the face of the solicitor. 'I do not have your propensity for humour, Victor,' he says.

'My dear friend,' says Victor, 'I'm surprised you have any sleep at all for the nightmares you must give yourself about Napoleon's machinations.'

When the two of them start talking like this, it's hard for Neva to bring the conversation back to the owner of the pebble. She is disappointed to learn so little about him and feels the chance of meeting him again diminishes with every month that passes. The only solid fact she gleans is that

Henri's birthday is 7th October, he has won a scholarship to go to Oxford this autumn, and his uncle refuses to support him financially or in any other way. Neva wraps Henri's pebble with the intention of giving it to Mr Gutteridge on the evening of the unveiling of the Weather Woman.

Mr Gutteridge enters the long drawing room where Elise and Cassie are waiting for the guests to arrive.

'This is a surprise, Mrs Gibbs. Will I at last discover how Victor knew about that hailstorm?'

'Perhaps,' says Elise, handing Mr Gutteridge a glass of champagne.

'Did you read the papers?'

'No, Mr Gutteridge,' says Elise. 'And tonight for once we aren't going to discuss Bonaparte.'

The next to arrive is Mr Ratchet with his dog, Old Bones. On seeing the solicitor he stays back, looking down at the carpet, as a thief might lower his eyes in a courtroom.

'Don't trust lawyers,' Elise hears him say under his breath to his dog.

Attempting to reassure him she says, 'I promise this one won't bite.'

Mr Gutteridge introduces himself and asks Mr Ratchet how he knows Mr Friezland.

'We go back far, sir,' says Mr Ratchet. 'You could say we are connected by law.'

Mr Gutteridge is keen to learn more but just then Mrs Dent makes her entrance. As always, she is dressed in such an extravagant manner that her appearance stops all conversation.

'Well, I never,' she says, embracing Cassie and looking around the room. She is full of praise. 'Why, this is delightful,' she declares and adds that she is very pleased to see a dog present. In fact, everything is much to her liking, even before the evening begins in earnest.

If anyone possesses a wooden spoon that stirs up company, smoothing out any awkward lumps in the conversation, then that spoon's owner is Mrs Dent. The atmosphere instantly changes.

Mr Ratchet moves to the centre of the carpet and, addressing Mrs Dent, says abruptly, 'I remember Lord Sutton. A most honourable man if I may say so, madam.'

'My dear sir, he was indeed,' agrees Mrs Dent.

Mr Cutter comes in, apologising for being late. Wearing a brand-new velvet waistcoat, he is a raisin that has been left out of Mrs Dent's pudding and she immediately gets to work, stirring him into the company by making the necessary introductions. Soon you would believe everyone present had long been acquainted.

Cassie and Elise serve drinks, but when Neva enters, the conversation falters. Mrs Dent, who, since their first meeting, has known Neva was destined to be a beauty, is now even more enamoured by her looks. At eighteen, tall and elegant, Neva is unaware of the effect she has on people, especially tonight when her only concerns are the demonstration of the Weather Woman and giving Mr Gutteridge the package for Henri Dênou.

Mrs Dent, observing Neva, asks if she will sit beside her during the unveiling.

'I can't, Mrs Dent,' says Neva. 'I have to help Papa.'

Elise smiles to herself, knowing none of the guests are prepared for what they are about to see. Neva goes to have a word with the solicitor.

'This is for Henri Dênou for his birthday. Would you be so kind as to give it to him as soon as you can?'

'I'm seeing him tomorrow. Shall I convey your regards?'

'No, the package, sir, just the package.'

She turns from him, claps her hands and asks everyone to follow her to the workshop. Carrying their drinks, the guests walk out into a fine October evening and along a candlelit path.

'Oh my, can it be any more charming?' asks Mrs Dent.

In the workshop the little group eagerly sits down. The chairs are in the light, the rest of the space in shadow. An oriental carpet marks the boundaries of the stage and at the centre is a structure on wheels.

In the gloom there is little to be said about it, thinks Neva. The audience can't see that the bottom section is a cabinet, about three feet tall, made of red lacquered wood with a glass front. Neither can they see what is standing, hidden by a curtain, on top of the cabinet. Either side of the cabinet are two narrow tables, covered in floor-length black cloths, angled towards the audience, and on each is an unlit candelabrum. With each table is a chair and on one sits a young man with a cello.

Neva and Victor wait out of sight at the back of the workshop. Victor takes out his fob watch. Seven o'clock. Neva rings a bell and the cellist begins to play. That is her cue. Holding a taper, she walks to the tables and lights all the candles in the candelabra.

Now the audience can see the glass-fronted cabinet and the wheels, wires and cogs within. Neva lights the oil lamps at the front of the oriental carpet, revealing it to be a proscenium arch with a curtain. It looks like a child's toy theatre and the guests are baffled. The curtain is embroidered with the words *The Weather Woman* but what lies behind it and how such a thing might tell the weather is a mystery.

Neva and Victor have spent many hours rehearsing what follows.

'Tonight, ladies and gentlemen,' says Victor, 'we will demonstrate the Weather Woman. She has the capacity to predict the weather and I can assure you she has never been wrong. But you are asking yourselves, "How is it going to be done?" I will enlighten you. As you can see, on either side of the curtain are two vertical panels. To the right is written...'

'The weather,' says Mr Cutter.

'Indeed it is. At the top we have Sun, then Sun with Cloud, Cloud, Light Rain, Heavy Rain, Moderate Wind, Light Wind, Gale Force, Light Snow, Heavy Snow, Hail, Fog, Thunder, Lightning.

'On the opposite panel, where Neva is standing, is written the temperature, from Freezing, Icy Cold, Chilly, to Mild, Clement, Warm and Hot. At the top of the proscenium arch is a clock that tells the time and below is a rotating calendar showing the day of the week and the month. But what's behind the curtain? Neva, will you please show us?'

On cue, the cellist comes to the end of his piece.

Neva pulls the curtain aside and the audience gasp. Standing upright is a beautifully carved and painted wooden doll. She wears a lace bonnet and a Madonna-blue dress which Cassie has embroidered with stars. She looks straight at the audience, her eyes shining, her hands by her side. In each is a wand.

'When the Weather Woman has calculated her prediction she will point to the relevant words with her wands. To Heavy Rain on the panel on your right, for example, to the temperature on the panel on your left. She may well point to more than one word: say, Heavy Rain and Thunder; but if her hand stays in position for more than five seconds, then her prediction has been made.'

Neva lifts a candelabrum while Victor opens the front of the cabinet and invites their guests to look for themselves at the complex clockwork within.

Together Victor and Neva rotate the cabinet to show three large cranks and a pulley. Victor opens the back of the cabinet so the guests can see the inner workings, and only when everyone has returned to their seats do Victor and Neva turn the cabinet round so the Weather Woman is facing the audience again.

The trick itself is simple but Victor has told Neva they must make it look elaborate. Neva wishes she could give her predictions as she did before but Victor's pride in the Weather Woman prevents her from saying a word. And she knows Papa has done it all for her, to allow her to continue making her predictions while preserving her anonymity. And her safety.

'May I have a round of applause for my lovely daughter who has helped me display the machine to you?' says Victor.

As the audience clap, Neva takes her seat behind a table and relaxes when her feet feel the pedals hidden there. She is confident of her predictions for the following seven days. Despite herself she has to marvel at Papa's design. Connected to the two pedals are metal rods that run under the carpet to emerge through carefully cut holes beneath the cabinet. Inside the base of the cabinet itself they are attached to two levers and these levers act as brakes for the cogs. Victor has modified an anchor escapement, widely used inside grandfather clocks, so that by pushing the lever forward with the pedal, Neva is able to lock the cog in place, halting the Weather Woman's arm movements at the correct positions.

'May I have a date and a time?' says Victor. 'Any time in the next seven days. You, Mr Ratchet, sir, what will it be?'

'The weather when I walk Old Bones at eight tomorrow morning.'

'Eight o'clock tomorrow morning it is.'

Victor explains that Neva will set the date and time while he winds the first of the cranks. Neva rises from her seat, sets the hands of the clock to read eight o'clock and rotates the calendar until it reads 3rd October 1804. She returns to her chair where she sits demurely, placing her white-gloved hands on top of the table. She has a clear view of both panels. The eyes of the audience are fixed on the Weather Woman.

Victor stands back as suddenly the automaton begins to revolve. Her gown billows, displaying her petticoat and her pretty red slippers. When she comes to a halt she is facing the audience.

Victor winds up the next two cranks. These, through a system of pulleys, are connected to two brass cogs inside the automaton, which control the movement of the Weather Woman's arms. By simply winding the cranks, he raises two weights connected to each of the brass cogs. Once the cranks will no longer turn, he releases them and moves away, allowing the weights to slowly fall. As they fall the cogs connected to them turn, and the Weather Woman raises her arms.

Neva knows it only needs the gentlest of pressure on the pedals at her feet. She stops the right arm at Chilly and lets the left arm rise until it stops at Light Rain. After a moment it moves again to Sun with Cloud. The machine stops whirring.

Victor comes forward to announce the Weather Woman's prediction.

'The conditions for your walk tomorrow, Mr Ratchet, will be sunny with cloud *and* light rain with a chill in the air. You will not have long to find out if the Weather Woman is correct.'

Mr Gutteridge goes next and the demonstration begins again. Mrs Dent asks for a prediction for tomorrow afternoon and Mr Cutter for Friday at noon.

'Surely,' says Victor, 'you would like to see proof tonight that the Weather Woman is accurate.' He takes out his fob watch. 'It's a quarter to eight. Let's find out what the weather will be at half-past eight.'

The prediction is disappointing – the weather is just the same as it is now.

'Let's try at half-past nine,' says Mrs Dent.

The cellist is paid and goes home, and the party reassembles in the dining room.

At supper, Mrs Dent tells Victor that if it's raining at half-past nine as the Weather Woman predicted, and if she is always correct, he could become a very rich man. But she advises caution.

'It's charm itself, but of no use if it can't tell the weather accurately every time.'

'Whether it's accurate or not,' says Mr Gutteridge, 'there's no denying the Weather Woman is a masterpiece. I've never seen an automaton like it.'

Elise has just brought in a rhubarb crumble when the clock strikes the half hour.

Mr Cutter says, 'Is that rain I hear?'

Mrs Dent rises and goes to the window. 'I feel someone has just walked over my grave,' she says. 'This is most disarming. Mr Friezland, you must let me show it at one of my soirees – to a small audience, of course.'

'Well, so far that little Weather Woman appears to be accurate. If this is the case with all her predictions,' says Mr Cutter, 'the world is your oyster.' He lifts his glass. 'To Victor Friezland, the master clockmaker.'

II

October 1804

On the eve of his twentieth birthday, Henri Dênou visits his guardian, Mr Gutteridge, in the hope of raising enough funds to live a modest life as a student at Oxford. He has decided that whatever happens he will not return to his uncle's house, and if he can't raise the money, he will find employment. For too long he's been treated as a servant by Lord Wardell, and he has no desire to be a servant to spoilt young gentlemen at university. He has already drafted a letter to the college saying he is unable to take the place he's been offered. Such is his resolve that October morning as he enters Mr Gutteridge's chambers.

Henri likes the solicitor and is sorry to put him in such a quandary.

'Unfortunately, *Monsieur le Comte*,' says Mr Gutteridge, 'I can't allow you to access your inheritance due to your uncle's insistence that you do not receive a penny of it a day before you are twenty-five. And I should point out, in the light of Lord Wardell's... precarious pecuniary situation, that if, God forbid, you should die before that date, your mother's substantial dowry – which fortunately your late father put in trust for you here in England – will go to your uncle.

'Neither can I lend you money, as that would go against me should the matter go to court. So it's with a heavy heart that I say there's nothing I can do for you. Life is precious, but it isn't fair.' Mr Gutteridge unlocks a drawer in his desk and takes out a flat leather jewel case. 'But I do have a gift for you from your aunt.'

Henri is shocked by the solicitor's words and hardly knows what he's doing as he opens the case and from it lifts a fine pearl necklace. He runs the silk-smooth beads through his fingers and wonders if his uncle is capable of having him murdered.

'More than kind,' says Mr Gutteridge. 'I believe her circumstances in America are difficult – certainly not what she was accustomed to in France before the revolution. There is a letter.'

Mr Gutteridge sees the young count looks pale and, rising, pours two glasses of sherry.

'I imagine you will not be going to Oxford. May I therefore suggest that you live quietly, perhaps in another city for the time being. It's hard for a gentleman of little wealth to protect himself from…'

'From a murderous uncle?' says Henri.

'From an… accident.'

'And what if I were rich?'

'My dear sir, if you were rich I wouldn't be worried.'

They look at the necklace, both knowing it won't raise sufficient funds to support Henri at Oxford.

Henri finishes the sherry and, with as much good humour as he can muster, says, 'Thank you, sir, for your advice.'

He slips the jewel case inside his coat, bows, and reaches the door before Mr Gutteridge says, 'Oh, one minute, *Monsieur le Comte*. I nearly forgot…'

He takes from his desk drawer a small, immaculately wrapped package. On it, in beautiful italic writing, is his name: *Henri Dênou*.

'Who's it from?' he asks.

'Miss Neva Friezland. She asked me to give it to you.'

Henri has never forgotten meeting Miss Friezland and has long wondered when his pebble would be returned as he knew it must be. He has hoped it would be she who returned it but he takes comfort from the thought that there will be a note inside, or a card with a few words.

He opens the package. There's the pebble but no note, no card, no words. Henri folds the wrapping and throws it into a basket, thanks the solicitor and leaves. Rolling the pebble's familiar shape round his fingers, he walks as far as Fleet Street, surprised to find, of all the revelations this morning, the most distressing is that Miss Friezland hasn't written a message. A thought comes to him: she wrapped the pebble when she could have just asked Mr Gutteridge to give it to him. Henri turns immediately and almost runs back to Mr Gutteridge's chambers.

Mr Briggs, the clerk, is in his office. 'How can I help you, sir?'

'I threw some paper in Mr Gutteridge's basket and now I think it might be important.'

'He empties his basket onto the fire but you might be lucky – today isn't too cold. I'll go and see.'

Henri nervously moves the pebble through his fingers until the clerk returns.

'You're in luck, sir,' says the clerk, putting the basket on the desk.

Henri takes out the neatly folded piece of paper and puts it inside his coat with the jewel case. 'Thank you, Mr Briggs. Do you happen to know of a fair pawnbroker?' he asks.

'No, sir, I'm sorry, I can't help you,' says the clerk loudly, while writing the name of a pawnbroker in Clerkenwell on a scrap of paper. 'Mention my name, sir,' he whispers. 'That should get you a good deal.'

In a coffee house just off Fleet Street, Henri orders breakfast, savouring the moment when he will read Miss Friezland's message. But when he unfolds the paper there are no words of endearment such as a young girl might shyly write to a young gentleman. He almost laughs at what is written; at first it makes little sense.

19th October, from a quarter to midnight until a quarter to eleven on the morning of 20th October, strong gales of a violent nature, powerful enough to cause damage to buildings and to capsize low-lying vessels in the Thames Estuary.

28th October, thick fog starting at six o'clock in the morning. It will be dense enough to take away all buildings and bridges. It will leave on 1st November.

On 15th November, light scattering of snow lasting one day.

5th December, three o'clock in the morning, heavy snow lasting until after Boxing Day when there will be a slight thaw.

January will be warmer than usual; more rain than snow.

The Thames will not freeze over this year.

The Thames will freeze in 1811.

Henri reads the note again and again as if further reading will reveal what he is to do with the information.

He remembers his uncle had once lost a wager on the timing of a hailstorm. When Lord Wardell's luck was still holding, he would often say that life is a game of chance; if you don't throw the dice you can't win.

Except when the dice is loaded against you, Henri had thought.

The pawnbroker offers a paltry sum for the necklace until Henri mentions Mr Briggs. Henri knows it's worth more, but £12 is enough to rent rooms and give him time to find employment, but far from enough to keep him safe.

He thinks more and more about the words written on the paper and concludes it's not just a matter of throwing dice but being clever with the opportunities that are thrown his way. And he realises the risk Neva Friezland has taken. Whether she knows it or not – and he suspects she does – she is admitting she is able to predict the weather.

His education and intelligence tell him this is impossible, that it runs against the laws of nature. But he remembers their brief meeting at Mrs Dent's Magical Soiree, how accurately she had read the weather of his soul. That, too, went against nature.

She has sent him these predictions for a reason. The question is, does he have the courage to make use of them?

12

Henri takes rooms in Theobalds Road and puts a plan into action. He'd learned enough about gambling from observing his uncle to know it was necessary to find someone who would wager against the storm Neva Friezland has predicted. He goes to the gambling dens off St James's where he secures several small wagers amounting to £400. It's the most reckless thing he has ever done. Bravado and good looks have got him the chits to prove the wagers are honourable but if the prediction doesn't prove accurate he will end up in prison.

He likes the rooms he's taken; they're clean, the house isn't noisy and the old lady who runs it is a good cook and doesn't ask questions. By the evening of 18th October his heart is beating faster than it has since he was a child. He wonders if he has been an absolute fool to do what he's done and spends the night pacing back and forth.

The watchman calls in the new day. 'Five o'clock and all's well.'

Henri tries to reckon how many minutes are passing and it seems this is the longest hour of his life.

At six o'clock he hears rain falling hard and heavy. He runs down the stairs, two at a time, opens the front door and, in the darkness of a day yet to dawn, stands laughing in the downpour as the wind comes roaring in.

He now has in his possession £550, £50 of which he is determined to keep. At another gaming establishment he takes small wagers on the fog. He swears he will not become a gambler. He has watched his uncle lose nearly everything and knows it's a game the house always wins and you are deluded if you think you can beat it.

When the fog arrives on 28th October he's won a total of £1,000 – enough, he knows, to pay his fees at Oxford but not enough to keep him safe.

He's been reading up on card games. There are many gambling clubs his uncle never frequents; Mrs Leach's in King Street being one such house. Lord Wardell stays away because of the notorious Three Beauties, fondly known as the Three Witches. To enter the card room, a gambler must pass by them. Sometimes they take no notice and at others they take delight in predicting what the night holds. They are witty and enchanting.

Henri has planned for this evening. He wants a clear head and eats boiled chicken and plain toast for supper with a weak tea and takes no alcohol to fog his mind. He arrives at Mrs Leach's, hoping he might escape the attentions of the Three Witches, but it isn't to be. He is near the door to the card room when one of the beauties spots him and the three glide towards him, each singing a line in turn:

'All hail! Your lucky star
Tonight's fortune be your guest
Play your cards well
And you'll go far,

Worry not about the rest.'

And laughing they walk away to find their next amusement.

There are two tables in the card room; one, known as the Poor Man's Table, plays for twenty guineas and the second plays for fifty guineas. Here the player has to keep fifty guineas on the table before him. Henri sits down at this table, places his pebble on top of his stake, and starts with whist. By midnight he's well up and believes himself done when one of London's biggest gamblers sits down at the table. Finding no one in the mood for whist, he says he will play cribbage and is Henri up for that? Henri has a good memory for cards and a first rate brain for mental calculation. He also understands what many fail to recognise: that luck and chance are lovers who rarely leave each other's side and to deny them their role only leads to misfortune.

Tonight Henri has felt the lovers' benevolence but is wise enough to know it is a fleeting dalliance. He has no idea of the time and it is beginning to seem as if he has been at this table all his life, no longer keeping count of what he's won, but keeping his mind on the play. Dawn has just broken when a party of young gentlemen enter the card room. Henri doesn't look up – to him it's just noise. What he notices is that his fellow gambler orders himself a tumbler of rum.

'Anything for you, sir?' asks the waiter.

'No,' says Henri. His opponent has yet to win a game and this in itself is extraordinary; he's known as the luckiest of all the hard players.

'Last game,' says his opponent. 'Bet all your winnings tonight and I'll double them if you win.'

Henri sees desperation in the gambler's eyes, a madness. He knows the danger of such a look – he has seen it in his uncle often enough.

'Are you sure, sir?' he asks. 'Wouldn't it be better to—'

'Dammit, no.'

The game commences. Daylight is shining through the cracks in the shutters, birds can be heard singing, the room is pungent with tobacco smoke and stale wine, and the perfume of gamblers too long at the tables. The young dandies who had made their entrance leave, bored by the longevity of this play. Only one of them stays.

Henri feels himself to be not quite of this world; a boxer, punch drunk from too many rounds in the ring. The vast sum of money is unreal and the cards seem to swim round the room. But he is on the brink of winning. Quietly he lays out his cards.

For a moment the other player thinks he might have won, but the cards shine the truth at him. He has lost the game. He storms off to settle his bill. The amount Henri has won is beyond his comprehension. He has been keeping a firm calculation on the cards but not on his winnings.

The waiter says, 'Would you like anything to drink now, sir?'

'Coffee,' says Henri. 'I'd like coffee.' Unaware that there is still someone in the room he feels himself re-entering reality and realises everything has altered.

'Do you wish to cash in your counters, sir?' asks the waiter, returning with the coffee.

Henri nods and the waiter counts them out. Henri silently counts with him and can't believe the sum. It is nearly £85,000. He is phenomenally rich.

'Now, sir,' says a young gentleman who is lolling in a chair, 'the question is: are you going to gamble it all away tomorrow?'

Henri looks at him for the first time. He's well dressed and has a kind, cheerful face with bright blue eyes.

Henri sips his coffee and says, 'I was nine when my parents were guillotined. The executioner had hold of me when suddenly there was an explosion – fireworks, probably. People panicked and he lost his grip on my arm. I heard a voice say, "Jump." I jumped. A young gypsy caught me and wrapped me in his cloak. In a backstreet a dwarf stood waiting with a wine cart. The dwarf put me in a barrel and said he would be close by. I was in that barrel until we'd left Paris when I was able to sit with them.

'I remember the gypsy said to me, "We humans make love, eat and drink and gamble so we might never know the truth – that we're all animals, waiting for the slaughter."'

After a long moment the young gentleman says, 'My name is Bos.' He stands, holding out his hand. 'And if I'm not mistaken you are Henri Dênou, *le Comte de Vernon*. It is an honour to meet you, sir. Shall we collect your winnings?'

It is not quite the largest amount ever won at one sitting, but it's much more than Henri had imagined.

'You know, what you need is a bank,' says Bos. 'And breakfast. In the reverse order.'

'No,' says Henri, coming back into himself at last. 'What I need is a piss.'

A week later, Henri and Bos leave for Oxford, Bos having first laid two wagers for his new friend. One at White's, split between three gentlemen, betting the Thames wouldn't freeze that year. The second wager – that it would freeze in 1811 – is laid at the Cocoa Tree with an army general.

13

May 1808

All Lord Wardell hears that fine May morning is talk of the Weather Woman; after the war, it has become the Englishman's main conversation piece. Even his tailor speaks of it before the impudent, scissor-wheeling upstart brazenly says his new suit of clothes will not be delivered until his lordship's outstanding bill is settled in full.

Lord Wardell affects to take the remark in a spirit of humour; it is obviously an ill-judged statement to be instantly regretted by the tailor – if he has any sense. Lord Wardell takes out one of the Belgian lace handkerchiefs, embroidered with his initials, that he has sent to him twice a year. He waves away the remark, expecting his tailor to feel duly reprimanded.

The tailor is far from crestfallen. 'Your nephew was here earlier, my lord. A fine gentleman, with such an original understanding of the fashions of the day.'

'My nephew? Henri Dênou?' And then the folly of what the tailor has said makes him laugh. 'If you think he will pay you, think again. I know for a fact he hasn't yet come into his inheritance.'

'He has already settled his account, my lord.'

My lord's mouth falls open. 'The deuce he has,' he says.

Lord Wardell, who dislikes breakfast and the fuss surrounding it, now feels dearly the absence of nourishment.

Smooth as butter on bread, the tailor says, 'He asked after you, my lord. He's returning this afternoon for another fitting.'

The tailor opens the dressing room door and there stands the clerk, a pen in his hand, his small, gold-rimmed spectacles on the end of his nose. He holds out Lord Wardell's bill.

'It's been over three years, my lord, and we are not a charity.'

Although it's spring and not yet uncomfortably warm, Lord Wardell feels the room to be stuffy and all merriment of the season leaves him.

Worse, the clerk shows no remorse for his rudeness in presenting the bill but stares at him, unblinking.

It is Lord Wardell who looks away first. He has it in mind to tell the little pipsqueak what he thinks of him. He doesn't. There are two bills in life you must attend to: your tailor's and your club's and both are in need of immediate attention if he doesn't want his reputation to slip-slide the way of his finances.

He fares a little better at Lobb's and, though advised against it, he has taken the boots that now pinch his bunions.

His next call is his solicitor. At Mr Gutteridge's chambers he demands to be seen.

'Do you have an appointment, my lord?' asks Mr Briggs, the solicitor's clerk.

'I don't need one,' says Lord Wardell.

'I'm afraid today you do, my lord, as Mr Gutteridge is in court. He's expected back in the next half hour.'

'I'll wait.' He sees there's a fire burning in the clerk's office. 'Why in May do you have a fire?'

'The cold and the damp, my lord.'

'I wouldn't allow a servant of mine to be such a wastrel.'

The clerk shows Lord Wardell to Mr Gutteridge's room. There is a stone coldness to it and he feels his toes then his fingers go numb and wishes there was a fire lit there. The longer he waits the more he stews in the juice of perceived injustice.

When at last Mr Gutteridge returns he asks Lord Wardell, without preamble, the purpose of this unexpected visit. This is spark enough to ignite the tinder and Lord Wardell rages, demanding to know if the solicitor has given Henri an advance on his inheritance.

'No, my lord, I haven't,' says Mr Gutteridge, arranging the papers on his desk. 'And I advise you to choose your words carefully before you make accusations. Is there anything else I can help you with?'

'Dammit, sir – if not from you, where did the boy get his money?'

'As you know, the late Comte de Vernon's sister, the young count's aunt, escaped to America and feared her brother, sister-in-law and nephew to be dead. When she wrote to you, you replied that the boy had been saved but was... let me find the exact word...'

'Imbecilic,' says Lord Wardell.

'Indeed. The young count wrote to tell his aunt he had won a scholarship to Brasenose College, Oxford, and that you, my lord, had told him he must go as a servitor. His aunt was impressed to learn that this college gives a needle and thread to each student on New Year's Day to encourage thrift.'

'Yes, yes, but none of this answers my question, sir. How did my nephew come by his money?' Lord Wardell's blood, often simmering, now boils over. 'I demand an answer.'

Mr Gutteridge glances at the handsome clock on his mantelpiece before sitting down. 'I assume the answer lies with his aunt. A pearl necklace with a diamond clasp, once a gift to her from his father, was sent to him on his twentieth birthday. A generous gift, all things considered. And now, my lord, if you will excuse me, I have briefs to read.'

'Do you know he's in London buying suits of clothes?'

'No, my lord.'

'Thrown out of Oxford, I'll wager.'

'I very much doubt that. Good day to you, my lord.'

Here sits Lord Wardell at White's, ruminating on his misfortunes. Four years ago he was one of the wealthiest men in London, having had the wit to marry well, and marry well twice. His second wife was far richer than his first and he never thought for a moment the river of riches would run dry. He can now see the stony bed of the river and it looks like hell.

Still he can't fathom where Henri's wealth has come from. An undergraduate's fees are high and he doubts very much if a few pearls would cover them, let alone the tailor's bills.

At least this club is a place of sanctuary for English aristocracy. In its golden halls, members drink and dine, and win and lose. He has lived most of his adult life in that mystical place that lies between infinitesimal hope and sudden disappointment when you realise good fortune has left you, when Bacchus, your only comfort, sits in the shadows, waiting to drown you in one of his barrels. He wonders which of the ancient gods deals with feet, because his new boots are torturing his bunions.

'Weevil!' He looks up to see Lord Telford.

Cruikshank has recently drawn Telford as a jester with money leaking from every pocket. He takes the chair opposite Lord Wardell.

'New boots, Weevil?'

How he hates the nickname, a leftover from days at a school of purgatory and buggery.

His unwelcome companion orders champagne and Lord Wardell assumes the countenance of a man of great wealth and prosperity, which is wasted on Lord Telford who falls into a drunken sleep, leaving Lord Wardell alone once more with his thoughts.

What is to become of him? Every year prices increase and, because of the war, taxation rises, which falls heavy on the aristocracy. He's put down his carriage, dismissed the footmen, bricked up his windows – even at the front of the house. As for his daughters – if they don't find husbands this season they will sink. One glorious wager could reverse the ill-fortune which has attended him these past four years.

To distract himself he picks up a scandal rag. Usually there's something in the tittle-tattle to amuse him.

Courteous reader.

The brightest star in London this May time must be the enchanting Weather Woman. She is a scientific sensation, one not to be missed, and I recommend selling the Chippendales and the Gainsboroughs to purchase a ticket. She has been proved accurate in all her predictions but it is her means of delivering them that is nothing short of fascinating. She is shown to perfection by Mr Victor Friezland and his daughter. Miss Friezland near outshines the Weather Woman in beauty.

Tonight they have been invited to perform for the Duke of Boswell as I know for a fact because this fortunate writer has received an invitation.

For some unaccountable reason, Lord Wardell thinks of hailstones as he screws up the paper.

It is at this moment he notices an elegantly dressed young gentleman entering the club room. Lord Wardell, whose eyesight is not as sharp as it once was, recognises him and then thinks it's impossible; his nephew – who he realises he hasn't laid eyes on for nearly four years – would never be admitted to this club. As he comes closer, Lord Wardell sees quite clearly that it is indeed Henri Dênou, looking every inch the young aristocrat. The cut of his coat is immaculate and having a handsome figure, unlike Lord Wardell who has run to fat, he wears it with style. Lord Wardell thinks his nephew must have seen him and, irritated, stands and calls his name. Slowly, Henri looks round, seemingly neither pleased nor displeased to see his uncle. Just then the waiter arrives with the champagne so the meeting is awkward with a muddle about glasses and whether or not Henri will be joining them.

'Finished at Oxford?' asks Lord Telford who has woken up.

'Yes, sir. For the last year I've been working for Sir Edward Fairbrother. He—'

'The "natural philosopher"', interrupts Lord Telford. 'I hear he wants us all floating above the city in balloons. Ha ha! But a clever man, yes, a clever man indeed, if somewhat too obsessed with the workings of his internal organs.'

Before Lord Wardell can ask his nephew the question that has been occupying his thoughts since morning, Henri looks up, bows and excuses himself.

'There you are, Dênou,' calls a young gentleman and it is clear they are friends, not passing acquaintances.

Lord Wardell sees Henri's friend is the son of the Duke of Boswell. He supposes his nephew met him at Oxford.

'We shall be late for the Weather Woman and that will never do,' he says. He takes Henri's arm and they disappear into the spring evening.

What a bloody awful day it's been.

'Cheers, Weevil,' says Lord Telford, lifting his glass. 'Lucky devils. I'd very much like to see this Weather Woman. Never wrong, I hear. As reliable as my fob watch, which is no surprise as they were both made by the same man – Mr Victor Friezland.'

'Friezland,' says Lord Wardell slowly, and with a hornet's sting he remembers. The loss of the wager that marked the moment his luck began to run out. Victor Friezland is the man he holds responsible for all his misfortunes.

14

Outside White's, the Duke of Boswell's carriage is waiting for Henri and Bos. Henri sees it as a ship in full sail with a crew of footmen and runners. Both he and Bos would much prefer to walk but know if they did the coach would accompany them along the few streets to Brook Street.

'The only thing that makes the prospect of an evening in the company of my father bearable,' says Bos, 'is that we'll see the Weather Woman perform.'

Henri isn't fully listening. He's thinking about Lord Wardell, how bloated he's become. Even though he can't stand the man there's a sadness to his decline.

The spring evening is cloudy and it looks like it might rain.

'Sorry,' says Henri, 'what did you say? Who's beautiful? Are you talking about Kitty?'

Kitty is Lord Tillingham's daughter, and it is taken for granted – at least by the Duke of Boswell – that his son will marry the filly. The very thought of it is enough to cause Bos to become frozen with terror.

'Lord, no. I mean Miss Friezland,' says Bos. 'She has a sharp wit and doesn't suffer fools. Because of that, the young gentlemen of London are falling over themselves to woo her. And the marriageable young ladies are green with jealousy. For her part, she shows so little interest in either that she baffles them all. I've heard she had five marriage proposals last week alone. I swear there's no one to match her.' For a moment he's quiet, as if giving the matter some thought, before saying, 'Well, apart from you, perhaps.'

Henri laughs and makes light of the fact he met Miss Friezland four years ago at Mrs Dent's Magical Soiree when he was still in the employ of his uncle.

'Didn't you fall in love with her, then and there?' asks Bos.

He has no idea how accurately this has found its mark. Henri, on the verge of seeing Miss Friezland again, knows the question demands an answer but fortunately the carriage arrives at its destination and much fuss is made about the opening of the doors.

Torches light up the façade of the Duke of Boswell's house, which is one of the grandest in the street. From the entrance hall a grand staircase leads to the first floor, and although the building has fine proportions and many rooms, Henri has a feeling of a great weight pressing down on him. None of the windows has been bricked up, yet the atmosphere is gloomy. Bos walks slowly up the staircase to meet his father.

To Henri the duke looks as if he's made of granite. Immediately he sees Bos, irritation makes a winter of his features. Henri thinks that's probably the sum of their relationship: a father disappointed that his son and heir doesn't have a mistress, never gambles and is neither a rake nor a dandy.

'Here you are at last,' says the duke. 'You should have been here half an hour ago to greet your bride.'

His cheeks reddening, Bos says, as firmly as it can be said, 'She is not my bride, sir.'

'Then, sir, I suggest you get on with the thing. What the deuce is keeping you?'

'Love, sir,' says Bos.

'Love?' says the duke. 'Where do you get these ridiculous notions? A young woman of good breeding with child-bearing hips, that's what you need. For the rest, get yourself a mistress. Now, sir, I've had enough of your boyish complaints. I have guests to attend to.'

The room is packed. Henri, taller than his friend, sees Lady Tillingham and her daughter making their way towards them. He whispers a warning.

'Oh, hell,' says Bos. Only halfway across the room and Lady Tillingham is waving her small, gloved hand at him. Bos doesn't wave back. 'I fear that I'm going to be eaten alive until all that is left of me is a bag of bones. Sometimes I think there is no answer but to marry the wretched girl.'

'Don't do it,' says Henri.

There is, he thinks, so much misery to be found in this game of marriage. Pushy mothers with greedy eyes, greedy daughters who only want to outdo their friends. What would he do with a dull wife? He'd seen too many of his friends marry into misery. No, this is not to be his fate.

'Good evening, my lord,' says Lady Tillingham, pushing her daughter in front of her until Kitty is almost pressed against Bos. 'The duke was kind enough to inform us you were delayed – nothing of consequence I hope.' Seeing the open doors leading onto the balcony, she suggests Kitty would love to be shown the garden.

'I think that's an excellent idea,' says Henri.

'You do?' says Bos, surprised.

The balcony runs the width of the house and doors open onto it from two large rooms. Lanterns are being lit in the garden. Bos looks even more nervous for there is a willow tree and a shrubbery not too far away and a young marquess might innocently go into those shadows and come out engaged to be married.

Bos turns, saying it's going to rain, and goes back inside to the safety of the crowd, Kitty trailing after him. For a few minutes, Henri stays on the balcony alone.

He's about to join Bos when he stops. At the far end of the long balcony a young lady is looking out over the garden, lost in thought. Certain it's Miss Friezland, he steps back into the doorway. He's surprised at his reaction. Why not say something? This is the moment, the perfect opportunity to thank her, to ask her if it's the machine that predicts the weather or if it's really been her all along. But it's too late – she's gone.

That ball Bos batted at him in the carriage earlier still demands an uncomfortable reply, if only to himself. After the pain of losing his parents he never wanted to care for anyone again. But, yes, he has fallen a little in love with her. He even knows the lane near Tooley Street in Southwark where she lives. How does he know? Simply because often when he came down from Oxford and took one of his long walks, he had happened to find himself passing the Friezland house.

Rain, thinks Neva. She tilts her head up to the sky and smiles to herself. Tomorrow she will go with Papa to a lecture by Sir Edward Fairbrother and she will be able to wear her hair short with no need for ribbons and pins. Tomorrow she can be Eugene Jonas, her second skin that allows her to go where no woman is wanted. Papa has long given up finding objections to the disguise. It has been so elegantly executed and, so far, no one has suspected Mr Jonas is not what he seems.

She is being watched, a gaze of curiosity. She knows that gaze. Some look at her with longing, some with envy, some with lust. None of them has seen her. She takes a step back and knows whoever is standing at the other end of the balcony can no longer see her, though she senses he is still there. The rain falls heavy in puddles and splashes at the hem of her gown. She goes back into the room where she and Papa have set up the Weather Woman. A footman enters and closes the windows and the shutters.

The cellist is there, puffing on his pipe. They've gone through four such players over the last three years. This one has terrible breath, but he's without doubt the best musician they've had.

As the footman leaves and the double doors click shut, the cellist says, 'This is the most funereal of houses. You could almost call it a mausoleum.'

'Yes,' says Neva. 'I wonder why that is.'

'The walls are heavy with stale conversations. They weigh a house down.'

Neva examines the walls. They're decorated with a fresco which in any other house would look enchanting. A balustrade of painted stone runs round the room, behind which stand groups of gentlemen and ladies dressed in the style of the *Commedia dell'arte*. Harlequin drapes his arms round Columbine, Pierrot looks on jealously, and Punchinello bears an uncanny resemblance to the Mr Punch of her nightmares. There is a small dog wearing a ruff and even a dancing bear.

Neva shivers. At least she isn't hidden away like her mother.

Victor comes in, looking at his fob watch. 'Are we ready?' he says.

'Papa, do you think conversations seep into walls?' asks Neva.

'If the one I've just had with the duke is anything to go by, I would say yes. He's the most morbid of men. He has a bee in his bonnet about his poor, benighted son marrying a girl called Kitty.'

'That's money for you,' says the cellist.

To which there doesn't seem to be an answer.

The three of them turn as the double doors at the end of the room are thrown open and quickly they take up their positions. The cellist begins to play. Neva and Victor stand as they always do in the shadows behind the Weather Woman. They're used to assessing their audience. Tonight's guests are colourful butterflies that flutter into the room, flighty creatures feasting on the syrup of novelty. It's apparent to both Neva and Victor that if these ladies and gentlemen are not immediately captivated by the Weather Woman, she will be instantly forgotten.

Over the time they've been showing the Weather Woman, Victor has made some little alterations to her. Small things, he's discovered, make a big difference. She now opens and shuts her eyes, her head turns from side to side. This all requires different workings, but the winding and the moving of levers and cranks is what convinces the audience that it is indeed the machine predicting the weather. In addition, the Weather Woman has, thanks to Cassie, a more extensive and fashionable wardrobe.

At last, everyone is seated. Victor is about to step forward when suddenly and with a military step the duke comes towards him, raising his hand to silence the cellist.

He turns to face his guests, saying, 'Before we start, I have just a few words…' The few words go on and on.

Yes, thinks Neva, the walls are weighed down by laboured conversations that dampen the spirit. She looks out into the audience and feels a jolt of excitement. Isn't that Henri Dênou at the far end of the room?

Just then the duke says, 'And finally I wish to mention my dear friends Lord and Lady Tillingham. My son will very soon be making their delightful daughter his bride.'

There is a general murmur of approval. The blushing Kitty

gently fans herself and the door that has previously been closed is now abruptly opened and two gentlemen leave. One is Henri Dênou.

Before the murmuring builds and before the duke, now scarlet-faced, loses his temper, Victor gives the sign for the cellist to start playing again. Victor knows if he doesn't catch the audience's attention straight away then all is lost.

He puts energy into every word, the timing is perfect and the questions keep coming. The one question only Neva would like answering is why has Henri Dênou left?

Tonight there are so many guests and so many requests for predictions.

'Ladies and gentlemen,' says Victor, more than once, 'one at a time, please.'

Unlike the audiences at fairs and tea gardens they had once been used to, everyone here feels entitled to have their weather requests answered.

Neva is exhausted. The last question comes from a red-coated military gentleman. He stands and his voice booms a command across the room.

'Tell me if the Thames will freeze in 1811.'

For a moment Neva's foot nearly touches the pedal. Realising what she was about to do, she lets the Weather Woman's arms fall.

'Sir,' says Victor politely, 'as I said in my introduction, one week from today is as far ahead as the Weather Woman can see.'

By the time the curtain is drawn over the little wooden lady, Neva can't wait to be gone. There is a standing ovation, as there always is. A few people drift away but most stay to talk to Victor while the young gentlemen, fascinated by Neva, each try to outdo the other in flattery. She hopes Mr Dênou might return but he doesn't, and the unexpected feeling of disappointment confuses her.

She receives four handwritten marriage proposals. The idea of being married to any of these silly dandies fills her with a sense of dread. Tomorrow, she thinks, Papa and I will go to the lecture about the naming of clouds and in the role of Eugene Jonas I'll be safe from such nonsense.

15

May 1808 and March 1805

Looking back, Neva tries to remember the beginning of Eugene Jonas, the moment her imaginary friend, the cloud walker, came down to earth, wearing tall boots of gravity. In the tangle of years that have tied Eugene and Neva together it's hard to recall how the corporeal Eugene Jonas had started innocently enough with her wish to learn to row. It was during those lessons with Mr Cutter that he began to take on a human form. Until then he had been a figment of her imagination. Neva soon found in this role a freedom that no young lady would ever be granted in polite society. Now at the age of twenty-two, Neva has been playing the part long enough to do it with confidence. Eugene Jonas lives in the wardrobe. He comes to life with the knotting of the cravat, the buttoning of the waistcoat, with the tilt of the hat.

Eugene is everything Neva isn't. No matter how hard she tries, and she *does* try, Neva is taken no more seriously than a cut-out character from a toy theatre. She is looked down on by ladies of high society for her lack of breeding and looked up to by young gentlemen with fanatical notions of marriage. She is rarely asked an intelligent question about the Weather Woman.

But Eugene Jonas is seen as having a brilliant mind and his

witty observations on life and people are not to be missed. Slowly and imperceptibly, she has divided herself into two distinctly separate people. She worries occasionally that she is losing sight of who she really is and that Neva Friezland is becoming invisible.

But playing the part of the young man is a stimulant that fills her with excitement. A dancer on the edge – at any moment she might be discovered for who she is – and here she stops, for who is she? She now knows more about Eugene than she does about Neva.

No one tells Eugene Jonas his ideas are far-fetched, his notions on the weather fantastical. No lecture hall bars him; quite the reverse, he and his myriad questions are welcomed. No dinner club turns him away on the grounds that ladies are not allowed. Debates on natural science greet him with open doors. But all this, Neva knows, comes at a price.

It's too early to go downstairs. She puts on her dressing gown and looks out across the garden to the river. Night now has sung a languid goodbye to the moon. Silhouetted in the breaking dawn light are a multitude of ships of various build and rigging: sailing barges, brigs of war, fishing-smacks, schooners, sloop-rigged barges, oyster-boats and luggers. The river never sleeps. Neva could sit here in this moment forever on the cusp of a changing tide. She thinks of the time before Eugene Jonas became what he is today. She was nineteen, and the role she was playing demanded a better disguise. But Auntie thought it was time to put Eugene Jonas away.

'It was all right when she was younger,' Elise said one day over dinner. 'It was a good way to get her out of the workshop. But now...'

'But now what?' asked Neva.

'It might well be considered off-putting, you dressing as a boy and all the rest,' said Elise.

'Off-putting to whom?' asked Neva.

'Not to mention upsetting to a gentleman's natural intellectual superiority,' continued Elise.

'Intellectual superiority?' said Victor, laughing. 'Neva is far cleverer than nearly any gentleman I know.'

'But Auntie has a point, Papa,' said Neva, straight-faced. 'I did read a doctor's report that suggested too much study has a damaging effect on a woman's ovaries.'

'Not while we're eating, Neva,' said Elise, helping Victor to potatoes.

'That's terrible,' said Cassie, trying not to giggle. 'Neva, you must stop studying straight away.'

'Why? I don't want to be married, I don't want children, so dried-up ovaries are of no consequence.'

'Neva!' Victor and Cassie were both in fits of laughter. 'Stop it, all of you,' said Elise, though she was struggling to keep from laughing herself.

'The only part I'm displeased with,' said Neva, 'is the prospect of turning into an unattractive, wrinkled prune.'

'That's ridiculous,' said Victor, wiping his eyes.

'It was written by a doctor,' said Neva.

'A doctor with a small, inferior brain, I would suggest,' said Victor. 'You should see those comments for what they are: a man who is frightened of women. If we had a more equal society, there would be no need for Eugene Jonas.'

'Victor, you just encourage Neva,' said Elise. 'How is she ever going to get along in the world?'

'It's simple. Neva stays at home, Eugene goes out in society because no place is barred to him.'

Elise sighed. 'You're going to tell me that the benefits of keeping Eugene Jonas outweigh losing him.'

'Well, Auntie, what would Neva do?' said Cassie. 'Can you see her sitting demurely, doing needlework, painting flowers, learning to play the piano? Calling on other ladies, attending balls?'

'No,' said Elise, knowing she was defeated. 'Then I suggest, if you're determined to keep Eugene, a better disguise might be useful.'

It was at this opportune moment that Mr Cutter rang the bell at the garden gate. Being told of the dilemma, he said he knew of someone who would be able to help.

'It's a precaution,' said Victor, 'to make sure no one discovers Neva's true identity.'

And it was with this in mind that on a foggy grey morning in March Mr Cutter had taken Neva downriver to an inn in Deptford.

'Why are we going there?' asked Neva.

Deptford was known as the place of a hundred inns, taverns and public houses. Sailors and shipbuilders, captains and lieutenants, were all able to frequent an establishment to suit their sensibilities. In short, the class divide was maintained, the status quo undisrupted.

The sight of the Crooked Ship brought back distant memories to Neva, fragments of the night the inn at Rotherhithe crashed into the river.

'It doesn't look safe,' said Neva.

Mr Cutter laughed. 'Mr James built it that way so that when his customers are drunk they think themselves sober and the world level.'

'It's still not safe,' said Neva. 'Why are we here?'

'To meet Mr James,' said Mr Cutter.

'Is there a particular reason for this?'

'Yes. Mr James runs the Crooked Ship and is a barber on Wednesdays and Saturdays. Now hurry up and come ashore, or the boat will sink with the weight of your questions.'

The bar had the smell of beer and tobacco, mingled with the iron scent of the Thames. The floor had just been scrubbed and a large man with a fine beard and bushy eyebrows was putting down fresh sawdust.

'Good morning to you, Mr James,' said Mr Cutter.

Mr James straightened up. He had a ruddy complexion and Neva imagined he had spent most of his working life at sea.

'This is Eugene Jonas,' said Mr Cutter.

Neva was still none the wiser but it was apparent Mr James knew the reason for this visit. He put down the bucket of sawdust and stood there, legs akimbo, arms folded. He studied Neva as if she was a specimen in a museum. And occasionally he tutted. The tutting showed his two gold teeth.

'Hmm,' he said at last. 'She looks exactly what she is – a girl dressed as a lad. So you want to pass as a young gentleman, do you? Take off your hat.'

Neva hissed at Mr Cutter. 'Why did you tell him?'

Mr James cleared his throat. 'I said, take off your hat.'

Neva's lush, curly hair tumbled down her back. As she went to put her hat back on, Mr James said, 'No, I haven't finished.'

'Finished what?' said Neva, irritated that Mr Cutter of all people should have spoken of her as a girl.

Mr James walked slowly round her, ignoring her outburst.

He then took a deep breath and said, 'I don't like to disappoint, Mr Cutter, as you well know. But it would be wrong to encourage expectations that cannot be met. To be honest, I think there's very little hope of this project of yours succeeding. For a start we are dealing with a young lady who is beautiful and beauty cannot be covered up by whiskers and a wig. I wish you luck and I bid you good day.'

'Wait,' said Neva, 'you haven't asked me what kind of young man I want to be.'

'A good point, a good point. All right, what kind of young man are you?'

'I'm too slight of build to be considered manly. I'm too clever to be seen as incompetent. I cannot boast a beard like yours but I don't want to. I'm eccentric. I think I could pass as a young dandy. I can fight and fire a pistol, I don't gamble but I'll have a game of chess with you and if you're fool enough to bet on the outcome, that's your loss. I win every time. The knight is the most unexpected of all the pieces on the board. It's the one that wrong-foots nearly everyone.

'If I had a tailor, he would be interested in my designs. I like to have a pinched-in waist, baggy pantaloons, a high collar for my frock coat. I don't wear hunting boots. I don't ride but I like rowing.'

'Do you like women?' asks Mr James.

'No, I much prefer men. But on the whole, if asked, I would say I like my own company best of all, and that of Papa, Auntie and Cassie. And of course Mr Cutter, when he is not giving away secrets.'

'And how would you look the part?' asked Mr James.

'First, my face,' said Neva. 'I want blue-tinted spectacles.'

'Why?' asked Mr James.

'Light hurts my eyes and gives me headaches.'

'What would you have in your pockets?'

'A fob watch which is elaborate to say the least and phenomenally expensive. I would carry snuff on me for other people's pleasure but I really do not enjoy sneezing that much. A handkerchief.'

Mr James said nothing but in the silence came a voice.

'Charlie!' A woman appeared at the foot of a narrow staircase.

'Oh,' she said, seeing Neva. 'So she's the young lad. I'm Rose, Mr James's wife.'

'What do you think, sweetheart?' said Mr James.

'I think you have your work cut out, my love.' She put her arm round Mr James's waist and kissed him on the cheek. 'Don't be too hard on the girl. Remember, we all started somewhere. Can I get you a beer, Mr Cutter?'

'Let's leave now,' said Neva, pulling at Mr Cutter. 'Now you've told everybody, there's no point in...' The lump of rage in her throat choked her.

'What do you think Mr James is?' asked Rose.

'I don't know, it's not my concern. A bartender. I want to leave.'

'Mr James is a woman,' said Rose.

All Neva's fury melted away. She stared at Mr James.

'It's our secret,' said Rose. 'That's the way we wish to keep it. Put it this way: your secret is safe with us because our secret is safe with you and Mr Cutter. Charlie was born into the wrong sex. He's the love of my life. We've been married fifteen years.'

Mr James laughed. 'That's stumped you, hasn't it?'

Neva nodded.

'Well, we'd better get started.'

'Started on what?' asked Neva, knowing it was a foolish question.

'Learning to be a gentleman,' said Mr James and he told Mr Cutter to return at three o'clock when the inn opened for business.

Anxious at the departure of Mr Cutter, Neva found a piece of skin on her finger and pulled at it.

'You must stop that,' said Rose. 'You'll give the game away.'

'Now, to work,' said Mr James. 'Do you know what's between a man's legs?'

'No,' said Neva, blushing.

'Well, you have to know,' says Rose. 'This is what you're going to wear every time you come here.'

'What is it?' asked Neva.

'A penis and balls made out of calico,' said Rose. 'I made it specially for you. It's weighted with beans.' She strapped it round Neva.

'No one can walk with that dangling between his legs,' said Neva.

Rose laughed. 'It doesn't just dangle,' she said, and quietly explained with no embarrassment exactly what a penis does.

Neva screwed up her face. 'It sounds messy,' was her conclusion. But the appendage altered the way she walked.

For the next three months on Mondays and Wednesdays Neva learned to lower her voice, to walk with a stride, to carry herself with the attitude of a young gentleman.

In the meantime, Cassie ordered clothes to her own design, made shirts and cravats, purchased shoes, and all was assembled at the Crooked Ship. On the final day of Neva's lessons, Mr Cutter, who hadn't seen anything of her progress, sat sipping a beer, waiting for her to appear.

In the neat back parlour the final part of Neva's transformation was taking place. Mr James cut off Neva's pigtail, wrapping it carefully for a wigmaker to use to make the hairpiece she would need as Neva.

'I thought I would give you a Cherubim,' said Mr James. 'All these curls will make you the height of fashion.'

Now Neva no longer saw herself in the mirror. She saw Eugene Jonas smiling back at her as the scissors snipped away.

She thought, this is why men have so many thoughts in their head. They're not encumbered with the weight of hair that needs daily attention.

When Mr James had finished, Rose helped Eugene to dress, leaving him to tie his own cravat.

'Now,' said Mr James, 'go out the back way, come in and introduce yourself to Mr Cutter.'

Neva didn't feel she was acting as she walked into the bar. She knew she was not Neva, she was Eugene Jonas.

Mr Cutter nearly spat out his beer. Before him, wearing small, blue-lensed spectacles, stood a striking dandy.

Now, three years later, Neva knows despite all her acting on the stage of life, despite the many silent curtain calls, she is in a quandary. Women are attracted to Eugene Jonas, Eugene Jonas is not attracted to women. Neva has decided she will never marry, never have children. This is what she tells herself on the morning of Sir Edward Fairbrother's lecture.

16

May 1808

Neva goes down to the kitchen, the warmest room in the house this cool May morning. Cassie is there, waiting for the kettle to boil.

'What was it like at the Duke of Boswell's last night?' she asks. 'Were all the high and mighty there? All the *bon ton?*'

Neva sits down at the kitchen table. 'And good morning to you, Miss Lamb.'

'Yes, good morning,' says Cassie impatiently, jumping a little on the soles of her feet. 'I just want to know.'

'The house was made of iron,' says Neva as the kettle bubbles for attention.

'No it wasn't,' says Cassie, pouring the boiling water into the teapot. 'What was the house really like?'

Neva yawns. 'It felt as if the house was made of iron. The duke, who's made it so, is a tedious man and he wants his son to marry someone called Kitty.'

Cassie looks at her quizzically. 'You didn't say any of that aloud, did you?'

'No. I wouldn't.'

'You do sometimes. Who else was there?' asks Cassie, who

follows all the gossip pamphlets and scandal rags. She keeps a list of the great and important. If any of them had been there last night, it would be considered, by her at least, to be a noteworthy occasion.

'The duke's son was there, he who is being marched into marriage with someone or other.'

'With Kitty Tillingham, Lord and Lady Tillingham's daughter. They are well connected and own land in Somerset, as does the Duke of Boswell. And if his son marries—'

Neva laughed. 'Cassie – how do you know all this?'

'I study the papers.'

'Henri Dênou was there,' says Neva.

'Neva! Stop and start again,' says Cassie. 'You mean the Comte de Vernon, the young gentleman who gave you his pebble?'

'Yes.'

'And did you speak to him?'

'No. He didn't stay.'

'What did he look like?'

'The same as when I first saw him, just a little older.'

'You're being very light in your replies this morning,' says Cassie. 'I can't go to these things. You do, and I like to know what happens, who is there and what they wear.'

'I'm sorry,' says Neva. 'I think I was disappointed Mr Dênou didn't wait to see the Weather Woman. But now I think about it, it was probably for the best.'

'Why?'

'He looked a dandy and every lady in the room had an eye for him.'

Cassie laughs. 'Of course. All the young ladies want to marry him, he's a French count.'

'Anyway, he left.'

'That's a pity,' says Cassie.

Neva takes the four marriage proposals from her

dressing-gown pocket. After Victor has read them Cassie will stick them in a scrapbook.

'One day,' says Cassie, 'when you're an old maid, you'll look back at all these proposals and wish you'd accepted one of them.'

'No I won't,' says Neva firmly but Cassie isn't listening. She is reading.

'Oh my – this one's from William Watson Wilberforce. The Wilberforces call all their sons William Watson Wilberforce.'

'Please don't read it,' says Neva. 'At least not out loud.'

'But listen to this—'

'No.'

'Then I will just tell you. Wilberforce William Watson—'

'You said William Watson Wilberforce before.'

Cassie takes no notice. 'He has an estate in Sussex and six children. He needs a wife, and a mother for his children. I think you can cross out "wife". He has five thousand pounds a year for your entertainment. You know what that means – he's most probably as mean as a capon on Sunday.'

'Stop it, Cassie, please. They're all awful. They see me as nothing more than a… a princess from a fairy tale.'

'What will you do when you meet someone who sees you for what you are and you fall in love?'

'I won't. Love is for fools. *You* haven't found anyone.'

'That's because I am waiting.'

'For what?'

'For a knight. I said to myself when I came to live here I will never leave unless I fall in love with a knight and he falls in love with me. And as that's never going to happen, I'm very content to stay where I am.'

'I'm very content to stay here too.' Neva thought for a moment. 'I'm going to ask Papa if you can come to help set up the Weather Woman at our next performance.'

The bell rings in the kitchen, which means someone is at

the garden gate. Cassie goes to answer it and comes back carrying a cage with a canary in it and a large bouquet.

'It's very yellow,' says Neva, wiggling her little finger through the bars at the canary. 'And it's a rather beautiful cage.'

Sunlight is shining lazily through the windows directly onto Neva's mass of short, curly hair and as Elise enters the kitchen she thinks Neva looks like an enchanting imp. She smiles and the canary starts to sing.

'Well, at least it's not a puppy,' she says. 'I don't know about starting a flower stall but I think we should start selling animals. How many have we had so far?'

Neva has lost count. She has been sent horses, hens and one sheep and numerous puppies, all of which have been found homes. One admirer wished to present her with a tiger; another sent peacocks. The noise was terrible. They went to a menagerie and the tiger was politely refused.

Victor joins them for breakfast.

This is the time of day Neva likes best when the hours before them are patted out and organised into parcels of time. Without this, Neva is sure the day would roll away into a muddle.

Cassie asks Victor about last night's performance and he is more forthcoming than Neva and gives better descriptions. He imitates the dreadful duke and his poor beleaguered son before turning his attention to the letters in front of him. One is a wedding proposal from a Colonel Fitzpatrick.

'The colonel says he has enough money to indulge your every whim, Neva, and wants to know if you would do him the honour of accepting his hand in marriage.'

'Would one hand out of his whole body suffice?'

'I think you would have to take all of him.'

'Then he will never do. Anyway, I'm not sure having my every whim indulged would be a good thing.'

Victor passes the letter to Cassie. 'Another one for the scrapbook,' he says, and opens a note which arrived that morning by footman. 'Ah. This is more like it. It's from a Mr Henri Dênou.'

'The Comte de Vernon,' says Cassie.

'A count, is he?' says Victor. 'Well, he has excellent manners for a count. He apologises for his rudeness in leaving without seeing the Weather Woman perform, but he had to attend to his friend. He's very much hoping to see the performance next Wednesday and he might then have a chance to meet Miss Friezland and rekindle the acquaintance. He finishes with the usual salutations and all the rest of it. What acquaintance was that, Neva?'

'Oh, fee fi fo fum. Life is complicated,' says Neva.

'Perhaps we should invite him to supper,' says Cassie, slyly.

'No,' says Neva. 'That's a terrible idea.'

'Why?' says Victor. 'You'll meet him when we next do the Weather Woman.'

'Yes,' says Elise, glancing curiously at Cassie. 'Why not ask him to dine?'

'Because... because then, if he ever meets Eugene, he'll know it's me.'

'No one else has,' says Victor laughing.

'Mr Dênou is different.'

'So I see. That's why I'm going to invite him. No argument.'

'But Papa...'

Victor takes out his fob watch. 'We should get dressed. The lecture is at Bedford Square and starts at half-past eleven.'

'And this evening,' says Cassie, 'we're going to the theatre to see Grimaldi in *Mother Goose*. We have seats in the circle at Covent Garden, not in the gods as usual.'

'Soon,' says Victor, 'we might even have a box.'

★ ★ ★

There's no point worrying about what might never happen, Neva thinks as she dresses. The lapels of the frock coat and the cravat with its high neck are essential to her disguise. Her slim, boyish figure makes her a handsome dandy, if slightly feline. As Eugene she has the confidence Neva doesn't possess. So complete is her transformation that now Victor addresses Eugene in a manner he would never use to address Neva. No one apart from him, Elise, Cassie and Mr Cutter know about Neva's double life. Certainly not the coachman who assists Victor into his town carriage along with his business partner.

'What are you thinking, sir?' asks Eugene.

'I'm wondering if the time has come to buy a house made of stone and brick. A solid investment, Mr Ratchet says.'

'It's a good idea,' says Eugene. 'But to leave the river... I don't think Mrs Friezland would like that.'

'Perhaps you're right. And there is George to consider. He wouldn't want to come with us and we can't do without him.'

'Let's wait and see. What with this damn war and one thing and another... did you read about Madrid? Simply terrible – so many people dead.'

The room is full of fine gentlemen and learned scholars. Anyone with an interest in meteorological observations has been invited to the lecture. Eugene adjusts his spectacles before entering the fray. It's not only his elegant dress that's noticed; what makes Eugene Jonas instantly recognisable are his blue-lensed spectacles.

Sir Edward Fairbrother, a well-heeled, middle-aged gentleman, looks as if he has never been weighed down by anything more inconvenient than his own thoughts. These being far superior to anyone else's, he is confident he alone is master of his subject.

Already Eugene doesn't like him.

Sir Edward begins.

'In two or three of my preceding lectures I gave a few rules for judging the weather by the barometer or the weather glass, and in order to improve and complete what I have begun I now mean to enter upon a series of curious and useful speculations on the evaporation of rain clouds.'

It strikes Eugene that this is a long way round the subject and not for the first time he's frustrated that no one sees the sky the way he does.

He's lost in thought until Sir Edward, who is taking questions, says, 'I agree. Unless there's a system for predicting the weather, fishermen, farmers and seafarers have to rely on weather wisdom.'

'Or the Weather Woman,' someone calls out to polite laughter.

Sir Edward continues. 'We must move beyond observing the behaviour of animals, of the frog in the jar, the swallow in the hedgerow, in order to learn of impending storms. And yes, beyond even the Weather Woman. It's necessary for science to fill the gap.'

'How?' asks a gentleman. 'The idea is preposterous, almost laughable I would say. The heavens belong to chaos. It will always be that way.'

A scholarly gentleman is standing. 'Yes, sir?' says Sir Edward.

'We need a different approach to this science, sir. It would help if there was a way of communicating the weather conditions in the different regions across this great isle to a central location. Then it should not be too difficult to calculate meteorological predictions.'

This is greeted with a murmur of approval.

Eugene stands up. 'I would venture to say, there is another element to this problem: man himself.'

'What do you mean, sir?' says Sir Edward.

'I have noticed the smoke from the chimneys in London

is already affecting the clouds and I believe this will one day have a great effect on the weather.'

'Bunkum,' says the last speaker. 'I've never heard such rubbish in my life.'

'I'm afraid you are wrong, sir, but I will not be able to prove it. Only time will.'

'Time,' says the gentleman, laughing. 'I tell you, sir, what we do on the ground has no bearing on the clouds.'

Eugene is used to people staring, used to being seen as controversial.

Safe in the guise of Eugene, it never bothers Neva what the men of science think.

'I will ask my assistant to comment on this topic,' says Sir Edward.

The assistant says a few tactful words and Eugene turns to look at him. Neva feels herself blushing. 'Papa,' she whispers, 'we must leave straight away.'

'And that, gentlemen, ends this lecture,' says Sir Edward. 'I thank you.'

There's applause, chairs grind on the floor and chatter surrounds Victor and Eugene as they move towards the door.

'Mr Friezland,' calls Sir Edward. 'Good to see you here, sir.'

Too late, thinks Neva.

'A most enjoyable lecture, Sir Edward,' says Victor. 'May I introduce you to my business associate, Mr Eugene Jonas?'

'Pleased to make your acquaintance, sir,' says Sir Edward. 'And, gentlemen, this is my assistant, Mr Henri Dênou.'

'A pleasure, Mr Dênou,' says Victor, bowing.

'I'm delighted to meet you, Mr Friezland,' says Henri. 'I'm sorry to have missed your performance last night.'

Victor nods, is polite about the lecture and Eugene stays close by his side, aware Mr Dênou is looking intently at him.

'Yours was an interesting observation, Mr Jonas,' says Sir

Edward. 'Far-sighted perhaps. But it is a radical point of view with no scientific basis.'

'You may have noticed, sir,' says Eugene, 'that when it snows and when there is fog there are particles and flakes of soot in the air. This wasn't the case three years ago. I believe it has come about in part due to the burning of sea coal. We stand on the brink of a revolution of industry; factories pumping smoke into the skies. I think we should be more careful.'

Sir Edward, unable to reply to this, turns to Victor. 'I would very much like to know, Mr Friezland, how you have constructed this machine. I gather you are unwilling to have it examined scientifically.'

'The machine is more entertainment than science but that doesn't mean Mr Jonas and I have no interest in your findings.'

'Which university did you attend, Mr Jonas?' says Sir Edward. 'Oxford or Cambridge?'

'Neither, sir,' says Eugene.

Victor sees this as the perfect opportunity to depart but Sir Edward says, 'I wonder if you might like to come with us to the Greenwich Observatory tomorrow? We would have time then to continue this conversation.'

Eugene can see Victor is in a quandary. It's an irresistible invitation. He hesitates for a moment and then says, 'It would be an honour, sir.'

The time and the place are agreed and Neva feels an enormous sense of relief as their carriage pulls away from Bedford Square.

17

It is night and Elise expected Victor and Neva home hours ago. They were only going to Greenwich. But at midday a message arrived saying Victor was invited to dine with Sir Edward Fairbrother and would be home later. It didn't say how much later.

She has now convinced herself the reason they are not back is because Eugene's true identity has been discovered. She wipes the kitchen table again and tells the wooden surface she knew all along this would happen.

How could it be any other way? It's obvious to her Neva feels something for Mr Dênou and Neva reacts badly when her emotions are tangled.

She hears the front door open.

'Where's Eugene?' asks Elise, seeing Victor standing there alone.

'I'd hoped that Neva – Eugene – would be back before me,' says Victor.

'What do you mean? Surely she has been with you all along?'

Victor looks decidedly sheepish.

'Eugene went to dine with Henri Dênou.'

She can't believe he's allowed this to happen. 'Where is she, Victor?'

'Brooks's Club in St James's Street.'

Elise puts her hand to her heart. 'But that's a gentlemen's club. What on earth made you agree to such a hot-headed scheme? What will happen if they've discovered Eugene is a woman?'

'There was nothing I could do without giving the game away.' Victor pulls out his fob watch. Nearly half-past eleven.

'Victor, you are a very clever man, you could have thought of something.'

It has begun to rain.

'I'm sure she'll be quite safe with Mr Dênou,' he says, weakly.

Feeling the heat of her fury, he walks past Elise into the long drawing room, unbuttoning his coat. They have never rowed in all the years they've been together. Not once has he seen her lose her temper but now the air crackles with her rage.

'You let your daughter go to a gentlemen's club with a Frenchman you hardly know? Have you lost your mind?'

'Believe me, Elise,' Victor pleads, 'there really was nothing I could do. We saw the Observatory, it was a fascinating tour, and then Sir Edward invited me to dine. I think he meant all of us but Mr Dênou suggested he would leave us to our weighty discussions and take Mr Jonas to his club. And before I could think up an excuse it was decided. All I could do was ask Eugene to be home at seven o'clock.'

'"Home"? Is that what you said?'

'No, of course not. I said he shouldn't have a late night because we have business to attend to.' He pushes his hand through his thick white hair. 'What could I do? Eugene was happy as a lark and went off in Mr Dênou's phaeton at a devil of a pace.'

'Those contraptions,' says Elise, contemptuously. 'I've heard they go far too fast. Neva could be lying in a ditch for all we know. What happens if it's discovered Eugene is a woman, is really Neva? There'll be a terrible scandal. And think how it will affect the Weather Woman. You old fool – what have you done? You'd better put on your coat again and go and find her. Don't come back until you have her safe.'

Victor picks up his muffler and his hat and without saying a word leaves the house.

Elise sits at the kitchen table, brushing off invisible crumbs and fearing the worst.

'Where are you, Neva?' she says aloud.

She thinks back to the night before. They had all four gone to see Grimaldi in *Mother Goose*. Did anything happen there to encourage her to go off with Mr Dênou? It makes no sense. She knows Neva well and the very idea of being alone with a stranger would cause her great anxiety. Even as Eugene she has never experienced such an outing as the one she has now embarked on. Elise remembers how Neva reacted when she saw Henri Dênou in the audience.

She, Neva and Cassie were dressed in the most fashionable muslins – my three beauties, Victor had called them – and Elise had felt immensely proud of her little family as they sat at the front of the circle, looking down on the great and the grand. Cassie had said just seeing the ladies and gentlemen in all their finery was a performance in itself. And for once Neva didn't seem worried by the crowds as she often was when they went out. She and Cassie chatted happily, Cassie pointing out the famous people and who she thought they were. She said they had a better view than a bird up there.

Elise had particularly noticed a good-looking young gentleman in the middle of a group of young people because he was staring up at them. Neva hadn't seen him but it occurred to Elise that it might be Henri Dênou. It was Cassie who pointed out the Duke of Boswell's son in the same group and she was about to say something else when Neva abruptly moved back and sat upright, hiding between Victor and Elise, her fists clenched tight. Elise asked if that was Mr Dênou and took Neva's hand.

'Why is he looking up at us?' Neva had said.

At the interval she didn't want to leave her seat so Cassie and Victor went to find refreshments.

'Auntie,' she'd said, 'will I always be like this?'

'Like what, dear?'

'An outsider, both as a woman and as a man. The bit of me that fits in nowhere. The ringing I hear as I go round a corner, as if a bell is attached to me. I don't fit the square, I'm too irregular; I'm too angular for the curves. This age is not made for me.'

A single tear fell on Elise's hand.

Neva had left before the end of the performance. After the curtain came down, Mr Dênou was waiting for them in the foyer. Victor introduced Elise as his wife and Cassie as his wife's niece. Victor and Elise had been married for two years. It wasn't strictly legal but so far no one had noticed.

'Isn't Miss Friezland in your party? I was sure I saw her,' Mr Dênou asked.

'A slight headache,' said Elise, 'she's waiting in the carriage.'

'But, my dear sir,' said Victor, 'you will meet her at our performance next week. And I hope you'll have supper with us afterwards.'

Mr Dênou had enthusiastically accepted the invitation.

Did any of that signify? The one tear, she thinks. A raindrop goes unnoticed in a storm.

Sitting alone in the kitchen, feeling dawn belonged to another world, Elise thinks about the curtain descending at the end of the show. That's what we should do with Eugene Jonas, bring the curtain down, pack him up and put him away. She should have heeded what Neva said at the theatre.

'I wasn't paying attention,' she says aloud. 'We have both been careless with Neva's gift.'

And she feels the same twisted knot of fear as she did when she knew her baby, her precious little darling, was dead. That aching loss, that uncontrollable grief now stands as a ghost, warming itself by the stove.

The clock strikes midnight.

'This has to stop,' she says. 'I promise, dear Lord, no more Eugene Jonas if only you will bring Neva home safe. No good can come of this double life. It will break her in two. How can she possibly know who she is when she plays two roles – female and male?'

Cassie, who had long retired to bed not realising the extent of the drama going on downstairs, is only woken by the sound of the carriage leaving the stables. Unable to go back to sleep, she goes down to find Elise at the kitchen table, her head in her hands.

'Oh my lordy-lord – Auntie, what's happened?'

'Neva isn't home. Victor allowed Mr Dênou to take Eugene to Brooks's.'

'No! What was he thinking?'

'He wasn't. And I fear Neva's reputation is ruined.'

The clock chimes the half hour, the candles flicker in their holders. Still it rains. The two women sit, silently imagining the worst. Minutes wade through the mud of hours. Elise feels herself on the brink of the most irrational thoughts. Neva is her daughter, her child. It matters not that she was born to another, Neva was always hers. So where is her child? At two o'clock there is still no Victor, no Neva.

'I've decided, Cassie – this must be the end of Eugene Jonas,' says Elise. 'We're putting away those clothes whether Neva wants it or not. It's too dangerous; if she's found out, think what will... This situation would never have occurred if Victor hadn't encouraged her.'

'Auntie,' says Cassie, putting a pot of tea on the table, 'thinking about it, what was Uncle Victor meant to do? If Eugene is Eugene, it's nothing that he went out with Mr Dênou. It was only a generous invitation. If Uncle Victor had made a fuss, it would have been as good as confessing Eugene was a fraud. Try not to worry. When I worked as a lady's maid the young gentleman of the family rarely made it home until the birds had started singing.'

'But if it was ever discovered that Neva—'

'Neva would be lauded and vilified in equal measure for having broken into an all-male world and got away with it as long as she did.'

'I think she must tell Mr Dênou the truth. He's coming to supper next week.'

Cassie reaches across the table and takes Elise's hand. 'Auntie,' she says softly, 'Neva is never going to marry someone as high up the social ladder as Mr Dênou – the Comte de Vernon – just as I will never marry a knight. These things don't happen.'

At the sound of the carriage they run to the door. Victor looks exhausted.

'No. It's no good,' he says, shaking the rain from his coat. 'I've sent the coachman away. I'm sorry, it's all my fault. I'm truly sorry.'

Elise puts her arm round him. 'So am I,' she says. 'I lost my temper.'

'There was nothing else I could do,' says Victor. 'That's

what happens with white lies, the truth is lost. The Weather
Woman is a lie, Eugene Jonas is a lie, Neva is—'
'Don't say it. Go to bed.'
'I can't.'
She takes his hand and leads him upstairs. 'Have a few
hours' rest and the minute it's light you must go out again.'
The clock ticks on and still Elise and Cassie wait. It's gone
three o'clock when they hear singing.

> But when I came to man's estate,
> With hey, ho, the wind and the rain,
> 'Gainst knaves and thieves men shut their gate,
> For the rain it raineth every day.

Elise pulls open the front door. The moonlight is shining
on Neva as she walks unsteadily towards her.
'Auntie – shouldn't you be in bed?' she says.
Elise takes her into the kitchen.
'Here,' says Cassie, 'have some tea.'
'Who needs tea when there is Madeira!' she says, throwing
her hat on the table.
'How long have you been drunk?' ask Elise.
'Think I'm bad, should've seen the other fellows.'
'Was Mr Dênou drunk?'
'Not as much as me. I was trying to stay sober, honest,
Auntie. I won three games of chess, Henri one. He plays fast.
I like that. No messing about, no thinking, just moves.' She
looks at Elise and Cassie and notices their expressions for the
first time. 'Why the solemn faces?'
'Did you go to Brooks's?' says Elise.
'I did. It's full of farty old men.'
'And did Mr Dênou see who you really are?'
'No, no,' says Neva, laughing. 'And that was no small feat
on my part. The thing is... yes, the thing is... I didn't... I

was doing well – as well as a frog in a fountain – before sobriety forsook me and I became devilishly drunk. But no one guessed anything.'

'Do you know that for certain?' says Elise.

'What is certain is that a circle keeps on shining. No one knew I was Neva Friezland. Because after we'd played chess...' Neva's eyes begin to close and she shakes herself awake. 'Yes, after we'd played chess, I was on the point of going or is that coming... no, I was leaving when Sir Edward Fairbrother joined us. He claimed he was a chess master and he bet twenty-five guineas I couldn't beat him in under ten moves.' She giggles.

'And did you?' asks Cassie.

'Wait, both of you, or I'll spoil the story. Then Sir Somebody Know-It-All bet ten guineas, then others bet as well until there were more guineas than fowls. I didn't have any money on me but...' She puts her finger to her lips and wobbles back and forth.

'And?' says Cassie.

Neva takes from inside her greatcoat a handful of guineas and tosses them on the table. 'I won. And Sir Edward and everyone was impressed. Or was that unimpressed? Then it all went four-eyed.'

'Four-eyed?' says Cassie.

'Four-eyed. And I'm still seeing two. Two of you, Auntie, and two of Cassie.'

Having thrown her greatcoat on the floor, Neva empties her other pockets of coins. 'I won it fair and two corner square.'

Cassie can't help but laugh.

'I think I'm a nice drunk,' says Neva. 'Papa says a man's true colour lies in a wine bottle. After Sir Edward lost he bought champagne and asked me if I was engaged to be married. Then he said to all the gentlemen there that he knew my secret. That sobered me up, I can tell you.

'"What is my secret?" I asked. And he said, "You're engaged to be married to Miss Neva Friezland." I stood up, raised my glass and said, "She is the love of my life!" So in answer to your question, Auntie, no one suspected I was Neva. But now I know I am marrying myself, whatever or whoever myself is.'

18

Dear Mr Dênou,

I write to thank you for a most entertaining evening. I much enjoyed your company and the honesty of our conversation.

I have a confession to make and you may well find what I have to say unforgivable but it is only right that you of all people should know the truth. My sincere apologies for any distress it may cause you.

Neva screws up the paper and throws it in the waste-paper basket. With a sigh she starts again. She went to bed in her clothes and still hasn't changed. She feels dreadful.

Dear Mr Dênou,

It is not for the lack of paper or ink ~~but for the lack of the right~~ words that I am failing to write what I feel. Rather, what I feel so perturbs me that I wonder if it should be put down to a sore head. And it is my head, not my heart, that is the cause of my melancholy. I want to be honest so I must gather the words to break the spell.

There is no Eugene Jonas.

This letter too finds its way into the basket.

She puts down her pen, lowers her head into her hands. She feels nauseous. What are you doing? she asks herself. Write a simple thank you note, not a confession.

She's about to start again when Cassie knocks on the door.

'Uncle Victor wants to see you.'

'Is he cross?'

Cassie comes in. 'I would say more anxious than cross.' Neva goes to the door. 'Wait,' says Cassie. 'You can't go down as Eugene. That will set everyone off again. You've slept in those clothes, haven't you?'

Neva nods.

'Lordy-lord,' says Cassie. 'Come on, let's get you washed and looking respectable.'

She helps Neva into a day dress and brushes her hair.

'Ow,' says Neva. 'My head feels as if it is broken into many different pieces, each single one sharp-edged and none of them able to make a whole.'

With a sigh Cassie follows Neva down the stairs.

The house lurches as she knocks on the door to Papa's study. Victor is standing at the window looking out at the river. When he turns he's grim-faced.

The wind will be strong and the tide high today, Neva thinks.

'I'm sorry, Papa,' says Neva. Even her words are drums in her head. Victor's voice is a trumpet voluntary.

'This is to be the end of Eugene Jonas. He has served his purpose.'

'No,' she protests. 'No, please, Papa, let me – let Eugene go out tonight.'

'Tonight?' Victor, who has rarely been shocked by anything she has ever said, is horrified. 'Tonight? No. I forbid it.'

'But Mr Dênou is going to take me to White's. We're to play chess.'

'NO!'

Neva winces. This is decidedly too loud and bruises her head.

'How do we know you got away with your disguise last night? Even if by some miracle you did, I refuse to let you take the chance again.'

Neva sits down, defeated. The house feels as if it is indeed a ship navigating the high seas. Neva holds tight to the arms of her chair, looking into a deep, rolling void.

'If Brooks's wasn't bad enough, White's would be worse,' says Victor. 'It gave me nightmares to think what would have happened if you'd been discovered. It would have been ruinous for all of us – and you especially.'

Neva takes time to rise out of this wave of unbearable noise. When she replies it's as a drowning woman. 'What am I to do then?'

'I don't understand,' says Victor.

'What am I to do – as a woman? As Neva I'm constrained to lighting candelabra and am seen at best as a little eccentric. As a woman I can't be myself, I have to pretend. No one will talk to me about politics and science. They will ask if I'm engaged, and to whom, and where do I buy my muslin. Oh, I would scream if my head didn't hurt so much. Please, Papa, I won't go to White's, I promise, but let me still be Eugene.'

'No,' says Victor firmly. Victor has not often said 'No' to her. This 'No' has the finality of a jail sentence. 'You've spent too long as Eugene Jonas. I suggest you reacquaint yourself with Neva Friezland. Write to Mr Dênou by all means; a polite note explaining you have to leave to go to the north on business. And next week when he comes to supper he will meet Neva.'

Neva is on the brink of tears. 'Then all the ease between us will be gone. We will meet and mumble platitudes at each other, meaningless nothings and all...' She stops.

'All what?'

Her face is burning. 'All gentlemen and ladies' stifled conversations, the quadrille of steps that, if not performed in the right order, trip you up in the face of society. That's the reason for so many unhappy marriages, each the result of a dance done badly. The walls around women are thick and tall and unintelligent, built by men and reinforced by women, women too frightened to think what they would do with their own freedom.' She stands, unsteadily. 'I know this to be true, Papa,' she says as she leaves. 'I have played the role of a man well.'

She curls up on her bed, wondering if there is any argument that would make Papa and Auntie change their minds. The light is too bright and she pulls the covers over her eyes and thinks about last night. Oh, last night – she could live it again and again and never tire of it. For the first time – no, that's not true – it wasn't the first time that she had spoken of money, politics and war; she has spoken of these things with other men. But not as candidly or as easily as she had with Henri Dênou. And she cannot remember being listened to with such intensity. They'd dined at half-past four, and the food was sumptuous and Henri had told Eugene that it was said that 'Dining at Brooks's is like dining at a duke's house with the duke lying dead upstairs'.

Afterwards, Henri had asked if Eugene liked to gamble.

'Do you gamble?' Eugene had asked with interest.

'Once I did and because of the sum I won, I'm not pestered to gamble again,' replied Henri. 'I play chess.'

And such was the speed at which he played, the fashionable gentlemen left off the cards and gathered to stare in amazement.

Not once did Henri find Eugene's notions extraordinary. He was intrigued, and Neva felt herself to be alive, all of her present, her mind not wandering off to the weather. And not once did she feel bored, a state of mind that could ruin an otherwise perfectly good day.

Brooks's is grand with large, lofty rooms where gentlemen are protected from the outside world and definitely from the fairer sex. Neva doesn't give a fig about royalty but here it is, lounging in the chairs, scattered among politicians and gentlemen with more than a whiff of ermine about them.

But as she thinks more about the evening other details come back to her and make her anxious. Like a hard piece of skin she begins to pull at them. Had Henri suspected her? Was she fooling herself?

The skin on the side of her index finger comes loose. This will be a good long tear. She hasn't attacked herself for some time. As Rose James had said, it would give the game away. The truth is Henri would never have taken her to White's. He was just... and there's the sharp refreshing pain, then the quiet that comes from hurt. He was just laughing at me. The thought is realised in the throbbing of her fingers; the pain momentarily stops her thinking until she picks hard at her thumb, then her middle finger and the tag of skin that rises, waiting to be pulled. This one is deep and it hurts. Her fingers betray her agony. She falls asleep and dreams of a beach. It's crowded with people dressed for a dance.

'You can't join us,' says a gentleman in an old-fashioned wig. 'You have to find Henri's pebble first.'

'But the beach is nothing but pebbles,' she shouts.

She wakes with a start. It's already evening and there's a tray of food and Auntie with what she calls the finger cure.

Neva sits up. 'Did he send a note?'

'Mr Dênou? Yes,' says Elise, taking Neva's hand.

'You've read it?'

'Your papa did.'

'What did it say?'

'That he forgot he has an engagement this evening from which he unfortunately can't free himself but he hopes you might be able to join him tomorrow evening. You will write to tell him you cannot.' Elise bathes and dresses Neva's fingers. She stays until the note is written.

Dear Sir,

I thank you for your invitation but unfortunately I have been called away on business. I leave tomorrow and will not return to London until the end of the summer. I wish you well with your plans and look forward to meeting you again.

She writes it out once more without the looking forward.

'Good,' says Elise. 'It's for the best. Sleep – you'll feel better in the morning.' She closes the door gently.

Neva lights a candle and stares for a long time at the river until it falls dark and she can see her reflection in the glass staring back at her without the artificiality of disguise. It is her, it is Neva.

She goes to her desk and picks up her pen with fingers that hurt. There is blood in the words.

Dear Henri,

I am not who I said I was but does it matter? I was me, the truth of me that is only respectable when dressed in pantaloons and waistcoats, for I know when wearing muslin no gentleman would talk to me as frankly as you did and I would never have seen the truth of you. It would have been hidden behind layers of titles, possessions, things that mean so little and yet define a life.

What matters is the soul of us and I saw that in you and I liked...

★ ★ ★

This letter is written over a month and in that time it changes and gives shape to what Neva is tentatively beginning to understand – that what she feels is more than just a liking for Henri, it is something more profound. The part of her that pulls and picks almost laughs at such a notion and in her dreams the chess-playing bear tells her Henri is not interested in Neva Friezland.

Three days after the evening at Brooks's he writes to Victor to say he regrets he must now decline Mr Friezland's invitation to supper on Wednesday. When Victor asks if another day would suit, the message that comes back is final: he is leaving London almost immediately to embark on a voyage to Iceland with Sir Edward Fairbrother and furthermore he cannot attend the next performance of the Weather Woman.

Neva knows Henri is fast disappearing over the horizon of her life. The letter that will never be sent becomes her only comfort.

> *I was a fool,* she writes. *I was a drunken fool to say I loved Neva Friezland. I didn't see that it would mean anything to you and perhaps it doesn't. But Cassie who is older and wiser than I thinks that it was this...*
>
> *And now I hear you are leaving and I am full of regret. If I could speak to you, if you were sitting before me, what would I say? That this foolish heart, this unknown heart of mine with its mansion of unoccupied rooms, has a library of a million words I would use to tell you that I, Neva, Neva, Neva, I love you, Henri Dênou. And what would come of that?*

This too finds its way to the basket and Neva thinks no more of it. But the next morning Neva's basket is to be emptied, Elise is out shopping, Neva is in the workshop with

Victor, and it falls to Cassie to throw the paper away. But she stops when she sees who the letter is addressed to and having a sentimental heart decides to iron it, and telling herself that she won't read it finds it's impossible not to, and having read it and knowing she shouldn't have makes it much, much harder to know what should be done with it.

It's such an honest letter, so true to who Neva is, and that these words and sentiments might be swallowed in the flame is distressing to Cassie. An idea, small but undoubtedly provocative, comes to her.

She has read that Mr Dênou has a house in Berkeley Square. Is that enough? She folds and seals the letter and writes his full name on it, and underneath she writes *Berkeley Square*. And this she gives to the letter-carrier.

19

June 1808

It is two weeks since Henri left England as part of Sir Edward Fairbrother's scientific voyage to Iceland to conduct experiments with an atmospheric machine. The first week after they'd set sail he'd suffered from seasickness, which still affects Sir Edward badly. No one, apart from Henri, had left his cabin. Henri is now used to the heaving sea and has adjusted to living in a world that alters his sense of balance.

He sits drinking brandy with another of the explorers, who asks, 'What made you take up Sir Edward's offer?'

'A thunderous headache and too little sleep. You?'

'A mistress who wanted a ring.'

'There's a moral to be found in that,' says Henri.

There had long been talk of such a trip but Henri's decision to accept Sir Edward's invitation was made the morning after the evening at Brooks's. Henri now has all the time he needs to reflect on his decision for there is some sobriety in the rolling of these waves. Walking up and down the deck with nothing to distract him but a sea that reaches beyond the horizon, he has to admit that the reason he is here is simple and it goes by the name of Eugene Jonas.

Henri still can't fathom why he was so unsettled by the young dandy and a thought comes to him that's as roguish as the sea is wild: he was willing to be seduced by him. He has never been attracted to his own sex, unlike several of his friends. Unlike several of his friends, he has never been in any doubt it's women he loves. He enjoys their company, he enjoys their beds. But he has never been in love. Perhaps once, when he was a very young man, he'd stubbed his toe on the notion that he might have been. But it was only a fantasy he'd glimpsed when he gave a girl a pebble.

He thinks about it rationally. He has to analyse what has happened, for his reaction to Eugene Jonas surprised and still surprises him. He thinks they are two magnetic forces, too strong to be torn apart.

Lying in his cabin with little to do, he has time to look back on that night at Brooks's and on the morning after. He must have been very drunk indeed because he'd woken with a sore head and the dawning realisation that he was jealous. Jealous that Jonas and Neva Friezland were to be married and alarmed that he wanted desperately to be with Jonas again. Is that who I am? Henri asks himself, for there was no getting away from it – he was drawn to Eugene Jonas, a young man with a mind as fast as an arrow that could spin a thought, turn it round and make you see it through a different lens. Jonas had spoken fluent French with only the trace of an accent. It was so long since Henri had spoken his mother tongue that although they were drinking far too much, the language felt like clean water to a dry mouth. He hadn't known how thirsty he was.

He enjoyed the way Jonas played chess, and his views on different styles of chess player. Henri had felt rather naïve when he said he only knew of one style and that was to attack, to which Jonas had replied that attack was only interesting if played fast.

Henri had never played with anyone as fast as he'd played with Jonas. He had been tempted to warn Sir Edward he was up against no ordinary opponent. But he admired Jonas's insouciance at the amount of money on the table. It was almost impossible to beat a chess master in under ten moves but Jonas had managed it in five.

There was no doubt this young man had rocked the foundations of his soul. It had been with relief that Henri read Jonas's letter saying he was going away. It would be as well if he didn't hear from him again. Or so he had told himself. There was no point in meeting Miss Friezland, not now, and he was disturbed to find how sharply his interest in her had waned.

He wonders, tentatively, what it would be like to be loved by Jonas and finds he envies Neva Friezland. These private admissions jog his sense of himself and make him less certain of who he is. He knows he needs to dismiss the experience as a passing folly.

After the evening with Jonas, Henri had returned in the early hours to his house in Berkeley Square. It was a house he had never felt belonged to him and he was ashamed to admit he'd bought it for show. It had grand rooms and lavish furnishings and all of it seemed to him quite soulless.

It hadn't been an excuse when he wrote to Jonas to say he had forgotten he had a prior engagement that evening. An invitation to Lord and Lady Fenton's May Ball stood on his mantelpiece. It was the height of the season and soon after the Fentons' ball, society would be preparing to leave London and the young ladies who hadn't found husbands would be shepherded home to draughty estates. This ball held the last chance to catch an unattached gentleman who might on a moonbeam decide to marry one of the season's forgotten.

Henri rose about midday to find a despondent Bos waiting in the breakfast room.

He looked up as Henri entered and said, as a condemned man might, 'It's done.'

'What's done?' asked Henri. 'Be gentle, Bos, I've been up all night – bar a couple of hours.'

'Here. See for yourself.' Bos thrust a newspaper at Henri. That day's *Times* was folded to the engagements page.

Henri sat down and asked his butler to bring champagne.

'Read it first,' said Bos. 'We don't require champagne.'

'Oh, we do,' said Henri, reading the announcement. 'Champagne when you're down to buoy you up. Who put this in the paper?'

'Who do you think? My ridiculous father.'

Henri saw his friend was on the verge of tears.

'I know it's late to be having breakfast,' said Henri as the butler brought kippers, 'but often I find it to be the most comforting of all the meals, especially when one has a devil of a head. Or has received a blow.'

'I can't eat.'

'I made the marmalade,' said Henri.

'Did you really make this?' said Bos, momentarily distracted by the marmalade. 'It has no bits in it. I hate the bits in marmalade.'

'I make it every year if I can.'

They ate in silence until Bos said, 'There it is then. You see, I'm to be wed Tuesday week. I had no choice. It would've caused a terrible scandal if I hadn't asked for Kitty's hand, once it was in the paper. My dear father, dammit, thought of everything. He even left my grandmother's ring on a silver dish next to my coffee. The Tillinghams were all up and dressed and standing in the drawing room as if they'd been placed there by a theatre manager. They looked like ravens, though to give Kitty her due she looked like a canary. Kitty. If you say it enough it sounds remarkably silly. Kitty Kitty. I don't love her, I don't even know if I like her, but that really is by the by. According to my father, I was born and bred to marry her. There was absolutely no other purpose to my existence. It means a vast estate will be created and I will be an even wealthier landowner than I would have been. And Kitty Kitty Kitty will be married and it seems that's all Kitty Kitty Kitty wants.'

'What do *you* want?'

Bos thought for a moment or two. 'You remember the other night when we were at Covent Garden?'

'Yes, and you pointed out Miss Friezland.'

'It was a strange moment – there was a young lady with her. I don't know why I watched her but she had a sweet face and I thought I would like to be loved for who I am, not for the title, just for me. I don't think she had any great breeding but I thought… It doesn't matter what I thought. It's too late. Will you be here for the wedding?'

Henri closed his eyes. 'You are a lamb to the slaughter,' he said, 'and I don't think either of you will be happy. My dear friend, I'm sorry but I'm going away.'

'Not with Fairbrother? It's a madcap scheme and it won't last. Are you really going to do this? I tell you, something else will interest Fairbrother and home he'll come leaving everyone else to clean up. My advice is don't go. But if you are going, you'd better consult the Weather Woman before you sail.'

'I found out last night,' said Henri, 'that Miss Friezland is engaged to her father's business partner, Eugene Jonas.'

★ ★ ★

The ballroom in Lord and Lady Fenton's house in Grosvenor Square was ablaze with candlelight. The chandeliers glittered brighter than diamonds. All the newly engaged couples were there, smug with success.

Those young ladies who were on their second season and had managed to become engaged this year tried to disguise their relief at not being left on the shelf. And looking on with fixed smiles were the parents who had put their daughters on show for the third season without success; these poor girls looked as appetising as over-ripe peaches.

The orchestra drowned out the knife-sharp comments and not for the first time Henri congratulated himself on escaping the noose of the marriage tie. The very fact that he was still available made him fair game and no mama with an unmarried daughter would leave him in peace.

After supper had been served Henri took refuge in the garden and there on a seat he saw Lady Sarah Wardell and her sister Lady Jane. They stood and curtsied when they saw him and it was clear Sarah had been crying.

'Shall we walk?' he said and gently led them away from a conversation he soon realised was the cause of the upset.

'Lady Palmore was telling her friend Father is nearly bankrupt. That he'd lost two fortunes on the card tables.'

'It's what everyone's saying,' said Jane.

Henri had always been fond of his two cousins who had fared little better than he under Lord Wardell's reign of terror.

'And how is the marriage market going?' he asked.

'Like the weather,' said Jane, 'unpredictable. Both of us have met gentlemen who have made offers for us. But according to our father, marrying into trade is like marrying into dirt: it soils the name.'

'Our name is already soiled,' said Sarah, sadly. 'By Father's gambling.'

'My advice is don't marry for money,' says Henri. 'And don't look so sad.'

'But what will become of us?'

It was a question he decided to address and the next day he went to see Mr Gutteridge to make sure his affairs were in order. If the worst should befall Lord Wardell then the solicitor had his instructions.

'And how long will you be gone, sir?' he asked.

'Until I feel it's right to return,' said Henri.

Less than five days later the ship set sail.

20

September 1809

It is three in the morning and Lord Wardell sits in his study, the room lit with just one candle. Before him on his desk is a bottle of his favourite port.

So this is it, he thinks. No thunder, no lightning, no figure with a long beard to tell him the demons are waiting to drag him down to Hades. Just this. An empty house, a grandfather clock that hasn't been wound. No ticking, no striking of the hour. The heartbeat of the house has been silenced by his folly. All the servants have left. His wife is upstairs weeping. It was humiliating that he had to snatch her jewellery box from her. She refused to give him the key, her last act of defiance. It almost made him love her.

He contemplates his addiction to the cards, to that moment when all hangs before him, when the void is waiting to swallow him, the blissful release, the euphoria of a win, the small quiet when the urge to gamble has been nullified – until he feels it pulling at him again, tempting him to see what the darkest part of this might mean. And he played the cards to the edge of his existence.

And here he sits. This is where his gambling has led him, this… this nothing. Nothing to be done. Nothing to be said.

Only this loneliness of nothing. Even the port cannot disguise or twist the truth. Tonight he was thrown out of his club in disgrace, unable to pay his bill. He's known men such as he. They exiled themselves to France.

He can't do that. He hasn't even the courage to blow his brains out. And the tragedy is that no one gives a fuck what becomes of him as long as whatever he does is done in a quiet, dignified way. Even his friend – well, not his friend, obviously not his friend because a friend wouldn't suggest he did away with himself. After all he had done for Palmore. Even now Lord Wardell is looking for someone else to blame for his sins. He holds fast to the idea that none of this would have happened if he hadn't accepted the wager on the hailstorm.

'It's your fault,' he says to the empty room. 'Yes, Victor Friezland, it's your fault.'

His beloved sister would agree with him if she was still alive. His elder brother would have come up with a plan of action if he hadn't died in a hunting accident. And he finds himself weeping, not for them but for himself, for all he could have been and never will be.

Having run through the practical things he could do, he decides in the end to do none of them but to sleep in his chair until morning. He dreams he's been swallowed by a silver fish. Only his toes are left and even they aren't all there.

Daylight shines into the study and he wakes and looks round the room. Bathed as it is in the morning light it's one of the most beautiful rooms he owns. He straightens his shoulders, brushes down his frock coat and picks up his silver-topped ebony cane. There's no point changing his clothes, he has no manservant to dress him. He tucks his wife's jewellery box under his arm and goes down into the hall, a cavernous unoccupied space with one of the grandest staircases in the street. It was the staircase that had decided him to buy the house. His hat on his head, he opens his own front door and walks out into a day just shaking itself awake, forgetting – or not caring – to close the door behind him.

Out at sea, deep under the water off the Sussex coast, a young herring has slipped the net. It is only a year old and will take another four years to reach maturity. It has spent every day of its life avoiding capture either from above by the fishing boats or below where it is prey to any fish larger than itself. Its colouring is silver, the upper half of its body a dark, iridescent blue, paler underneath. With its forked tail the young herring moves as swiftly as an arrow towards its destiny.

Lady Wardell is already dressed when she hears the front door open and doesn't hear it close. Realising she is the only person left in the house, she goes downstairs and closes her front door. It is a small act, meaningless, and yet it's the first time that she hasn't had the door opened and shut for her by a footman.

Elizabeth Wardell has always been a practical woman, not given to flights of fancy. She would never have squandered her substantial wealth. She had been brought up to believe every penny counts and every penny has sweat and hard labour behind it. Her father had made a fortune in what the aristocracy disparagingly call 'trade'. To him it was imperative his only child should marry a title and she was sent to a girls' boarding school in southern England and taught all the social graces. She'd left with no hint of a Lancastrian accent, unlike her parents. Out of their depth in London society they retreated to their northern roots and left the finding of a suitable husband for Elizabeth to a widowed aunt who'd married respectably. During her first season in London, Elizabeth had met and fallen in love with Mr John Campbell, who wrote for a newspaper. She had also met and been remarkably unimpressed with Lord Wardell. It was well known that he had gambled his way through one fortune and, recently widowed, was on the hunt for another.

Her aunt had been horrified when she realised the strength of her niece's attachment to John Campbell. A hasty marriage agreement had been made with Lord Wardell.

Three days before the wedding, Elizabeth and her aunt were invited to Vauxhall Gardens. It was a large party and in the mass of people she saw John Campbell. He said he loved her and begged her to elope with him. Such was the desperation they had for one another that down one of the dark walks they went and she discovered what her mother and aunt had refused to tell her. When they returned to the party they found they hadn't been missed.

From the very beginning Elizabeth knew she had nothing in common with her husband who was married to his club, and gambling; his greedy mistress demanded his full attention. The art of love and love-making interested him not at all. It had to be done so the marriage held fast in the eyes of the Church. The only joy the newly married Lady Wardell knew was when she felt a stirring in her womb and sensed this baby was the child of John Campbell. She had never admitted it, even to herself, but this morning there was nothing more to lose and the truth might be the only solid stepping stone out of this house. Her strict upbringing had made her ashamed of her dalliance with John until she met him again three years later at a house party in the country. He was married by then and owned a newspaper, but the love they had for each other had not diminished. By the time the party left for London Elizabeth and John had become lovers again. She had entered the house in Pall Mall sure that her sin would be discovered, but she found that Lord Wardell had been away three nights playing faro and winning well. Such were his high spirits that he immediately demanded his marital rights, although

Elizabeth never doubted that John Campbell was the father of her second daughter, Jane.

Sitting on the third step from the bottom of the vast staircase, she revels in the thought that Lord Wardell may have her jewellery box but he has never had her jewels, her two daughters. Today this feels less like a sin, more like a celebration.

The knock is firm and assured. This is it, she thinks, patting down her dress. She glances in a mirror and opens the door. It is Mr Gutteridge who is standing there. He bows.

'May I come in, Lady Wardell?' he says.

'I am not receiving...' Her voice falters.

Mr Gutteridge gently manoeuvres her back into the hall and closes the door behind them. 'Is Lord Wardell here?'

She shakes her head.

'Your daughters?'

'No.'

'Good. There isn't long before the bailiffs arrive to repossess the house. Along with the properties in Norfolk, it will settle a fair amount of the mortgages. An inventory has been made of all the items here but I must ask if any are of value to you.'

This seems a ludicrous question given the circumstance and her answer surprises even herself.

'No. He took my jewels. There's nothing left that I want.'

'Do you know where his lordship keeps his papers?' Mr Gutteridge asks.

She leads him into the study and points at the desk. The solicitor rummages in the drawers and finally finds what he's looking for.

'Good,' he says. 'He definitely didn't keep his affairs in order. I take it you haven't eaten.'

Lady Wardell shakes her head.

'Would you mind taking a seat? I'm not good with fainting ladies and what I have to say may call for smelling salts, which I don't possess.'

'I'm not given to fainting, Mr Gutteridge,' says Lady Wardell, but she sits anyway.

'My client and ward, Henri Dênou, the Comte de Vernon, feels that you and he have been the victims of a tyrant. He has instructed me to offer you his house.'

'What do you mean, Mr Gutteridge, he offers me his house?'

'My client is away travelling and his house in Berkeley Square is at your disposal. He wanted to be sure you and your daughters would have somewhere to live if events should take an unfortunate turn.'

Lady Wardell is stunned by Henri's generosity.

Mr Gutteridge continues. 'My client gives you permission to use what he calls your "latent artistic sensibility" to make his house into a home for you and your daughters. There is one stipulation.'

'And what is that?'

'Lord Wardell is never to set foot inside it.'

'I understand. But he is forceful.'

'That my client knows all too well. At present there is only a caretaker staff at Berkeley Square. I have asked Mrs Dent to call on you there this afternoon.'

'Mrs Dent? Lord Sutton's...' She stops herself.

'She will help you employ servants to protect you, for I don't doubt Lord Wardell will try to claim his right to live there. I believe you will in time be free of him. Meanwhile I recommend good locks and patience.'

By the end of that day, Lady Wardell is settling into the house in Berkeley Square and a message has been sent to Lady Sarah and Lady Jane. She feels that fate, for a reason she cannot fathom, has given her a second chance at life.

Downstairs the new servants are gathered in the housekeeper's office off the main kitchen. The discussion is on how best to keep her ladyship and her daughters safe.

The maid who was kept on after Henri departed for Iceland is on the point of leaving for her new position when she remembers the letter. It had arrived a month after the master left and she doesn't know what she should do with it. She knows she's at fault. She'd put the letter in her apron and forgotten all about it and now there's no one to tell. Or rather she's too embarrassed to tell the new housekeeper. She could leave it on the table in the hall but decides against it, not wanting the housekeeper to find it and think badly of her. She decides it would be for the best if, while no one is looking, she hides it. By the time it is found no one will think to blame her.

21

September 1809 to Spring 1810

Aubrey Friezland in his time had worn a blue coat and a red coat and now he wears a second-hand frock coat bought in Seven Dials which is where he met Mrs Phipps who runs a gambling den. When she had all her teeth she used to run a brothel but now she finds it easier dealing with gentlemen's wallets rather than their breeches.

Mrs Phipps had been looking for someone to help with her more troublesome clients, most of whom were desperate gamblers looking to recover their fortunes.

'They're wasting their time coming to me, love,' Mrs Phipps told Aubrey. 'My house rarely loses.'

Aubrey is about thirty. He is a thin man, his thin skin pulled tight over a mean skeleton as if there isn't quite enough flesh to cover his bones. His eyes are big, insect eyes, his mouth a thinly drawn line. He doesn't look as if he smiles much. His hair, which still has some ginger in it, he wears tied back in a greasy pigtail. His hands, his mother considers, are his best feature, which isn't saying much. His fingers are long, square-shaped and they are what people notice about him if they notice him at all, for he prides himself on being unmemorable. It's an asset in his line of work.

So far Mrs Phipps has no complaints. Aubrey is good at bringing in the customers and making them feel secure. He's nifty at picking pockets when necessary and good at making the customers pay. Oh, how he makes them pay.

Aubrey had no interest in his father until he realised the relationship might be worth something and that only occurred to him after he heard about the Weather Woman.

He is thinking how he can squeeze his father for the odd guinea. He starts making enquiries about the clockmaker around Tooley Street where he's seen to be quite a hero – he and his daughter.

'Daughter? What daughter?' says Aubrey to himself, feeling something cruel and jealous rise up in him. And then he gleans a piece of information as good as finding gold on the banks of the Thames. Apparently his father has got married again, to his housekeeper. Now, in Aubrey's books that's called bigamy.

His mother, Mary, whom he dislikes enormously and who can't read or write, has no idea where the certificate of her marriage to Victor Friezland is and doubts she ever possessed it. She thinks they got married in Camberwell, or possibly Hastings. No, Camberwell.

'Think, Mother. Did you marry Victor Friezland in Camberwell?'

Mary tries to correct herself. 'No, it wasn't Camberwell, it was Hastings. Oh, I don't know.' And those were her last words on the subject.

Aubrey sees this as a once-in-a-lifetime opportunity and desires to do the thing properly. For that he needs facts. And evidence. He knows he's about to play a subtle game. There must be vulnerability in the victim, enough to hook a guilty conscience with.

Things are already looking promising when, early one September morning, Lord Wardell walks into Mrs Phipps's gaming establishment.

★ ★ ★

When Lord Wardell leaves his house with the front door wide
open he has not a penny to his name and the only place where
he knows he's guaranteed a welcome is Mrs Phipps's gambling
den off Maiden Lane. He remembers this area from his youth
with sentimental affection. Now it's run-down and smells of
rotting vegetables and crumbling brickwork. No sane man
would think of walking there holding a jewellery box unless
they hoped to be mugged or murdered. But that morning Lord
Wardell doesn't look sane. He's talking to himself – or talking
to the devil – for he addresses whoever it is as Beelzebub. Here
is that rare thing – a well-born man with nothing to lose.

Mrs Phipps is a large, buttery woman, a muffin left too
long in a baker's window. She's lazy, and once in her chair
near the door she has little inclination to stand up or to
do anything more than raise an arm. The energetic part of
the business is all Aubrey's. Mrs Phipps is nearly as wide as
the door she guards and is only ever seen in a cloud of pipe
smoke. She plays the little old lady card while keeping a knife
in her garter. Mrs Phipps is surprised when Lord Wardell
materialises through the smoke.

'Pardon me, my lord,' she says, 'but is everything all right?'

'All I have left in the world is in here,' says Lord Wardell,
shaking the jewellery box. 'But I can't open it.'

'You need a key for that, my lord.'

'I don't have one, you see.'

Mrs Phipps is undecided if Lord Wardell has only
temporarily lost his mind or whether it's a more permanent
state. But whatever his condition, he's the fattest fly they've
attracted to their jam jar for some time. Before she's even
called for Aubrey he's there. She introduces them. For the
briefest moment Lord Wardell looks at Aubrey with a spark
of interest.

Aubrey eyes up the jewellery box as he shows Lord Wardell to a seat in a basement alcove. It smells of damp London clay.

'So many doors are closed to me,' says Lord Wardell.

'This one ain't,' says Aubrey. 'My lord,' he adds quickly.

'I haven't got the key,' says Lord Wardell.

He's talking too loudly, his words echoing in the empty, cavernous room.

'What's your tipple, my lord?' asks Aubrey.

'Port.'

Lord Wardell puts the box on the table and spreads himself out as if wanting to own the space around him. Aubrey brings him a tankard of port laced with laudanum. He knows the exact measure to put in. Some clients are better unconscious, others semi-conscious, it depends where you have to move them to. This one will go upstairs until Aubrey has decided how to handle him. One thing he knows is that having caught this fly he's not going to let him go.

'What you got in there then?' asks Aubrey, his face stretched tight into a smile as Lord Wardell takes a drink. 'You look hungry, sir.'

'Yes. Yes, that's what I am, hungry,' says Lord Wardell. 'Jewels. In here.'

'Stolen?' asks Aubrey.

This ruffles the feathers of his lordship. 'Dammit, man! They belong to my wife.'

'I could help you open that box,' says Aubrey. 'You look like a gentleman who could do with some help.'

'Bugger off,' says Lord Wardell.

Not such a pussy cat after all, thinks Aubrey. He'll enjoy making this buffoon beholden to him.

'What's your game?' he asks. 'The cards, I mean.'

The maid unceremoniously dumps a plate of food in front of Lord Wardell and it's Aubrey who arranges the knife and fork. Like bloody babies, he thinks. All that coddling, all those bleeding servants. No more 'bugger off' now.

Lord Wardell is taken aback that someone cares enough to straighten his plate, to hand him his napkin. Aubrey sits and listens and watches his fly buzz drunkenly round the jar. By the time Lord Wardell is muttering about Victor Friezland, his words are slurred, his eyelids heavy.

'You've no idea,' says Aubrey as Lord Wardell falls into a stupor. 'You've no idea, you arrogant shit, what you've got yourself involved in. 'Cos I don't think anyone is looking for you.'

Aubrey doesn't like aristocrats. He doesn't like generals. He doesn't like the silver spoon, the privilege, the arrogance. He feels it a shame there hasn't been a revolution in England as there was in France. He would happily see heads roll. But he thinks if he could get this Lord Wardell on his side, his knowledge of all those fine houses groaning with treasure would be an insurance in case his plan to negotiate with Victor Friezland fails.

Mrs Phipps closes the door.

'How much d'you reckon?' she says when Aubrey has opened the jewellery box.

'Most of these are paste,' says Aubrey, disappointed. 'Looks like her ladyship's outwitted him. I think we'll get about twenty guineas for the lot.'

Mrs Phipps puts down her pipe. 'A good morning's work, I'd say,' she says, dusting her hands. 'But what do we do with him?'

'I think,' says Aubrey, 'this Lord Wardell may turn out to be more valuable than either of us yet knows.'

As the year draws to a close and the London season is under way once more, what has happened to Lord Wardell is a matter for speculation. He hasn't been seen, no body has been found, and his disappearance has caused endless problems, for no one is sure of the correct protocol around Lady Wardell and her daughters. Just when it has been decided that the best way to deal with the scandalous Wardell family is to simply ignore them, something extraordinary happens.

Sir John Campbell, the newspaper mogul, has heard about the disappearance of Lord Wardell and calls on Lady Wardell in Berkeley Square. An article printed in one of his papers has shamed those who've been quick to judge and now Lady Wardell and her daughters are invited everywhere.

The seasons pass, winter gives way to spring and a series of disturbing burglaries in big houses takes place. Whoever the thief is, he seems to have an uncanny knowledge of where the strong box is kept and, most importantly, which items are the most valuable. And there's a whisper, only a whisper, that it has to be someone in the know.

22

Spring 1810

Aubrey has embarked on his many ventures too fast and with not enough thought and that, he thinks, is why they've gone awry. This time he'll be careful. He'll ask questions, gather the evidence.

This he does, and he finds his father, Victor, is something of a celebrity due to the phenomenal success of the Weather Woman. This delights Aubrey. Victor, he's sure, will be arrogant enough to not want to lose his reputation. Now all Aubrey has to do is wait for an opportunity to find Victor alone.

It comes one afternoon when the whore, as he thinks of Elise, the usurper, Neva, and her companion leave in the carriage. He reckons he has an hour or two. He doesn't need long. Extortion is the sweetest of crimes, the cream on the tart. He's done it many times. Once he went in a little too hard and the stupid fool blew out his brains. He doesn't want that to happen.

He wonders about taking his mother with him, just for effect, but when he thinks about it he knows she would be more of a hindrance than a help. It's that voice of hers that riles him, the high-pitched screeching. Just a light touch is all it needs, he tells himself. And he mustn't lose his temper.

The house is protected by a high wall.

'What are you hiding, Father?' he says under his breath as he picks the lock of the garden gate and lets himself in. He wants to creep up on Victor, give the old man a shock so he knows who's the guv'nor. He stops, surprised. His mother always told him the house was a disgrace, that she couldn't live in it. He stares at it, open-mouthed. Washed in the light of a spring afternoon it's a piece of heaven. Only one word comes to his mind: beautiful. You have to have an imagination to build a house like this, he thinks, and in that moment he catches a glimpse of what might have been. Aubrey jumps. Victor Friezland is standing, unseen, beneath a tree not far away, studying him.

Victor is unruffled. 'Most people ring the bell. You decided to pick the lock so I can only think that you intend to be threatening. Am I right?'

'Do you know who I am?' says Aubrey, pulling himself together.

'A man who picks locks instead of ringing a bell.'

'I'm your son.'

Victor's expression doesn't change. 'If you're my son, why did you feel the need to break in?'

This isn't going to plan, thinks Aubrey.

'I knew you would come one day,' says Victor. 'I thought you might have come before – but not for the reason you are here now.'

'You don't know why I'm here.'

'I think I do. Neighbours and friends told me someone has been lifting up stones, hoping to find grubs of information about me. I suppose that was you.'

'No,' says Aubrey, slightly too fast.

'I have made enquiries about you,' says Victor.

'You... what?' says Aubrey.

'I followed your career when you were in the army but

lost track of it since you became…' Victor pauses. 'Whatever it is you are today. Before we go any further, let's just get something straight. If you have come to say you heard I married my housekeeper, then you are correct.'

'It's bigamy,' blurts out Aubrey. 'You married my mother in Hastings and you abandoned us.'

It wasn't Hastings, thinks Victor. But he says, 'Shall we go into my workshop?'

Aubrey is rarely speechless but Victor's workshop is magical and at the far end stands the Weather Woman. When Victor asks if he'd like to see her move, Aubrey can only mutter, 'Yes.'

'Take a seat, Aubrey.' Victor brings out wine and some biscuits and winds up the automaton.

Aubrey is transfixed. 'How does she tell the weather?' he asks in a voice that is almost childlike.

'You'll have to come and see her perform,' says Victor.

'I heard there was music.'

'There is.' Victor pulls up a chair quite close to Aubrey and sits down. 'I paid your mother an allowance until you turned sixteen, when I hoped you might find me of your own free will.'

'You paid for me?' Aubrey says, baffled. 'Where did the money go?'

'That is a question only your mother can answer,' says Victor. 'Or Lieutenant Letchmore.' He pours Aubrey another glass of wine. 'Aubrey, I don't think there's a court in this land that would find me guilty of bigamy. I haven't seen your mother nor heard from her, not once in nearly thirty years. I've only ever heard from the lieutenant. Is Mary still alive?'

'Yes.' Aubrey remembers himself when he was small and vulnerable, and hoping to God Letchmore wasn't his father. 'You paid for me?' he repeats. 'I didn't know. The cow, the cow!' He tries to calm his mind, to remember his plan, why he is here.

Victor says quietly, 'I was born in Russia, and until my parents' untimely death, I was a privileged little boy of a wealthy family. But I didn't have what I wanted, needed, which was to be loved. When I met Mary, I was twenty. I believed we would be happy together, that we would make a family. It soon became very obvious she was in love with another man; it also became obvious she was with child. I thought – foolishly as it turned out – that loving her would make it right. I told her I would look after her and the child. The child was you. She took you to her parents and then ultimately to live with Letchmore. There was nothing I could do. He wrote to me several times asking for money. I paid so that you could join the redcoats but I gather that didn't suit.'

Aubrey stands up. He has to get out of there.

'There's something in everyone's life they can be tormented with,' says Victor. 'We should start again, get to know each other better. I would be delighted if you would come to supper and meet my family.'

Family. Aubrey feels a flash of jealousy. He can't breathe. He mumbles something and once outside, with the gate closed, he realises he's crying. It's too late. Nothing can make him clean, the dirt is too deep within him. He finds a gin shop. Victor Friezland has cast a spell, he thinks. He's a magician.

After his visit to the clockmaker, Aubrey finds he hasn't enough words to elaborate on what he's feeling. He just knows the anger in him is growing, accompanied by a deep sense of injustice. There's some irrational release from his rage in beating up Lord Wardell, but it's not enough. His fury boils over when he thinks of his mother – she who kept telling him he looked just like his father, just like Victor Friezland.

Now he knows he looks nothing like Victor Friezland.

'You are so like your daddy,' his grandmother would say, and, it turns out, she didn't mean Victor Friezland. What riles and rattles him is the money Victor says he sent Aubrey's mother.

'Pennies,' she pleads, when he finds the old bitch drunk in an inn near the Old Bailey.

'One day, Mother, they'll hang you for a liar and a thief.'

'I'm telling the truth.'

'So you never married that shit of a lieutenant?'

'No – I married Victor Friezland, and it's written in a church register, all proper.'

'How would you know? You can't read or write, you ignorant cow. Where was this church?'

'Camberwell.'

'You said Hastings before.'

'No, I never.'

'And that fucker the lieutenant – is he still alive?'

She wavered.

'Is he?'

'No.'

If he's dead, all the better, let him stay that way. If he's not, Aubrey will willingly make him dead.

'If your mother was indeed legally married to Victor Friezland,' says Lord Wardell when he has recovered from the beating, 'the church register will be proof that Victor Friezland is a bigamist. And when he dies, no matter what his will says, no court would find in favour of his second wife or his so-called daughter over his rightful heir. Patience, Beelzebub, patience.'

Shut it, shut it. Shut out all the voices in his head. Aubrey, you are better off dead, shut it. His mother lied about the house. It is the most beautiful house he has ever seen. As for

Victor Friezland, he is the mildest of men. A kind man. But Wardell might be right. The only calm thought in Aubrey's turbulent brain is the memory of the Weather Woman. He feels she understands him, she alone can see the injustice of his fate.

Wardell whispers, 'Beelzebub, it was the Weather Woman who had the power to see a hailstorm. It is she who Mr Friezland used to cheat me out of my money and my good fortune. So you see, Beelzebub, we must make Mr Friezland pay. It's him you should be angry with.'

Aubrey knows his success with Lord Wardell is due to what he puts in his drink. Too much laudanum and Wardell is asleep all day, too little and he is itching for the cards. It's this, and a generous helping of sudden violence sprinkled with the occasional word of kindness, that keeps him on his knees.

Aubrey gets much pleasure from humiliating him. The lieutenant taught him about humiliation, how to make someone feel no bigger than a worm. Unlike a woman, Wardell never complains, even when Aubrey loses his temper and goes a little too far.

Lord Wardell says, 'Beelzebub, you are right to punish me, make me worthy of your forgiveness.'

Aubrey can't believe how easy it is to control him. He had thought it would take longer to pull the arrogant poser down, to make him utterly beholden to him.

It never crosses Aubrey's mind that Lord Wardell is play-acting.

Aubrey can't go back to see Victor Friezland. It hurts to thinks about him. He tells himself one day the Weather Woman will be his, his compensation for having suffered so badly as a child. His salvation.

Mrs Phipps has told him she's had enough of Lord Wardell lodging in her premises. There are too many eyes, eyes with ears, ears with mouths and some of them with tongues that are talking. Aubrey and Lord Wardell have to move out of Covent Garden. Aubrey has rented rooms in a rat-infested house not far from the Fleet River. It stinks as the weather warms up and the crowded conditions fuel the anger in him, the noise bounces off the walls of his mind. At least they have the attic with a view over the rooftops.

Aubrey sits looking out of the filthy window. He can see the dome of St Paul's. He can hear the neighbours fucking, giving birth, fighting, screaming – all the states of being human are played out from the bottom to the top floor. He looks at the wreck that is Lord Wardell lying on the bed and Aubrey thinks he needs a barber. He wonders about chaining him up. It's what he usually does before he goes out but he doesn't bother now as it looks like he'll sleep until tomorrow. Anyway, Aubrey won't be long.

At Mrs Phipps's there's a party upstairs and he's not invited, not even offered a drink. Mrs Phipps takes him into the empty gambling room.

'You let him go then, have you?' she asks.

'Who?'

'You know who. That Lord Wardell.'

'No.'

'Why not?'

'Because he's still useful.'

'I doubt it. That last burglary was botched and you were lucky not to be caught. If you let him go, prison will be waiting for him. You're soft on him, aren't you?'

'No! Why do you say that? I like women.'

'I doubt that too,' says Mrs Phipps. 'I don't mind who you

like. But I won't have him back here. If you want to keep him, you should make him pay.'

'Come on, we've done well out of him.'

'We need to do better. And you need to stop putting your fingers in my purse. Personally, I think you should get rid of him.'

'You mean, kill him?' says Aubrey.

Aubrey walks back to Farringdon, wishing he had the money to buy food and more drink. He stops and looks in a print shop window displaying the latest cartoons. One is of Wardell. It's called *The Vanishing Lord*.

He manages to steal a loaf of bread and a snuff box. Not a bad piece, he thinks. Gold, worth a bob or two. Still Mrs Phipps's remark scratches at the thin walls of his sanity. Soft on Wardell. What made the old bitch say that?

Aubrey hasn't enough words in him to know what he feels for anyone. His language, like many things in Aubrey's life, like love itself, is impoverished. He has no understanding of the subtleties of his emotions; he's only aware of its high notes of fury, of lust. He knows one thing: the aristocratic prick is his slave to do with as he, Beelzebub the master, sees fit.

He thinks of the women he's lain with, who've caused nothing but trouble. Leaky, needy vessels. They go soft at the wrong moments, cling to you and want a wedding ring. Wardell doesn't even cry out when he's gone a little too far. He's not soft, he's hard and it's thrilling. It makes him feel... what does it make him feel?

The street and the people come hurtling back to him. Anyway, Wardell hasn't complained and it hasn't happened again, not for a while, not since seeing his father. He looks again at the snuff box. This will be the end of it. But he knows it's like the drink. In the morning you tell yourself you won't drink again and come the evening you can't stop yourself. He can't give this up. He'll make sure Wardell keeps taking the medicine.

And a thought, knife bright, comes to him. If there wasn't Wardell, who would there be? The answer shocks him. There would be no one.

He climbs the stairs to his lodgings, passing the endless chatter and shouting. At least the top floor is his. But the door is wide open and Wardell has gone. Aubrey runs down the stairs. Out in the street there's no sign of him. Panic floods him. He has a wild imagining of Wardell in the dark, stinking water of the Fleet. It's nearly ten o'clock when Aubrey returns home in need of a drink. He walks wearily up the stairs to find candlelight coming from the room and on the table is a bottle and a pie. Lord Wardell is sitting bolt upright on the bed, waiting.

'Mr Beelzebub,' he says, standing. 'Where have you been?'

Aubrey stares at him. Wardell's wearing a new set of clothes and has been to a barber.

'Close the door and sit down,' says Lord Wardell. Aubrey does as he's told and Wardell pours him a drink then goes to the door and locks it. He puts the key in his pocket. 'I've enjoyed our games. I like the way you play, Mr Beelzebub. I'm cured of one demon and obsessed with another. You're no beauty – you have the face of a ferret. I suppose when your hair was red you might have been considered good-looking. But that's of no importance.'

Aubrey is speechless. In all the time Wardell's been with him, he's hardly said a word.

'Have you turned me in?' Aubrey asks. 'Are they coming for me?' He pulls his knife from his belt but Wardell catches his wrist with more strength than Aubrey would have imagined he possessed and the knife falls.

'Beelzebub,' says Lord Wardell, 'let me finish what I have

to say. I went to Seven Dials and bought myself a suit of clothes. They're not new but passable.'

Aubrey laughs. 'You daft old bugger – where'd you get the money?'

'When you're gracious enough to let me gamble, I keep some of my winnings. With the coins that roll from your pocket I had enough for the clothes, some groceries and the essential ingredients of your brew: laudanum and rum. Tell me – would you have missed me if I hadn't come back?'

Unguardedly, Aubrey says, 'Yes.'

'Good. Because I've never enjoyed myself as much as I have with you. Your games stop me thinking about gambling. Shall we eat?' Aubrey stares incredulously as Wardell cuts the pie. 'I've noticed, since your visit to the clockmaker, that you've lost your zeal.'

'My what?'

'Precisely.'

'Why did you want to come back here?' says Aubrey. 'I'm cruel, I humiliate you and I—'

Lord Wardell interrupts him. 'We are the head and the tail of the same coin. My dear Beelzebub, you are just what I've always wanted, what money never bought me. But we can't live here, it's too gross. I think you should burgle Sir Richard Palmore's house. I can tell you exactly what to take and where it is. I thought tomorrow night. Let us have supper and talk about the future, and what other games we might play.'

'Games?' says Aubrey. He sits stock still. This is a revelation. 'You call what I do games?'

'You're very good at them. Now, to inspire you to further monstrous behaviour I have a present for you from a favourite shop of mine.'

'Did they recognise you?'

'Of course. When I was addressed by my title, I said I

was always being mistaken for Lord Wardell. Do you have anything for me?'

Aubrey gives him the snuff box.

Lord Wardell opens it. 'Not bad. Good gold – though not inscribed to me. But I'm being discourteous. What does Mr Beelzebub do when I'm discourteous to him?'

Aubrey isn't sure if he's comfortable with this. Wardell hands him a slim leather case and inside, nestling on red velvet, is a small whip.

'It's supposed to have belonged to a great whore,' says Lord Wardell. 'It was used, I'm told, on the backsides of aristocrats.'

Aubrey takes it from the case and flicks it. A smile crosses his face and his tongue flashes out to wet his lips.

'That's more like my Beelzebub,' says Lord Wardell.

23

Spring and Summer 1810

Aubrey's visit has given Victor much to think about and the knowledge that Mary is alive concerns him greatly. He can see her son might well persuade her to bring a lawsuit against him for bigamy.

It is shortly after this on a sunny morning in May that he goes to consult Mr Gutteridge at his chambers in Lincoln's Inn. Mr Briggs, the clerk, shows him into Mr Gutteridge's room and here he waits. The solicitor's chambers, even in fine weather, seem to lack sunshine. The brightness of the day outside only emphasises the gloominess of the place within and Victor thinks all the lugubrious conversations must have crept like dry rot into the walls. Victor sees the room as a tomb that only time could extract him from.

Something has changed in Victor. He doesn't know if it's due to the regret he feels about Aubrey or the guilt he feels about Neva.

Cassie has confided in Elise that, two years ago, Neva wrote Henri Dênou a letter, a confession, a declaration of love, and Cassie posted it without Neva's knowledge. As there was no reply she concluded that Mr Dênou hadn't received it before he set sail. Elise made Victor swear he would keep Cassie's secret but it has had the effect of sobering his thoughts.

He jumps when he hears a most unexpected sound, so at odds with his surroundings. He spins round to find Mr Gutteridge holding out what Victor believes is a fob watch.

'What is it?' asks Victor. 'What is making that sweet music?'

The solicitor smiles. 'Indeed,' he says. 'What is it? A musical watch without a face to tell the time.' He hands it to Victor who opens it and as he does the music begins again.

'It's enchanting. Where did you get it?'

'A client brought it from Switzerland.'

'I want one.'

Mr Gutteridge's low laugh, rarely used, sounds rusty. 'That, my dear friend, can be arranged. Now, musical boxes aside, how can I help?'

Victor is so lost in admiration of the small musical fob he has almost forgotten the reason he's here.

'I'm not convinced that Mary's case would stand up in a court of law,' says Mr Gutteridge after Victor has told him of his concerns. He says it in the soothing voice he uses in his most difficult cases. 'Especially because for these past thirty years you have not been sure if she was alive or dead. Added to that is the fact you suspect she was already married to Robert Letchmore before she married you. If that's the case, it's Mary who should be worried. It would be helpful, of course, if there was evidence of said marriage rather than mere speculation.'

'I intend to find it. Something Aubrey said makes me think they were married in Hastings,' says Victor. 'But there is something else. I want to be sure Elise will be financially secure if anything were to happen to me.'

'You must have your will watertight,' says the solicitor, 'otherwise the estate might pass to Aubrey and his mother.

You could leave a sum of money to Aubrey, who, after all, you previously acknowledged as your son, and the rest to Neva. Do you think Aubrey would be satisfied with that?'

'No,' says Victor. 'He will plague her life. What if I left the bulk of my estate to somebody else?'

'Why? Who would you leave it to?' asks Mr Gutteridge, perplexed. 'But first, Victor, you must find proof of Mary's previous marriage. That's what I counsel you to do.'

Victor says goodbye to the solicitor and sets off for Cheapside to call on Mr Ratchet. Victor wonders if Aubrey or his mother have paid him a visit recently. He finds Mr Ratchet, hat in hand, at the door of his premises.

'There was I,' he says, 'about to put on my hat and stretch Old Bones's legs by way of a walk down to the river, there to find myself a ferryman to take me to Mr Friezland's abode. I told Old Bones we'll warn Victor Friezland what my nephew and half-sister have planned. No sooner had I told him than Old Bones sniffs and there you are. Come on in, sir.' Mr Ratchet puts down his hat, closes the door and takes Victor upstairs.

'My dear Mr Ratchet,' says Victor. 'I thought they might come to see you. Was it about bringing a case against me for bigamy?'

'No. But they came to see me all right. Not because of you being married to Mrs Friezland, and not because they haven't seen me in near on twenty years and wanted to enquire after my health or even pay back some of the funds I so generously lent them in the past. No, no. I was on the brink of telling them they could take a paper boat down the Thames for all I cared, when another thought, more productive, took its place. If I have their confidence then perhaps I would have knowledge of what they're up to.

'Aubrey asked if I was on speaking terms with you and then had the insolence to suggest my loyalty should be to my family. They're worried in case Victor Friezland should die and leave all his money to his well-beloved and hard-working daughter, who so diligently helps him run his business, and not to his wastrel of a son. My half-sister wants an insurance policy. "What kind?" Only my help to have Miss Friezland committed to an asylum when you are dead and gone. They have even been to the trouble of finding one in Highgate. A bit expensive, but they've been assured their clients usually only manage a year or two before death comes to take them home.'

'Oh God,' Victor says and sits down heavily.

'A drink,' Mr Ratchet says and pours two glasses of brandy. 'Now, what you have to ask yourself is, where did those two deluded imbeciles get such a notion? Or perhaps the question is, how did *Aubrey* come up with such a poisonous plan? Mary hasn't the wit, the gin has taken that from her.' He hands a glass to Victor. 'There's a rumour the missing peer, Lord Wardell, and Aubrey Friezland are in a fiendish partnership. Who is running whom is a matter for conjecture.'

The brandy warms Victor but in the heart of him is an icicle of fear. 'I ruffled his feathers,' he mutters to himself.

Mr Ratchet gets up from his seat and for a minute or two disappears. He comes back with biscuits and cheese on a tray.

'You look pale, Mr Friezland,' he says, putting the tray down in front of Victor.

'Do you know if Letchmore is still alive?' Victor asks.

'I couldn't say. I asked Mary and she looked sheepish. As well she might. I knew him, a nasty piece of work, and Aubrey looks just like him.'

'What if I left Aubrey a goodly sum, do you think he would be satisfied?'

Old Bones farts and Mr Ratchet smiles. 'That's what he thinks of the suggestion and I'm upwind of it. To be honest, if you left them the moon tied up with a bow, it wouldn't be enough.' He finishes his brandy. 'It might be to our purpose if they don't know of the high regard in which I hold you.'

'You are a good friend, Mr Ratchet.'

'I'll do my utmost to help you, Mr Friezland.' Mr Ratchet coughs, then says, 'I only tell my first name to my closest friends. I'd like it if you would call me Ebenezer.'

Victor walks back towards the river and wonders, would Aubrey have turned out differently if he had been raised by kind hands? Victor had felt a stirring of regret when he saw Aubrey look longingly at the Weather Woman, his face lighting up like a child's. At that moment Victor would like to have felt affection for the man he had wanted to believe was his son. But now he knows this man intends to have Neva committed to an asylum.

'Is it because of Aubrey's visit that you're not quite yourself?' Neva asks Victor when they're alone in the workshop.

'Are my colours that pale?' he asks her.

'They are overcast,' says Neva. 'How did you meet his mother?'

Victor is taken off guard by Neva's question. After a moment he says, 'I was younger than you are now. I went to a house in Kennington to deliver a clock – one of the first I'd made, in fact. Mary was a housemaid there and I fell in love with her in an instant.'

'The word "fell" is interesting,' says Neva. 'You fell a tree, it dies. You fall, you hurt yourself, few are caught in the fall. Falling, on the whole, is not a good thing. That makes me think that falling in love might be the same; the emotion is subject to pain.'

'You're right, Neva. I fell in love with something that wasn't there and I hurt myself badly. But it wasn't the same when I fell in love with Elise – that took time and it was the most wonderful thing to happen to me in all my life: I had found a kindred spirit.'

'I imagine Mary was as pretty as a picture and that's why you stumbled.'

'I wanted the family I'd never had. When I asked her to marry me she called me a noodle, which there can be no disputing – a noodle I was. Then she left her employer and disappeared. I was heartbroken. She came back, saying she loved me. She was older than me, but not much, definitely a little sadder, but not much, and I married her much, much too soon.'

'When I pick my fingers,' says Neva, 'I tell myself I am making them perfect. I know I'm not. I know the pain it will cause me, yet still I can't stop. Perhaps that's what your love for Mary was like.'

'You mean it was nothing more than a sore finger?' says Victor, laughing. 'But you're right. It was my fault. I refused to see what I didn't want to see. I worshipped Mary. When she told me she was with child, I knew it wasn't mine, it couldn't have been mine. Nevertheless, I was delighted. My uncle had recently died and left me a little money, just enough to buy this plot of land. The minute the baby was born, Mary demanded a wet nurse, saying if you suckled babies yourself you lost your figure. I was patient; I heard it said that some women become a little odd after giving birth. But three months later she left with the baby and I soon found out she had gone back to her lover. I suspected at the time she might have already been married to him and now I feel positive that's the case. Aubrey said his mother had told him we were married in Hastings. We weren't. We were married in Camberwell. I'm planning a visit to Hastings.'

24

January to Summer 1811

Victor's colours have faded; there is a foggy blue and a yellow in them that weren't there before and it worries Neva. There is something Victor is not telling her.

She wishes things were simpler. How is it that a gift such as hers, which demands nothing other than eyes to see and a voice to speak, has become so submerged in Papa's inventions? Far from freeing her, they've become a prison.

He's talking about a complete redesign of the Weather Woman and Neva sees a desperation in him that wasn't there before.

'I thought we were only going to improve her,' she says.

But Victor says he fears a servant or footman in one of the grand houses and assembly halls where they perform will have watched them setting up and worked out how the predictions are made, and the mystery of the Weather Woman will be revealed.

'The aristocracy seek novelty,' he tells Neva. 'They've seen the automaton and now we must do something else.'

Neva tries to tell him how she feels. 'Papa, can't I just do my weather readings for the people who need them? None of the *bon ton* could care less about the weather unless a hat is

191

ruined by rain. But there are those who risk their lives every day—'

'We will use smoke,' says Victor.

Neva sighs. 'Smoke,' she repeats and can see that it is useless to protest.

Victor's new idea involves a magic lantern and a speaking tube. 'The art is to make the light in the lantern as bright as possible so it can project the image onto smoke.'

'You're talking about a phantasmagoria show,' she says.

She remembers going to the Lyceum in the Strand with Papa and Cassie to see the ghost show. She had found it truly terrifying. As skeletons rose above the audience, people screamed and a woman fainted. Neva wanted only to leave. And this is Papa's plan?

'Not skeletons,' he says. 'Just one apparition and that will be you.'

'Me,' says Neva, who likes the sound of this less and less.

'There's an artist who paints on glass and makes the slides. We'll project your image onto the smoke.'

Victor is adamant this is how to reinvent the Weather Woman. He's bought a magic lantern and a speaking tube to demonstrate what he has in mind. First he makes a smoke screen, mixing potassium nitrate with sugar and heating it slowly until it goes brown, then pouring it into a glass jar. He waits until the sun has gone down, and when it's dark he sprinkles the contents of the glass jar with potassium permanganate and glycerine. There's a burst of flame then smoke billows from the jar and forms a ball. On it the magic lantern projects an image of a bear. An unfortunate choice.

Neva stands in the darkness, her hands over her eyes. All around her, or so it seems, there are unearthly sounds. She jumps as Papa's voice appears to come from next to her, when she knows he is behind the lantern at the end of the workshop.

She begins to count her steps. Even in the dark she has the measure of the workshop, as she does the rest of the house. She knows how many steps each room requires. She feels safe knowing that if all the light were to be snuffed out she wouldn't lose her bearings. But now she wonders if there is something she's missed, for Papa's voice seems to be moving away from her in invisible steps.

'What has this to do with the Weather Woman?' she says, reaching the oil lamp and lighting it. She's relieved that, although the workshop is full of smoke, there's order again in the light. But the strange and unsettling feeling in her doesn't leave. The question she asks herself she can find no answer to: what is the point? What is the point of this terrifying apparition?

Victor looks thrilled with the experiment. 'The sound you heard came from an instrument made of glass. What do you think?' he asks. And not waiting for her reply, he continues, 'You see, you can speak your weather predictions, even sing the rain, without the inconvenience of wheels and cogs. I think it's going to be sensational. Of course, we must design it so the lantern isn't seen. In fact, the whole setting needs to be considered.'

Neva agrees with that but asks, 'What are you going to do at the end of the show when the audience call for Victor Friezland, the inventor of the Weather Woman? And who is going to speak to them and address the apparition, if you are operating the magic lantern and I'm talking down a tube?'

Victor looks baffled. 'We'll work something out,' he says.

Neva, who hates change, is forced to push any doubts she has to the back of her mind. Somewhere between the automaton and the magic lantern her gift is wasted, so wrapped in Papa's plans that it can hardly be seen. Even her mother, sewn into the chess-playing bear, was more visible than she is.

It had been an enormous blow the day she'd been forced

to put Eugene away. He had been the perfect mask to hide behind. Now Victor has to be alert when people call at the workshop and see Neva there. When that happens they pretend she was bringing him a book, a cup of tea, a plate of biscuits. What Victor cannot say is that it's Neva's idea to line the inside of the lantern with polished tin, Neva's idea to devise a screen to hide it in such a way the audience won't notice the hole the lantern shines through.

This new Weather Woman is a creature of darkness and illusion, a trick of the light. She demands the night in order to perform, smoke to fool the eye's lens and a voice that seduces and terrifies its audience. Neva feels she is drowning. Again she thinks of mariners who sail into storms and ships that are wrecked on rocks. What use is this gift, what use? she asks herself. And the answer is, you are an amusement, a freak of nature.

Victor hires a carpenter and an artist. While the carpenter is working in the workshop, Neva has to stay in the house with Elise and Cassie. They watch her pace back and forth. 'What do women do all day?' she asks.

The artist who paints her is a small man. She stands on a wooden crate in the long drawing room, draped in white muslin, a veil over her face.

'You look like a ghost,' says Cassie.

'I think that's the idea,' says Neva.

'Please stay still, Miss Friezland,' says the artist. He is supposed to be the best in his field at painting images on glass. 'Please stay still,' he says again.

Neva longs to move. In her mind and in her body, stillness is for the grave.

The carpenter builds the screen and a free-standing frame, and a low circular dais which is the stage.

Because Neva can't be seen in the workshop, Victor is back in the house every other minute asking her advice.

Elise looks at Neva astounded, as if she hadn't realised before just how vital Neva is to Victor's work.

Only when the carpenter has gone and the artist has left the two painted images, do Neva and Victor stand in the workshop, looking at what they have. Victor is pleased to tell her he's found a way to manipulate the glass slides to give the illusion the Weather Woman is moving.

'So now it's a matter of making all these pieces work together,' says Neva.

'And I've had an idea,' says Victor. 'As you pointed out, we need someone to present the apparition. I thought Cassie would be perfect.'

'I'm not sure she'll agree,' says Neva.

For the first time, Victor invites Cassie and Elise to watch a demonstration of the new Weather Woman.

They take their seats and Neva extinguishes the oil lamps. Cassie has made curtains for the workshop windows so all light is blocked out.

The apparition of a ghostly woman appears, hanging lugubriously in the centre of a circle.

'Cassie,' calls Victor, 'go up and ask her a question about the weather.' Tentatively Cassie makes her way to the wooden dais, nearly tripping on the outer rim. 'Sorry,' she says, uncertainly.

'Ask her about the weather,' says Victor.

'What will the weather be like in three days' time?' Cassie sounds stiffer than a plank of wood.

Neva's voice makes her jump. It's coming from inside the apparition. Cassie backs away.

Elise says sternly, 'Victor, light the lamps. I don't like this.'

'There's nothing to worry about,' he says.

'This is the most terrifying thing I've ever seen. And what's it got to do with predicting the weather? That's what I want to know.'

'Neva will be free to make her weather predictions and she won't have to sit at the front of the stage, apparently doing nothing, and being stared at.'

'It won't matter what Neva says, all eyes will be on the apparition.' This is what Neva has been thinking all along. 'Personally,' adds Elise, 'I preferred the automaton.'

Neva can see how disappointed Victor is at Elise's reaction. As he locks the workshop door that night, he says, 'It will run smoothly once we've rehearsed properly.'

'All work and no play makes for dull companions,' says Elise at breakfast one morning. She fears the new Weather Woman has too much to do with darkness. 'It's summer,' she reminds Victor.

'So it is,' says Victor, who has yet to persuade Cassie to try to present the Weather Woman again.

'I have a plan,' says Victor. 'We'll become tourists in our own city.'

On a warm July day he hires a waterman and arranges for them to be taken to Greenwich.

Neva longs to row as she once did. 'I miss being on the river,' she says.

They have a picnic at the top of the hill in Greenwich Park from where they can see the dome of St Paul's and all the church spires of London in the distance. Even on a fine day the smoke rising from the many chimneys into the clouds dims their brightness.

'You can see what the smoke is doing,' says Neva. She is lying on her back on the grass with Cassie next to her.

'I can't,' says Cassie. 'All I see is windmill clouds.'

'You can't see the smoke is staining the sky?'

'You know that's beyond me,' says Cassie, laughing. With half-closed eyes she watches a Red Admiral fluttering round them. After a moment she asks, 'What do you miss most about Eugene?'

Neva feels on days like this that time has gone to sleep. She sits up and pulls at a blade of grass. Chewing the end, she says, 'What I loved about being Eugene Jonas was discussing my findings and observations with people who were interested. My women's clothes don't allow me that freedom.' Until then, she had been unaware Victor was looking at her. 'Papa, what are you thinking about?' she asks.

'I'm thinking how beautiful you are,' he says. Which he isn't, but nevertheless it's true. His mind has drifted back to the time when he first saw her. He thinks of it as one of the luckiest days of his life.

He watches the two young women laughing as they run down the hill and, taking Elise's hand, he kisses her cheek.

'What's that for?' she says.

'Nothing. Just that I love you.'

Elise pulls back a little and looks at him. 'You're not ill, are you?'

'No,' he says, taking her in his arms.

'Victor! What will people think?'

'Do you really care?'

'No,' she says, and he kisses her again.

On overcast evenings they go to the theatre. Victor tells Neva he feels these outings are particularly important for Cassie, who loves the theatre.

'Uncle Victor – I'm no actress,' Cassie says when Victor asks for the umpteenth time how she feels about presenting the Weather Woman. 'I love going to the grand houses and helping you set up but I couldn't... *perform.*'

Victor looks at her gravely. 'There's no one else I want,' he says.

'I came here as a maid of all sorts,' says Cassie, laughing at the memory. 'Not a blooming actress.'

'Some might call it a golden opportunity,' says Victor.

'Not me,' she says cheerfully.

But for all her protests Cassie spends most evenings rehearsing with Victor and Neva and the more they rehearse the less stiff and nervous Cassie becomes.

The summer is drawing to a close and the new season will soon begin.

Victor gives Cassie one instruction: when they perform in public she should be outrageous.

'What do you mean?' she asks.

'I mean you read the scandal rags and the newspapers and know the society gossip. My suggestion is you use that knowledge to make fun of society – which you're very good at doing.'

'What if someone gets up and punches me on the nose?' asks Cassie.

'I can promise you they won't.'

Cassie finds herself smiling. It's an entertaining thought.

Neva isn't sleeping well. Her nightmares are usually about the chess-playing bear but now they're about a sinking ship. Papa is standing on the water as the mist comes in.

'I tell him to hold on,' he says, 'but the water is cold. I tell him to think of Neva, to remember the knight is the most unexpected of all the chess pieces.' And she hears singing about Davy Jones and all is lost in the roiling waves.

25

October 1811

The Marquess of Smedmore is attending Mrs Dent's soiree in Harley Street. The new Weather Woman is to perform and he, like many of the *bon ton*, is curious to see what all the fuss is about as Mrs Dent has made much of the fact that no one will have seen her like before. Bos doubts that anything could be better than the original automaton, which he considered to be one of the most riveting things he had ever seen, and even if one isn't impressed by the Weather Woman, the accuracy of her predictions is a wonder in itself.

Bos has been married now for three miserable years and the only joy they've brought him is a daughter named Camille. If the marriage was meant to bring Kitty and Bos together, it has had the reverse effect. Kitty told him recently all the 'bed stuff', as she calls it, can stop and he should take a mistress.

Bos has never wanted a mistress. His father had a constant stream of them while his mother had endless flirtations. He had grown up in the ha-ha of their dalliances, left in the care of nannies, governesses and boarding school. He was unloved – forgotten.

Tonight he stands alone at the back of Mrs Dent's large drawing room and thinks himself resigned to being alone all his life. Love, he tells himself, is for other people, not for him. Friendship will be his solace and in this at least he has been lucky. There is one friend he sorely misses. In his pocket he has a recent letter from Henri Dênou saying that he's in New York, staying with his aunt, and that he has become fascinated by what is called there 'natural physical amusements and diverting experiments'. Henri is interested in how science and mathematics are combined to form something called 'conjuring' which becomes entertainment, an illusion, a trick of the light. He writes of coming home and hopes to return early next year, fearing that relations between America and England are on the point of breaking down.

America seems so unimportant. All the British papers speculate on is the Corsican ogre Bonaparte's next move. There is a rumour that his army is now intent on taking Russia.

All the chairs in Mrs Dent's drawing room having been taken, Bos has positioned himself out of sight, or so he thinks, by the doors. Here he has a perfect view of the proceedings.

The stage is very simple and not particularly interesting. A circular dais has been placed in the middle of the floor, raised at a slight angle to give the audience a good view of it. The outer rim has been painted with the weather symbols, and in the middle the sun and the moon are masterfully rendered. Hanging behind the dais is a black velvet drape. To the right is a painted screen and in front of that a small round table on which has been placed a single candle. He hopes the performance isn't going to be as obvious as he thinks it might be, with someone hiding behind the screen. It's a pity there's no cellist. He feels that the show is going to be a great disappointment and perhaps he should make his exit while he has a chance and go to his club. Then he sees the unmistakable figure of his father sitting three rows from the front.

Having absolutely no desire to talk to him, he turns to

leave just as the footman closes the drawing-room doors and to escape now would only draw attention to himself, and that he doesn't want to do.

Bos and his father have not been on speaking terms since the duke made it quite clear the main reason for the marriage, in fact the only reason for any marriage, is to produce a son. On hearing Bos had a daughter, he pronounced that girls take money from powerful estates like his. Boys bring it back and men know how to keep it.

Kitty is pregnant again. She lies in bed on doctor's orders, eating French pastries amid a pile of cushions and pillows. She reminds her husband of the story of the Princess and the Pea. This baby, she assures him, will be a boy. The duke has already told everyone there is soon to be an heir to the estate.

Bos now has no choice but to stay and watch the performance. At least when the doors open at the end, he can be the first to leave and an awkward meeting with his father will be avoided.

The room is crowded. So many people have returned from exile in the country, no doubt thrilled to be back in a city where there are theatres, gambling tables, shopping and mistresses, political intrigue and a new season of marriageable young women.

Mrs Dent stands in front of the audience dressed in a confection of colours. Bos thinks she looks like a sweetshop.

'My lords, ladies and gentlemen,' she says, 'may we have quiet please.' The talking dies down. Only one gentleman is still mumbling to someone. 'I ask for quiet,' says Mrs Dent again. Finally, there is that rare thing among the aristocracy, silence. 'Tonight, we have for your amusement a novelty I believe will intrigue you all. So, without further ado, let me introduce Miss Cassandra Lamb, to present Mr Victor Friezland's latest creation.'

From behind the screen comes the young woman Bos

remembers seeing at Covent Garden three years ago. She has his full attention and that of the rest of the audience. There is something mesmerising about her; he would not call her beautiful, but her face possesses a natural loveliness.

She stands on the wooden dais, her features drained of colour. She appears to be frozen to the spot and he wonders what will happen if she can't move. Later that evening when he writes to Henri, he tries to describe this moment. It feels as if she has been standing still like this for at least an hour, when it could be no more than twenty seconds.

Then, as if coming up for air, she starts. 'My lords, ladies and gentlemen. I am Cassandra Lamb.' Her voice gains strength with every word. 'For your entertainment and delight tonight, and without intending offence to the Lord of the Heavens, I present to you one of the wonders of the world: the Weather Woman. She, unlike gentlemen of science, can predict the weather, not just a week but fourteen days into the future. She can also sing the rain. The doors will now be locked. After all, we can't allow her to escape.'

A familiar voice calls from the audience and Bos's heart sinks.

'Before you turn out the lights, I want to know—'

'Hold your horses, sir,' says Miss Lamb. 'I haven't finished yet. When the Weather Woman appears, I'll ask you to give me a date.'

'I want to know—' repeats the gentleman.

'Yes, sir, and I want to know where your "please" is,' says Cassie, smiling. It's such a winning smile no one could possibly be angry.

'Still,' says the gentleman, 'I should go first.'

'A "please" and you might, sir,' says Cassie, to hoots of laughter.

Someone says, 'That's right, tell his grace to mind his manners.'

'How *gracious* are you, sir?' says Cassie, not missing a beat.

'I am the Duke of Boswell!'

'So you are!' says Cassie and drops a deep curtsey. 'I'm a cockney sparrow and most honoured to meet you, your grace. Shall we begin? Is everyone ready to be amazed, amused and astonished?'

The lamps are extinguished, the key turns in the lock and the room falls silent. There is a loud rumbling, a flash of yellow lightning and the sound of thunder roars about the room. Someone screams.

Miss Lamb lights the candle on the table then steps up into the circle where she throws down fire from her hand. There is a flash of blue, a flicker of flames leaps up and dies as smoke begins to rise.

She waits until the cloud is thick, then says, 'Weather Woman, will you show yourself?'

And there she is, a ghostly apparition.

'Now, your grace, the Weather Woman will give you her prediction. What day and time?'

His grace, like the rest of the room, is silent.

'Come on, your grace,' says Miss Lamb, 'don't be frightened. She isn't the ghost from *Hamlet*, she's the Weather Woman.'

Bos has never seen anyone be disrespectful to his father before and lived to tell the tale.

Finally the Duke of Boswell says, 'I would be pleased if the Weather Woman would tell me if it will rain or shine in one week's time when I intend to ride out in Hyde Park.' His voice is less assured than before. 'Please,' he adds to nervous laughter from Mrs Dent's guests.

'I bet you look a picture, your grace,' says Cassie.

'I do,' says the duke, who is beginning to be charmed.

'Tell us, Weather Woman,' says Miss Lamb.

This is not what Bos had been expecting. The Weather

Woman speaks in a low, seductive voice, her prediction quite clear, then the room fills with the sound of rain. The audience gasp.

'She's alive,' shouts someone into the darkness.

'Ladies and gentlemen, please do not alarm yourselves,' says Miss Lamb. 'Just watch – I promise no harm will come to you.'

With every prediction Miss Lamb extracts from the Weather Woman, Bos falls a little more in love with her.

A footman lights the lamps and Miss Lamb folds away the screen to the side of the room. There is nothing there. The doors open and there is Victor Friezland. The audience are on their feet, the applause deafening.

The art of the performance, Bos writes to Henri that night, is that it borders on the terrifying while Miss Lamb has the timing of a comic.

People leave Mrs Dent's drawing room murmuring that they have just seen the work of a genius. Bos avoids his father in the stream of people making their way downstairs for a light supper.

Now there is no one else in the drawing room apart from Miss Lamb. He goes up to her.

'I saw you once at Covent Garden, Miss Lamb,' he says, 'and I wondered what it would be like to be loved by you. You might think me mad for saying so. The worst part is I can do nothing about what I feel for you: I am married and I don't want a mistress.'

He realises he has been saying this to his shoes. He looks up and sees Miss Lamb is watching him intently.

She seems to have frozen again. At last, she says, 'I didn't think I could do the performance, I was that scared. Then I saw you at the back of the room and I thought if there is only one person this show is for, then it's for you.'

26

October to Christmas 1811

'What kept you so long?' asks Neva as George Cutter helps Cassie into the carriage. She sits next to Neva and says nothing. Neva sees that the colours she always associates with her have changed. She has been constant in the mellow sunshine of her yellows, the brightness found in buttercups, the softness of daffodils. But this evening a bright purplish-red has streaked through the yellow of her colours. Cassie is unsettled.

'Everything's packed away safely,' says George.

'Good,' says Victor. 'Let's go home.'

They now have two carriages, one for themselves and the second to transport the equipment. Victor has had a sign-writer write *The Weather Woman* on this carriage in gold letters. George Cutter feels it's a mistake to advertise her but Victor is sure that advertising is essential. They agree to differ.

'I'll see you at home,' says Victor to George whose journey has to be taken slowly if the lantern isn't to be damaged by the movement of the carriage and the uncertainties of the roads. 'You'll stay and have a bite to eat?' says Victor, knowing Elise will have a sumptuous supper waiting for them.

Of course he will, thinks Neva. He's as much a part of the family as anyone could be.

Cassie still says nothing. Neva takes her hand and squeezes it as if to make the reds go away. Cassie turns to her, smiles, and looks out of the window again. Still the reds shine out.

The carriage lurches to the side as Victor climbs in. 'Too many wholesome pies,' he says, patting the front of his waistcoat. He sits opposite Neva and Cassie and taps the roof of the carriage with his walking stick.

'The Lamb was not slaughtered,' he declares. 'Cassie, you were magnificent. A little slow to start with, but you reeled in the audience. Many congratulations.' Before Cassie can say anything, he turns to Neva. 'Did you mind not being front of stage?'

'Not in the least, Papa,' she says. 'There's a definite freedom in being behind the screen. Though it's strange not to see the audience.'

'I agree,' says Victor. 'But the most important thing is that the new Weather Woman works.'

'That's because Cassie is brilliant,' says Neva. 'And because we have a system of codes.'

'Codes?' says Victor, slapping his leg and laughing. 'What codes?'

'We had to practise to get them right,' says Cassie.

'Are you going to tell me what they are?' he asks, intrigued.

'It's simple,' says Neva. 'Because I can't see who is asking for a prediction, I can't gauge their mood. The code tells me whether it's a gentleman or a lady, difficult or not difficult.'

'I say "So" if it's a lady,' says Cassie, 'and "If" if it's a gentleman. "Well I never" for a difficult one, and "Tell me" for a young lady of marriageable age.'

Victor looks amazed. 'I hadn't realised. Are there more?'

'Of course there are,' says Cassie. 'But we don't want to give away all our secrets, Uncle Victor.'

Still laughing, Victor says, 'Tomorrow we will be inundated with demands for the new Weather Woman.'

Elise has indeed laid out supper for them.

'A feast,' says Victor.

'Nothing less than you all deserve,' she says.

George arrives, Victor helps him unload, and then there is champagne and everyone talking. Neva, watching this happy scene, worries that nothing can ever stay the same. This perfect evening is destined for memory, to be elaborated upon by those who watched the Weather Woman. Victor is in the middle of a story about one of Mrs Dent's guests when the bell rings at the gate.

'Who can this be at such an hour?' he says, putting down his napkin.

George stands up. Knowing of Aubrey's visit, he's on his guard.

'Please sit down, George, I'll go,' says Victor.

He returns a few minutes later carrying an enormous bouquet of yellow roses. The colour is perfect for Cassie. Who is this suitor who knows Cassie so well? In the centre of the bouquet is one of the reddest roses Neva has ever seen, purple-red with a velvety quality to it. Cassie has been constant in her determination never to fall for anyone. To Neva these roses look dangerously like the edge of a cliff.

'Oh my,' says Elise. 'Do we have a vase big enough?'

Victor rests the bouquet on a chair while a vase is found. Among the roses, Elise finds a card. 'They are for Miss Cassandra Lamb,' she says, smiling.

'For me?' says Cassie.

'Yes, of course they're for you,' says Neva, laughing.

Cassie is genuinely flustered by the roses. Elise notices the thorns have been snipped off.

'Come on, Cassie, tell us: what does the card say?' asks Neva.

'It says, "From your greatest admirer",' says Cassie. 'And the initial "B".'

She turns it over. In gold lettering is the name *Marquess of Smedmore.*

That night when the family has gone to bed, Neva waits. She knows Cassie will knock on her door. There it is, a light tap.

'Neva, are you awake?' Cassie whispers.

'Yes.'

'Can I come in?'

'Yes, Cassie.'

'I just wanted to know,' says Cassie, going in, 'if you were all right, being hidden backstage.'

'No, you didn't,' says Neva. 'You just wanted to tell me about the titled gentleman who sent you the roses.'

'The Marquess of Smedmore. I read that his friends call him Bos.'

'What did the Marquess of Smedmore say to you?'

'He said...' Cassie pauses. 'He said that he had wondered what it would be like to be loved by me. And that he was married and didn't want a mistress.'

Neva sighs. 'Cassie, I'm afraid this sort of thing is not unusual. The minute you are on show everyone thinks you are theirs for the taking.'

'Not him,' says Cassie.

'Remember how many proposals I received? All those silly gentlemen said the same kind of rubbish.'

'Oh,' says Cassie, crestfallen. 'I hadn't thought about that. I thought he meant it. Of course he didn't.'

'Oh no, Cassie, I'm sorry. It's very thoughtless of me.'

'That's not unusual either,' says Cassie.

'What do you mean?'

'You often don't think before you speak and a lot of what you say can be taken as thoughtlessness.'

'I am trying to think more before I speak. But I don't want your heart to be broken. He most probably is very much in love with you – who wouldn't be? But he's married and he doesn't want a mistress. Which makes it a difficult situation for both of you, don't you think?'

Cassie smiles.

'There are a lot of very foolish gentlemen in the world,' says Neva, 'though I grant you not all possess glasshouses full of roses, and grand carriages to deliver them at near midnight.'

'When we all turn into pumpkins,' says Cassie. 'Would you mind if I slept with you tonight?'

'Yes,' says Neva, 'because I hate sharing my bed. But for you I'll make an exception.'

'Thank you. I won't wriggle.'

'Neva,' says Cassie sleepily as they lie in bed together, 'do you ever think about Henri Dênou?'

'No,' says Neva. 'Well, only now and then. Nothing good can come of it. Falling in love must be painful – the heartache, I believe, is awful. I'm very happy not feeling anything except some mild irritation at having to share my bed with you.'

Cassie giggles. 'You are a card, Neva.'

'Is that a good thing?'

'It is if you're the Ace of Spades.'

The bookings for the new Weather Woman come in so fast the following day that there isn't a moment when a footman isn't running to or from the garden gate. The sums of money on offer are beyond even Victor's expectations.

Elise becomes quite giggly when he turns down Lord Telford. 'Are you sure? After all, he is a Member of Parliament.'

'Even more reason to refuse him,' says Victor. Two hours later the duke's messenger returns to ask if Victor might reconsider treble the first sum offered.

'Money makes whores of us all,' says Victor. Taking Elise by the hand he dances with her round the kitchen, saying, 'Do we mind? No, we don't. Yes we do, no we won't.'

What follows are the most profitable months Victor has ever known. It is Mr Ratchet who advises Victor where best to invest and bank his money.

By Christmas of 1811, Victor and Cassie have seen the inside of countless private rooms, halls and salons, and the Weather Woman who terrifies, delights and amuses has caught the imagination of London. Miss Cassandra Lamb is a star.

At nearly every performance, the Marquess of Smedmore is to be found in the audience. He often stays behind after the show to have a word with Cassie. Both look shy and both look as if they should be with the other. Then at the last performance before Christmas, Cassie sees his wife, the Marchioness, is with him in the audience.

'What's wrong?' asks Neva in the carriage going home.

'I'm a fool,' says Cassie. 'A daydreaming fool.'

'Do you know the proverb,' asks Elise, one bitter December night, '"If you would live in health, wear the same garment in summer that you wear in winter"?'

'That's why the English are never prepared for winter,' says Victor. 'You know, we Russians are accustomed to stoves and furs. The thing that surprised me most when I came to this country was that men wore the same clothes all year round. The cold in this country can be intense but because it's not severe enough to nip off a man's nose when he puts it outdoors most Englishmen take no precautions against the weather and therefore suffer more than the Germans or the Russians.'

This is the first time for a long while, thinks Neva, that she remembers neither she nor Victor was born in London.

'Do you have any memory of Russia?' Cassie asks her.

'Only that Andre Tarshin named me after the river Saint Petersburg is built on,' says Neva. 'I wonder if I'll ever see Russia again.'

'I know I won't,' says Victor.

This Christmas the air is so full of soot the snow is already soiled as it falls. Victor and George Cutter climb onto the roof of the workshop to shovel it off.

'Go and tell them to come down,' says Elise.

Neva wraps her shawl around her. Only George is on the workshop roof.

'Where's Papa?' she shouts.

'We were nearly done, but he said he had to get down.'

'Why?'

'Something about a bird.'

Neva finds Victor by the river. 'What are you doing, Papa?' she asks. Not for the first time she thinks he's keeping something secret. 'Papa, are you all right?'

'Yes, Neva, yes,' he says, turning to her and smiling. 'It's nothing. A magpie caught my eye, that's all.'

On Christmas Eve, a slim box arrives for Cassie from a Bond Street jeweller's.

'Very smart,' says Victor. 'Jewellery makers to the Queen, no less.' Cassie stares at the box.

'If you're not going to open it,' says Neva, 'shall we try to guess what's inside? You go first, Auntie.'

'A ring,' says Elise.

'I don't think it's a ring,' says Neva.

'Earrings,' says Victor. 'Much more appropriate.'

'Stop it,' says Cassie.

She opens the box and puts it down as if there's a wasp inside. Lying on velvet the same red as the single rose is a delicate gold chain on which hangs the most exquisite little sparrow. Suspended from the gleaming bird is a tiny red gem that seems to possess a light of its own.

'It's paste,' says Cassie. 'It must be paste.'

'Would it matter if it was only paste?' asks Neva.

'No. It would still be the most precious present I've ever been given.'

'Then it definitely won't matter,' said Victor, 'if I tell you the bird is gold, studded with diamonds, and that red gem is a ruby. The necklace must have cost a fortune.'

It's the note that accompanies the gift that breaks Cassie's heart. It reads:

There is nothing I can do about my situation and I cannot come again. Think no more of me,
  Yours always and forever,
  Bos

Too late Neva realises Cassie is in love with the Marquess and she hadn't seen her fall. She thinks Cassie must have done it silently when no one was looking. And all the colours in her that shimmered so brightly have turned brown.

'You never know,' says Neva, 'he could have been a terrible bore. And he probably snores.' It being too cold that December to sleep alone they're both tucked up warm in Neva's bed, the glow of the fire lighting the room. 'All will be well,' she adds, to comfort.

'You don't know that,' says Cassie.

★ ★ ★

On Christmas morning, the bells of London ring out, St Paul's calling to his brother and sister churches. Cassie and Neva go in the carriage to Cheapside where shop windows are filled with large plum cakes, encrusted with sugar and ornamented in every possible way for the festival of the Three Kings.

They find mince pies, cheese and sweets of all sorts of delicacies for the table, and make their way home as the black-spotted snow begins to fall.

There's a merry party at the Friezland house. Victor has insisted on decorating the mantel shelves with candles and greenery, and making an elaborate garland for the front door. George, Mr Gutteridge, Mr Ratchet and Mrs Dent join them for dinner and Elise serves roast beef, plum pudding and mince pies. Victor pours a good burgundy.

Neva would like to believe she is content with life, at peace with the burial of Eugene Jonas in the wardrobe. But she knows she's not at ease with being unable to make predictions as she did when she was young, predictions that helped people whose living relied on the weather. The Weather Woman is merely a fantasy for rich people's entertainment. But what can she do? It's Papa's creation and to complain would be ungrateful. After all, he built the Weather Woman for her. And what would have become of her if he hadn't found her all those years ago, and given her a home, given her love? She can imagine many things but not life without Papa. Life without Eugene Jonas, yes. As for her gift – what does it matter? It's no more than a novelty.

Victor stands, glass in hand. 'I have a few words – not many. Here's a toast to my love Elise, here's to our family and friends, and here's to the Weather Woman. Merry Christmas, everyone!'

Mrs Dent insists there should be singing. Mr Gutteridge plays the piano and plays it so well that there's not only singing but, after the rolling back of the carpet, there's dancing too.

Victor brings out the wassail bowl, the mulled wine hot and steaming and, as Cassie says, smelling of Christmas.

It has begun to snow again, the river is slowing, ice tinges the water. Neva knows it will freeze this year. A frost is coming, she can feel it, and the world is changing.

Part Three

27

December 1812

Henri doesn't know how long he's been in the sea. Neither is he certain if he still has legs. He can't feel them and his arms are going the same way. He wonders what makes him cling to the broken mast but cling he does and a sea shanty goes round and round in his head.

> She dressed herself up like a sailor
> In her jacket and trousers so blue.

The waves have died down, the storm has passed. It had brought its vengeance on them, its white-foamed horses relentlessly destroying the ship.

For ten days they were tossed and thrown by unimaginable seas until Henri dismissed all rational arguments and became convinced this was the work of the ancient god Poseidon, the king of storms. The deity of tempests was playing with them for his own amusement until the package ship was wrecked and all the letters it was carrying, all the words it had in its hold, were washed away and only mermen and mermaids might glimpse a sentence. The god of storms by then had lost all interest and raced on to his next victims. Henri thought he would never look at weather in the same way again. Had the Weather Woman predicted this tempest?

'Good morning to you, sir,' says the bosun as he drifts out of sight.

Mrs O'Donnell, returning to Ireland from Boston, is holding onto the broken mast with Henri.

'Don't let go, hold on,' he repeats until he's too cold to speak.

'You will have to excuse me,' she says at last and disappears.

He tries to find her but a wave pulls him away.

His mind is jumbled with a shipwreck of images and fragments of sound.

She dressed herself up like a sailor
In her jacket and trousers so blue.

'Sherry, Mr Dênou?' says the captain.

Why has he tied himself to the table? Henri is thrown across the cabin, his head hits a cabinet. 'Bring the glasses,' says the captain.

Was it this morning? Was it Christmas Day? When was Christmas Day?

'We are bound for the bottom of the deep, deep sea,' says the captain. 'My advice, sir, is to get drunk.'

The sailors are exhausted. The carpenter is washed overboard. This leaky old vessel is no match for Poseidon.

'Not enough lifeboats for everyone,' says the captain. He takes the stopper from the sherry decanter, pours the golden liquid into two impossibly small glasses and drinks them both. He puts the decanter to his lips and gulps the sherry as if it were water. 'How much salt do you think is in the sea, Mr Dênou?'

Henri is swimming for the steps. The captain can't move, bubbles come from his lips, the water swirls this way and that as if the god of storms is rinsing a fly from a bottle.

Henri pulls himself up onto the deck. It's ankle deep in water. Passengers and sailors are fighting about who will go in the three lifeboats. Mrs O'Donnell says, 'I can't abide crowded spaces.'

A lifeboat is launched. It is carrying about twenty-five people. It is only fit to take ten.

Still Henri clings to the broken mast. 'Hold on,' he repeats. Am I the last one? Why not let go? It will be so peaceful. Perhaps there'll be mermaids. The thought is comforting.

His parents' heads float past, their eyes closed.

And there is Eugene Jonas, standing on the water, looking up at the sky.

> She dressed herself up like a sailor
> In her jacket and trousers so blue.
> Three years and a half on the ocean
> She spent with her young sailor bold.

The dwarf says, '*C'est un tour de lumière*. You aren't truly looking at him.'

> Three times her true love got shipwrecked;
> Each time to him she proved true.
> Her duty she did as a sailor
> In her jacket and trousers of blue.

'Am I dead?'

'Not yet,' says the dwarf. 'Soon. I'll be close by.' He floats off. 'Look out for the dog,' he calls.

A bright green apple bobs past. Henri grabs it. He's struck by the outrageous colour in the grey water. It makes him laugh.

It won't be long before he joins Mrs O'Donnell.

She dressed herself up like a sailor
In her jacket and trousers so blue.

'You aren't truly listening to it,' says Eugene Jonas.

Henri is tired, his arms are weak.

Am I dead? It seems like a sound explanation because coming towards him out of the sea fret is a rowing boat. Now he's certain he's dead. There's a dog in the prow, looking out to sea.

Henri hasn't the strength to climb in. The dog hauls him into the boat. Like a dead fish, he thinks. The dog says nothing. Is it a real dog or is it his imagining? Does it matter? Floating past him is a bottle of sherry. He pulls the cork. Along come two more bright green apples. He gives one to the dog though he's sure it's a figment of his imagination.

He lies at the bottom of the boat, looking up at the sky and its whirling clouds. He is in a floating coffin, he is frozen, he is dead. He's as small as the stars, a speck on the horizon, he's lost at sea. He will never drink sherry again.

28

January 1813

If the sun has risen this January day, it has done so in such a half-hearted manner that it has hardly been noticed. It seems the sky might tumble at any moment, snuffing out what little light there is. On the river, where such mists are often to be found, the fog is gathering an army of particles. Collectively they hang ominously over the water, climbing the rigging of the tall ships at anchor in the Thames. The white smoggy blindness moves up the river steps and like the tide itself it is changing, thickening.

Victor Friezland's house in the lane off Tooley Street is lit with candles though it is barely twelve o'clock. The furniture, bookshelves and ornaments that used to lend charm to the long drawing room are now shrouded in wintery glumness. The temperature outside hovers around thirty-two degrees fahrenheit and the well-stacked fire makes little difference to the bitter chill.

Surplus chairs have been placed against the bookshelves and the double doors at the end of the chamber are left open so that the jewel box of a dining room can be seen with its galleon window. This is where Neva stands as the fog rolls in, looking out at the fast-disappearing view of the garden. All is still, as if the house is holding its breath, uncertain if the nails, wattle and plaster that hold this ship together can bear the weight of so much sorrow.

A violent storm of grief threatens to blow Neva away, the unbearable emptiness turn her mad. He is not in the workshop, he is not in the house. He can't be found in the kitchen. He is no longer in the bed he shared with Elise. This is the first day he sleeps in the grave.

Victor, so full of life, is lifeless. Her papa, her anchor, is dead. There is no one to rescue her. Everything is motion, everything is falling. He must have known, she thinks, he must have.

The week before he died, he seemed anxious that his affairs were in order.

They had taken the boat out on the river.

'Why so serious?' she had asked and to her surprise he suggested she think again about marriage.

'I'm now considered an old maid,' she'd said.

'You are one of the loveliest old maids in London. And you have so many admirers,' he said. 'Think again.'

'I don't have to – remember I married Eugene Jonas.'

She was rowing and he had placed his hand on hers and asked, 'Do you think of him?'

'Who,' she said, 'Eugene Jonas?'

'Henri Dênou.'

It shocked her to hear his name. It was as if Victor knew her heart. She had never said a word about him, not since the day she'd put Eugene Jonas away in the wardrobe.

'Papa – that's a strange question. But, yes, I do.'

'Marry him.'

'How could I do that? I hardly know him. And he only knows me as Eugene.'

'I believe he's in New York. But given the war between

England and America it is very likely he will try to come home.' Neva said nothing. 'Life is but a turning of a leaf, too short to understand, too long for regret,' said Victor.

Oh, where have you gone, Papa? Try as she might to banish her tears, like rain they have become the weather of her.

She turns to see Elise in the doorway, her black gown accentuating her pallor.

'Mr Seaton is here,' she says.

'Auntie, how do we carry on?' Neva asks.

'If we don't,' says Elise, 'all Victor's kindness, all that was wondrous in him will be lost. You are the Weather Woman – he made you that.'

Neva has not let anyone touch her since Papa's death but now she holds tight to Elise.

Mr Gutteridge comes into the long drawing room. He has been with them all day, as had the many friends and neighbours who attended the funeral. The church was filled to the rafters. Now they're gone.

Elise asks Mr Gutteridge, as she has a hundred times, 'Why didn't Victor make his will with you?'

'For some reason I don't understand,' says Mr Gutteridge, 'Victor chose to draw up his will with a local solicitor. I can only think it was because there was something he didn't wish to tell me.'

On cue, the solicitor, Mr Seaton, joins them. He's wrapped as tight as a Christmas pudding and looks not unlike one. Introductions are made.

'I have a delicate throat,' he says by way of an explanation no one asked for.

The garden gate bell rings again and Cassie answers it. Two people are talking loudly in the passage. One is a woman with a voice that would put a peacock to shame.

The door bursts open and there is a thin, badly dressed man who announces too loudly to a room that has been shrouded in silence and whispering voices, 'I'm Aubrey Friezland and this is my mother, Victor Friezland's one and only wife, Mary Friezland. Heaven help you if the will says anything different.'

Mary is a plump woman, the shadow of her prettiness now lost in a double chin that rolls down her neck and over the top of her too tight and inappropriate gown. She shivers and wraps her shawl about her for the cold.

Mr Seaton is puzzled. 'I only have one Mrs Friezland named,' he says.

Mr Gutteridge closes his eyes.

'There is mention of a Mary and the name is Letchmore.'

'Well, that's wrong for a start,' says Aubrey. 'That was the name of the lieutenant and he...' He stops, suddenly aware that he might have said too much.

Mr Seaton is quite bothered by this intervention. Mr Gutteridge pokes at the fire that shows no inclination for life.

'No,' says Aubrey as Elise takes the front chair. 'That's where Mrs Friezland should sit, not my father's mistress. Here, Mother.' He pats the chair.

Elise's white face is stoic. Cassie is on the point of saying something but Elise shakes her head.

Mr Seaton looks at his fob watch.

Inside her black gloves, Neva's fingers have been picked into constant pain. She sits with Elise and Cassie, and even though she is in the shadows the light longs to find her for her beauty has no passing moment.

The clock strikes once on the half hour.

'Shall we proceed?' says Mr Seaton.

He takes the will and his spectacles case from his inner pocket. Everything he does is methodical and slow. He carefully sets his spectacles on his nose.

'Wait,' says Aubrey. 'One always needs a full glass of wine

when listening to a will. We haven't had any refreshments or sweetmeats.' He turns to look at Elise. 'Did you hear me, woman? Wine.'

His mother squeezes his arm and tries to hint at letting the solicitor speak. 'After all, that's why we're here,' she inadvertently adds.

'I didn't ask for your opinion, did I?' snaps Aubrey.

'No, but—'

'Well then, Mother, desist from giving it.'

The atmosphere in the room is brittle. Neva says nothing. Cassie gets up and takes out the wine and pours a glass. She looks so furious that for one moment Neva can see her pouring the rest of the decanter over Aubrey.

'What about me?' says Mary. Cassie ignores her and puts the bottle down. 'Did you see that, son? Did you see—'

'Shut it, Mother,' says her son.

Mary looks wounded but smiles. No one smiles back.

'What are you waiting for?' asks Aubrey, basking in the full attention of everyone. 'Before you start, or whatever it was you just said – *proceed* – that's it, before you *proceed*, what I want to know is…' Aubrey turns and points his finger at Neva, 'what's *she* doing here?' He has a shockingly white hand and he moves in such a jerky manner that he spills his wine over his mother's skirt. 'You're always so clumsy, Mother, and thick as a brush to boot,' he says, elbowing her. 'I want to know what she's doing here.' He points again at Neva and, once more, wine is spilt. 'She shouldn't be here; she's a usurper.'

Mr Gutteridge has had enough. 'Mr Friezland, this is the day of your father's funeral, a funeral which you did not attend. You could at least show some respect.'

'Oh, highty-tighty,' says Aubrey.

'Thank you, Mr Gutteridge,' says Mr Seaton. 'I am here to read your father's will, Mr Friezland, and I have no interest in whether you have a glass of wine or not, sir.' He says this in a most commanding voice. 'What concerns me is that I return to my chambers before dark.'

Neva supposes Aubrey was in the army long enough to be wary of generals. Mr Seaton continues. '"In the name of God, Amen. I, Victor Friezland, formerly Viktor Morozov, of the parish of Southwark in the County of Surrey being in perfect health and of sound and disposing mind, memory and understanding and to prevent any disputes that might arise after my death, do make this my last will and testament, making null and void any will written before this date."'

'Wait,' interrupts Aubrey. 'When was this will written?'

'Two weeks ago, Mr Friezland.' Mr Seaton takes a deep breath. '"First and principally, I commend my soul to God and my body to the earth to be decently interred at the direction of my executors. I desire that all my just debts and funeral expenses be fully satisfied. To Aubrey Friezland, I leave the sum of five hundred pounds."'

Aubrey smiles. 'No less than I deserve. You see, he did love his son. I've taken the lion's share.'

'"To Mary Letchmore, née Kydd, who claims to be my wife, I leave the sum of one shilling for candles, she having lived well off the generous maintenance I freely paid her over the years, and with which she sought her own benefit over the education of her child Aubrey for whom the money was intended."'

'I never had a penny,' says Mary. 'Honest. That's a mistake. If I'd had that money my life would've been—'

'Shut it, Mother,' says Aubrey.

The solicitor clears his throat. '"To my true wife Elise, née Rose, formerly Gibbs, I leave the sum of two thousand five hundred pounds per annum, so she may live comfortably."'

'Wait!' says Aubrey. 'What do you mean, he leaves her two thousand five hundred pounds? That can't be right. My mother was his one and only wife and the whore and the usurper took advantage of my father. Because of them I never saw him. That woman...' he points his finger at Elise, 'she's nothing more than a trollop.'

'Will you please be quiet, sir,' says Mr Seaton. 'I will not ask you again. If you interrupt me once more, I shall not continue with the reading of this will. It will be done in my chambers.' Aubrey sinks down into his chair as the solicitor clears his throat again. '"To Miss Cassandra Lamb, I leave the sum of one thousand pounds per annum, and to Mr George Cutter, I leave the sum of six hundred pounds per annum."'

'He what?' says Aubrey.

'Sir, will you listen quietly. "To my beloved child, Neva Tarshin Friezland, I leave two thousand five hundred pounds per annum. I also hereby give her all household goods, furniture, plates, linenware, and goods and chattels."'

'You mean,' Aubrey stands up and belches, 'you mean he's left all of this to the usurper and the trollop? Everything? Chairs? Paintings? Everything? What about the house itself? He's left it to me, hasn't he?'

Mr Seaton takes off his glasses. 'Sir, will you show some respect for the dead.' He gives Aubrey his most withering look. Aubrey sits down again.

'"This foolish world being but a dream and no more than the stuff of sleep, I therefore leave to Eugene Jonas my personal estate including my business and property for as long as he be above the ground, and in the event of his demise his said portion will pass to my daughter, Neva Tarshin Friezland. I go, but I leave, I hope, my reputation, my clocks and my automatons behind me."'

Neva feels a jolt as if she has been struck by lightning. This is most unexpected and immediately explains why Papa didn't instruct Mr Gutteridge to draw up his will. But the danger of it going wrong – if Eugene Jonas is found to be her – is a terrifying prospect.

'Where is this Eugene Jonas?' shouts Aubrey.

'Abroad, sir,' says Mr Seaton.

'And that's it? I challenge the will. For a start, I'm his only child, his right and proper heir, and this woman – my mother – is his true wife.'

Mr Seaton looks at his fob watch.

'How much, just out of interest, is this house and the workshop worth? I mean, he made clocks.'

Neva is glad Aubrey has no idea of the value of the Chippendale chair he's sitting on, or of the Hogarth paintings decorating the walls.

'And the Weather Woman – how much is that business worth? Well?' says Aubrey. 'How much?'

This is what Neva has been dreading.

'The business is worth around forty thousand pounds a year, sir, subject to the continuing involvement of Mr Jonas,' says Mr Seaton.

There is silence for a moment.

'Did you just say forty thousand?' says Aubrey. 'Did you? Well, I think you will find all of it is mine. He made a mistake to put Child in his will and Wife. He was badly advised, Mr Seaton. I think the court will find in my favour. And by the way, Mother, you can pay me back all the money you took.'

Mr Seaton puts away his spectacles and the will, does up his coat, wraps his muffler several times round his delicate throat and says, 'Mr Friezland, you have been left a goodly sum of money, some would say a fortune for a man estranged from his father, with whom he had nothing to do and as an adult saw once. You can, of course, argue this in the courts if you wish. It would mean that your inheritance will be in probate until the case is heard and if you lose there will be legal bills to pay which could be half the sum of money you would receive. It is up to you. I suppose the question is how much in need of money you are at present. If you wish to claim that Mr Friezland was not in his right mind, your argument would fail, for the will was signed in my presence as well as that of his physician, Dr Richards of Wimpole Street, Mr Cutter of Jamaica Road and Mr Ratchet of Cheapside.'

'My uncle was a witness?'

Mr Seaton goes to Elise. 'I am so sorry for your loss, madam,' he says.

'What about me?' says Mary.

'The behaviour of you and your son this afternoon is nothing short of a disgrace. My advice, sir,' he says, turning to Aubrey, 'is to accept what you have been so generously given and to accept it with gratitude.'

'Gratitude? You talk of gratitude when it is I, his son, and my mother, his wife, who have been grievously abused and neglected. So yes, Mr High and Mighty Lawyer, we are taking this to the courts. Come on, Mother, we're leaving.'

'I wouldn't mind a glass of wine,' says Mary.

But Aubrey has her by the wrist and pulls her out of the house.

Mr Seaton also takes his leave and Neva accompanies him to the garden gate.

'Thank you for all you've done, Mr Seaton,' she says.

'Mr Friezland had hoped the money left to his son would be enough to satisfy him,' says Mr Seaton. 'But it doesn't look as if that is the case. Your father was convinced Mary Letchmore was already married when he and she were wed. He didn't know it at the time, of course. If we can find proof of that earlier wedding then the will stands.'

Neva has turned to go back to the house when she changes her mind and walks down the garden, past the workshop. There, on the bank of the Thames, where the rowing boat is moored, she looks up at the sky and sees the mauve stain rising from the chimney pots, bruising the clouds above the city. She feels Victor beside her, gently whispering to her soul. 'Be strong, Neva.'

29

January to February 1813

'D o you know this Mr Eugene Jonas?' Mr Gutteridge asks Elise while Neva is accompanying Mr Seaton to his carriage. 'Because it's a mystery to me why Victor has done this.' Neva comes in, bringing with her a blast of freezing air that makes Elise shiver. 'Mr Jonas,' the solicitor continues, 'is, by all accounts, a remarkable young man, or so my client, Mr Dênou, told me. He went as far as to describe him as brilliant.'

Neva is trying to coax the fire into life and is shaken to hear Henri's name in this context. She feels herself blush.

This is not what she wants to be talking about, not now. The timbers of this ship she lives in, which have felt so solid to her, are beginning to tremble around her. Nothing is stable. The tide has turned, the clouds are too low and she is lost in a fog of grief. The chess-playing bear is standing in the shadows behind Mr Gutteridge.

Henri Dênou, long banished from her mind, has, in the space of ten days, been mentioned twice.

'He spent an evening at Brooks's in Mr Jonas's company. Mr Dênou was under the impression Miss Friezland was engaged to him. Are you, Miss Friezland?'

'No,' says Neva, slightly too quickly.

'Then this is most untoward,' says Mr Gutteridge, 'and it makes me wonder if we should trust Mr Jonas if he can mislead Mr Dênou in that way. But of course, circumstances may have changed.' He looks questioningly at Neva. 'This was, after all, four and a half years ago, just before Mr Dênou departed on that ill-fated voyage.'

Neva is confronted with a merry-go-round of emotions. Even if she might never wish to see him again she would be sorry to hear of Henri meeting with a fatal accident.

'I hope Mr Dênou is well,' she finds herself saying. 'Did the ship arrive at its destination safely?'

'Oh, it was damaged in a storm and limped into harbour in Denmark where the expedition was eventually abandoned and Sir Edward Fairbrother returned home. I always thought that gentleman had more words in him than actions and this apparently proved to be the case. Mr Dênou went on to New York to visit his aunt – his father's sister. When I last heard from him, he was hoping to find a passage home to England.'

Cassie can see Neva is longing to know more. 'What will happen to him if he can't get home?' she asks, hoping to tease further information out of the solicitor.

'I beg your pardon, Miss Lamb?'

Cassie repeats her question.

'That is a question I'm not qualified to answer.' It is obvious to everyone that what concerns Mr Gutteridge most is Victor Friezland's will. 'We must hope Mr Jonas has the moral strength to exert his rights and maintain his hold on the property and business. Whether he will be generous to all of you, there is no knowing. It is, in short, most unsatisfactory. Do you know where Mr Jonas is?'

'Yes,' says Elise, to Neva and Cassie's surprise. 'I wrote to tell him of Victor's death. He's been travelling but is due back soon. Now, Mr Gutteridge, if you don't mind, I'm too exhausted to talk further. It has been a long day for all of us.'

'Forgive me, Mrs Friezland, I've been most insensitive,' says Mr Gutteridge. He retrieves his walking stick, hat and muffler, and bows low. 'My dear lady,' he says, 'you know you can call on me at any time.'

'At last,' says Elise when she hears the garden gate shut. She sinks into a chair and turns to Neva. 'Were you aware your papa intended you to become Eugene Jonas again?'

'No,' says Neva. 'It was as much of a shock to me as it was to you.'

'A shock?' says Elise. 'How on earth did Victor think this subterfuge would work? It's bound to be discovered and then what? And, Neva, it's been an age since you masqueraded as Eugene and... What was Victor thinking? If this goes to the courts...'

Neva kneels beside Elise. 'What else can we do, Auntie?'

'I suppose it's the only way to try to secure Victor's work,' says Elise. 'But if you're found out? You'd go to prison. Or be deported. And more than likely so would I.'

They all jump when the garden gate bell rings. The three women look at each other, dreading the return of Aubrey and his mother.

'Leave it to me,' says Cassie and goes to answer it. She returns a few moments later with George Cutter.

He, too, seems diminished by Victor's death.

We are drowning, thinks Neva, clinging to memories to stay afloat, not knowing if we'll survive.

'Please forgive the intrusion,' he says, turning his hat round and round in his hands.

'It's no intrusion,' says Neva.

'I saw Mr Gutteridge as he was leaving – he told me Mr Friezland remembered me in his will,' he says.

'It's no more than you deserve, George,' says Elise.

Ever since the dreadful morning of Victor's death, George Cutter has been a quiet presence in the house, helping with the undertaker and the arrangements for the funeral. He should have been here for the reading of the will, Neva thinks. Without him they would be even more adrift than they are.

He clears his throat. 'Knowing Aubrey Friezland and his mother would be here for the reading of the will, I thought it best to stay close by, in case they turned nasty. I followed them when they left until they disappeared in a hackney carriage then I came straight here. Elise, I've had a good look at that Aubrey Friezland. He's no son of Victor's, and I don't trust him an inch. I'm going to have some of the lads from my boxing school keep an eye on things here.'

'Do you think that's really necessary?' says Elise.

'I do,' he says with such sadness. He stops, fearing he might have said too much.

Elise nods, too drained to argue. 'You're a good man, George. And a trustworthy friend. Victor has surprised us all with his going, and with the will. To be honest, I don't know…' Her voice trails off. 'I think,' she says, 'I've run out of words.'

'You know I'd do anything for all of you,' says George. 'You're my family, I'd defend you with my life.'

'Oh, I hope it doesn't come to that,' says Elise. 'But you should know – Victor has left the business to Eugene Jonas.'

'Well, thank the Lord for that. I feared he might have left it to you and Neva, in which case—'

Elise interrupts him. 'But Eugene Jonas – why bring him back?'

'I suppose,' says Neva, 'if he'd left the business to us, there would be a danger of it being stolen by those two rogues.'

'Neva's right,' says George, 'and she's more than capable of playing the part. You might not feel it now, Neva, but wait until you've had a few lessons and a haircut. When you're ready, I'll ask Mr James to call. You're not to worry. Apart from Mr James, no one will know about this but ourselves.'

Slowly, Elise rises to her feet. 'I hope for all our sakes you're right,' she says, and goes into the kitchen, where she feels in charge. Alone at last, she closes the door.

'I thought,' she says to the empty room, 'we agreed there would be no more Eugene Jonas. Why didn't you tell me what you planned?'

Victor has just been buried but Elise knows he is still with her. He has told her as much.

'Where I come from it is believed the soul of the dead stays with the living for forty days.'

'I wasn't prepared for you dying. We weren't prepared for this,' says Elise to the well-scrubbed table top. 'I thought I would end my days in this house with you. I thought we wouldn't have to worry about Aubrey and his mother. What have you done, Victor?'

Her mind drifts back to the morning Victor died. It was two days after Christmas, 27th December. She had woken to his 'kisses and a good cuddle' as he called it. At seven she was in the kitchen, making him coffee as usual. When she returned to the bedchamber, he was dead. She'd known straight away.

She'd gone to him, laid her hand on his chest. His heart had stopped and in that instant her own heart broke.

'Don't leave me, my love, stay,' she whispered as she lay down beside him. 'Come back to me – oh Victor – come back.' She'd wrapped her arms round him but there is such a difference between the living and the dead. His body no longer housed his soul.

This is the weather of grief, thinks Neva – a violent storm. There's no knowing where it ends. It has capsized all those who loved Victor. Trees upended in the hurricane, lives upended by grief. Their house – their ship – has been sunk by this unfathomable tempest. Throughout her life, what Neva had dreaded most was Victor not being there. Not dead, but not there, and this, his dying, was worse, far worse than the vague memory she had of losing her parents. Victor was her sanity, the person who had helped her make sense of the world. Now her old fears are back and the chess-playing bear is growing in size, waiting until it is big enough to eat her whole. What will she do without Papa, he who rescued her, taught her; he, the inventor of the Weather Woman? It is this, his legacy, she must keep alive for him.

The house feels soulless and time is without meaning. Neva longs to curl into a small ball and let the waves roll over her, for in the debris the tempest has left unsaid secrets. Auntie talks of a baby girl, asks when Victor is coming home. Neva realises Elise is drowning. It's inconceivable to her and Cassie that Elise, so steadfast and strong, could be so broken.

She won't eat and stays in the kitchen, staring at the door expecting him to come in from the workshop. When he doesn't she takes to her bed. She says Eugene Jonas shouldn't be allowed in the house, that he isn't welcome.

Cassie tries to coax Elise to eat, but she won't. She says she's waiting for Victor to come and take her home.

Neva sings Russian lullabies to her which seem to calm her but still she asks, 'Where's Victor?'

Mr Cutter understands for he too near lost his mind when he discovered his wife and child buried in the graveyard. It took him all his strength to remain sane.

'And I'm still haunted,' he says to Neva.

'How did you find that strength?' she asks.

'I just did, because there was nothing else.'

Mrs Dent comes to see Elise. She sits with her a long time. Elise says nothing as Mrs Dent holds her hand and tells her not to wander into the dark woods of her mind.

'You don't want to get lost in there, my girl,' she says quietly. 'You must find your way home.'

Mrs Dent recommends a doctor. 'And don't leave it too long.'

Neva thanks her and doesn't say she is worried Elise might tell the doctor about Eugene. But she isn't getting better and Neva can see her following Victor to the grave. She stops eating and wanders at night. More than once Neva finds her by the river, half-frozen. Now none of them are sleeping.

Mrs Dent comes again, bringing the doctor. He's a calm, quiet man and speaks to Elise with a kind but firm voice as if she's a child. Cassie and Neva are surprised when Elise listens and does as she's told. She takes a bowl of soup and bread-and-butter, and some colour returns to her cheeks. Neva and Cassie stay in the room as he examines Elise. She says nothing and looks exhausted when he's finished. And asks, as she asks every day, when is Victor coming home?

In the long drawing room the doctor explains that with rest and a light diet she should get better. He leaves bottles of medicine and now at least Elise sleeps.

'Perhaps,' says Cassie, 'it's happened this way for a good reason. I thought it would be you who'd become ill. I think Uncle Victor knew that and leaving his will the way he did means you have to be strong. He was a clever man.'

'We must plan,' Neva says to Cassie a few days later. 'Becoming Eugene is beyond me at the moment. I can hardly remember who he is, and what I do remember I don't much like.'

'Fortunately,' says Cassie, 'it's four and a half years and I imagine he's grown wiser and become more serious. He's a little more sober and, obviously, his heart is broken by Victor's death.'

'Not only by Victor's death but by Neva Friezland refusing to marry him!'

They laugh but their laughter sounds strange to them.

'This is folly,' says Neva.

'I agree it would be folly to bring Eugene home at this moment,' says Cassie, 'but we should set a date for his return – May perhaps – and hope Auntie is better by then.'

'Why May?' says Neva.

'The apple blossom's on the trees, the wisteria's blooming, life's beginning again.'

Neva shakes her head. This is the greatest challenge Papa has ever set her. She crawls out of bed every morning. Every morning she wants to hide from the day.

In April Elise rises from her bed. She's lost a lot of weight and doesn't say much but she no longer asks where Victor is.

She says, 'Forty days have passed, long passed and Victor has gone.'

She likes being in the kitchen and quietly she starts cooking and polishing and neither Neva nor Cassie stop her.

Mr James arrives by boat to cut Neva's hair. Elise sits at the kitchen table and watches.

'So,' she says, when Neva's thick black hair is lying round her feet, 'Eugene Jonas has come home.'

'Yes, Auntie,' says Neva, turning to face her.

'About time,' says Elise and with that she is back with them again and appears to have little memory of the weather of grief. But the brightness has gone from her.

30

April 1813

Mr Gutteridge is even more perplexed now the snow has melted from his dear friend's grave. He still cannot fathom why Victor didn't consult him. He would not have advised him to word his will in such a way. The folly of it is beyond his comprehension. Something must be done, because Aubrey Friezland will win the case, unless it can be proved he is illegitimate. The idea that Elise and Neva might be left penniless is too dreadful to contemplate.

A daring notion occurs to him, perfect in its simplicity; a thought as arousing as it is unbalancing. If Neva were to accept the offer of his hand in marriage, he would be in a good position to defend Victor's last wishes. As for the age difference – there are many such marriages in society.

There is only one impediment to his scheme and that is Eugene Jonas. He suspects that Mr Jonas had an attachment if not a love for Neva. And perhaps in their shared grief at Victor's death love between the two might be rekindled.

Mr Jonas is all I have to contend with, he tells himself. He remembers seeing him once, several years ago. A personable young man; at the time he thought him far too young to be

Victor's business partner but Victor was adamant that the young gentleman was supremely clever.

None of this dampens Mr Gutteridge's enthusiasm for his plan.

On a Monday in late April, with good intentions and an engagement ring in his waistcoat pocket, he calls on Elise. Mr Gutteridge is a man with little instinctive understanding of the complexities of human emotion and he fails to see these are not the circumstances in which to make his proposal.

He asks if he might have a quiet word alone with Elise. Once the kitchen door is shut he lays out his brief before her, emphasising the advantages of such a match.

'Of course,' he says, 'the wedding would be at an appropriate time, after the official period of mourning has passed, though I recommend in the meantime that the engagement is announced in *The Times*.'

Elise looks at him as if he has lost his mind. She says, 'You can ask her, I suppose.'

He finds Neva in the long drawing room, crouched in front of the fireplace.

'Good morning, Mr Gutteridge,' she says. 'The wood is damp.' She manages to light the kindling and stands to face him only to find him on one knee. 'Mr Gutteridge, I can light the fire – I don't need any help.'

'Marriage,' says the solicitor, maintaining his position at her feet, 'is the most important undertaking a young woman can make. It is, without doubt, the defining moment in her life. It not only shapes her future but that of her intended.'

Neva suddenly realises where this is leading.

'Please, sir, will you stand up? You look quite ridiculous…'

She stops and puts her hand to her mouth; Mr Gutteridge cannot tell if in horror or to stifle laughter.

Nevertheless, he continues. 'It would be the greatest honour of my life if you would accept my proposal. I can offer you safety, companionship and financial stability without fear of poverty. I know there is an age difference but my position in society will afford you...' and on he goes.

Whatever reaction Mr Gutteridge expected, it wasn't this:

'Congratulations! You have played your knight well and wrong-footed me. Perhaps, sir, you should apply that same skill when playing chess.'

With a groan, Mr Gutteridge stands up. 'Neva,' he says, 'I am asking you to marry me.'

'And my answer is no, Mr Gutteridge. In all honesty I would make you a wretched wife and we would both be miserable. I thank you for your offer, sir, but no.'

'Are you rejecting my offer because of a commitment to Mr Jonas?'

'No,' says Neva.

'He allowed Mr Dênou to think you were engaged to him and I take his deception as proof, if proof be needed, that Mr Jonas cannot be trusted. My advice is that you take your time to consider my proposal.' He only now notices that Neva is staring out the window at the river. 'Neva, your only hope – and I mean *only* hope – is that you accept my proposal and I, as your husband, protect you against Aubrey Friezland and take Mr Jonas to court if he fails to be generous to all of you.'

'Mr Gutteridge,' says Neva, 'I thank you again for the honour you do me but I will not marry you. Please do not ask me again.'

Elise has come into the long drawing room. 'Perhaps, Mr Gutteridge, that is enough,' she says.

There is great relief when the garden gate closes on him.

31

June 1813

Elizabeth Wardell is in the garden of the house in Berkeley Square this June evening. The change in her over the past five years is remarkable. No longer subject to the constant winds of her husband's rage, she, like this garden, has blossomed. She has become that rarest of women, one who finds herself amusing and puts those around her at ease with her humour. Henri had given her *carte blanche* to make his house into a home and she has discovered she has a natural talent for design. Her daughters, Sarah and Jane, are married and now she is less concerned about what society might think and more given to laughter at the folly of it all.

In her mind she is divorced from her husband and her friendship with Sir John Campbell has become more important as time has passed. He has been widowed eighteen months and, through hard work and enterprise, has become rich and influential, and Elizabeth knows her friendship with him is part of the reason she is still invited to the grandest parties. After all, breeding accounts for a great deal but money accounts for a great deal more.

★ ★ ★

Sir John is first to hear of the shipwreck of the *Sea Wind* and finding Elizabeth's nephew, Henri Dênou, was on the passenger list decides to withhold the news. In his long experience ships go down, people are lost at sea and sometimes, surprisingly, people reappear. Through one of his reporters in Ireland he hears the story of a young man found half-dead with a dog in a rowing boat. He had been rescued by a fishing vessel. Sir John has made enquiries and discovered the article is several months old and Henri is now in Dublin. Only now does Sir John tell Elizabeth what he has learned. Quite how Henri got to Dublin or what has happened to him in the intervening time is still unknown. A month ago he sent a message to say he is on his way back to London.

On this pleasant evening as jasmine scents the warm breeze, Lady Wardell wonders if he will approve of the alterations she has made.

Even as she's thinking of him, there he is at the French windows with the evening light on him. Her nephew looks thin but is far more striking than she remembers; his travels have chased away the remains of the boy in him.

He bows. 'My dear Aunt,' he says, 'you look in better health than when I last saw you.'

'Henri! Why didn't you send word of your arrival?' says Elizabeth, going to greet him.

'I sent three messages but the footman told me only one arrived. Your butler, Morton, has shown me the house. I think he takes personal credit for the improvements.'

'The old devil,' says Lady Wardell, laughing. 'Do you like them?'

'Very much.'

'How long have you been here?'

'Long enough to have bathed, changed my clothes, examined my rooms and come to the conclusion I possess a rather talented aunt.'

Under the cherry tree there are a table and chairs and here they sit as Morton brings champagne.

'I take it Wardell has vanished into a whirlwind of gossip,' says Henri.

'Yes, he has vanished – but there are rumours,' says Elizabeth. 'You will be pleased to know he has never turned up here.'

The evening being warm and his aunt so eager to know of his adventures, and with a good champagne to keep the mouth from becoming dry, Henri tells of his journey from Denmark to New York where he stayed with his aunt and her husband, Nathaniel Stanton II, and Henri became fascinated with the conjuring world. Only when they sit down to supper does he find himself in London again without once having mentioned the shipwreck.

'What happened when the ship was wrecked?' asks Elizabeth.

'Sir John has been immensely helpful in getting me and the dog home.'

'Where is the dog?'

'In the kitchen with Morton. The dog is always hungry.'

'Does he have a name?'

'No. He should have. I've always called him Dog.'

There is a silence in which much could be said and much isn't.

'Now, tell me your news. What is the London gossip?'

'Oh… where to start? Much of the gossip has recently centred on me and Sir John Campbell. There is much speculation as to the nature of our friendship.'

'Which is?'

'Carnal, of course. What else could it possibly be?' Lady Wardell laughs at the shocked look on Henri's face. 'What an expression! Don't we all desire – and deserve – some love?'

Henri leans towards her. 'You are a wicked woman,

my dear aunt,' he says. 'But talking of love, how are my cousins?'

The conversation is interrupted by the arrival of Sir John Campbell. He is a good-looking gentleman, heavy of build, well dressed, with eyes that have a decided twinkle to them. His dark hair is streaked with white and in the candlelight Henri thinks he looks like an amiable badger.

'*M'sieur le Comte*,' he says, bowing to Henri.

Henri stands. 'Just Dênou,' he says. 'I am the Count of Nowhere and of Nothing.' He returns the bow. 'I have to thank you for all your help, sir. Without it my time in Dublin would have been much longer.'

'Delighted to be able to assist you, sir,' says Sir John. 'When you have fully recovered from your experiences, I would very much like to write an article about how you survived the sinking of the *Sea Wind*.'

'I'll think about that, sir. There were, I believe, no other survivors.'

'None,' says Sir John.

Henri feels the room is too small, his feet too still. He turns to Lady Wardell.

'If you will excuse me, Aunt,' he says, 'I should take the dog for a walk.'

32

Henri walks to St James's Street on the slight chance he might find Bos there. He is constantly restless. Perhaps, he thinks, it's the consequence of so much movement; his soul has yet to settle. The dog possesses no collar, no lead. Henri feels it would be wrong. He stays firmly at his side and Henri wonders if the dog is as haunted by what has happened as he is.

He was pleased when he found Mrs O'Donnell's sister. She lived in Dublin, a surprisingly wealthy woman with mean eyes that didn't flicker or blink when he told her the news. She'd simply said, 'Kathleen was always clumsy.'

Henri likes the sound of his boots this evening, walking click-click on the pavement, going faster, stepping harder, wearing out the shoe leather.

He is genuinely surprised by how much London has changed in a relatively short time. There seem to be more people, more dirt and more dust than before. London sounds like a wheezy old lady gasping for breath. Even the darkness is slowly dissolving into the sparkling lights of this monstrous city whose main ambition, it seems, is to outshine the moon itself.

There's a certain novelty in seeing a place you know well with fresh eyes. London has a peculiar fragrance all of its own, an unmistakable perfume more pronounced in the summer months and not to every man's liking. The further he walks the more he thinks and this time it is of Eugene Jonas. He thinks of Eugene married to Neva Friezland. In his mind Henri has long told himself the story of their marriage until he has turned them into the most perfectly matched couple imaginable.

If it hadn't been for Mr Jonas, Henri knows he wouldn't have travelled so far, been gone so long. Sir Edward Fairbrother had turned out to be one of England's most boring hypochondriacs. He didn't just have seasickness, no, he was terminally ill. He had sailed for home as soon as he arrived in Denmark, believing he was dying. And Henri had gone on to New York.

The doorman at Brooks's greets Henri warmly, saying he is pleased to see him safely back from his travels and hopes he won't be going away again, the world being such a dangerous place. 'Is that dog with you, sir?'

'Yes,' says Henri and, taking no notice of the look on the doorman's face, enquires if the Marquess of Smedmore is in. The doorman of this club, like the doormen of all London clubs, including the Houses of Parliament, is not supposed to say if a member is there. Today he makes a rare exception for Henri.

'I believe he is here, sir,' he says.

'Would I be pushing my luck to ask if Sir Edward Fairbrother is in the club this evening?'

Having exceeded his duty by answering one question, the doorman shakes his head. Henri smiles. It is a winning smile.

'But dogs...' says the doorman.

'It is a male dog,' says Henri.

The club this evening is speckled with that breed of men among whom Henri does not count himself: the fashionable. These gentlemen, as far as he can see, scale the heights of folly and judge a man on nothing more than the cut of his frock coat. As for the rest of the company, they are the usual dandies and gamblers, and the ancient gentlemen to be found in the Great Subscription Room. They look no different from the ancient gentlemen who were there before he left and Henri wonders if the ancient gentlemen have ever been home in the intervening years. They look as if they are folded away into a cupboard at night.

In the club he sees several faces he recognises and at last spies Bos alone in a corner, reading a newspaper. Bos looks up and at the sight of Henri and the hound nearly upends the table in front of him.

'You're back,' he says, stating the obvious. 'When did you return?'

'Today, late afternoon,' says Henri. 'My dear friend, it's good to see you.'

Bos puts the paper aside and asks if Henri would like a glass of champagne.

The five intervening years have changed him into a quieter man and in that they have something in common, both more thoughtful, less talkative. The waiter takes his order.

'What kind of dog is that?' asks Bos.

'A very loyal, shaggy dog with long legs. I don't think any one breed would claim him. He's a muddle and a mixture,' says Henri. 'But how is Kitty?'

Bos is silent for a moment. 'She died about four months ago.'

'Oh, my dear friend, I'm so sorry. I didn't know.'

'No. Why should you?'

'How are you?'

'If I'm honest, not well. It was for both of us a wretched marriage. We had nothing in common. I had the idiotic idea that at least there might be some comfort in the bedchamber but Kitty thought making love was unbearable. When there was no sign of a son and heir, the Bishop – as I called her mother – told her to apply herself to the act.'

Henri smiles. The dog looks up from where he is sleeping then puts his head down with a sigh. 'I'm sorry, Bos, do you really call Lady Tillingham the Bishop?'

'It's rude to speak ill of the living,' says Bos, 'but she's one of the most sanctimonious women I have ever had the misfortune to meet. Totally dogmatic. I blame her in part for Kitty's death.'

'That is a strong accusation to make,' says Henri.

'Oh, my dear Henri, I told the Bishop exactly what I thought of her. She called me diabolical.'

The waiter places two glasses of champagne before them.

'We had a daughter, Camille,' Bos continues. 'She's now four. And after that there was no intimacy between us until the Bishop said her duty as my wife was to have a son. Once that had been completed, we could, in her words, live separate lives in separate wings of the house. Consequently, I was allowed another chance in the bedchamber. It was even worse than before. I felt like a brute. But she lost that baby. When she found herself with child again and was certain she was past the worrying time and the baby was showing, she told me I could take a mistress, in fact she would be grateful if I did. And she promptly returned to the Bishop in Dorset. Her parting shot was that she would have been happier as a nun as long as she could have continued shopping and was never made to wear the ugly clothes.' A smile crosses his lips. 'I'm afraid she was as empty-headed as a hat shop.

'My father was a perfect idiot. He prematurely announced that the expected baby was a boy, claiming he was never wrong in these matters. I went down to Dorset several times to try to persuade Kitty to come home to London where there were doctors who knew what they were doing. I believed it would be safer if she wasn't so isolated. The Bishop said, "Tish-tosh, what rubbish" – she'd never had a problem giving birth so why should Kitty?

'Near her time I received a message to come immediately. It wasn't an easy journey; being winter the roads were bad. I took with me a London physician. When I arrived Kitty had been in labour five days with only a country quack in attendance and a midwife who looked terrified. The physician I took down from London told me the baby was the wrong way round and that Kitty was very weak but he would do his best.

'Kitty clutched my hand and told me she didn't want to die. Two hours later she gave birth to a baby girl. I stayed with her and thought she might pull through. She told me she'd been an idiot, she was sorry and could we start again? We had three days of what I would call genuine mutual affection. I could even see the possibilities of loving her, but she died in my arms at three in the morning on the fourth day. The baby died a day later.

'The Bishop said, "All that for a girl – just another girl." Sentiments echoed by my father. At least I have Camille. I love her dearly. I'm sorry, Henri, enough of me, I want to hear about your adventures.'

'Another time,' says Henri. 'So many women die in childbirth.'

'Yes, but the tragedy is that Kitty could have been saved with the right care.'

'What of your father?'

'We're not on speaking terms.'

'And where do you live these days?'

'I have a house in Cheyne Walk.' The dog sits up and puts its head in Bos's lap. 'Does the creature have a name?'

'I call him Dog,' says Henri. He changes the subject. 'Do you, by chance, know what's happened to Wardell? Aunt Elizabeth has successfully washed her hands of him.'

'There are three theories,' says Bos, smiling. 'You can have the mild version, or the scurrilous or the absolutely outrageous.'

'I don't think I would believe the mild, so let's start with the scurrilous.'

'Very well. This version has it that your uncle is controlled by a nasty piece of work who claims he is the son of the late Victor Friezland.'

'Victor Friezland is dead?'

'Yes, he died last Christmas. Apparently he left his business and property to a Mr Eugene Jonas.'

'Did Mr Jonas marry Miss Friezland?' asks Henri.

'That, my dear friend, I cannot answer,' says Bos.

Henri says, 'And the absolutely outrageous?'

'Lord Wardell is behind a spate of burglaries at fine houses.'

'I can't see my uncle having the energy for burglary. Tell me – is the Weather Woman still giving predictions?'

'No. Miss Cassandra Lamb has let it be known she doesn't wish to continue now Mr Friezland is dead.'

'I'm sorry, Bos, the name means nothing to me.' Henry has a feeling that there is something Bos isn't telling him.

'Up until Christmas,' says Bos, 'Miss Lamb was presenting the Weather Woman, no longer an automaton, but an apparition that hovered in the room like a ghost and spoke the predictions. It was a sensation.'

'And where was Miss Friezland?'

'I don't know. Perhaps she married Mr Jonas and retired.'

'Are the predictions still accurate?'

'Yes, I believe so. But honestly, the Weather Woman was so mesmerising that in a way the weather was by the by.'

'What a pity,' say Henri. 'As I discovered, the weather is never by the by; at least only for those whose lives don't depend on it.'

Bos sees from the expression passing over Henri's face that he has inadvertently opened Pandora's Box and says gently, 'Drink up, my friend. I think the dog needs some fresh air.'

They part at Bos's carriage. As Bos is climbing in, he stops. 'By the way,' he calls after Henri, 'I have a substantial sum of money for you – the Thames froze in 1811.'

Henri and the dog walk back to Berkeley Square. In a way, he thinks, Bos and I have both been shipwrecked.

His nightmares return that night. He is fighting his way out of the ship as it sinks, he is swimming up the stairs that lead to the main deck, the hatch slams shut with a bang.

By the time dawn breaks he is wide awake. He watches the maids working in the hush of a house which is being visibly goaded into life without the inconvenience of waking its inhabitants.

Morton wonders if Henri requires coffee. 'We aren't serving breakfast for a few hours, sir,' he says. 'The oven is yet to heat up.'

'No, thank you, Morton,' says Henri. 'I don't want anything.'

Picking up his hat he decides to go on one of his long walks. In New York he found walking was the best way of seeing the city, of knowing its people, and though he pretends this morning he has no ulterior motive and no particular destination, he knows exactly where he's going. With the dog at his heels, his feet lead him to St Paul's and Paternoster Row. Even here he is too early, the bookshops are still closed.

He finds a coffeehouse and spends an hour or two reading the paper and after perusing the bookshops he walks as far as the Tower of London and then back to London Bridge. People used to believe this bridge went from one world to another, and possessed magical properties. In its heyday, Henri has no doubt, it was one of the wonders of the world.

It is about eleven o'clock when he and the dog find themselves down a lane near Tooley Street, outside the gate of the Friezland house. He wonders about ringing the bell and leaving a card, and finds himself embarrassed that he is there at all. He walks away, then justifies the folly of it by telling himself it would be proper to offer his condolences to Mrs Friezland. He turns, and is walking back again when the garden gate is flung open. A young woman rushes out and, seeing him, she stops.

'Oh sir, please, sir – help us,' she says.

33

Henri and the dog follow the young woman into the garden and, if he's not mistaken, standing with her back to him is Neva Friezland. In front of her a thin, drunken man is swaying, a knife in his hand. He stabs the air as if trying to pin the words down; he goes closer but still she doesn't back away.

'This is my house,' he shouts. 'I'm the rightful heir, not you, you usurper, you – you – you madwoman!'

What surprises Henri most is Miss Friezland's defiant stance. Most women Henri knows would have fainted at the sight of the knife. In this moment, the dog takes off with a loud bark. This dog, who has never shown any sign of aggression, leaps through the air and sinks his teeth into the drunken man's arm. The knife falls to the ground, the dog clings fast to his prey. The man cannot free himself of the hound and as Henri picks up the knife and moves in on him, the man shouts to someone on the riverbank. The dog still has his teeth sunk into his victim's arm when a single gunshot pierces the air. The dog lets go and the thin man runs down the garden and throws himself into a ferry boat.

The dog gathers his strength and is set to jump in after him only to be stopped by Henri, who curses the fact that the man has escaped and he hasn't a collar or a lead for the dog. Holding the creature still between his legs, Henri looks out across the river, following the line of the ferry boat which is being skilfully sculled and is now midstream. It strikes him there is something familiar about the other passenger in the boat. Perhaps it's the tallness of his hat or the sudden glint of light from what Henri suspects might be a silver-topped cane. He flings the knife into the river.

The dog, defeated, wriggles free and takes himself, panting, back into the garden to Miss Friezland. Henri slowly follows. Five years have passed since he last saw her. He can't recall if he has ever known a more arresting woman. Neva Friezland is tall with a strong face that demands attention; dark, intelligent eyes, a straight nose, full lips, arched eyebrows. So enchanted is he by her that for a moment he can't think what his tongue is for.

She curtsies. 'Thank you, Mr Dênou, for your assistance,' she says and her voice is calm with no fear in it.

It is the other young woman whose voice betrays her fear.

'We are much obliged to you, sir,' she says with a slight tremor. 'It was more than fortunate you were so close by.' She curtsies. 'I'm Cassandra Lamb.'

Henri knows he's heard that name recently but he's not taking in Miss Lamb. It is the image of Miss Friezland he doesn't want to let go.

There is a moment's silence in which he realises how immature he was when he glimpsed her on the terrace at the Duke of Boswell's house. What a fool he'd been. He wonders if he should address her as Mrs Jonas. He decides to try it.

'Mrs Jonas,' he says, 'do you have anyone to protect you?'

The calmness she showed throughout the exchange with

the drunk disappears. Flustered, she says, 'I am plain Miss Friezland, sir.'

There are many words to describe her, Henri thinks, but plain would never be one of them. He wants to laugh at how idiotic he has been. Of course she isn't married. She could never have been married, not to Eugene Jonas.

He is surprised by how lightheaded the thought makes him.

'To answer your question, yes, we do – Mr Cutter. He's gone out for an hour. But why did you think I'm married to Mr Jonas?'

'Mr Eugene Jonas himself led me to believe he was engaged to you. I presumed then that in due course you would be married.'

Miss Friezland pulls at her fingers and he thinks he sees her blush.

He says, quickly, 'My mistake, Miss Friezland.'

She is looking down at her slippers and he has a sudden recollection of her doing just that when he first met her, when she was a girl.

'Who is that man?' he asks.

Miss Friezland looks up. She has regained her composure. 'He claims to be Victor Friezland's son and he is determined that all this...' she gestures at the garden, the house and an outhouse of sorts, 'will be his. Papa's will has gone to probate. I think Aubrey Friezland is short of money and that's why he has become ever more desperate.'

Henri feels somewhat out of his depth.

Miss Friezland changes the subject. 'Is this your dog who so valiantly saved the day?' she asks.

'Neva,' says Miss Lamb, 'it wasn't only the dog.'

Henri finds himself laughing. 'He has been with me a while.'

'Did you have him as a puppy?' asks Miss Lamb.

'No. You could say we found each other.'

'Has he a name?'

'No. I'm not sure what to call him.'

Miss Friezland puts her long fingers on the top of the dog's head. 'Jetsam,' she says.

Henri considers the name and thinks it suits him. 'He's definitely not Flotsam,' he says and is delighted to see Miss Friezland smile.

'Would you care for some lemonade, sir?' asks Miss Lamb.

'No, thank you,' he says, feeling it's best to leave before the situation becomes awkward. 'Will you be quite safe if I go?'

Miss Friezland is silent as if thinking about something. Whatever it is, it is not much to her liking.

'You were in a storm, your boat shipwrecked.'

Henri nods.

'I read it in the newspaper. It didn't name you but it said you had a dog. When was the storm?'

'It was Christmas.'

How interesting, he thinks. She shows no reaction to the knife that could have harmed her and yet mention of the shipwreck causes her to pull at her fingers.

She says not to him, but to herself, 'It's pointless.' Staring at him she asks, 'If the captain had known there was a storm coming, he wouldn't have set sail, would he?'

'No.'

'What use is the Weather Woman?'

'Neva,' says Miss Lamb. She says it sharply, as if to break a trance.

Miss Friezland looks right into the heart of Henri. 'How many drowned?' she asks.

'All except me.'

'Oh lordy,' says Miss Lamb.

Henri is careful how he words his question. 'Did the Weather Woman anticipate the storm?' he asks.

'Yes,' says Miss Friezland.

'I think,' says Miss Lamb, 'we shouldn't dwell on the subject.'

But Miss Friezland is still looking at Henri. It's hard to break that look but not to do so would be thought unbearably rude. If there was no one else here, if it was just him and Neva Friezland, he would put his arms round her and kiss her. Her look is inscrutable. She shakes her head as if steadying her thoughts.

'Mr Dênou,' says Miss Lamb, 'would you join us for supper on Wednesday?'

'It's an irritating day, with an unnecessary "e",' says Miss Friezland. She turns to go into the house and the dog follows her.

'Here, dog,' Henri says. When the dog ignores him, he says, 'I don't have a collar for him.' He hesitates, then adds, 'Jetsam has always done what he chooses.'

'Bring a collar for him on Wednesday,' she says.

And with that Neva Friezland and Jetsam disappear into the house.

Miss Lamb accompanies Henri to the garden gate and locks it after him.

Only then does Henri realise he hasn't offered his condolences. And he wonders how many hours there are until Wednesday.

Court has been adjourned and Mr Gutteridge is in his chambers. It's a sunny day but the rooms are dark and perpetually cold, and a small fire is burning in the grate. Quite why he should notice the cold now when he has occupied these chambers for more than twenty years somewhat worries him. He gazes at the few coals and the flames they let off. The death of Victor Friezland has made him feel more lonely than he had ever realised he was. Now there are no Mondays at the Friezland house, no games of chess with Neva.

He has always considered himself a bachelor and set in his ways. But death has a way of altering the scenery of life. Victor's has made him feel closer to being erased and forgotten.

His name, written in gold paint on the front door, would be immediately painted out like his father's was, and another solicitor's name would take its place. The sandstone steps so used to his tread that he likes to think he has left an imprint on them would be moulded by other lawyers' boots. All the love in him has been left unwritten. Is it too late? Neva has sent no word and until he hears from her he believes there might be hope.

For the first time it occurs to him that he was a little jealous of Victor's contentment. Emotions buried in the silt of his soul have been dislodged and confuse his rational mind until understanding dawns on him. Deep down, he knows he's in love with Neva Friezland. Victor's needless abandonment of him hurts more than anything else. How could Victor have gone to another solicitor? Why hadn't he trusted him with his will? He would have advised against mentioning Aubrey Friezland; he would have ensured the will did not go to the Ecclesiastical Courts. The worst part is that the major portion of the estate is left to Mr Eugene Jonas. What Victor has done, in Mr Gutteridge's considered opinion, is an act of complete folly.

He jumps when Mr Briggs puts his head round the door.

'Mr Dênou is here to see you, sir.'

Mr Gutteridge is so surprised that he goes to the door and nearly collides with Henri.

'My dear Mr Dênou,' he says. 'The money arrived?'

'Yes, thank you, Mr Gutteridge, it did.'

'I didn't dare mention your predicament to Lady Wardell

and I know Sir John Campbell was careful to keep your name out of the papers. It's a terrible business, terrible. I gather there are no other survivors.'

'No,' says Henri. 'Only the dog.'

Mr Gutteridge opens the door as if expecting the dog to walk in and, seeing no dog, asks Mr Briggs to go out and buy a bottle of champagne.

'No need, sir,' says the clerk. 'The minute I heard Mr Dênou was safe I made the necessary arrangements.'

'I sometimes think Briggs knows exactly what I'm thinking, which is alarming,' says Mr Gutteridge.

A moment later, Mr Briggs returns with the champagne and two glasses.

'Were you badly hurt, Mr Dênou?' says Mr Gutteridge.

'I was ill for a long time and not being able to remember anything was a blow. But it would have been worse if not for your help. However, that's not why I'm here. Yesterday, on hearing of the death of her husband, I went to express my condolences to Mrs Friezland only to find a man there threatening Miss Friezland with a knife.'

'That would be Aubrey Friezland,' says Mr Gutteridge.

'So I discovered. Can't something be done about him?'

'I don't, as you know, talk about a client's business, but in this instance I can for the simple reason that Victor Friezland isn't my client and he didn't make his will with me. It's a most unfortunate state of affairs. What I can tell you is that Aubrey Friezland is contesting the will and it's likely he will be found to be the rightful child of Victor's first marriage. In which case, Aubrey will inherit a substantial amount of the estate, but not all of it because a considerable portion is left to Mr Eugene Jonas. The sums Victor left to Mrs Friezland and Miss Friezland are in doubt. But Aubrey is playing a far nastier game and that is to have Neva committed to an asylum for lunatics.'

Henri is shocked to hear this, so much so that he asks Mr Gutteridge to repeat what he's just said.

It is the look of concern on Henri's face that makes the solicitor realise the true obstacle to his marrying Neva is not Eugene Jonas. It is Henri Dênou. In that instant he sees the hopelessness of his marriage proposal, the dust of his dreams.

Mr Gutteridge takes a sip of champagne.

Henri, believing the solicitor to be grieving the loss of Victor, says, 'I imagine Mr Friezland was a good friend of yours.'

Mr Gutteridge nods and smiles sadly. 'I want to say one thing to you, Henri – an apology. When you came to me at the time you hoped to go to Oxford I pompously told you I could not lend you money. I have long regretted it.'

'*I* haven't,' says Henri. 'It was the making of me. But I thank you, sir.'

'I fear I'm beginning to resemble Malvolio,' says the solicitor.

Henri is perplexed. 'I don't see it, sir.'

'Well,' says Mr Gutteridge, raising his glass. 'Your health, Henri. I'm glad you're home, safe and sound.'

Henri walks across London with long strides, his thoughts on Aubrey Friezland. He concludes that the rumours regarding his uncle are true for he can see his cruel thinking at work. He always was a master manipulator. He fears that Neva, tall, defiant, beautiful Neva, may be no match for Lord Wardell.

His tailor is delighted to see him and Henri explains he is in need of a new wardrobe as his clothes are being worn by a merman.

'Oh, so droll, Mr Dênou,' says the tailor, clapping his hands. 'It's most gratifying to see you have neither drowned nor run to fat like many gentlemen given to following the Prince

Regent. Your timing is most fortuitous – we made clothes for a client who has just gambled away his last carriage at White's.'

A few alterations are necessary but Henri agrees that whoever this young gentleman is he has good taste.

'No, sir, he had a good tailor.'

34

That night, Henri sleeps well, undisturbed by nightmares, and wakes surprised by the lateness of the hour. The clarity of his thoughts is not clouded by ghosts and it comes to him almost the instant he is awake: a revelation.

He puts on his dressing gown and, barefoot, goes down the stairs two at a time to find Morton standing in the hall holding a breakfast tray.

'The dog hasn't come back, sir.'

'No,' says Henri. He hadn't expected him to.

'Your breakfast, sir?' says Morton with a nod to the tray.

'The study, please,' says Henri, opening the door for Morton.

He hasn't been in this room since the day he left for the voyage with Sir Edward Fairbrother. It's been repainted and like all the rooms is much improved for its decoration. His desk is waiting for him. It has two drawers, each with a little key hung with a green tassel that complements the colour of the walls.

Morton puts the tray down on a round table. 'Is there anything else you require, sir?'

'No,' says Henri and he is about to close the door when Elizabeth comes in.

She's surprised to see he isn't dressed. 'Good morning,' she says, looking round the room. 'Flowers. I should have told the housekeeper. Though she's given the room a thorough spring clean and all the books have been aired.'

Henri is suddenly anxious lest the drawers too might have been spring cleaned.

'No,' says Elizabeth. 'But she found this posted inside one of the books.' She hands Henri a letter.

'I suppose whoever it's from and whatever it says is irrelevant now.'

'Most probably,' says Henri, putting the letter in his dressing-gown pocket.

'I wanted to tell you Mrs Dent is expected and I would love you to meet her. She sent a message this morning saying that she hoped she might have a word with you. She has become a great friend – a remarkable woman. I don't know if you remember – we went to her house in Harley Street and saw Mr Karavino's Mysterious Cabinet.'

'You're wrong. I remember her well and I remember we didn't see Mr Karavino's Mysterious Cabinet due to my uncle's appalling behaviour.'

Elizabeth laughs. 'You're right!'

'I will be dressed in time to meet her,' he says, shepherding his aunt towards the door.

Finally alone in the study, as foolish as it seems, he finds his heart beating faster as he opens the first drawer. And there is Neva's note with the predictions that changed his life. The second drawer is jammed and he has to look under the desk to see what the problem is. There is a letter wedged at the back of the drawer and it is a delicate operation to extract it without tearing. It is the letter Eugene Jonas wrote to him after the evening at Brooks's. He takes both letters to the table and pours a coffee before carefully flattening them.

They were written by the same person.

That Neva Friezland is Eugene Jonas answers many questions but asks many more of him. In the silence of this well-ordered room he bitterly regrets his ill-judged decision to go abroad. It was his pride and confusion that made him run. He laughs at his stupidity. What a fool he has been.

He can see clearly that all hopes of forming an affection with Neva will be impossible. How can she allow herself to feel anything for him when she has to assume the mantle of a warrior, protecting her family, her father's name? Yes, he will go to supper with her on Wednesday and he predicts it will be a stiff and awkward occasion and Miss Friezland herself will put an end to all further meetings. What else can she do? This is what her father has left her; his will deemed it so. He can see she must continue to play the part of Eugene Jonas to perfection – it is her only protection against Aubrey Friezland's claim.

If he could roll back time, he would have stayed in London, accepted Victor Friezland's invitation to supper and met Neva. But he allowed Eugene Jonas – that bolt of lightning – to dislodge his reasoning. The weather is not just what we are subjected to outside, he thinks – we carry it within us. Passion, love, despair, male or female, it fogs all rational thought.

He is dressed an hour later; it's a long time since he has been this well turned out. Henri doesn't wear breeches; he wears trousers and a frock coat, a beautifully embroidered waistcoat and an elegantly tied cravat. His shoes are well polished and his watch, which stopped when the ship sank, is hanging on a gold chain across his waistcoat. His dressing gown is put away and the letter in the pocket is as forgotten as it was in the bookshelves.

Mrs Dent looks like a rare butterfly. Her clothes are such

a confusion of style and colour that the effect is to make you more aware of the clothes than the woman wearing them. But on closer inspection she has a bright, intelligent face, her sharp, green eyes flecked with brown. Henri suspects Mrs Dent misses nothing. He bows.

'I imagined you would be a handsome man, Mr Dênou,' she says. She rises from the sofa and curtsies to him. 'I like a well-turned-out gentleman. This new fashion for trousers has divided the young men from the old who still favour breeches and riding boots. I think it's a very good thing that legs are not so much on display as they were. Few men can boast elegant calves. Trousers, I believe, are the future.'

'Perhaps this time the future is here to stay,' says Henri.

She has an infectious laugh. She pats the sofa and Henri sits down beside her.

'Did you ever see the Weather Woman perform?' she asks.

'No, much to my regret I didn't.'

'I'm very friendly with Elise Friezland,' she says, 'as I was with Victor. I watched Neva become the woman she is today. This is a very sad business. With Victor's death so much rests on her shoulders.'

'So I understand,' says Henri.

'The will is more than a little worrying. Lady Wardell tells me you were at the Friezland house yesterday and Aubrey was threatening Neva.'

'News travels fast.'

'Bad news travels faster,' says Mrs Dent. 'You are interested in meteorology, I believe.'

'I was returning with a paper I had written on vapours and that, like everything else, is at the bottom of the sea being nibbled by fish.'

'It must be hard being the only survivor.'

'I have twice cheated death. These things go in threes. The next time—'

Mrs Dent interrupts him. 'Next time you will be the right age to meet him.'

'The storm made me review my thoughts on the weather,' says Henri. 'But you don't want to be bored by this – forgive me.'

'No, tell me. I'm more interested than you might think.'

'I believe the weather is fundamental to our survival, it is the roof of our planet.'

'I'm glad I wasn't wrong,' says Mrs Dent.

'What do you mean?' asks Henri.

'If you weren't interested in the weather then what I have to show you would be of no consequence to you.' Beside her on a small table is a leather-bound notebook. She opens it and on the flyleaf in spindly writing are the words *The Weather Woman's Predictions*. 'I thought you might like to see this.' She hands it to Henri. 'Lord Sutton was interested in astrology; we would look at the stars together and both of us put great value on meteors and eclipses of the moon and the sun. I dabble in casting horoscopes – I have done for years. I don't do them for just anyone. I do them for people who interest me.'

Henri is only half-listening. He is lost in the book. 'This is very well observed,' he says.

'I attended many performances. As you can see, in one column I wrote every question the Weather Woman was asked, the answers in the second column and in the third if the prediction was accurate.'

'This is a phenomenal record,' says Henri. 'It is almost unbelievable none of the predictions were wrong.'

'Alas, the Weather Woman was not acclaimed for the accuracy of the predictions,' says Mrs Dent, 'but for the entertainment. But the Weather Woman made Victor a very wealthy man. The second Weather Woman was a showpiece, unlike any seen in London. Now, I ask you this question: do you have any interest in Neva?'

'I do, madam, but I doubt she has any interest in me.'

And he finds himself telling Mrs Dent what happened the night he met Neva and about the pebble. Then he returns to the book and works through the years. There's not one mistake in all the predictions. He comes to the date he's been looking for: Christmas 1812. The question doesn't relate to London. The question is, will there be a storm in the Atlantic? To which the answer was, there will be high energy out at sea midway between America and Ireland with gale force winds, and torrential rain will blow all shipping off course. The storm will be strong enough to wreck ships and will last ten days, making landfall in Ireland.

'Who asked this question?' says Henri.

'I did,' says Mrs Dent. 'Your aunt was very concerned about you.'

Mrs Dent turns herself on the sofa so that she might have a better look at Henri. 'Victor Friezland claimed to have invented a machine that could predict the weather. He did it once with the automaton, he did it again with a spirit-like creature, but I don't believe it was he who did it at all. Neither do I believe that Cassandra Lamb is the Weather Woman. I think you and I both know it was Neva. But I'm very worried about her and what Aubrey Friezland has in mind. There is one way to save Neva: marry her, Mr Dênou, get a special licence and marry her.'

35

The inside of the inn is so smoky it's hard to tell the season, let alone the weather. As for recognising a face, it's best not to. The inn smells of unwashed clothes mingled with tobacco, stale beer and overcooked vegetables. The sawdust on the floor is old, the tables sticky and behind a screen in the corner sits Aubrey Friezland's mother, Mary. She is, as usual, a little worse for the drink and has no idea of the name of the gentleman she's talking to but he's got a clean face and is well dressed for such a dirty bar as this.

'You a stranger round here?' she asks.

'No,' says the gentleman, 'I know this area well.'

'You're too smart to be in a high-class establishment like this,' she says and laughs. If she doesn't concentrate, there appear to be two gentlemen where there is only one. Mary has had a difficult day. She feels on her own, alone. Sometimes the gin gives her the sense there might be a future. Other times... This is one of the other times.

She had been awoken this morning by Aubrey and that snake Wardell storming into her rooms.

'How're you paying for these rooms, Mother? Been out whoring again?'

She'd told him, 'None of your business. And you should have a bit more respect.'

The mad glint came into his eyes. 'Respect? Was it respect when you left me with that shit of a lieutenant? I was only ten years old and you, you bitch, ran off with yet another man.'

'Aubrey, darling Aubrey,' said Wardell. 'He has such a commanding voice.' And he smiled as he put his hand to Aubrey's face. 'Remember, be a good boy.'

Aubrey moved his neck from side to side as if realigning his broken brain, then, taking a deep breath, he spoke in the calmer voice his mother knows is altogether more worrying.

'You see, Mother, my business is connected to yours and I need to make sure my investment is going to come good.'

'What... investment?' Aubrey is full of long words these days.

'The will. Remember, my father's will?'

She'd almost forgotten about the will. Aubrey had dragged her out of this inn in January and given her some money to smarten herself up. She was to look crestfallen to hear Victor Friezland had died. Oddly enough she was. He was a good man.

But this morning Aubrey had come back, threatening that if she were to talk to anyone about the will, about Victor Friezland, about anything, he would kill her.

'Oh, no,' said Wardell in a long, low voice. 'I would recommend cutting out her tongue. You don't want to swing for a mother.'

She had a row of little animals, china things that had belonged to her mother. Everywhere she lived, Mary put them up on a shelf. She liked to imagine her mother might come into the room and tuck her up as she used to when she was a little girl. The one part of the room that felt like home was this shelf.

Aubrey was wearing gloves, she noticed, as he knocked all the little ornaments off the shelf. He broke every single one then Wardell brought his boot down on what remained. Nothing was left.

'I hope we've made it clear,' said Aubrey. 'No talking, Mother, to anybody. Or you will end up in the asylum with the usurper. Do you hear me?'

She'd laughed as they slammed the door but after they'd gone she'd sat on the edge of her bed and wept.

She has no money, she's living in a room she can't afford, the workhouse looms. She feels her life is over. She has made so many wrong decisions, so many bad choices. Too many men, all of them have led her to this inn, to this corner, with a glass of gin and this gentleman.

'What's your name?' She thinks she might have asked that question before and he might have answered it.

'Does it matter?' he says.

For a moment she can't think what he's referring to. She hopes he'll buy her another drink, she needs another drink.

'No, it doesn't matter.'

'Do you want another?' he asks. 'Water with your gin?'

'Yes,' she says, though she likes it neat, hits the spot faster.

She watches him get up and go to the bar. She thinks to herself she should have a piss. She shouldn't leave it too long. Last time she wet her drawers.

He brings the drink to her and settles in his chair again.

'Are you married?' he asks.

'No.' There's a silence after that and she thinks he might leave. She tells herself it doesn't matter but hopes he paid for the gin, that's all.

'Were you ever?'

'Ever what?' she asks. 'Thank you,' she adds.

'A pleasure. Married,' he says.

Have they had this conversation? She can't be sure. The gin muddles your mind, makes everything fuzzy. Her legs feel hollow. If she closes her eyes she could float. It would be funny if you could float up to the ceiling.

The gentleman is looking at her. He takes out his pipe and carefully puts tobacco in it. She likes a gentleman who has a pipe. It takes away the fumes of this place. She likes his company. She wouldn't want him to go now. All she's got to go home to is an empty shelf and a carpet of broken china.

'Bet you can't guess how many times,' she says.

He lights the pipe then glancing up at her, says, 'How many times what?' as if he too has forgotten what they were talking about. He puffs on his pipe; the smoke has a sweet smell to it. 'No one should get married more than once,' he says.

'Not any sane woman,' says Mary.

'You mean you've been married more than once?' he says, laughing.

'Three times,' she says.

'That must be hard,' says the gentleman, 'must be very hard, being widowed three times.'

'I know I was widowed twice, but as for the third – I don't know. But that's a riddle for you.'

'I like riddles.'

'The one I don't know about – he was my first husband.'

'I don't follow you,' says the gentleman.

She changes the subject. 'Do you have any children?'

'No, do you?'

'One son, a cruel man. He's grown up just like his father. He came to see me this morning. He smashed up all the little ornaments my mum gave me. They were precious to me. They were more precious than he is.'

'Who was his father then – the first, second or third?'

A sudden wave of sobriety hits Mary. She remembers what

happened this morning and what they threatened. 'Why are you so interested?'

'I'm not,' he says. 'It's just chit-chat, nothing to it, nothing in it. Are you hungry?'

He orders a plate of food and she watches him make a joke with Jim, the barman. She tells herself there's nothing to be worried about. He's just a stranger, just company for the night. Better than going back to the empty room, to the empty shelf. She eats like a wolf. She hasn't eaten for a day and a half. The plate is hot and she holds onto it as if expecting someone to snatch it from her.

'Are you paying for this?' she asks with her mouth full.

'Yes, it's all paid for. There's pudding if you want.'

'I'm not talking any more about my husbands,' she says.

'You brought them up, not me,' says the gentleman. 'I say, who needs to rummage in the past? Best to look to tomorrow and not dwell on yesterday.'

But as Mary thinks about it, there's nothing in tomorrow to look forward to and yesterday seems so full of everything. There's been no one to talk to for a long time.

'The one I truly loved was my third husband, Sam.'

'What happened to him?'

'He was murdered. Never proven. He was found down by Fish Island. They said he could've drowned, then they said it was suicide, because his feet were tied, as were his hands and he had stones in his pockets. Back then I believed in justice, so I said, how could he tie his feet with his hands behind his back? They said the case was closed.'

'That's a sad tale of injustice,' says the gentleman. 'You were divorced from your second husband then?'

Mary laughs. 'Do you think I'm dripping in gypsy gold? The law has it that I'm still married to the first.' She changes the subject. 'I was once, you know, a pretty lady.'

'What makes you think you aren't now?'

'Flatterer. I know I'm not. I was fifteen when I first got married. Fifteen. What the hell did I know about life? He looked so smart in his uniform, I thought I would die if I couldn't be with him. Every time I fell pregnant he beat it out of me. I thought I couldn't have children after that. Then, when I was seventeen he went away with the army. That was the best time of my life. I went to work in London where I met a clockmaker. He was soppy-silly about me – that was the trouble. I thought he was weak. I knew where I stood with violence, but not what to do with love. It's a bit like saying you like rain and thunder but are lost when the sun shines.

'He came back, the lieutenant, and my parents were daft enough to tell him where I was. My father was a Bible man and once married you were stuck, for better or worse. I was taken back to Hastings, then he was off to fight in the bloody war. Part of me wanted him dead and another part of me loved him. That's a stupid pickle to be in.

'Then I discovered I was pregnant. I had no choice. I went back up to London and found the clockmaker. That's what I did. I did it so I could keep the child. I think now I should have flushed him out. I made bad decisions, bad decisions. I don't know why I went back to him really...' She stops. 'I thought the clockmaker's house was bloody ridiculous.

'The lieutenant found me. He said he would change, be a better man. I told him about the baby. He told me he would be a good father, that he was my rightful husband and if I didn't go back to him straight away he would tell the clockmaker what I'd done. I left the baby with my parents and followed the lieutenant up north. By then I hated him.'

The gentleman says, 'Would you like a pudding?'

'I've been boring you,' says Mary. 'I'm sorry for wittering on like that.'

'No need,' says the gentleman. His pipe has gone out and

he taps it on the table and empties it into a dish. All that's left is a little pile of dried-up ash.

Mary stands unsteadily. 'Just going outside for a piss,' she says. She knows he'll be gone when she comes back, and gone he is.

She goes up to the barman, who usually has no time for her. 'If I owe you anything, you'll have to put it on a tab whether you like it or not. I haven't anything to pay with.'

Jim smiles at her. 'For once, Mary,' he says, 'you don't owe me a penny.'

It takes a moment to sink in. 'What, nothing?'

'It's all paid for, and your tab.'

This cheerful news makes Mary feel sick. What has she done? Who has she talked to?

She walks unsteadily past the other drinkers with their heads down. At her seat there is a fresh drink waiting for her and, under the tankard, money and a little card. She looks at its raised words. What has she done? What has she done?

'You all right, Mary?' says Jim. 'You've been sitting like that for hours, just staring at your drink.'

'Can you read?'

'I can.'

'And can you keep quiet about what you read?'

'How do you think I keep this place going? By keeping my gob shut.'

She hands him the card and Jim reads the words to her.

'"If you need any help do not hesitate to contact me."' He turns it over.

Mr Briggs, Clerk to
R. Gutteridge Esq., Solicitor.
5 Lincoln's Inn

'What the fuck have I done?' says Mary, aloud.

36

July 1813

Neva hasn't foreseen the pamphlets would be quite as popular as they are. Cassie has gathered several on her shopping trips and shown them to Neva. Papa and Auntie's so-called bigamous marriage and the lie that Mary and her son were treated cruelly seem to be the main topics of interest.

If that isn't enough for Neva to worry about, there's the lack of money. But most concerning of all is the reappearance of Henri Dênou.

Neva climbs onto the workshop roof and lies there as she did as a child, staring up at the sky, listening to the weather talking. For a moment she forgets everything except the clouds. A fog. A fog she hasn't seen before, a fog unlike any London has ever experienced. But when?

The thought of Henri brings her back down to earth with a jolt. This can't happen. She can't fall in love again with Henri. But that's a lie, she has never not been in love with him. At any other time, this would... Stop it, stop it. Stop thinking this thought. It's over, it has to be over.

And what of the fog? Can she trust that?

Jetsam is on the lawn, howling up at her. Neva climbs

down, strokes his head. 'Don't you ever tell your master I love him,' she says as he follows her into the kitchen.

Pans are steaming and the table is overflowing with baskets of vegetables, fruit and two lifeless ducks.

'I thought sorrel soup,' says Elise, busily plucking a third duck.

'This isn't meant to be a festival, just a light supper. He isn't the Prince of Wales,' says Neva, a little too harshly.

But Elise is lost in what she does best when she puts her mind to it.

'Surely no one will believe this rubbish,' says Cassie. She rolls up the newspaper she's reading and swats a fly. 'There's not one grain of truth in it, just a cat's cradle of lies.'

'In the newspaper?'

'Yes, look,' says Cassie.

Truth, Neva knows, is the last thing any newspaper wants to publish.

'And how dare they say you're mad!' says Cassie.

'It's not the first time,' says Neva. 'The difference is that then the rumour travelled round the neighbourhood, not the whole of London.'

'When was this?' asks Cassie.

'When I was a child.'

Cassie shakes her head, picks up a knife and starts to chop vegetables.

'What about Hastings?' she says quietly after a few minutes of furious chopping.

'I am still going, of course,' says Neva. 'I'm determined to find proof of Mary Letchmore's first marriage and then all that...' she gestures at the newspaper, 'will go away.'

'When?' asks Cassie in a whisper.

'At the end of this month.'

'Take George with you.'

'No, I'm going as Eugene Jonas and I am taking Neva Friezland with me. I've already booked a room.'

'What will Auntie say?'

'Not worth buying, not worth reading and not worth worrying about,' says Elise.

'What isn't?' asks Neva.

'The future,' says Elise. 'It's so contrary, even if we could see what was coming, it would have changed its mind by the time it found us. Better we concentrate on this evening.'

Later, when everything is ready and Jetsam is asleep on Neva's bed, Cassie comes into the room to find Neva staring out of the window.

'I'm worried that Auntie isn't well,' says Cassie.

'None of us is,' replies Neva.

'Neva,' says Cassie, 'what are we to do for money until the will is settled? There's very little left in Uncle Victor's strongbox. How will you pay for the room in Hastings?'

'I don't know yet,' says Neva, biting her bottom lip. 'I think he's married.'

'Mr Dênou?' Cassie laughs. 'No, he's not.'

'How do you know?'

'I would have read about it. And you don't really think so. Did you feel nothing for him when you saw him again?'

'No. Except to wonder if he was married. Tell me – what can I feel for him? If he found out who Eugene Jonas is, what would happen?'

'If he loves you, he would understand.'

'What – that I deceived him? It would be better if he wasn't coming to supper this evening.'

'I thought him more handsome than I remembered.'

'Stop it, Cassie. If he's not married then every unmarried young lady will be after him. Anyway, I'm far too old now. We're both old maids, you and I.'

Cassie thinks about this for a moment. 'No, we're not. I

thought he looked quite smitten when he saw you.' She helps Neva into her gown. 'You were once in love with him.'

'How do you know?' says Neva.

'You told me when you were drunk.' Cassie blushes a little at the lie but the truth would be more difficult to explain and Mr Dênou will be here in ten minutes.

Neva isn't being honest either. 'I'm not in love with him. I never was,' she says, hoping a lie might be her best protection. 'And after the scandalous things that are written about us in the newspapers, I doubt he will want any more to do with us. And he certainly won't want to marry an insane woman.'

'I hear mad wives are all the fashion,' says Cassie, and Neva feels a lump of rage in her throat for not being able to laugh at herself and at the folly of it, and at her need of him.

Since Papa's death she has been telling herself a story of herself and Henri. It's a story that makes her smile. He plays the role of a hero, he sees through her disguises and loves her. Here in the world of clouds and imagination she finds solace. What she hadn't expected was the reality of him and that her heart, which had almost forgotten what it was like to love him, would be so quickly set on fire.

The table has been laid in the garden, which has been hung with little oil lanterns. It looks like the perfect setting for a romantic evening. Henri is punctual; Elise is delighted to see him and shows him the house then the workshop, talking more than she usually does. And by the time she has finished Cassie has brought the punch bowl out to the garden. Neva is the last to appear with Jetsam. He has a ribbon round his neck.

'He has taken to us, Mr Dênou,' says Elise. 'He won't leave Neva's side.'

At the sight of Henri, the dog charges one way then another, ears back, tail wagging, round and round him then running to the bottom of the garden to do the whole thing over again before coming to a sudden and exhausted halt at Neva's feet.

Henri says he hopes it's not been too much trouble, and no one is sure if he is referring to the dog or himself. He has brought a bouquet of red roses for Elise and two identical boxes, one for Elise and one for Cassie, each containing a beautiful enamelled brooch.

'There was no need, Mr Dênou,' says Elise, her face a picture.

'It is precisely because there is no need,' says Henri with a smile Neva thinks could break her heart.

She stands back, hoping that he hasn't brought her a brooch. She doesn't like them, they always get lost. It seems women are destined to be given rings and small things then spend most of their time looking for them, as if they haven't enough to do. He hands her a velvet box, slightly bigger than Cassie's and Elise's; she opens it cautiously, aware he is watching her. Sitting on a dark velvet cushion is an amber stone, an exact replica of his pebble. She holds it up to the evening light. It glows and inside she can see the smallest insect.

'It's millions of years old,' says Henri. 'And it wasn't formed in the clouds, as alchemists used to believe.'

Neva is silent.

'Or perhaps it was,' she says at last.

It's the most perfect gift she has ever been given. She looks up, blinking tears from her eyes, and is relieved Henri is bending down to put a collar on Jetsam and hasn't seen them. She manages a thank you.

Supper is as awkward as any meal could be.

It's a warm evening, the sky is full of colours and London is magical, bathed in reds and golds and flashes of yellow, reflected in the ripples of the Thames.

Yet for all the beauty of the garden and the sky, the deliciousness of the food, the plentifulness of the wine, the conversation is stilted. No matter how many stories Elise and Cassie tell with Neva at the heart of them she refuses to join in.

Henri takes out his watch that doesn't tell the time and says he has another engagement, which is a relief for everyone. Elise thanks him for coming and hopes he will come again. Cassie thanks him once more for his timely appearance when Aubrey was threatening them. Neva says nothing.

Henri calls to the dog. 'Are you coming, Jetsam?' The dog looks at him apologetically and stays next to Neva.

'If he changes his mind, I'll come back for him.'

Neva at last speaks and thanks him for the amber pebble. For a moment the two of them stand in a silence heavier than lead.

Henri says, as if it has just come to him, 'I could escort you, Mrs Friezland and Miss Lamb to Bermondsey Gardens. I think Jetsam would like a run there.'

Neva bites her lip and nods. She watches him walk to the gate with Elise who is talking about flowers and how they grow all their own vegetables. Neva can hear her artificially cheerful voice.

Cassie has taken in the plates and Neva sits down at the table, rests her head on her arms and for the first time in a long while she weeps. She weeps for all that could have been, for all she has so successfully put an end to this evening.

When Elise and Cassie have joined her again, the garden gate opens and George Cutter comes in with one of his men.

'Did you arrange a cart?' Neva asks him.

'A cart?' says Elise. 'Why do we need a cart?'

George, having no wish to become embroiled in an argument, shrugs and looks at Neva.

'All the precious furnishings and pictures are going to be stored,' she says.

'Neva, is this necessary?' asks Elise.

'Yes,' she says. 'We can't risk Aubrey stealing them. It will leave the house looking bare, I know, but they're valuable. Papa had a good eye.'

She reaches for Elise's hand. 'They'll be back, Auntie, I promise.'

'Unlike Mr Dênou,' says Cassie.

Henri had been prepared for this evening. It had gone exactly as he thought it would. The only surprise, the only hint of optimism, was the tear in Neva's eye. That he hadn't expected. He had watched her nearly all evening as the amber pebble danced through her fingers. He had been fascinated by her stubborn silence and the way every question he asked her was so swiftly batted back at him. No woman had ever made it clearer that she didn't want to see him again. Yet Henri felt full of love for her. He could see the precocious Eugene Jonas hiding in her and he understood that everything Jonas was, everything that made him so intoxicating was what no clever woman like Neva could ever be in public. The world is lopsided, he thinks; we put value on things that have no value at all: sex, colour, beauty – all transient, and in these we imprison women and enslave men.

Elizabeth is a perceptive woman. She had to be to survive her dreadful marriage. She is very much alive to the moods of others and she can clearly see Henri has been downcast since the supper at the Friezland house. After her careful prodding, he reluctantly tells her of his first meeting with Miss Friezland. He leaves out the part about the gambling and goes on to say he'd never forgotten the unusual girl and since meeting her again has discovered he has an affection for her. He doesn't tell his aunt about Eugene Jonas.

Elizabeth is also a good listener. She concludes he hasn't

told her everything and from this she surmises he is in love with Miss Friezland and she with him.

'How you deduced this I have no idea,' says Henri. 'But you are right: I am in love with her. And you are wrong: she isn't with me.'

'Then my suggestion is we invite them to tea,' says Elizabeth.

Henri is pacing the drawing room. 'They won't come.'

'Oh, an invitation to tea is incredibly tempting – especially when hosted by a good-looking, wealthy young gentleman with a house in Berkeley Square.'

'I don't know if I can wait very long to see Miss Friezland again.'

'A pamphlet I saw the other day claimed she's insane, and now it's in the newspaper,' says Elizabeth. 'I assume she's not.'

'I can assure you of that,' says Henri. 'Who put the story out, I wonder?'

'Well, it wasn't John. But he heard a rumour about it.'

'Which is?' asks Henri.

'That it came from Wardell. He's borne a grudge against Mr Friezland ever since he lost a wager to him.'

'And now he's hounding him with slander beyond the grave,' says Henri.

'May I suggest,' says Elizabeth, 'that if you genuinely feel something for Neva Friezland, then you must pursue her. Persistence often pays off and if she's the one, Henri, make sure you are at least engaged before the next season, for her sake and yours. Otherwise you will be devoured by every mother with an unmarried daughter accomplished in the pinning of butterflies.'

Henri sits down. 'I can't imagine anything worse.'

'I agree it is terribly harsh on the butterflies.'

Henri smiles.

★ ★ ★

He hears nothing from Neva Friezland but news of his return reaches the inhabitants of London's finest addresses. He is inundated with invitations for balls, for dances, for teas, for dinners, to make up a party to Vauxhall Gardens, and so it is for the next three weeks by which time he has come to the conclusion that he could live his entire life without once inconveniencing his staff by eating a meal at home. He's only sorry he's been unable to visit Bos in Chelsea.

He is most entertained by the way that Elizabeth and Sir John conduct themselves. Even after he has spent the entire night with Lady Elizabeth – not one, Henri supposes, spent talking about politics or the state of the newspaper industry – Sir John leaves by the tradesmen's entrance only to go round to the front of the house where Morton opens the door and lets him in for breakfast. The element of farce entertains the three of them and Henri wonders who exactly Sir John thinks he's fooling.

One morning, Sir John says, 'I met a fascinating young gentleman at the meteorological society last night. I don't often use the word "extraordinary", but extraordinary he was, without any doubt. A brilliant mind. I invited him to dine with me at the Garrick. That buffoon Sir Edward Fairbrother was there. We dined at the members' table.' Sir John laughs. 'Mr Jonas gave him a run for his money. Sir Edward was no match for this young gentleman, who knew more about the weather than that pompous fool. We were onto the port and I hadn't noticed old Telford because he had his back to us. He turned round and said he remembered being at Brooks's when this young whippersnapper beat Sir Edward at chess.'

'You're talking about Eugene Jonas,' says Henri, attempting to disguise his amazement at Neva's nerve. And an idea comes to him. There's no point seeking out Neva Friezland but perhaps he might meet Eugene Jonas again.

'You know him?' asked Sir John.

'I was at Brooks's that evening. He beat Sir Edward in fewer than ten moves.'

'Sir Edward said it was a fluke and calm as can be Mr Jonas said he could beat him in five. Sir Edward is an ass. We all duly went upstairs where the chessboard had been set up. I can tell you, there was quite a crowd. Mr Jonas went first playing black; the final fatal move was the queen and checkmate. Five moves and forty guineas won. It was the highlight of the evening and when it was over Sir Edward, trying to regain ground, grudgingly invited him to a lecture he's giving next week at the Royal Society. He invited me too, but I haven't time to attend.'

'Would you mind if I took your ticket?' says Henri.

37

Neva is up early the morning of Sir Edward Fairbrother's lecture. It was her original intention to go as Eugene Jonas, listen to the talk, ask one question then take the carriage on to Hastings – no need to change. This plan, as good as it was, had to be put aside for it occurred to her there was a high chance of running into Henri Dênou and she couldn't see him again. She wasn't sure if her resolve would hold. She was uncertain what to do about Jetsam. If she took him with her to Hastings, he could be a hindrance. To leave him with Auntie and Cassie would never do. The best solution was to return him to Henri Dênou, although that might encourage questions best not answered. Jetsam follows her mournfully from one room to another as she packs to leave.

'My shirt...' she says, going down to the kitchen where she finds Elise seated at the table in the exact same spot as she had been last night. A shaft of light shines on her. Neva suspects she never went to bed. She looks like Mother Winter who the sun could never thaw.

Yesterday Elise had burst into tears when Neva told her of her plans.

'But Auntie, what else can I do?' Neva had asked.

'I don't know,' said Elise. 'Take Cassie.'

'If I do there will be even more talk. Better we say Neva is staying with an acquaintance in Deal. That's quite respectable and understandable in the light of the newspaper articles.' Neva softened her voice and said, 'I am doing this for you and for Papa. Once we have proof Mary Kydd married Lieutenant Letchmore before she married Papa, as his legitimate wife, you will be able to keep the money he wanted you to have.'

'There's no point to my existence,' Elise had said. 'I'm useless, I would be better off dead. I have no part, there's nothing for me. Whatever I suggest, you do what you want. You always do.'

Neva had tried to tell her it wasn't so. But Elise was once again becoming lost down some dark corridor of her mind.

The shaft of light that now shines so obligingly through the window illuminates how unkempt Elise has become. Her realm has always been this room, the heart and soul of the house. As a family they had spent more hours here than they had in the long drawing room. For the first time since Victor's death Neva takes a good look at the kitchen. Once it had been methodically tidy, well organised and spotlessly clean. Now it's dusty and as untidy as old memories. Neva should have noticed. Cassie and she have tried to keep the house up to Elise's standard but Neva would never say housework was her strength and it fell more to Cassie. Neither of them dared touch the kitchen. They didn't possess the keys to Auntie's realm and she would always tell them to leave it be.

'Oh,' says Cassie, coming into the kitchen for the first time that morning and, like Neva, seeing Elise where they'd left her. 'A cup of tea?' she says. 'Would you like that, Auntie?'

'How long do you think you'll be gone?' asks Elise when the tea is put before her.

'I'm not sure,' says Neva. 'If I find the church and the register, it will be simple and I will come straight home.'

Elise suddenly brightens. 'What if George went with you?'

They'd been over this last night, but Elise appears to have forgotten. 'George is needed here, Auntie, to look after you.'

Cassie is holding the shirt Eugene is about to put on when the garden gate bell rings loudly.

'If it's the butcher, tell him I'll pay him on Monday,' says Elise.

Neva looks at Cassie.

'I'll answer it,' Cassie says, 'and if it's anybody alarming I'll shout, "Oh my word".'

Elise is starting to dig at the wooden table, a habit she's had since shortly after Victor's death. It's not a good sign.

'Oh my word,' shouts Cassie from the garden and it sounds as if a whirlwind is fast approaching the kitchen door. Neva runs up the stairs so as not to be discovered in trousers.

'Well,' says Mrs Dent, brushing her shoes briskly on the kitchen mat. 'There you are, Elise. The garden and the house, outside at least, are charming.' She looks around the kitchen. 'But this is not how I remember it. No, it's not.'

'It's hard to live up to Auntie's standards,' says Cassie, nervously. It's only now she notices that there's a maid with Mrs Dent and she's buried under a collection of clothes.

'May I ask why you're holding a man's shirt?' says Mrs Dent.

Cassie says, 'It… belongs to one of Mr Cutter's lads.'

'Does he make a habit of using you to do his laundry?' says Mrs Dent. 'Leave the shirt, girl, and take Annie here up to Neva.'

Cassie can't remember the last time the kitchen door was closed but the second she is out of the room it bangs shut.

Mrs Dent walks slowly round, opening cupboards and drawers, running her beringed fingers across the surfaces.

Coming to a halt in front of Elise, she says, 'You've got to snap out of this, girl. You hear me? Enough. Too much is at stake and unless you pull yourself together you'll become one of the sad, homeless old cows finding solace in an inn, talking about the days when you had a house. Are you listening to me?'

It's a hard voice Elise hears, a voice of command. She's heard it before and knows no one disobeys it.

'Victor belongs to the dead and the timeless, you belong to the living and the tick-tock of the clock. He went to a lot of trouble to protect Neva, to protect you, and this is the way you honour his memory, by letting yourself go? Look at you, you should be ashamed. You once ran a good house, I was impressed. What is it? What is it, Elise?'

'I'm not like you, Cora,' says Elise. 'I don't have your iron spirit.'

'That's a load of bull. Forgive my French, but it is. One blow and that shit Aubrey and his mother – with the help of Wardell – will take the lot. All Victor and Neva worked for, and you'll let it happen.'

'I'm not so pathetic. You're being extremely rude. I didn't invite you here.'

'Go on. Yes, I'm being hurtful but I've woken you up, haven't I? I think Henri Dênou is in love with Neva and if she's got any sense she'll be in love with him. He can thwart Aubrey's intention to put her in an asylum. What are you going to do? Mope around the kitchen, become a dishcloth on everybody's floor?'

'No.' There's silence and finally Elise says, 'I'm tired.'

'Grief does that, it exhausts you. When did you last bathe?'

'I can't remember.'

'I can tell you this: you need a bath. Get out of those clothes and when I come back after the lecture, I want to see you looking sprightly, smelling sweet, and with a glass of champagne in your hand.'

Annie, Mrs Dent's maid, is like her mistress, a powerful and determined little woman. She has her orders and they will be carried out to the letter. She has no interest in whether or not Neva wants to wear a brand-new gown and her determination seems to work.

Cassie gasps when she sees Neva standing on the top step. 'Oh lordy-lord,' she says.

'My sentiments completely, girl,' says Mrs Dent. 'Now let's see if that doesn't shatter some hearts.'

38

Henri arrives at the lecture hall a little late. It's already crowded and among the many people there he cannot see Eugene Jonas. A colleague from the days when he worked with Sir Edward says, 'I don't think he's here. He's unmistakable in those blue spectacles.'

To Henri's surprise there are ladies in the audience and this has been permitted at Sir Edward's request. Indeed, Sir Edward's own wife is sitting in the front row. Searching the faces Henri is disappointed not to see Eugene Jonas.

There's a sudden rush and a crowd forms round the entrance to the lecture hall. Someone of note must have arrived. From the middle of the crowd comes the inimitable voice of Mrs Dent.

'Gentlemen,' she says, laughing, 'give us a little space please.'

Henri takes one look and then another. It's Neva Friezland who's caused the commotion. She's wearing a dark grey muslin gown, ribboned with black velvet, long, dove grey gloves and a black hat with three elegant black feathers. A small white Pierrot ruff frames her face. Although the dress is half-mourning, there's something daring about Neva's appearance. She looks and is the height of fashion.

Henri hears some voices in the crowd.

'Who is she?'

'I think... it's Victor Friezland's daughter.'

'No! You mean the mad...'

Henri sees there's no hope of reaching Neva without pushing several men to the floor. A path is at last cleared so Miss Friezland might reach her seat. She looks at no one, or so it seems, until she's seated. Mrs Dent stands guard, searching the room for someone and, spotting Henri, waves and calls him over.

'Mr Dênou, I took the liberty of reserving this seat for you.' She pats the chair next to her.

Henri has a strong feeling his aunt and Mrs Dent have contrived this meeting. Nevertheless, he is immensely grateful. There may be a chance to talk to Neva once the lecture is over. Patience, he tells himself, patience. But it's an awkward arrangement. Mrs Dent is in the middle, Neva to her left and Henri to her right. He has to lean across to speak to Neva.

'Miss Friezland,' he says, 'may I compliment you on your gown. You look—'

Mrs Dent interrupts. 'Miss Friezland has a question she would like you to ask on her behalf.'

'If I asked it,' says Neva, turning to look at him, 'it would confirm that I am indeed mad.'

She passes him a piece of paper.

'It will be a pleasure, Miss Friezland.' She turns away from him. 'This will upset the apple cart,' he murmurs to himself.

A man comes onto the stage and moves the lectern a few inches.

'Next he'll be polishing it,' says Mrs Dent.

Sir Edward Fairbrother enters to polite applause and positions himself at the lectern. He's clutching a bundle of notes. The one thing Henri knows about public speaking is never carry notes if you don't want your lecture to be so dull that half the audience fall asleep. Sir Edward gives an incredibly uninspiring lecture about what makes a storm. When finally he concludes quite a few people leave. Sir Edward asks if there are any questions. A woman's hand goes up but he ignores it and goes on to take a question from a man.

Henri raises his hand and asks Neva's question. 'Sir Edward, do you believe the wind has an innate intelligence and the same could be said for the weather as a whole?'

Laughing, Sir Edward says, 'I would have expected a more insightful question from you, Mr Dênou.'

'The ancient Greeks,' says Henri, 'believed in Zeus and Poseidon and credited each weather system to gods and goddesses. In New York I was fortunate enough to meet Algonquin Indians. They have an instinctive understanding of weather patterns unlike anything we can claim in this country. We ought to have a more rounded approach to the weather; it's one of the great powers of this earth and it shapes our lives.'

'The answers, sir, lie in science not in hocus pocus or the beliefs of uneducated people,' says Sir Edward, looking around desperately for another raised arm.

But Henri is still standing. 'You, Sir Edward, have never suffered a violent storm. You've never lived through winds that can tear a ship to pieces, never seen waves as high as mountains and then wondered at the sudden stillness of everything. Yes, science has a role to play. We need a better understanding, greater knowledge. But to arrogantly believe that by doing so you will have some control of the weather is folly. Too many lives depend on the sky above us. We must learn to understand it – with the use of science, certainly – but also with the insights of those who have a natural instinct for weather patterns beyond the perceived rationale of this day.'

Sir Edward Fairbrother laughs loudly but no one in the audience joins in. 'If we may return to the practical experiments I undertook,' he says. 'When I was in Denmark I was able to do an experiment with Professor Heidleman which we called the Birth of Thunder.'

This is too much for Henri who is on his feet again. 'You seem to have forgotten I accompanied you to Denmark, Sir Edward. My memory is that you believed you were terminally ill after a choppy sea voyage and you begged to return to England. You were there less than twelve hours. Professor Heidleman was in Germany at the time you were doing your fantastical experiments.'

This shocking moment divides the audience. The young gentlemen in trousers leave. Older gentlemen in breeches stay to congratulate Sir Edward.

Mrs Dent turns to Henri. 'Most impressive, Mr Dênou. Wouldn't you agree, Neva?'

Neva says quietly, 'You've not only upset the apple cart, you've driven it off the road into a deep ditch – and I would say it's irretrievable.' She laughs and her face brightens as if the sun has peeked out from behind a cloud.

Mrs Dent gets up to leave, saying that next week Henri must come to her Magical Soiree where Neva will be performing. She says it with a naughty twinkle in her eye and it obviously takes Neva by surprise because the sun goes in. Henri accompanies Mrs Dent and Neva to the door of the lecture hall. But the bombshell he's dropped means he's now surrounded by people wanting details about the Denmark expedition. His last glimpse of Neva is as she's leaving. She turns and smiles at him. He thinks if he ever has her portrait painted he will make sure the artist captures that smile. And it is this one smile and the single tear that give him hope.

He returns home to be greeted by Morton.

'No dog, sir?'

'No dog,' says Henri.

Morton hands him a message. Bos has invited him to dine at three o'clock.

Henri walks to Westminster Stairs and asks the ferryman to take him close to the Old Chelsea Bun House. From there, it's a pleasant walk along a river unfettered by too many buildings. Here there are more cows than people. At least in the countryside the noise of the city fades and the waters of the Thames are less grey. Birdsong can be heard, no longer drowned out by street criers and horses' hooves. Swallows swoop and dive across the water.

Bos's house in Cheyne Walk has none of the pomp and ceremony of his father's house; there is an air of charming absent-mindedness about it. Bos's daughter looks exactly like her father only with dimples.

All thoughts of grown-up matters are lost in the hurly-burly of hide and seek. The three of them spend a happy afternoon causing chaos until at last order is restored with the return of Camille's nanny and the little girl disappears upstairs to the nursery, full of tales about the smallest place where she and her father have hidden and the kindly dragon who lives in the airing cupboard.

'Oh yes, the dragon,' Henri hears the nanny say. 'What colour is it?'

'She's an enchanting little girl,' says Henri, 'and very lucky to have you as her father.'

'She is,' says Bos. 'And now, a drink.'

They sit in the garden and Henri has begun to tell him about calling at the Friezland house to offer his condolences when Bos interrupts him.

'I just wondered... did you... did you happen to meet Miss Cassandra Lamb there?'

'I did,' says Henri.

'And is she well?'

'I believe so.'

'Good. That's good.'

'Bos,' Henri says gently, 'is Miss Lamb important to you?'

After a pause, Bos says, 'Yes. Yes, very important. I'm in love with her. I have been, I think, since I first saw her at Covent Garden. I should have done something about it then and now... well, I...' He stumbles over his words and then manages to say, 'It was after a performance of the Weather Woman. Nothing happened. I told her what I felt and that I was married.'

'Do you still feel the same way?'

'Apart from my daughter, I have only loved once,' say Bos. 'If I wasn't in full mourning, I would give away my dukedom to be married to her. I don't give a damn for the ermine and etiquette. There, Henri, I've shocked you.'

'No, not in the slightest.'

Henri takes a ferry back to Westminster Stairs. The tide is in his favour but the sky darkens, the rain pours down and by the time he's reached his house he's wet through. Morton opens the door.

'A miserable evening, sir,' he says. 'Lady Wardell and Sir John are at the theatre.' The butler smiles broadly. 'The dog is back.'

'Who brought him?' says Henri, surprised.

'A young gentleman in blue spectacles.'

'Where is Jetsam?'

'In the kitchen, sir. Shall I bring him to you?'

Henri has shed his wet clothes, bathed and is in his dressing gown before he and Jetsam go to his study. He pours himself a whisky. The windows look out onto the garden and he sees his reflection marked out in raindrops. He lets Jetsam out; the dog does a quick round of the rose bushes and comes back inside, shaking his shaggy coat. Henri closes the door.

On his desk is a pile of letters. The top one is from Miss Cassandra Lamb writing on behalf of Mrs Friezland, Miss Friezland and herself. Regretfully they must decline his invitation to tea.

He leans back in his chair, stuffs his hand in a pocket and finds there the letter that Lady Wardell gave him on his return from Dublin.

He looks at it and looks again at Miss Lamb's letter. Both were written by the same hand, postmarked five years apart. Why on earth did Miss Lamb write to him five years ago? It is with some trepidation that he opens it.

But inside the letter, the writing is Neva's.

And now I hear you are leaving and I am full of regret. If I could speak to you, if you were sitting in front of me, what would I say? That this foolish heart, this unknown heart of mine with its mansion of unoccupied rooms, has a library of a million words that I would use to tell you that I, Neva, Neva, Neva, I love you, Henri Dênou. And what would come of that?

39

Henri has hardly slept and now he walks back and forth the length of his chamber. He wishes he could roll back time. He thinks how different his life would be. After a few more turns of the room he's convinced himself it's too late, five years too late. There's so much that goes against him; not only time but his ingratitude to Neva. If only he had accepted Victor Friezland's invitation to supper. If only he had asked the simplest of questions – who is Eugene Jonas? Jetsam glances up at him with a sigh, as if to say he wouldn't have wasted so many good dog years. Henri takes out his watch, forgetting it no longer tells the time, and promises himself that if Neva will give him a second chance he will have it mended.

The sky has a half-rinsed look to it as if there are more showers to be wrung from the clouds. Henri wonders, not for the first time since reading her letter, if Neva will only greet him with indifference. But nevertheless he will apply for a special marriage licence. He wonders how long it will take to organise such a thing.

Such thoughts consume him so that he is unaware of how fast he is walking or how soon he has arrived at the lane off

Tooley Street. St Saviour's bells have just struck ten o'clock, too early for polite society, which only receives visitors after eleven. But he is outside the Friezland house, it has started to rain, and Jetsam, who has no interest in manners or the rights and wrongs of the hour, begins to bark.

He hears Mrs Friezland hurrying to open the gate. 'No, no, no,' she says, 'I thought...' and stops, surprised to see Henri.

'I'm sorry to call on you so early, madam,' he says, realising Jetsam has already run into the house.

Elise smiles at Henri sympathetically and says, 'Come in, Mr Dênou, you'll get drenched in that coat.'

In the kitchen it is warm with the smell of bread baking.

'Is Miss Friezland at home?' asks Henri.

'No, she left yesterday,' says Elise.

'Left?' says Henri. 'Where has she gone?'

'Hastings,' says Elise, bending to lift the bread out of the oven.

Cassie comes hurrying in. 'How did Jetsam get here?' she asks and stops on seeing Henri. 'Oh. Oh, good morning, Mr Dênou.' She curtsies.

Henri bows. 'Good morning, Miss Lamb. I came to see Miss Friezland but I understand she's gone to Hastings.'

Cassie shoots a look at Elise and says quickly, 'Mr Jonas has escorted her to Deal to stay with a cousin of his.'

Elise puts butter and damson jam on the table and says, 'You'll have breakfast with us, Mr Dênou?'

'Yes, Mrs Friezland, thank you.' He stares intently at Elise, hoping she might contradict Cassie but she puts out plates and pours boiling water into the teapot. Henri sits down, thinking about the house and what it must have been like growing up here, in a place full of love. Few people, no servants, but love.

'Butter,' says Elise, passing it to Henri. 'I always think if I had to choose between butter and cheese, it would be butter every time.'

'I agree,' says Henri.

The bread is cut, the tea is poured and the damson jam put before him. Henri realises he's hungry.

'Is Miss Friezland away for long?' he asks.

'We're not sure,' says Elise. 'I think until this nonsense about her being mad has died down and that may well not be until after probate is granted.'

'Mr Friezland's will is going to the courts,' explains Cassie.

'It's not what Victor would've wanted,' says Elise. 'Nor would he have wanted that solicitor to go making Neva a marriage proposal.'

'Auntie!' says Cassie.

'Well, it's the truth.'

Henri is astounded. 'Solicitor? Do you mean Mr Gutteridge?'

Jetsam trots into the kitchen looking dejected. He has searched everywhere for Neva and now, defeated, he sits beside Henri.

'Cassie,' says Elise, 'would you fetch my shawl for me? I left it upstairs.'

'It's quite warm in here, Auntie,' says Cassie briskly.

'I'm not as young as you and I feel the draught.'

Cassie stands for a moment. 'Shouldn't we just see if Mr Dênou—'

'My shawl, please, Cassie,' says Elise.

Elise waits until she hears Cassie's footsteps on the stairs. 'Hastings,' she says.

Henri nods. 'Mrs Friezland, is Miss Friezland considering Mr Gutteridge's proposal?'

Elise laughs. 'No, Mr Dênou.'

They can hear Cassie running down the stairs and into the kitchen. She glances at Elise suspiciously as she hands her the shawl.

Elise looks out of the window. 'A blustery old day. It's been a wet summer so far. If you will excuse me, Mr Dênou, I have things to do. You are always welcome here.'

Henri stands, thanks her and sits again as she leaves the room.

'She hasn't been herself since Mr Friezland's death,' says Cassie.

'I'm sorry to hear that. But she seems in good health today.'

'I think she has a soft spot for you, Mr Dênou.'

'Miss Lamb,' says Henri, 'yesterday I received the letter.'

'Our reply to your invitation?'

'The letter you sent me five years ago, the one that Miss Friezland wrote and you sent after I'd left for Iceland with Sir Edward Fairbrother.'

'That feels like a bird flown backwards,' says Cassie.

Henri laughs. 'What does that mean?'

'If a bird could fly backwards, so could time,' says Cassie, smiling. 'Mr Dênou, I shouldn't have sent that letter, it was meant for the waste-paper basket. But those words were so beautiful, and she was so done in by that evening and having said—'

'Having said he, Eugene Jonas, was in love with her, Neva Friezland?'

'You know?'

Henri nodded.

'Neva lost so much that night.'

'So did I. I'm very glad you sent the letter, even if it didn't reach me in time.'

'The post is a little slow round here,' says Cassie.

'Do you think Miss Friezland feels the same way about me now?' He corrects himself. 'No, not the same way, that would be impossible. But do you think there is any hope for me?'

'I shouldn't say this,' says Cassie, 'but yes, most definitely, yes.' Her face is screwed up and her eyes closed as if saying it that way might be better than looking at Henri. 'She's in Hastings, lodging at the Beach House.'

'Disguised as Eugene Jonas, I take it.'

Cassie's eyes are now wide open. 'Yes, but if anyone knew...'

'No one will. Out of interest, how many people do know?'

'Auntie and I, and George Cutter.'

'Not Mr Gutteridge, I take it.'

'No. Please don't tell her I sent you the letter. At least not yet.'

The rain has stopped and Henri retrieves his hat and his dog. 'Your confidence deserves one in exchange.' Cassie looks puzzled. 'But first, may I ask you, Miss Lamb – and I know you will answer honestly – if you have affection for my dear friend, the Marquess of Smedmore?'

She stifles a gasp and Henri sees her hand go instinctively to her pretty necklace. 'Yes, yes, I do, but I haven't...'

'He is still in love with you.'

'He is?'

'Yes. But he's in mourning and there is nothing he can do – as yet.'

Cassie is about to say something and at first thinks better of it. Then, in a rush, 'But Mr Dênou, what does it matter if Bos is in love with me or I with him? I'm no lady.'

'No, Miss Lamb,' says Henri. 'You are a duchess.'

40

July 1813

Ebenezer Ratchet is at his desk amid piles of boxes, going through his books. As is his way he occasionally looks out of the window. It's not the cleanest of windows but it's dirty by design because he can see enough to watch the passers-by.

Now the moneylender makes out the unwanted silhouettes of Aubrey Friezland and Lord Wardell, seemingly loitering with intent. Wardell is upright, his right arm swinging out, his hand on his silver-topped ebony cane. Even though his clothes are falling apart the man's arrogant stance hasn't changed, while Aubrey, who was once just as upright, now looks as if he has collapsed into himself. He's thinner and his clothes looser. He looks meaner. Mr Ratchet watches them with interest.

'How much do you think they're after this time, Old Bones?'

The dog doesn't move.

Mr Ratchet has no doubt they are summoning up the nerve to come in. They've walked past three times and each time Old Bones growls softly under his breath. But now the dog is on his feet.

'Yes, Old Bones,' says Mr Ratchet. 'We're going to have visitors.'

Lord Wardell enters first and Aubrey, sniffing, follows close behind. Both smell none too sweet. Old Bones bares his teeth and is ready to spring.

'Charming dog,' says Wardell. 'Do you think you could call him off?'

One word from Mr Ratchet and Old Bones retreats to his basket.

'Good morning, gentlemen. What can I do for the two of you?' asks Mr Ratchet. Last time they'd called he had sent them away with a flea in their ear.

'Well, Uncle, as you know...' Aubrey stops to wipe his runny nose on his sleeve. 'As you know—'

Lord Wardell interrupts. 'Victor Friezland's will is to be heard by the Ecclesiastical Courts in November. It is now nearly August and we are in need of a loan of two hundred pounds, after which you will be truly reimbursed.'

'You are expecting me to wait until November before I get my money back? Any idea of the interest I would charge on that? Your ebony cane isn't worth that much.'

Lord Wardell puts a piece of paper before him and taps it with a long fingernail.

Mr Ratchet reads, then reads it again.

'It is all above board and properly signed by blue-blooded gentlemen,' says Lord Wardell. 'Whatever happens, I will be paid two hundred and fifty pounds in September. It is guaranteed. You can see the signatures.'

Mr Ratchet can and Mr Ratchet wonders if his lordship is losing his mind.

'And if I manage it, which of course I will, eight hundred pounds is promised by Sir Richard Palmore.'

Mr Ratchet is stunned. What he's looking at is a list of peers and knights whose houses are rumoured to have been burgled by Aubrey. It's obvious this is their attempt at revenge.

'If I understand it correctly,' says Mr Ratchet, 'these personages – all of whom have had property stolen from them at your behest – are prepared to pay you this sum of money if you swallow a live fish.' The folly of it makes Mr Ratchet roar with laughter. At the same time he can see the justice in it. 'You don't think they're doing this as retribution?'

'Of course not,' says Lord Wardell. 'I had nothing to do with their unfortunate losses.' He looks around, noting there is nowhere for him to sit.

'What size fish are they expecting you to swallow?'

'I don't know,' says Lord Wardell. 'It will be fish-sized, I imagine.'

'There are a lot of fish in the sea,' says Mr Ratchet. 'Some quite big ones and others quite small. From what I read here, you have to hope the fish they serve up that day is a small one. There's no mention of size.'

'Is there not?' says Lord Wardell. He glances at Aubrey. 'But I'm not showing you this for your opinion, only as proof you will be repaid.'

'What about the rest of the money you owe me? Will that be repaid too?'

'Of course it will in due course, Uncle,' says Aubrey. 'Once the will is sorted out and we get what is rightfully ours.'

'Due course costs money,' says Mr Ratchet. 'And may I ask what you mean by "we"?'

'I mean me,' says Aubrey. 'When I come into my father's estate.'

'What about your mother?'

'What about the old cow?'

'Put her out to pasture. That's what I would recommend,' says Lord Wardell.

'It would've been better, Aubrey, if you'd taken the money

Victor Friezland so generously left you, then Lord Wardell here wouldn't be putting his life at risk by swallowing a live fish of uncertain dimensions.'

Lord Wardell takes offence at this. 'I could swallow a fish with ease,' he says.

'You've been practising then?'

'No need, Mr Ratchet,' says Lord Wardell.

'If I were you, I'd find out what kind of fish they're expecting you to swallow.'

'Oh, it will be the catch of the day.'

Mr Ratchet thinks about it for a minute or two, then says, 'I'll lend you thirty pounds but I want it back by the end of September. You're familiar with my terms and conditions.'

'But, Uncle, we need more than that,' says Aubrey. 'You've got the list of pledges, and when I get my inheritance—'

'All this on a fish and a wish,' says Mr Ratchet.

'You,' says Lord Wardell, pointing his silver-topped cane at Mr Ratchet, 'you, you upstart, you forget who you're talking to.'

Old Bones growls loudly and Lord Wardell backs away.

'Twenty. And another word from you – *my lord* – and it will be ten. Here you are, now scarper.'

'What about the sherry?' says Aubrey.

'I wouldn't waste good sack on you.'

'That's not nice, Uncle,' says Aubrey. He's started to shake. 'You should show more respect, you bloody well should.' Old Bones's growls are turning into barks. 'All right, all right – SHUT IT,' he shouts at the dog.

They take the money on offer and leave. Mr Ratchet stands in his doorway, watching them go, knowing full well he won't be seeing a coin of the £20 again. He returns to his desk.

An hour later he is thinking of the dinner waiting for him upstairs. A good loaf of bread and some fresh cheese, not to mention a cold pork pie. He's just closed his ledger – which always makes good reading – when the doorbell rings. Old Bones barks once. There is Mary.

'If you've been sent by those two clowns...'

'What clowns? I don't see anything funny about coming here.'

'You sure that son of yours and his fine friend aren't waiting outside?'

'No,' she says. 'Why?'

'They came this morning wanting fish money.'

'I don't understand.'

'Money to buy a fish with.'

'Oh...'

'It doesn't matter, Mary,' says Mr Ratchet.

'I didn't know they'd been here, honest.'

'And that's something, Mary, you're not.' Mr Ratchet produces a chair for her.

'Not what?' she says. Old Bones goes and sits beside her and she strokes the top of his head.

'Honest.'

She takes no notice of what her half-brother has said. She says, 'I can't afford the rent and they'll throw me out if I don't pay up. The workhouse is waiting for me, brother.'

Silence. Mr Ratchet remembers his sister as a chatterbox, never quiet for a minute, always with something to say. He used to wonder if her mouth ever got tired of all those words. This silent Mary is one he doesn't know but he likes her a lot better.

Finally she says, 'Aubrey broke all those china figurines that belonged to Mum.'

With a sigh, Mr Ratchet locks the shop and takes her upstairs. He puts out the bread and cheese and pours her a sherry. Her hands are shaking so much she spills some and he pours her another until the shakes stop.

'Thank you,' she says. 'It tastes good. Better than gin.' Then she says, 'I think I'm in trouble.'

'I think you are as well,' says Mr Ratchet.

'A man, a lawyer man – I talked to him without thinking. He asked me about my husbands.'

'What did you tell him?' Mr Ratchet pours her another sherry.

'I told him the truth. And Aubrey will kill me if he finds out.'

'The truth. Which is?'

'Could I have some of that bread and cheese? I haven't eaten for a while.'

'You're falling to pieces, girl. What's happened to you? You're made up of lies and fabrications. I want you to tell me the truth.'

'I'm sorry, I can't think straight, I'm that hungry.'

'Eat slowly,' says Mr Ratchet.

Watching Mary stuffing food into her mouth makes him lose his appetite. He's never liked eating with other people, he's never understood the attraction of it. He thinks he'd rather have a conversation with a friend sitting on a chamber pot than have a meal with him.

'You not eating?'

Mr Ratchet thinks of the pork pie in the larder. 'No,' he says.

Mary tears the loaf into pieces and spreads it thick with butter and hunks of cheese. At last there's nothing left but crumbs.

'Listen to me, Mary,' says Mr Ratchet. 'I'll pay for your room and give you an allowance, but you must give me the certificate which confirms your marriage to Robert Letchmore.'

'What makes you think I have it?' she says.

'Because you're not stupid, you never were.'

'I need to think,' says Mary.

'Where are you living?'

She tells him.

'I'll speak to the landlord. But I want that certificate.'

'Aubrey said he'll kill me if I talk, if I tell anyone he isn't Victor's boy.'

'Mary, no one would ever think he was Victor Friezland's son.'

'He's deranged,' says Mary.

'He's certainly dangerous,' says Mr Ratchet. 'I'm told he threatened Miss Friezland with a knife.'

Mary stands up and with her middle finger she presses the few crumbs left on the board and eats them.

'Thank you,' she says. 'I've not been a good sister to you. I always called you the Rat.'

'That you did.'

'It was my father. He was a cruel man.'

'That he was. Here, take this.' Mr Ratchet gives her two guineas. 'Try not to drink it all away. In one month bring me the certificate and I will look after you until the sun sets on your days. But if you don't bring it, you're on your own and at the mercy of those two villains.'

'It was the candles that angered me,' says Mary. 'I would rather Victor hadn't mentioned me at all than leave me a shilling for candles.'

'One month,' says Mr Ratchet as he lets her out.

He clears away the board and the plates and wipes the table. Putting on his hat, he calls for his dog.

'Come along, Old Bones, let's take a walk. We have a lawyer to see.'

Part Four

41

July to August 1813

This is the first time Neva has been out of London alone. As Eugene Jonas she had hoped to go unnoticed, make her enquiries then leave. But it proves impossible in this small seaside community of summer visitors whose curiosity knows no bounds. Mr Eugene Jonas is too much of an enigma to go unremarked.

Mr Eugene Jonas is not staying at the Crown Hotel, nor the Swan where apparently people of quality stay. Mr Eugene Jonas is lodging at the Beach House where those of humbler purse and less refined taste find rooms. Neva's room boasts a sideways view of the sea.

On the first day, having breakfasted, she sets off, her blue spectacles firmly on the end of her nose and in her pocket the amber pebble and a list of churches in Hastings. Lost in her own thoughts, she has no inkling of the interest Mr Jonas is causing, for as he walks down George Street, he looks like an exotic bird released from a cage. Some fear that he's an escaped prisoner-of-war. Everywhere Mr Jonas goes, Mr Jonas is noticed, but Neva is oblivious of the gossip about him.

The first church on her list is All Saints, but it is only when she is shown the church register that she realises the size of the undertaking. The parson is helpful but vague.

'The records before 1800 are somewhat free, shall we say, in their descriptions of the marriages,' he says. 'I take it the marriage is before that date, Mr Jonas? There is also a book of banns but even if the banns were read it does not necessarily follow the wedding went ahead.'

Neva realises she was naïve to think her task would be easily accomplished in a week. It could take a month.

As she's leaving, the parson asks, 'Are you sure you have the right church, sir?'

'That's the problem. I don't know in which church it was that the marriage took place.'

'Oh dear. Should you wish to come back this afternoon, I'm afraid we have choir practice. Perhaps tomorrow?'

Neva walks along the seafront, her head aching from reading so many entries through blue lenses in the gloom of the church. Some of them are sketchy to say the least. One parson had written that the couple were most ill-suited and the groom was drunk. All Saints is just one church. She should also investigate St Clement's, and St Leonard's Church in Hollington.

Her solace is the library tearoom on the seafront with a view out to Beachy Head. Neva sits at a window and takes in the vastness of the sea and sky. Perhaps she should admit defeat and go back to London. Yet there is a peace in being away from the city, away from Henri Dênou. Where he's concerned she is perched on the rim of herself, a wingless bird in love with him and lost.

It will get better, it will, she repeats to herself. The more she says it, the less she likes Eugene Jonas with his blue gaze on the world. Perhaps she will give him up for good. He has brought her nothing but trouble. She should never have said he was in love with her. When this is over, she will bury his clothes and send him back to the clouds. This will pass, this love. Passion is the weather of our souls and this is a stormy afternoon. It will pass.

The next day she is back at All Saints Church, going through the dates but finding nothing of Miss Mary Kydd. The parson has been unable to discover anyone who has a memory of a Lieutenant Letchmore. The militia were based mainly in Brighton, he tells her. The headache returns.

Again the church is busy that afternoon and it is as she's leaving that the parson introduces her to Mrs Bickerton.

'A welcome visitor to our parish, whose generosity to this humble church is boundless,' he says.

Neva bows and excuses herself, saying her head is splitting.

She has no appetite for dinner and no desire to spend more than she needs to so she returns to the library tearoom and orders coffee. It's a warm day and she sits at the table by the window, her eyes closed, enjoying the sun on her face.

'Excuse me, Mr Jonas.'

Someone is blocking the sun. Neva opens her eyes to find it is Mrs Bickerton.

'Mr Jonas,' she says, 'what a happy coincidence. I've sent an invitation to your lodgings inviting you to join me for tea this afternoon.'

Neva rises to her feet. 'Thank you, madam, but unfortunately I have a headache.' Mr Jonas bows and hastens away.

The following day, Mrs Bickerton rushes up to Mr Jonas in George Street as he's making his way to All Saints Church, which this morning the parson has said is all his.

'Mr Jonas, how delightful,' says Mrs Bickerton. 'Perhaps today you are free to join me for afternoon tea?'

Again Mr Jonas makes his apologies and hopes this might put an end to Mrs Bickerton's interest in him. But she proceeds to inform those who are curious and those who are not that Mr Jonas is here on account of his eyes, hence the headaches which result in a slight shortness of temper and the need for the blue spectacles.

At breakfast the next day, Neva's landlady hopes Mr Jonas's vision is improving in the sea air. This ridiculous notion of Mrs Bickerton's works in Neva's favour and she would be the first to agree she sees things differently from most people.

Neva decides to go to St Leonard's Church at Hollington.

The church is locked and a gravedigger tells her the parson is away attending a dying parishioner.

She walks back to Hastings and stops to have a cold drink at the library tearoom. There's no point to this, she thinks, and calculates how soon she can return to London. Everything here is too small, too close. She calms herself, letting the amber pebble dance through her fingers. This world is a lonely place without Papa, he who had long protected her from the humdrum nature of life, who had allowed her to dream, given her the freedom to become Eugene Jonas. And here is Jonas lost inside a whale of grief.

The tide is out and through her blue lenses it appears the sky and the sea have merged and everyone looks as if they are underwater. Only half-listening, she overhears a lady talking loudly to a gentleman with an ear trumpet.

'We have a new visitor at the Swan,' says the lady. 'He came down last night from London in his own carriage with a fine pair of black horses. He's taken three rooms.'

'Three?' repeats the gentleman. 'What kind of bounder is he?'

'A very handsome one,' says the lady. There's a pause and Neva awaits the 'but'. 'But he has a foreign name.'

Neva stops herself from laughing aloud. Tomorrow none of this will matter, she will be on her way home. She finishes her drink and is leaving the tearoom to book a seat on the coach to London when she hears a dog bark. For a moment she thinks her spectacles are deceiving her eyes. Bounding towards her is Jetsam. He comes to an abrupt stop, panting and furiously wagging his tail. He jumps up, licks her then sinks down beside her as if to say, 'See, I found her.'

She bends down to stroke him. 'Jetsam, where did you come from?' she says.

'London.'

Neva looks up, the sun in her eyes, and there, in a halo of blue, is Henri Dênou.

She isn't prepared for this. Of all the possibilities she has rehearsed, this is not one she has considered. Fully aware everyone is watching, she stands up and bows. 'M'sieur Dênou.'

'Mr Jonas,' says Henri, bowing. He smiles.

Neva has forgotten how powerful that smile is.

'Shall we walk? I believe the tide is going out.'

Their feet crunch on the shingle, away from the bathing machines until they reach the sandy foreshore. The sea is as still as water in a bowl.

Jetsam runs into the gently lapping waves and chases the pebbles Henri throws for him.

Only now does Neva breathe. 'Why are you here, Mr Dênou?'

'To see you,' says Henri. 'What other reason could there possibly be? And to ask you a serious question.'

'I can't answer any questions until we've taken a hundred steps.'

They walk along the beach while Neva tries to calm herself and fathom the reason for his visit. They both speak together.

'Why are you here?' asks Neva again.

'I wanted to ask...' says Henri.

And they laugh because they've both arrived at a hundred steps at the same time.

'Please – you first,' he says.

'I ask in earnest, why are you here?'

'And in earnest I tell you it's because of Neva Friezland.'

'Neva?'

'Yes. I hope you will be able to give me the answer to my question. I want to know if Neva Friezland has any feelings for me and if there is a hope of my seeing her again.'

What would it be like to be kissed by him? To touch his skin, to be held?

Neva can think of nothing else then realises she is walking fast and he isn't. She stops and waits as he catches up. 'Why do you want to see her?'

'I want to tell her I'm sorry.'

'Sorry for what?'

There's a long silence.

She's not sure if she hears him right when he says, 'I don't want to play games anymore. I must be truthful with you.'

It feels as if the tide is no longer going out but is rushing in on her.

'Five years ago we dined together at Brooks's,' says Henri. 'It was the most exhilarating evening I've spent in anyone's company. I fell in love not with Neva Friezland but with Eugene Jonas. I was so confused by what I felt and why I felt it that I did what all fools do – I ran. If I'd had the wit to slow down, if I hadn't frightened myself, if I'd looked at the note Neva sent me when she returned my pebble and the letter Eugene sent to tell me he was going away, I would have realised I was in love with Neva.

'I have given this a lot of thought. The world is run by men and for a clever woman it must be completely frustrating. For an extraordinary woman? I have no idea what it must be like. What your father gave you I have no wish to take from you. I want to marry you.'

'Marry,' she repeats.

He is studying her face, waiting for an answer.

She turns away from him. Jetsam is digging in the sand, his

tail wagging, and she thinks dogs live in the moment, they don't weigh the present against what has been, what might be, what could be.

Finally she says, 'My heart broke that night. I lost you. I lost Eugene Jonas too. He was to be buried for good. Now I have him back I don't know what to do. He's stuck, weighed down by how others view him.' She pauses. 'I don't know where to hide.'

'I understand that,' says Henri. 'I have a special licence. We could be married tomorrow.'

'No,' says Neva. 'I'm too odd, my mind is broken. I'm strange, I don't like being touched – and yet, and yet – I don't know what to do with all my love for you. Perhaps I *am* mad.'

'Neva,' says Henri, 'I feel the same. But I have an idea – we could get married and then...'

'That's all too proper, full of impossible teasets and teaspoons. It's ridiculous. We can't marry unless it works physically between us. It would be unfair, a life of misery. I won't do that. I can't do that.'

'What are you saying?'

'I've shocked you.'

'No, Neva – I just need you to explain.'

'I'm not going to marry you unless I've been to bed with you and we know that part works for us.' Henri stares at her. '*Now* I have shocked you,' she says.

He laughs. 'Yes, you have. It's most unconventional.'

'I had an unconventional education,' says Neva.

'Let me rephrase this so I'm sure I understand,' says Henri. 'You want to go to bed with me and for me to make love to you. If you find it bearable, you will consent to marry me. Yes? Have I understood you correctly?'

'Not quite. It has to be more than bearable. Is that so very shocking? Surely if you hope to spend a lifetime with someone not knowing if this part, this most important part of a relationship works, what is the point of all the words of love? You might as well become a nun or a priest, put your mind to higher love and let your body go cold.'

Henri looks out to sea. 'I could be seen as taking advantage of you.'

'How, when it is my suggestion?' She pauses. 'Why did you take three rooms?'

'Because I thought if you consented to marry me, you would need a maid...'

'At Brooks's,' says Neva, 'I found your true spirit. I met you not as you are in the society of ladies, I met you, just you. What if I stayed with you as Eugene Jonas? We could go to bed together and if it doesn't work we are free to go our separate ways and no one can accuse you of seducing Neva Friezland.'

He shakes his head. 'And if you find you're with child?'

'Well... then we would have to think again.'

'But if it works between us, then it wouldn't matter,' he says.

'Yes and no,' says Neva. 'I would rather not have children. Is it agreed?'

'Agreed. And you can always change your mind.'

'But I won't. Why would I?'

They don't speak as they walk back towards Hastings.

'Can I send someone to collect your bag?'

'No.'

'You won't run away?'

'No, I promise. You'd better put Jetsam on the lead otherwise he won't go with you.'

'Tonight at six.'

Before she walks off, she says, 'I want a bath.'

'That can be arranged. I love you, Neva Friezland.'

His words trail after her and make her smile.

At the Beach House she packs and sits on the bed. There are too many hours until she sees him again. Her world is spinning fast, she is falling and she doesn't care.

42

That same summer's afternoon, Elise opens the garden gate to a man who bows and introduces himself as Briggs, Mr Gutteridge's clerk.

He presents his card, and after Elise has examined it she says, 'You'd better come in, Mr Briggs.'

'I'm hoping to learn the whereabouts of Mr Eugene Jonas.'

'Why do you want to know?'

'It's a matter of some importance concerning Miss Friezland. Is she at home?'

Alarmed, Elise says, 'No, she's staying with a relative of Mr Jonas. She isn't in any danger, is she?'

'I couldn't say, Mrs Friezland.'

'I think you could, Mr Briggs, but you choose not to.'

'Mrs Friezland,' says Mr Briggs, 'Mr Gutteridge wishes to write to Mr Jonas. Time is of the essence.'

Elise offers the clerk tea, and when it's made, she takes the tray into the garden.

'May I speak frankly, Mr Briggs?' she says.

'You may, Mrs Friezland.'

'I don't know if you are aware that Mr Gutteridge has

asked for Miss Friezland's hand in marriage. Quite what led him even to consider such a far-fetched notion I cannot think. I've always thought him to be a clever man and this obsession he has with Miss Friezland and Mr Jonas isn't good for him. I believe its roots lie in grief at the loss of his friend, my husband. But it would be better all round if Mr Gutteridge would stop interfering in our affairs. Mr Seaton is dealing with the will so I ask you again: is it really necessary to contact Mr Jonas urgently?'

'I suspect not, Mrs Friezland.'

'Thank you, sir. I will ask Mr Jonas to call on Mr Gutteridge when he returns – and when that will be, I don't know.'

Elise wishes him good day and sees him to the gate. She goes back to find Cassie looking into an empty teapot.

'Who was that?' she asks.

'Mr Gutteridge's clerk. It was nothing important.'

Elise sits down. She wonders what Victor would say and her heart knows the answer: it's time to drown Eugene Jonas. He's not going to stand up in the courts; he's only stopping two lovers from being together.

'What did you say, Cassie?'

'I said I wish Mr Dênou had never said anything to me about Bos, for nothing will come of it and there is nothing I can do. And it's too heavy to think about any further.'

'Come here,' says Elise and she puts her arms round Cassie.

'No, don't, Auntie. I'm going to cry. It's foolish. It doesn't matter. Bos would never marry me, it's just a dream, that's all.'

'We build our lives on dreams,' says Elise. 'We punctuate them with "it isn't possible". We give weight to etiquette that has no gravity to it. Or to the Lord above who never blushes at the cruelty of men to women and of both to children. Victor's dream was that Mary would come back to him. I don't think she was a bad woman. He remembered her as being pretty and kind, flirting with everybody, full of laughter. The woman who turned up at the will reading was a completely different soul, a dreamer whose dreams had been wrecked. I don't think your dream is impossible. My dream certainly wasn't – it was just delayed a little longer than it should have been.'

'What was your dream?' asks Cassie.

'That Victor might love me and my bastard of a husband might die.'

Cassie smiles. 'Thank you,' she says.

'Just wait and see. And keep dreaming.'

43

Henri doesn't know what to do with himself in the intervening hours – these interfering hours – until six o'clock. He stops at a tailor's shop in George Street and buys a dressing gown and a shirt. He can only guess at Neva's measurements but he knows she is slim and as tall as he is. In the barber's he buys some good soap and eau-de-cologne. He goes into a draper's shop and makes another purchase. He walks to the top of the West Hill and he walks down; he walks to the top of the East Hill where he looks out towards France. The sky has changed; there is a stream of light that seems to flicker on the horizon. One day he would like to go home. He hasn't thought of France until this moment and he realises he has long missed his mother tongue. His problem is with the people, the barbarity that lies beneath the surface. He fears large gatherings and the crowd's susceptibility to strong words; the madness of the mob baying for blood. His mother had wept when she'd heard of the September Massacres. They had lost relatives, young cousins, a nephew. This is what he's thinking as he looks out to sea towards the country of his birth. He has twice stared into the hollow eyes of death, twice believed himself gone; now his life is beginning again. He hasn't felt this excited for a long time. He hums to himself.

She dressed herself up like a sailor
In her jacket and trousers so blue.

'Dear Mrs O'Donnell,' he says to the summer breeze, 'I would like to tell you I'm here, I've found her.'

As he descends to the town, he's relieved to see the church clock says five. Back at the Swan he requests supper to be served in his room and a bath to be put in the room next to his.

'Are you expecting your fiancée's party tonight, sir?' asks the landlord, remembering that's the reason Henri gave for needing three rooms.

'No, she will be coming later. I'm expecting Mr Jonas. He is a friend of mine.'

The landlord looks surprised. 'Do you mean the young gentleman with blue spectacles?'

'I do,' says Henri.

'I've heard he's unwell on account of his eyesight which results in blinding headaches.'

Henri hadn't heard this helpful piece of gossip.

'Indeed,' he says. 'Tonight he must rest. Hence the bath.' And with that he goes up the stairs two at a time, followed by Jetsam.

He hears the bath being filled and the chatter of the servants and when all is quiet he opens the interconnecting door. The bath is ready. He leaves the two packages on the bed with a note. *They are for you.*

He returns to his room and closes the door. Jetsam is whimpering softly. Henri is nervous – and not just slightly nervous. He has been to bed with numerous women but never once with a woman he was in love with. For a long time he had argued love didn't exist.

Jetsam barks. Neva must have entered the hotel. Henri knows the dog will whimper until he can be with her and he lets Jetsam into her room.

He hears her come up the stairs, Jetsam's wail of excitement, then her soft voice as she greets the dog.

The landlord follows her and asks if everything is to Mr Jonas's liking and Henri stays completely still, waiting to hear Neva's reply, but she says not a word. He hears her movements in the room and then there's silence.

At seven o'clock he's still waiting for her and now he's worried she's had a change of heart. If that is the case, he will say he understands.

The maid brings the supper: lamb chops, new potatoes, gooseberry pie. The champagne is on ice and still no Neva.

The minutes roll by and he convinces himself she will not come to him. Why would she come? She said something brave on the beach and time and the tide has washed it out to sea. In truth, he thinks, this is not the way a courtship should be. They should be married before doing this.

Twenty-past seven. Now he knows he's compromising her. And while he's at this low ebb the interconnecting door opens and she's there, her hair wet, the dressing gown loosely tied. He suspects she has nothing on underneath. That she can be this unabashed thrills him. He hands her a glass of champagne.

'Good evening to you,' she says and, in her fluent French, proceeds to talk to him in a language he hasn't used for years. 'I think love sounds much better in French. Do you miss France?'

Jetsam goes to his basket.

'Yes.' Henri feels he will have to close his eyes in order to stifle his desire for her. 'We had a beautiful château. Whether it is still standing I have no idea. My father tried to protect us but he didn't believe the French were capable of such brutality. He was proved wrong.'

Neva lifts the domes from the food. 'There's going to be a storm in an hour's time,' she says.

Henri looks out of the window. There's no sign of rain and he laughs. 'I laid bets on all your predictions, you know. Those and a night at the gambling tables made me a wealthy man. But I've never thanked you, although I thanked you in my heart every day I was at Oxford. How is it possible that you can tell the weather?'

'I don't know.'

They sit down to eat.

Neva's dressing gown loosens as she drinks the champagne. Henri can't take his eyes off her. He pours her another glass.

'What are you thinking?' she asks.

He swallows and says, 'About making love to you. And the thought is making me wild.'

There is no shock on her face, only a smile. 'You're very restrained for a wild man. And too well dressed and proper. Is anyone coming with more dishes?'

'No, I told them we would need nothing else.'

'Good, because I'm not hungry. I think it's the sitting and standing that is making our conversation so stilted. When I go cloud walking I lie down to study the clouds.' Neva takes a sip of her champagne. 'I think we should lie down, I think we would speak better if we were lying down.' She pauses. 'With no clothes on.'

Henri thinks he might have lost the power of speech altogether. Finally he finds his voice. He goes to her, she takes his hand and he kisses her gently on the lips.

'Is that... bearable?' he asks. Her eyes are closed.

'More than bearable,' she says and he kisses her neck.

'Stop,' she says.

He does. He pulls back.

'Oh no – nothing's wrong. It's just you are still dressed and we are standing up.'

'Would you take off your dressing gown?'

Biting her bottom lip she lets the gown fall and lies on the bed.

Slowly he undoes his cravat, unbuttons his shirt and his trousers and takes them off while she looks at him. He stands before her naked.

'When I was learning to be a boy,' she says, 'I was given home-made cock and balls to wear. They were leaded to give them weight and I was told the cock on a man went up and down. I couldn't think how. Now I know.'

Henri laughs and lies down beside her.

'It was a poor imitation of the real thing,' she says.

He kisses her again, his skin on hers, and she folds herself into him.

'Will it hurt?' she asks.

'A little,' he says. 'I will stop if it's unbearable.'

She kisses him, his tongue dancing in her mouth, his fingers gently caressing her skin. Down he goes, in between her legs, touching and kissing the softest parts of her until she moans and says, 'Wait...'

He stops. She rolls him onto his back and runs her fingers down him and round his cock. 'It's so beautiful. Far more pleasing than a home-made set.'

'I'm glad to hear it.'

'Is it all right if I kiss it?'

He nods.

With her lips on the tip of his cock he has to concentrate on holding himself back. She tastes him for the first time.

He has never been with a woman so innocently instinctive as she.

Now she sits on top of his legs and feels him hard between her thighs.

Breathless he asks, 'What are you going to do now, my lady?'

She leans forward and he kisses her while she guides the tip of his cock into her. The pleasure is exquisite, almost agonising. She sits up, the tip of him still inside her.

'Give me your hand,' she says and kisses his palm.

All he has to do is thrust once up into her and she would be fully his and he knows she would not be his at all. He feels as if time is standing still, waiting for her. He looks up into her face which has a quizzical expression as if she is trying to work out something that she hadn't known before.

'Yes,' she says to no question he has asked.

With her eyes closed, she kneels so as to be in a better position to take him, and she lets him go deeper inside her. The pleasure of this moment is beyond anything he has ever experienced, as she rises then goes down a little further until she is at the very hilt of him. She opens her eyes, amazed by the simplicity of an act that has given them both so much pleasure.

Startled, she says, 'What do I do now?'

The rain arrives just as she has her first orgasm. He sees her lose herself in it and having held back for as long as he can he too finds release. She holds him so tightly he cannot break free and he spills himself deep into her. He looks nervously at her as she unwinds herself from him. She's beginning to own her body, to understand the power of it.

'I never thought it would be as mystical as that,' she says. 'You go somewhere else while at the same time being present.'

'Did it hurt?'

'Yes, but not unpleasantly so. I throb where you've been.' She props herself up on her elbow. 'You're very good at it. Have you done it many, many times?'

'I have never before made love to you, so in that respect I was a virgin.' And he laughs.

'I thank all the ladies who taught you to make love to me so well,' she says. 'The trouble is, I don't think I could do without this now I've tried it. I want to learn more.'

'Does it mean you're going to run off with every man in London?' asks Henri.

'It means I'm going to be very demanding.'

'I can make love to you every day,' he says.

'Only once a day?' She smiles. 'I need you at least twice a day. Could we put that in the marriage contract?'

'Yes. Absolutely, yes,' he says.

They eat the gooseberry pie naked and then lie in bed. Henri takes out a little cheroot and lights it.

'Can I have one?' she asks.

'Certainly.'

She smokes it with one leg swung over the edge of the bed. He lies beside her; her hand is on his stomach.

'I wonder why such a fuss is made about something so natural,' she says.

'Because it isn't always a success between couples,' says Henri. 'Or because of beliefs and prudishness. Or because it's abused.'

'If I was buying a house,' says Neva, 'I would say this one is perfect for me.'

'Then marry me and the deeds of this house are yours.'

She is silent. The room is becoming dark and Henri gets up and lights the candles. Jetsam is curled up asleep.

'How do you do it?' he asks. 'Tell the weather, I mean.'

'I walk the clouds.'

'Is that hard to do?'

'When I was little I thought everybody could do it.' Neva runs her fingers down to below his navel. 'What happened to you after the storm?'

Henri is lying on his back looking up at the canopy of the four-poster bed with its folded fabric that neatly pleats itself into a button, and against his will his memory conjures up fractured images. Avoiding her question, he says, 'I tried to save a woman, a Mrs O'Donnell, but I didn't succeed. Everybody drowned but me.' He closes his eyes. 'I think it was when I was in the sea that I realised you were Eugene Jonas but after that my memory was lost in a fog of illness. When I could remember I found it too horrific to think about. All the sailors – their families, the children who will never have a father.' He says this and he feels a knot in his chest and gasps for breath. 'I'm sorry,' he says, embarrassed to find himself suddenly crying. He hasn't cried for such a long, long time. The ferociousness of the tears shocks him.

She doesn't say any of the unhelpful things other people have said to him, but curls herself into him and silently rocks him until he is quiet.

'Your colours are blues with soft purples that bleed into red,' she says. 'Colours of sorrow.' He has wet her face with his tears.

She gets up, goes into the adjoining room and comes back with a facecloth. She washes his face.

He says, 'There's another sea no one talks about, the sea of sorrow. It's filled with the tears of those who mourn the drowned. It's so salty no one can sink in it; they just float on its unbearable surface.'

'What colour is its sky?' she asks.

'Yellow.'

She lies down next to him and puts the amber pebble on his chest. It is cool.

'I was worried you might have found someone else,' he says.

'There's no one else I love,' she says. 'I have loved you since I first saw you. I will always love you.'

'I don't know why you do.'

Her face serious, she asks, 'Do you think me mad?'

'For loving me? Yes. But no, you're unique. You're unlike anyone else I've ever met. That is something to celebrate.'

'I think I was born into the wrong age,' she says. 'I don't even have the right body for today's fashions.'

'You, my love, have the perfect figure.'

'Near flat-chested, with a boyish look?'

'Wrong,' he says with a deep, passionate kiss. 'You are the most desirable woman I have ever made love to.'

'Or the most desirable boy?'

'The only boy. I love the way you are made – you have perfect breasts.'

'What if I grow a big bosom and become fat?'

'Then,' he says, gathering her to him, 'I will love every extra pound of you.'

He is hard again. She bites her bottom lip.

'You're not too sore?'

'Oh no,' she says, 'let's go cloud walking.'

'You think it's possible to take me?'

'You must let your mind jump over the fence of all you believed impossible.'

'Such as loving you...'

'No, you ninny, that was never impossible. But perhaps such as believing you had a right to survive.' She kisses him. 'Let's try by making love.'

He is inside her. The deliciousness of this he relishes.

She whispers, 'Let go.' In the heat of their passion, she says, 'Come with me, come with me.'

He is with her. Their love-making rolls to the rhythm of the thunder and for one infinitesimal moment he catches a glimpse of what is possible in a world flooded with colours and clouds. It takes his breath away. She cries out and he explodes into the infinity of her.

44

Henri opens the door to his chamber and two maids nearly fall on top of him.

'We were sent up to see if you want breakfast, sir,' said one of them.

'I could eat a good breakfast,' says Eugene Jonas, standing behind them on the landing, buttoning his waistcoat. 'With coffee.'

'The same,' says Henri and the maids go down the stairs, giggling. 'That shows us we should leave tomorrow, before any more maids fall in love with you.'

They strip the sheet from the bed and put the evidence of their love-making at the bottom of Henri's valise. He produces the replacement he'd bought at the draper's shop a day earlier.

'What foresight, sir,' says Neva.

Henri is serious. 'We have to be scrupulously careful not to leave any evidence that might compromise you, my love.' He puts on his linen coat and says, 'If ever it becomes known that you are Eugene Jonas, all hope of securing your inheritance will be lost.'

It is a day of a perfect blue sky. If summer could be bottled, she thinks, this would be the day to do the bottling. They set off with a picnic in no particular direction, following Jetsam who seems content to wander down unfrequented paths. They find themselves deep in woodland, well away from the sea. The sun is high and in this hazy light there stands a stone-built house with tall windows, grown over with ivy. They think the house is occupied until they come across a walled garden left to the butterflies. Raspberry bushes and rhubarb have grown wild, and thistledown blows in the breeze across a garden of majestic weeds. It was sunshine catching the glass in the windowpanes that had made them think the place was occupied. They walk around as if it is a puzzle to be solved. Henri tries the front door and to his surprise it opens. It's cool inside the beautifully panelled hall. In the ballroom a chandelier, festooned with cobwebs, reflects the light from the elegant windows, sending sparkles round the room.

'Will you dance?' says Henri.

Neva bows, then laughs and curtsies. 'Wait,' she says, takes off her jacket, pulls out her shirt, and they dance, whirling up the dust while Jetsam watches them.

'It isn't haunted,' says Henri.

'How do you know?' asks Neva.

'I've always known when places are haunted.'

They walk carefully up the stairs to find there are still pieces of furniture: the frame of a four-poster bed, mismatched chairs, a child's rocking horse, and scattered pages covered with illegible writing. In one room, Neva finds, standing on a table, a broken ship that had once been in a bottle, the glass now lying shattered on the bare wooden floor. Henri opens one of the shutters and looks out. Down past what once were lawns is a pond.

They sit at the foot of the marble stairs in the hall and have their picnic.

'What would you say happened here?' asks Neva.

'Dice. Or cards,' says Henri. 'Let's swim. There's no one about.'

That same day, at the same time in the house in the lane off Tooley Street, Cassie is alone. Elise is dining with Mrs Dent and George has gone downriver to see Mr James for Neva soon will need another haircut. There is nothing for Cassie to do but daydream about Bos.

The bell rings at the garden gate. She is in two minds about answering it, fearful the visitor might be Aubrey Friezland, but she calls out, 'Hallo, who's there?'

'Cassie? It's me.'

And she feels as she opens the gate that she's conjured Bos from her imagination. But there he is, looking down at his shoes, stumbling over his words, hardly daring to look at her.

What does it matter if this man standing before her will never marry her? She loves him, has loved him for so long she can hardly hear what he is saying.

'I've lived in fear all these months that you would be married by now. But Henri told me you still care for me. Cassie, I want us to be wed, as soon as I'm free.'

She smiles at him. 'I don't think a woman who once was a lady's maid can marry a marquess.'

He looks up from his shoes. 'I don't give a damn about all that. I want to be with you. I was going to ask Mrs Friezland if she would give me permission.'

'I don't need anyone's permission,' says Cassie. 'My answer is "yes".'

'You will marry me? Really? Oh, are you sure? You don't need time to consider? May I kiss you?'

'Oh, yes.'

It is such a deep kiss, filled with longing, and he is surprised that she is equally passionate, although Cassie finds she doesn't quite know what to do, where to put her hands. He kisses her again, pressing her to him, and she can feel his arousal.

'I'm sorry,' says Bos, stepping back a little. 'I was carried away.'

And Cassie, mistaking his meaning, says, 'It doesn't matter – I wouldn't hold you to marrying me.'

'No, no,' he says. 'Carried away with my kisses. Kitty always said I overdid everything.'

'Your kisses make me want more, but more of what, I don't know. I only once saw a... a man,' she says, 'when I was a lady's maid. The master came up to our room and...'

'You were that maid? Who he laid a bet on?'

'He didn't win the bet and if it hadn't happened I wouldn't have met Victor Friezland and I wouldn't have met you.'

He takes from his pocket a little box. 'Miss Cassandra Lamb, will you do me the great honour of becoming my wife?'

'Yes... Lord Smedmore... with all my heart.' But when he opens the little box she says, 'No!'

'You don't like it?'

'It's the biggest bloody diamond I've ever seen.'

'It belonged to my great-grandmother. She was an actress and my great-grandfather watched her perform every night. He said there wasn't a diamond worthy of her and then this was brought to him.' He puts the ring on her finger. 'We will have to wait until I'm out of mourning.'

'Yes, I know. But what will the duke say?'

'Can I swear? Will you be very shocked if I do?'

'No, Bos,' she says, laughing.

'Fuck the duke.'

★★★

Jetsam is in the pond before Henri and Neva have reached it. They swim then lie on the grass in the sun.

Henri says, 'Last night when we made love, I caught a glimpse of how you saw the clouds.'

'For a moment,' she says, her eyes closed, 'you were with me.'

It's impossible, he thinks, it's a metaphor for their love-making.

'We could be from another century, lying here without our clothes.'

He runs his fingers down her spine and kisses her bottom. 'Which century would you choose?'

'The future. But in one way it will be no better for the clouds will lose their colours.'

'That's how you see them? Are the clouds more colourful to you than to me?'

She rolls over. 'They're patterned as well. It's why I love being up there.'

'Do you walk on them?'

'Yes,' she says.

'Take me again.'

He kisses her – down, down, down.

As they walk back to Hastings the sun is setting.

Henri asks, 'Do you want to go back to London tomorrow?'

'No, I don't want our time together to end.'

'Neither do I.'

He finds a thin twig from which he fashions a ring.

He takes her hand, kisses her fingers and says, 'With this ring I promise to be truthful to you in all I say and do. With my body I thee worship – and I will make love to you every day as much as you wish.' He puts it on her ring finger.

'If we weren't both dressed as gentlemen, I would kiss you,' she says.

Jetsam looks up hopefully at a passing cart and Henri stops the driver and asks if he would take them to Hastings. They sit apart, and as the house disappears Neva thinks about the ballroom and their steps left in the dust, about the tall grass by the lake which carries an imprint of where they lay together.

Henri asks the driver about the house.

'It belonged to a sea captain, sir. It was just finished when he went and lost the whole lot, they say, on the roll of the dice.'

As soon as they are back in Hastings, Henri says he has to go out for short while.

'What are you up to?' she says, half-suspecting.

'Wait and see,' he says.

He returns for supper looking extremely pleased with himself.

'In less than a week, my lady, we will be married.'

'Where?'

'Can you bear a surprise?'

'Oh, yes.'

That night Henri beats her at chess.

'You only won because I was distracted by a mixture of desire and curiosity,' she says.

'I fear that might be true,' he says and takes her to bed. 'This afternoon I wasn't in the clouds, was I?'

'No,' she says, kissing him. 'You were lost in the waves.'

In the slowness of their love-making, in the depth of his cry, in the shadow of a tear, in the strength of her being she raises him out of the sea of sorrow.

45

Not far from the Old Bailey, down a muddle of lanes, live Aubrey and Lord Wardell. They have taken rooms above a second-hand clothes shop and the owner is pleased to have such a well-spoken, trustworthy gentleman living above her premises. The last vestige of Lord Wardell's aristocratic background is his voice. It has traces of the silver spoon in every vowel. Such a refined voice is rarely heard in these streets and definitely not in her shop. She has a daughter, a plain, dull little creature whose one ambition is to be an actress. Her mother is certain that if her voice sounded less like a market stallholder's, she might well stand a chance of starring on the stage.

In lieu of rent, Lord Wardell offers to give her daughter lessons, guaranteeing these will turn the girl into an actress. He claims to have brought about many such transformations.

What he enjoys most about the lessons are the cake and Madeira wine the mother leaves out for him. In turn she deeply respects the fact he has never laid a hand on her precious little girl. Lord Wardell thinks the child has less talent than a dishcloth and for his entertainment he has her read Shakespeare to him. She stumbles over every word and it makes him laugh out loud.

'Excellent,' he says, wiping tears from his eyes, 'excellent.'

'What's so funny?' asks Aubrey.

'The butchery of the Bard, my dear,' says Lord Wardell. 'And the child reads it all without one ounce of grammar.' Aubrey finds it impressive that she can read at all and he remembers when he too was in awe of the way Wardell spoke. Now he hates the sound of his voice even more than he hates the man himself.

How dare he talk of Victor Friezland the way he does; his father, one of the greatest automaton makers of all time, his father, who invented the Weather Woman?

Aubrey has recently been thinking. Thinking and walking. He has walked down to Limehouse where he met a Chinese gentleman selling dreams in a pipe. And there in this enchanted castle Aubrey has seen her again in his mind's eye. The Weather Woman. 'Your freedom lies with me,' she says to him and in her soft, calm voice there is redemption. With the opium pipe comes a stillness in his head; all the chatter stops and that in itself is a miracle. He knows what he's going to do. He has never felt love for anyone; what does it matter if she is made of wood, he has had enough of flesh. She whispers to him about the future. He hears her and now Aubrey knows how to rid himself of Wardell: he places a bet on a fish.

Wardell misses his past life, feels bereft of money, of culture, of society. If he had known it would come to this, he would have taken better care of his finances. But then perhaps he wouldn't. He hopes, once Aubrey has secured his inheritance, that he will be free to start over again. The first change he will make after putting Victor Friezland's daughter into an asylum will be to extricate himself from Aubrey. That shouldn't be difficult. Just a little too much laudanum one night.

Then he will make his wife pay for her dalliance and for forgetting him so easily. In the meantime, he is grateful for Aubrey. He feels he can read him like a weathervane. All that needles him is the swallowing of the fish. It is four weeks away, but once that is done the rest of his plans will fall into place.

It irritates Lord Wardell that no matter how many times he repeats himself Aubrey doesn't do as instructed, for example when they went to the Friezland house. He had expressly told Aubrey what to say, that he should be just a little menacing, hinting only at the possibility of Miss Friezland being committed to an asylum. But no, he had drawn his knife and shouted at her. The most aggravating part of the whole affair had been the arrival of his nephew, Henri Dênou. He had hoped the war would keep him in America and the fact he was there in the garden with Neva worries him greatly.

'Why?' asks Aubrey, childishly.

'Because if my nephew marries Miss Friezland, we have a problem.'

'Why?'

'Because no one has the right to put another man's wife in a madhouse, my dear ignoramus.' He doubts Aubrey will understand the meaning of that word and he is right.

But Aubrey says, 'I never thought it was the brightest idea in the first place.'

Wardell is astounded. 'You didn't?'

'No. You see, I've a better one.'

'Would you share your wisdom with me, my dear Beelzebub?'

From below, the shopkeeper calls up to them. 'I'm shutting up now. Goodnight, your lordship, Mr Friezland.'

'You have a better plan?' says Lord Wardell with a certain amount of cynicism.

'Oh, I have,' says Aubrey. 'In case you're looking for it, I used all our money to place a bet.'

This takes Lord Wardell's breath away. 'What do you mean?'

'It's quite simple, Wardell. "I used" – you understand that part?'

'Of course I do.'

'Good. "All our money"...'

'What?'

'"What" belongs with "Why",' says Aubrey.

'So now we have no money at all?'

'None,' says Aubrey. 'None. Or rather you have none until you swallow the fish.'

Aubrey picks up his hat, dusts it off and places it on his head at a greyhound angle. Whistling – a habit Lord Wardell cannot abide – he leaves, closing the door to their rooms. Lord Wardell hears him trotting down the stairs then all is silent. Just when he thinks Aubrey has gone, the door flies open.

'No one,' Aubrey says, pinning Wardell against the wall, 'talks to Beelzebub as if he was a child, and no one calls Beelzebub an ignoramus. No one.'

The shop is empty and Wardell's cries go unheard. When Aubrey leaves an hour later, he says, 'You made me do that.'

Lord Wardell is chained to the bed. Church bells ring midnight over the city, a drunken man in the street shouts out, a woman screams, then all is quiet. Lord Wardell wonders if the devil is going to come back, and if he doesn't, he will have to wait for the shopkeeper to open up and face the humiliation of being found naked and in chains.

Three o'clock in the morning and he is alive to every noise, the mice behind the skirting boards, the cockroaches scampering across the floor. At last a thin, rainy light shines through the shutters. The watchman has called, 'Four in the morning and all is well.' A new day is dawning. Lord Wardell has never felt this wretched. Then there is a sound on the stairs, a slow thump-thump.

Aubrey is carrying something heavy. It has taken some manoeuvring to get it up the stairs. The door opens. He is as pale as moonlight and has a smile on his face. At his feet is what looks like a child's body wrapped in cloth.

'Oh God, what have you done?' says Lord Wardell. For a moment he sees the shopkeeper's daughter. Would he put murder past Aubrey? No, he wouldn't.

'I went and took what is mine,' Aubrey says. Carefully, he sits the body on a chair and wordlessly removes the layers of cloth.

Wardell wishes he could put his hands in front of his eyes. It's the calm side of Aubrey that Lord Wardell finds the most concerning and this silence concerns him deeply.

Aubrey, intent on the job before him, takes no notice. In the cool light of a summer morning he unwraps Victor Friezland's greatest creation, the Weather Woman. The wooden doll's serene face stares back at him.

Aubrey sits on the bed next to Wardell and says, 'I've never been fond of all those long words of yours. They go nowhere, they're meaningless. This silent woman is the future, this quiet whisperer of the sky says more to me than you ever have. She speaks of love.'

'Are you going to unchain me?'

'Why did you buy the arsenic?'

A week later, Lord Wardell is feeling sufficiently himself. Aubrey has been relatively kind since the arrival of the Weather Woman.

Seeing the childish look on Aubrey's face as he gazes into the glass eyes of the Weather Woman reminds Lord Wardell of the day he and Palmore went to the frost fair on the Thames. Their pockets were full of gold and they played for twenty guineas each against an old fleabag of an automaton, the chess-playing bear. A detail of that memory comes back to him. When Palmore had lost and Wardell sat in front of the bear to play he'd caught a glimpse of a child whose ebony eyes looked straight through him. Why should he think of it now when so many other things had happened and that day is nearly rubbed out in his memory?

Now he says – instantly regretting that the words have so easily slipped from him – 'Of course the Weather Woman won't work without Victor Friezland, or his daughter.' He holds his breath.

'No,' Aubrey says. 'Neither of them. The person I need is Eugene Jonas. Only he knew how to talk to the Weather Woman, though every day she tells me more and more. Soon, she tells me, we'll be ready. In fact, the moment after you've swallowed the fish.'

'How so?'

'"How, why, what,"' Aubrey laughs. 'Because then I'll have the whole machine. The clockwork is delicate and I left it where it will be safe until I have the money to buy it.'

There is no point asking what he means and for the first time Lord Wardell knows he is truly frightened of Aubrey.

The sea is wide, the sea is vast.

Out in the Atlantic, the herring has made the long migration of over twelve hundred miles from the feeding grounds to the spawning grounds, just as it has every year of its life. At present it is off Dogger Bank. The summer is drawing in and September will find it in the shallow waters of the east coast of England.

In Hastings a fisherman has agreed to a challenge laid

down by a coachman from London. On 13th September the coachman will return. He requires a fish of a certain size; it must be alive and the fisherman must accompany it to London. If the fish is still alive, the man will receive one hundred guineas.

'London,' repeats the fisherman. One hundred guineas is enough, he thinks, to put some of the past right.

46

For the following five days Neva only sees Henri in the evenings. She doesn't ask why he is so occupied and her lack of curiosity fascinates him. He tells her he has never met a woman who didn't have a thousand questions about where he has been or what he has been doing.

Neva says, 'If we don't trust each other then we shouldn't be married.'

Eugene Jonas goes to the library, reads, and sits watching the sea and drinking coffee. Neva has given up hope of finding the entry she was searching for in the marriage registers and instead enjoys the time on her own, knowing what the evening will bring. She wonders at her own happiness.

In a shop on George Street she buys a notebook, some pens and coloured inks, and begins to write down what the skies are telling her about the coming winter. But her freedom is curtailed thanks to Mrs Bickerton's inventive mind. She has cast both Mr Dênou and Mr Jonas in the roles of French spies.

Henri wonders if it would be advisable for Neva to stay in their rooms as it appears that most of the town is gossiping about them.

'No,' says Neva. 'Eugene Jonas is not so easily defeated.'

On the third day Mr Jonas goes to the Crown Hotel where Mrs Bickerton is holding her weekly coffee morning, a perfect meeting place for Mrs Bickerton's small mind and extensive imagination to take its daily constitutional.

She is in the middle of recounting what she had seen yesterday '… and I ask you,' she is saying, 'what is it that Mr Jonas is writing in that book of his?' when this most interesting topic of conversation appears before her.

'Good morning, Mrs Bickerton,' say Mr Jonas, bowing. 'I have listened to your slanderous allegations quite long enough. You have ruined my stay here and your persecution of me has caused the headaches I suffer from to increase. I came down to Hastings to take the sea air for my health and I have had to deal with your ridiculous accusations that I am a spy. Unless you retract them and send me a formal apology, you will be hearing from my solicitor, Mr Gutteridge of Lincoln's Inn, for I will not hesitate to bring charges against you for defamation of character. I trust I make myself clear.'

Mrs Bickerton withdraws into her wingback chair, shaking. Even the coffee cups shudder.

'No one has ever spoken to me in such a manner, sir,' she says, placing both hands on her heart.

'More's the pity,' says Mr Jonas. 'I recommend that you write the letter and that you learn that you cannot go around slandering people for your own amusement. Good day to you, madam.'

'What does a wife do?' Neva asks Henri on the eve of their wedding. 'I'm not good at small talk or pretending I'm only interested in embroidery.' She brightens and says, 'Though I am becoming more convinced of the power of a well-designed gown.'

'Just be you,' says Henri. 'You are all I want. And the rest we'll work out between us.'

The following morning, Henri's carriage arrives at the Swan bringing with it a parcel from Brighton.

'I don't think you can be married in trousers,' Henri says as she unwraps it. Inside is a simple muslin gown embroidered with hundreds of wild meadow flowers which seem to fall from the bodice onto the skirt. It's the most wonderful gown she has ever seen. She hangs it up and it looks like a butterfly, almost too delicate to wear.

'Who made this?' she asks.

'I have to admit that I wrote to consult my tailor and he recommended a dressmaker in Brighton. I told her it was to be a gown a wood nymph might wear to be married in.'

'You will have to help me into it.'

'With pleasure, my lady.'

When he has finished, Neva looks at herself in the mirror and is silent for a long time.

'My reflection keeps on surprising me,' she says at last.

'Don't you like it?'

'I do, I do, it's just... it's me, it's Neva. I'm here and there is no Eugene Jonas waiting to take centre stage.' She puts her arms round him. 'Am I really going to marry you today?'

'I hope so, Neva Friezland.'

'Are we coming back here after the wedding?'

'Wait and see.'

If anyone bothers to look closely at Mr Jonas as he leaves the Swan in Mr Dênou's carriage that morning, they might catch a glimpse of muslin under the long linen coat. But his hat and his famous blue spectacles lead Mrs Bickerton to pronounce that indeed it was Mr Jonas and she only hopes he has received her letter.

The carriage starts moving accompanied by the screeching of seagulls, and once it is on the road to St Leonard's, Neva feels safe enough to take off her spectacles and her hat. She runs her fingers through her short hair and, resting her head on the edge of the carriage window, she looks out onto a still, grey sea that the day has yet to turn blue.

'Neva Dênou.' She says it over and over again and decides it has a nicer ring to it than Neva Friezland.

Who was that foolish young girl who said she would never fall in love, she wonders, and laughs as she thinks of it. Could it possibly have been her? In the rolling of the wheels and in the jingling of the bridle she hears Henri's name.

'Papa,' she says quietly, 'I am marrying him.'

She lets down the leather strap on the window and, having torn the letter to pieces, she lets the wind carry away Mrs Bickerton's profuse apologies.

The carriage has gone some little way and Neva is wondering if they are going to London when they turn off onto a small country lane that she recognises. It leads to St Leonard's Church. She had walked there hoping to see the marriage register.

The church is set in ancient woodlands where the late-rising sun gives an early morning yawn of light that dances among the shadows of the trees and over the tops of the gravestones. There being no sign of the vicar or the groom, Neva, still wearing Eugene's boots, goes in search of wild flowers.

Her only regret is that Elise will be sad not to see her wed, Cassie perhaps even more so. But if she married in London there would be such a fuss, something neither Henri nor she would like.

The timeless silence is broken only by the hurly-burly of birds, the horses snorting and the occasional rattling of their harnesses. She changes into her slippers and takes off her linen coat. Just when it feels as if the clock will never strike another hour there come the sound of wheels and the clip-clop of horse's hooves. A country trap arrives, driven by the vicar with his wife beside him and their maid in the back.

'My word,' says the vicar, 'what an exceedingly lovely bride you are, Miss Friezland. Exceedingly lovely.' He turns to his wife. 'Wouldn't you agree my dear?'

'I've never seen such a gown before,' says the vicar's wife. 'And your hair, Miss Friezland, such an original style.'

The maid sniffs into a handkerchief.

'Weddings always make her cry,' says the vicar.

The gravedigger turns up for work and, taking off his hat, bows to Neva saying he will willingly be another witness if needed and all agree it would be most useful. The vicar ushers his wife, the maid and the gravedigger into the church then returns to the porch. He is telling Neva about the church being in the Domesday Book when coming down the lane they see a small man clutching sheet music under one arm and holding onto his hat with his other hand.

'I'm late,' he calls.

The vicar is surprised to see the organist.

'But the organ is out of tune,' protests the vicar.

'It was yesterday, but I spent the day making sure it was in tune for the wedding this morning.'

'And who paid for this extravaganza?' asks the vicar.

'The gentleman who is to be married,' says the organist.

'A miracle,' says the vicar.

And now Jetsam is bounding down the lane towards her, with a bell and flowers in his collar, and behind him is Henri, elegantly dressed and handsome.

Neva thinks, this is who I'm going to marry. This beautiful man.

The vicar greets him. 'A special licence, Mr Dênou. You don't see many of these outside London.'

Half an hour later, Henri and Neva are married, the register signed and with heartfelt thanks on one side and good wishes on the other the couple and Jetsam climb into the carriage. It's only after they've gone a few miles and Neva is still amazed by the wedding ring on her finger, in the shape of the twig ring Henry had made for her, that she looks up. The carriage is pulling into the driveway where five days ago they had found the deserted house. Now it appears less abandoned. The carriage stops at the front door and the coachman unloads the trunks Neva had not noticed were strapped on the back of the carriage. As soon as they are stacked in the hall, the coachman turns the carriage round with a cheery salute and it disappears down the drive.

Henri watches Neva explore the house which in the space of five days has been transformed. The glass has been swept up, the broken ship rests on a mantelpiece, the wooden floors are gleaming in the sunlight. The ballroom and its chandelier have been cleaned, the windows have been washed and everything has lost its layer of neglect.

Upstairs the four-poster bed, minus the bed curtains, now has a mattress and has been made up with new linen. A large vase of flowers stands by the fireplace. Otherwise, the chamber is empty.

'What did the owners say about you taking the house?' says Neva.

'They were pleased,' said Henri, bringing two glasses and a bottle of champagne. 'I put in an offer to buy it.'

'Buy it?'

'It's my wedding present to you. I hope it meets with your approval.'

'You bought this for me?'

'I didn't buy it for Jetsam,' says Henri. 'Though he does seem to like it here. I've had all the provisions we might need delivered.'

'And no servants?' asks Neva.

'I thought we could do for ourselves. Is that to your liking?'

'Yes. There really is no one else here?'

He lifts her up and carries her to bed.

Later they take a picnic basket down a steep, stony path that leads through the woods to the sea. The tide being out and no one around, Neva takes off her gown – a much simpler one than the wedding dress – and naked she wades in. Turning, she sees Henri watching her and goes back to him.

'Come,' she says. 'The sea's calm. Make your peace with it on our wedding day.'

Reluctantly he takes her hand. They swim and he begins to rediscover the joy of being in the water. He catches her and holds her tight.

'You're a water nymph,' he says.

'I'm Neva.'

Neither bother to dress and they search for shells among the pebbles.

Outside the window of the bedchamber is an oak tree in full leaf and in the darkness of a midnight blue sky it appears to them that the stars have nestled in the leaves.

'The clouds all have names,' says Henri.

'And each of them has a message,' says Neva.

'Tell me what you see, how you see them.'

'I see you.'

Henri doesn't ask her again.

He teaches her how to waltz and in the evening he lights all the candles in the chandelier and they dance in the ballroom. They cook simple meals which they eat outside, they go on long walks and talk half the night away and still Henri's question remains unanswered.

She writes in her notebook and Henri marvels at the beauty of her drawings of the clouds.

'They look like fishermen's nets in the sky,' he says and tries the question again. 'Is this how you see the clouds?'

There's no answer and he leaves it.

On a hot night when the flowers have died and the petals lie scattered on the wooden floor of their bedchamber, she says, 'You're interested in science and accurate observations. What I do doesn't come into that. I tried to explain it to Papa. I think it worried him and I left out the main part. I knew he would have preferred that my gift, as he called it, went away. He never said so.'

'What is the main part?' asks Henri.

She begins to pick her fingers and he takes hold of her hands. 'Tomorrow,' she says. 'Tomorrow.'

But tomorrow the weather is too warm, the grass is grown dry, the thistledown floats across the garden, and it's too hot to be bothered with answers.

A gale blows up; they have gone to bed and lie listening to the wind as it whistles through the house. Outside the oak leaves rustle and the moon makes momentary appearances from behind the clouds. All the candles in the chamber flicker in the draught.

Henri asks her, 'How did you know exactly when the gale would start and, more importantly, how strong it would be?'

The darkness is the perfect cover for a difficult answer.

'There was a frost fair on the Thames when I was small. I remember I could hear the ice singing. I knew it was melting. I can remember so little about being small, but I do remember the sound – the high-pitched song of the ice. I couldn't understand why no one else heard it. But they didn't. Since then I have always heard the weather. Sometimes in London it's harder due to the noise and the dirt that goes into the sky and muffles the sound. When that happens, I rely on clouds. But they don't look the same to me as they do to you.'

'Can you explain that?'

'You are interested in meteorology, you're a mathematician. What I'm now about to tell you cannot be proved right or wrong by science. I now understand what I do belongs to a world no educated man recognises. I could well be seen as insane. I knew this even when I was a child. I know how you and others see the sky and the clouds by the paintings in the Royal Academy. But that's not how I see them. To me the clouds have many layers and I can see the patterns where they have joined to other clouds. Even small clouds carry messages. And none of this is what anyone in science is interested in. I can't understand why no one can predict the weather. Auntie and Papa were worried I would be seen as a freak. Have I frightened you?'

'No, far from it. You are a visionary. I don't think you should hide, I don't think your way of seeing the sky should be dismissed. You are the only person I know who accurately predicts the weather.'

'There will be thunder.'

'You hear it?'

'Yes.'

'It must be noisy, hearing so much weather.'

She nods. 'I think you do understand. That alone is enough of a reason to have married you.'

'Any others?'

'Oh yes,' she says and kisses him.

She lies in his arms. 'Can you hear that?'

'No. What?'

'Thunder. It's summer saying farewell.'

47

September 1813

The tide is pulling the shoal of herrings away into deeper waters. A harvest moon hangs heavy, pregnant with the summer light in its luminous belly. Unable to take up its throne in the night sky, it sits on the horizon as the waves argue with the shore. Under the dark waters the herring has reached its prime. It's been feeding off plankton and now it's not far below the surface. It was nearly caught once. It breaks away from the shoal to greet the lord of all tides, the great fish eye of the night sky. It is about to depart with the current for wilder seas when it catches a glint of a sprat. Just one more and it will join the ribbon of herrings.

Too late. The vast world of seas drains away as the herring is hauled from the water, its breath stolen.

The herring is alone in a tomb, swimming back and forth, bubbles churning the water in the darkness. This, the herring knows, is the end, but in every silver fin and scale, its instinct is to fight for life.

The tomb, the tank, has been specially constructed for the purpose of keeping the herring alive. It is strong enough to contain seawater and a pump worked by hand to keep the water oxygenated. The fisherman who caught the herring has also caught live shrimps and sprats to feed it on during the journey. If all goes to plan and the fish arrives alive, in good condition, the fisherman is guaranteed to receive one hundred guineas. A catch has never been this valuable.

The fisherman is unaware of the amount of money still being taken in bets on tonight's entertainment.

In his opium-soaked mind, Aubrey sees the future. The Weather Woman sits before him in all her splendour, speaking to him, telling him how his fortune might be made.

'Yes,' he says, as she comes near, her arms out to embrace him. 'My love,' he says. Her words whisper of an icy winter to come.

'Get up.' It is Wardell, prodding him sharply with his silver-topped cane. 'Get up.'

And Aubrey finds himself dragged from the castle of dreams. A slap wakes him further.

'Do you know what day it is?' he says. 'Look at you, look at you. I am to swallow a fish to save you from the debtors' prison and where are you?' Aubrey doesn't reply. 'I've been searching the dens of this Godawful place to find you and I am hiring a waterman at vast expense to take us to Black Lion Stairs.' Aubrey isn't walking, he is floating. 'If we don't hurry we will be late. And the sooner this is over...'

Wardell's words strike Aubrey and in them he hears the leaden weight of reality. He is surprised to find he hasn't yet said a word. In his head there is peace, there are no voices to drive him crazy.

The air is full of autumn and the nights are getting colder. The Thames, which in August stank as bad as smelling salts, now smells sweeter. Wardell and Aubrey are sitting beside each other on the ferry. Aubrey's fingers find Wardell's hand and he's glad there's no resistance. For once they're quiet in each other's company and Wardell turns to say something but stops.

At Covent Garden Aubrey says, 'We're early now. Always advisable to be a bit late.'

'For old time's sake, shall we call on Mrs Phipps?' suggests Wardell.

The place is empty. 'Where is everybody?' asks Aubrey.

'All gone to bet on some blithering fool who says he can swallow a live fish,' says Mrs Phipps. 'Whoever he is, he's a first rate idiot.'

'It's Wardell,' says Aubrey.

'You are joking,' she says and looks over to where Wardell sits. He's a sorry sight, his clothes much the worse for wear. He still has his ring and that silver-topped cane, she notices.

'I wonder if we could have a room,' says Aubrey.

'You can have a room, love, and a bottle of my second-best champagne. He'll need it. I'm going to shut up shop and put a bet on a fish supper.' She heaves herself out of her chair and lumbers away. 'Won't be long,' she calls back.

Aubrey takes two glasses and the bottle and leads Wardell up the stairs. 'I thought you'd like some privacy,' he says, as he closes the door.

Lord Wardell puts his hand on Aubrey's cheek and kisses him.

'What would you like,' says Aubrey, 'if we could be kind and not revolted by each other?'

Wardell's eyes fill with tears. 'For you to make love to me and it to mean something that isn't hate.'

'Sweet lady, drink up,' says Aubrey.

Lord Wardell and Aubrey are now late. A crowd of people is

standing in the street outside Mr Jobe's Boxing Club and so many men are trying to push or bribe their way in, it's nearly impossible to reach the door.

'Wardell, wait,' says Aubrey, but Wardell isn't listening. His commanding voice booms out and brings silence.

'Let me pass. I am the man who's here to swallow the fish — so let me pass.'

Aubrey doesn't like this, it's not what he's imagined. When it was first proposed, things were different, he'd had enough of Wardell, would willingly have seen him dead. But tonight there was redemption in their loving.

Inside, the place is packed. A gallery runs round the wooden walls high above the boxing ring. There stand the barons and dukes whose houses Aubrey knows better than he should. They are all searching the crowd for Wardell. Aubrey can see shadowy figures on the building opposite, staring in through the glass roof. Gentlemen from all walks of life push and jostle round the ring to get a better view of the proceedings.

Now a sense of dread fills Aubrey. With Wardell at Mrs Phipps's, he'd experienced something new. He's unsure what to call it; some might call it love, a tenderness filled with hope. He thinks if they get out of this place they could go somewhere else, Liverpool perhaps. He's jostled aside and momentarily loses sight of Wardell. Then he sees him, too far off to catch hold of. He wants to tell him he regrets ever thinking this was a good idea. But the noise of the chatter in this cavernous building is deafening, worse than a battlefield.

The atmosphere is tense with the anticipation of the lost lord's reappearance. It's hard to believe that after all these years he will finally show himself. Aubrey is desperate to reach him, for a thought comes to him, as deep as a well and just as dark: Wardell is his sanity.

'There!' shouts someone from the gallery.

'That's him,' shouts another.

Sir Richard Palmore has put up the money to rent the club for one evening. He had never imagined so many people; the arrangement was for secrecy and he can see perfectly well the situation is out of control.

'Where is he then?' asks Mr Jobe, a big, bald man whose clothes barely contain him. In his day he was a champion boxer.

'I thought I made it clear this was not a public event,' says Sir Richard. He can feel the perspiration on the back of his neck.

Mr Jobe laughs. 'You expect me to turn away all these paying customers?'

Mr Jobe is a head taller than Sir Richard and looks as if he could crush his skull between his fists. 'He'd better show up, sir, that's all I'm saying, because everyone is impatient for it to start.'

Sir Richard is becoming fearful Wardell and his friend are not going to show, when Aubrey takes him by surprise.

'This isn't what we agreed,' says Aubrey.

'Mr Friezland,' says Sir Richard. 'Where is Wardell?'

'There's no end of gambling going on in the street and in the pub across the road – all betting on the fish,' says Aubrey. 'I'm telling Wardell he's not doing this.'

Sir Richard anticipated there might be a problem when Aubrey saw the size of the fish, not when he saw the size of the crowd.

Sir Richard looks over his shoulder and nods to a heavily built man who moves slowly towards Aubrey. Then to his relief he sees Wardell. He is shocked by his old friend's appearance. He remembers when they were young with guineas in their pockets and the best tailor in London. How has he been brought so low, this man of breeding, of education, who once possessed superb taste, who is now in the company of a weasel?

'Good evening, Wardell,' says Sir Richard.

Aubery sees Wardell being pulled back into a past long gone.

'This way, sir,' says Mr Jobe as he lifts the ropes of the ring.

But Aubrey takes hold of Wardell's frockcoat.

'Let's go,' he whispers. 'Let's get out of here.'

'No,' says Wardell, patting him gently on the cheek. He climbs into the ring amid cheers and boos and stands in the middle, a fighter. 'I see more dukes, marquesses and knights up there in the gallery than ever grace the plush seats of the House of Lords.'

This is greeted by hoots of laughter and, finding he has his audience, Lord Wardell is determined to perform.

Aubrey sees the tank containing the fish. Beside the tank sits a thin man, his red hair streaked with grey. Everything stops and Aubrey can only hear the throbbing of blood in his ears. Sweat forms on his forehead and the noise comes rushing back in.

'What's he doing here?' Aubrey says to Sir Richard Palmore.

'Who?' says Sir Richard.

Aubrey points.

'Oh, he's the fisherman. He caught the fish and brought it up from Hastings.'

The voices in Aubrey's head that had been quietened all afternoon by the opium, by Wardell, begin again, nibbling at him.

'He has come to beat you up. He has come to eat you up.' They shout, 'Father's come home. He's going to kill you.'

Aubrey climbs into the ring, keeping his back to the fisherman. Wardell is all smiles and waves occasionally at a face he recognises.

'We're leaving,' says Aubrey. 'Now.'

'No, Beelzebub, no.'

'You can't do this, it's a trick, that's what it is.'

'Calm yourself, my dear.' He touches Aubrey's arm and the voices stop for a moment.

'I will do this and we will be free of debt. No fuss, Beelzebub. A wager is a wager. Here, take my ring and my cane and this letter – they're all yours. Be a good boy and don't do anything silly. Remember, you have the Weather Woman.'

The heavily built man pulls Aubrey away.

Sir Richard Palmore climbs into the ring and stands next to Wardell. The place is silent and he begins to read out the rules of the wager .

'The fish must be alive. There will be six attempts to swallow the herring and if, after the sixth attempt, the fish has not been consumed, then the wager is lost. If the fish is partly swallowed, no assistance may be given until the entire fish is gone. At no point may anyone intervene. Is this agreed, Wardell?'

'Agreed,' says Wardell and they shake hands.

The doors to the club are closed.

Wardell finds Aubery in the crowd and doesn't take his eyes off him, while the fisherman puts the herring, still alive, into a pail and carries it into the ring.

Sir Richard insists the fisherman stays, in case the fish escapes his lordship's grasp.

This is Wardell's moment. Ever the showman, he removes his frock coat and hangs it on one of the posts. He takes a gulp from his hip flask then, with far more precision and delicacy than anyone would have imagined, he picks up the impossibly large herring. On the first attempt he gags and loses his grip. The fish flops onto the sawdust. Aubrey is about to shout when he feels a hand over his mouth and a knife at his ribs.

'One word, Mr Friezland,' says a brisk voice, 'and I will kill you.'

Aubrey's tears soak the hand clamped across his mouth.

Three times Wardell tries to get the fish down his throat. It curls in on itself, wriggles free, falls again onto the sawdust, bending and arching its back. The fisherman rinses it and puts it back in the pail.

'He can't do it,' shouts a man in the audience.

'Give him a drink – no one can swallow with a dry throat.'

A bottle is handed up to Wardell. He drinks and lifts the herring by its tail fin. The fourth attempt.

'Big fish, big fish,' he says.

The fish isn't moving as much as before and Wardell now has hold of it at the right angle. He thinks it might be easier to swallow this time. To his amazement the herring starts to slide down his throat, diving deep into him.

'Yes, yes!' Shouts come from the crowd. 'Yes!'

But it sticks in his windpipe and goes no further. His muscles clamp round the herring, he is gasping for breath, but the fish has filled his throat. Wardell flaps his arms, the herring's tail protruding from his mouth. He clutches his neck, but Sir Richard refuses to let anyone help him. The fisherman steps forward and is warned, bluntly, 'Raise one hand and not a penny.'

Wardell is on his knees in the sawdust, his long fingers feebly pulling at the fish, his eyes bulging from their sockets, the veins in his neck turning blue.

'He's pissed himself!' someone shouts.

'Is he dead?'

Beside Aubrey is a doctor, drunk and most probably useless. He wobbles into the ring, lifts up Wardell's arm and says, 'Not quite, though the fish is.'

'Then stand back,' says Sir Richard Palmore.

Minutes later, the doctor announces, 'He is dead.'

★ ★ ★

If Aubrey had a pistol he would shoot them all. After it is over, he collects Wardell's things and looks for the last time into the ring where he lies, eyes open and staring. Aubrey can't see his fisherman father anywhere, perhaps he imagined the likeness. He walks away from Covent Garden to Charing Cross, where he sits on Black Lion Stairs. It begins to rain as he opens the letter Wardell gave him. Folded inside is a betting slip. Wardell has bet against himself.

Make the most of the Weather Woman, Beelzebub. I won't be jealous. I have loved you and that is enough.

By the waters of the great river, Aubrey weeps.

48

Mr Ratchet is asleep. It is three in the morning and he surfaces to hear the watchman call, '... and all is well.' But there is another sound nudging him into consciousness. And Old Bones is growling.

Outside someone is calling his name, repetitively, softly, persistently. Mr Ratchet is loath to leave his warm bed; he can feel a nip in the air. The voice outside doesn't stop. Reluctantly Mr Ratchet gets out of bed. The floorboards are cold and he puts on his Moroccan slippers and goes to the window. He can't see anyone in the street below. It's as empty as a street should be at this time of the night. Then he hears his name being called again.

'Ebenezer, open up.'

Mr Ratchet is rather proud of his sash windows, which go up and down easily, never jamming. He thinks vaguely that's what money does, it makes windows rise and fall smoothly.

He lifts up the window until he can stick his head out, still not knowing who's calling him. But then he sees a figure swaying in the moonlight. He looks drunk. It's probably someone who didn't like his terms and conditions.

'Go home,' says Ebenezer Ratchet. 'I don't do business in the middle of the night. If you have a grievance, come in the morning and it will be attended to.'

And he's about to let the window slide gracefully down when the voice says, 'Ebenezer, it's me, Bob Letchmore, Mary's husband. You remember – the lieutenant.'

Now Mr Ratchet is wide awake whether he likes it or not. 'What do you want?' he says.

For a moment Mr Ratchet thinks Bob Letchmore has gone away and he is about to pull the window down and climb back into bed when the disembodied voice says, 'I've got something for you.'

'I'll be down,' says Mr Ratchet. Old Bones is up and at his side. 'What do you think, Old Bones?' He puts on his paisley dressing gown over his nightshirt. The fabric is not cheap but nothing that Mr Ratchet owns is. He has a good understanding of the finer things of life.

'Old Bones, my wise friend, you're not to do anything untoward.' Old Bones doesn't like being woken in the middle of the night. He looks up at his master, hears the knocking on the door and decides to go back to his basket.

Mr Ratchet pats him on his head. 'A good decision, if I may say so.' He takes the pistol from his bedside cabinet, slips it into his dressing-gown pocket, and makes his way down the wooden staircase to the shop.

'All right, all right, stop your banging, I'm coming.' He lights all the oil lamps for he would rather see this gentleman in full light than in the shadows of his shop. One of the lamps starts smoking and he thinks to himself that the minute gas comes in for households, he will be the first in Cheapside to have gas lighting.

'Stop your banging,' he says again, 'or I'll call for the watch.'

The one thing Mr Ratchet hates is people demanding his

attention. He has hated it since he was a small boy. Long ago he decided he liked his own company. He definitely doesn't like being told what to do by anyone and this banging on his front door is getting on his nerves. When he opens the door, Bob Letchmore falls into the shop.

'I thought you weren't coming,' he says by way of an apology.

'What is it you want at this ungodly hour?' says Mr Ratchet.

The man is in the shadows. Mr Ratchet would prefer he walked into the light and says as much. Bob Letchmore looks as if he's been in a fight: one of his eyes is swollen and there's a drop of dried blood at the corner of his mouth.

'I ask you again: what do you want?' says Mr Ratchet briskly, trying to wake himself up. He feels he should have his wits about him more than he does at the moment.

'I must get back to Hastings. I have to get out of this godless metropolis, this place of vice and vipers. And men like that.'

'Like whom?' asks Mr Ratchet.

'That Sir Richard-bloody-Palmore. I've seen men like him on their horses watching the foot soldiers do what their kind never would. After all, they weren't bred to have blood on their shiny boots.'

'I can't say I know what you're on about,' Mr Ratchet says. He was once very frightened of this man but now he only sees a pathetic drunk.

'It's made me think, this night has,' says Letchmore. 'It's made me think a lot.'

It's apparent to Mr Ratchet that he's not going to get a word of sense out of Bob Letchmore until some of the alcohol has worn off. Reluctantly he offers coffee and adds, 'Whatever weaponry you have on you, I would be grateful if you would put it on my desk.'

'You're right. In the past I would have been carrying a pistol – like you are now – and it's likely I would have beaten you. But that's the past. I did some bad things I'm not proud of. Alcohol. This country is awash with alcohol. It only lacks decent water to drink. The water in the Thames is vile.'

Mr Ratchet can see this meeting is going to become maudlin. He indicates the staircase concealed behind the panelling and makes sure Letchmore goes first. He sways and Mr Ratchet gives him a moment to take the first two steps, time enough to note how well dressed he is. His boots are new, as is his coat.

Old Bones struts into the room to growl menacingly at the stranger until Mr Ratchet says, 'Basket.' Reluctantly the dog returns to the bedchamber.

'You have a fine place here, Ebenezer,' says Bob Letchmore as they sit down at the table. 'And indeed, some very fine objects, very fine.'

The coffee is hot and strong. Old Bones is anxious. He comes in and flops at his master's feet.

'With deep respect, Ebenezer,' says Bob Letchmore, 'I thank you for letting me in. And I don't want money if that's what you're thinking. I've made enough tonight on one herring – one hundred guineas, and more besides.' He gulps his coffee. 'But Sir Richard Palmore made me stay in the ring and I watched – I had no choice – as a gentleman died there, trying to swallow my fish for a wager.'

Mr Ratchet pours more coffee for his guest. So Wardell went ahead with his mad enterprise and predictably failed in the attempt. How long, he wonders, before Aubrey is at his door again looking for a loan?

'My fish, caught by my own skill, a fish that was never meant to be swallowed alive. That gentleman died with his eyes popping out of his head. But do you know what alarmed me most about what I saw? Not the dead gentleman, no. It was that the gentleman had been brought there by my son. Yes, my son.

'It riled me when I heard him addressed as Mr Friezland. He's my son, he looks like me, or rather he looks like I did a long time ago, when I was angry. Afterwards, I followed him and found him sitting by the river, weeping. I said I had sympathy for him and it was a terrible end for both man and fish. He told me to fuck off.

'But I wanted to apologise, and I told him I was ashamed of the way I treated him, my son. He wasn't having any of it, told me to stay away from him, that he wasn't my son and I wasn't to interfere.

'I thought of all the lies he'd been raised on and that was the worst. He is my son, no man has looked more like me, and my pride will not let him claim to be another man's child. I was married to his mother and I can prove it. We were wed in Hastings, in the eyes of the Lord. And while I was away fighting for King and Country, what did she do? While I led my men, with their blood on my boots? She ran off to London and claimed my son was another man's child.' Bob Letchmore rests his head on his hands and for a moment Mr Ratchet thinks he's about to fall asleep. But he sits bolt upright and says, 'Yes. A young gentleman came down to Hastings and the parson was making enquiries on his behalf about a certain marriage. He wore blue spectacles. The parson, who, let me tell you, is a good friend of mine, wondered why. As do I.'

'Why he was wearing blue spectacles?'

'No, why was he wanting the proof? And when Aubrey wouldn't tell me...'

'Was it Aubrey you had a fight with?'

'Yes. He ran away. So I reasoned and reckoned with myself that if my son is claiming his name, this has to be about Victor

Friezland. Would I be right in thinking Victor Friezland has died?'

'You would,' says Mr Ratchet.

'And his estate is worth money?'

'It is.'

'Then this is all about avarice, the devil's work.' Bob Letchmore takes from inside his coat a folded, slightly dog-eared document and pushes it across the table.

'It's the marriage certificate. You'll know what to do with it,' says the lieutenant. 'You don't have a drop of brandy for the coffee?'

'No,' says Mr Ratchet.

'A pity. Here,' he says and puts twenty guineas on the table. 'That's for Mary.'

'May I ask,' says Mr Ratchet, 'if you took the money Victor Friezland sent for Aubrey when he was a boy?'

Letchmore stands and pulls himself up to his full height. He looks like an overgrown weasel. 'I'm not proud of what I've done, not proud I took that money. I saw it as mine.'

Mr Ratchet looks at the twenty guineas on the table. 'I would say it's small change for the grief you've caused.'

The day is dawning. Bob Letchmore puts on his hat and says, 'Thank you for listening and for the coffee without brandy. There's another thing you ought to know. The young gentleman who came down to Hastings went by the name of Eugene Jonas. Aubrey told me he was looking for him. Something to do with a weather woman, whoever she is.'

When Letchmore has left, Mr Ratchet locks the door and he and Old Bones go back to bed. Mr Ratchet falls into a fitful sleep.

The nightwatchman knocks on the front door of the house in Berkeley Square. Morton is always up at this time and he answers the door with the same calmness as if it had been nine in the morning rather than five.

'I am sorry to call at such an early hour,' says the watchman. 'It's an important matter. Might I have a word with Lady Wardell?'

Morton knows what this is about. The news of Lord Wardell's death reached him an hour after it happened and he quietly informed Sir John Campbell. Sir John immediately left the house for his office and only returned three hours later. He hasn't woken Elizabeth. She has sleepily wrapped an arm round him as he lies wondering how soon they could be married. At last he will be able to acknowledge his daughters. They have all waited long enough. Tomorrow his newspaper will carry an article with the headline *Lord Wardell Dies Swallowing a Live Fish*.

It is always a delicate matter waking her ladyship. Morton knocks on the door of her bedchamber and says quietly into the darkened room, 'Your ladyship, the nightwatchman wishes to speak to you.'

The watchman is surprised to see Sir John Campbell, in his dressing gown, accompanying Lady Wardell.

'Has something happened?' says Lady Wardell, fearing the watchman's visit concerns Henri.

The watchman clears his throat. 'Your ladyship, I'm sorry to inform you I've learned from the watchman in Covent Garden that Lord Wardell is dead. I thought I should tell you.'

There is complete silence in the room and he has the distinct impression Lady Wardell is trying very hard not to laugh.

Fortunately Sir John Campbell is more composed than Lady Wardell. He thanks the watchman.

Elizabeth interrupts him. 'How did Lord Wardell die?'

'Trying to swallow a fish,' says the watchman. 'A herring, so I'm told.'

'A herring?' she says, incredulously. 'A whole herring? Poached or pickled?'

'The fish was alive, my lady, brought up from Hastings.' The bizarre nature of this conversation does not encourage solemn faces.

'And where did this fish-swallowing take place?'

The nightwatchman fortunately has no sense of humour. 'What I heard,' he says and goes on to recount the details, ending with the information that Lord Wardell's eyes nearly popped out of their sockets. 'It sometimes happens to dogs,' he adds.

Elizabeth is now biting her tongue and trying to concentrate on the saddest thing she can think of, which is not the manner of Lord Wardell's dying. With eyes streaming, she says, 'Do dogs often try to swallow live fish?'

'I couldn't say, your ladyship,' says the watchman. 'But I knew a lady in this very square who had a King Charles spaniel and its eye popped out.'

Elizabeth holds her breath until she hears Morton compensating the nightwatchman for his trouble and closing the front door on him. Only then does she shout with laughter.

'You knew,' she says to Sir John. 'You rogue, you knew and you didn't tell me.'

'It was busy last night and you looked so delectable when I got back that it completely escaped my mind.' He puts his arms about her. 'Shall we get married?'

'Yes, John,' says Elizabeth, 'and yes again.'

'Then this morning I will apply for a special licence. Unless you think that's inappropriately fast.'

Laughing, she says, 'It cannot be an hour too soon.'

49

Elise can't be sure exactly when Mr Gutteridge took on the role of Friezland family guardian, though she dates it from the time Neva left for Hastings and the garden was full of sorrel, lettuces and cucumbers. Since Mr Briggs's call, the solicitor has either written or visited Elise every week with the same graveyard expression etched onto his features. She wonders where his sense of humour has gone and comes to dread his unmistakable double ring at the garden gate. Whatever sympathy she might have felt for him quickly wanes when he well-meaningly points out the dire position in which she and the girls, as he calls Neva and Cassie, now find themselves.

'It is very hard – I would say near impossible – for a widow and two unmarried ladies to navigate the waters of polite society on their own. In short, you need a man to act for your family and I urge you to make Neva reconsider my proposal.'

A week later he is there again, this time concerned about where Neva is staying and with whom.

Elise speaks vaguely of Mr Jonas's cousins in Deal.

'Madam,' says Mr Gutteridge with deep solemnity, 'I

advise you to take better care of Neva's reputation. I am somewhat taken aback that you didn't provide a chaperone to accompany her to Deal but left these precarious arrangements to Mr Jonas. It was not wise, madam, not wise at all.'

Then news reaches Lincoln's Inn that the Marquess of Smedmore has become engaged to Miss Cassandra Lamb and Mr Gutteridge wastes not a moment before once again ringing the bell and explaining to Elise and Cassie the impropriety of such a marriage. Both are left speechless.

Now the apples are ripening in the orchard and not a week has gone by without a letter from Mr Gutteridge expressing his deep anxiety over Neva, or over Mr Jonas, or over Neva and Mr Jonas in combination.

Not wishing to cause Neva anxiety, Elise hasn't written to her about the solicitor's calls and letters – or about the theft of the Weather Woman.

Elise's joyful consolation was Neva's letter telling her she was married to Henri Dênou. She wrote,

I thank you and Papa for allowing me to grow up to be my idiosyncratic self. It is because of you that I have found a man who suits me mentally and physically. I am more than fortunate.

More recently her letters are about the house Henri has bought and its refurbishment.

Elise thinks this should be the happiest time since Victor's death – Neva married and Cassie engaged. But this engagement is now the source of much unhappiness.

Ten days ago Bos left for Dorset to take his daughter for her annual visit to Lord and Lady Tillingham.

'You will write to me every day? Promise you will,' he'd said to Cassie before he left and Cassie has.

But there hasn't been a single letter from Bos, not one. Instead there was a letter from the duke's solicitor so full of intimidating words that Elise had to ask Mr Gutteridge to look at it. The solicitor read from the thick, embossed writing paper carrying the ducal coat of arms.

'... and his grace concludes, "I will not stand by and watch while a housemaid seduces my son into marriage." And he advises Cassie to free the marquess rather than see him ruined.'

'Ruined?' said Elise. 'How dare he! The marquess came here to declare his love and honourably propose marriage.'

'Mr Gutteridge,' Cassie said, 'I'll give back the ring the marquess gave me. He just has to ask me himself.'

'Ruined,' repeated Elise. 'There's only one person who is ruined and it isn't the marquess.'

For the first time, Mr Gutteridge took his leave with speed. Elise asked herself why she hadn't told him of Neva's marriage.

Two letters arrive this morning, one post-haste but it is not for Cassie. She is at the garden gate to greet the letter-carrier as she has been every day. She puts the letters on the kitchen table.

'Never mind, my dear,' says Elise. She opens the letter from Neva. 'Oh my, Cassie, they're coming back today. But I don't understand what...' She hands the letter to Cassie, who reads it aloud.

> *Henri and I are returning to London and hope to be there this evening. I am sure you will understand, in light of the shocking news, that we must first see Lady Wardell.*

'What shocking news?' says Cassie.
'I have no idea,' says Elise.

Cassie puts on the kettle and sits down at the table. 'What does the judge-and-jury man want now?' she asks, seeing Mr Gutteridge's unmistakable hand on the second letter.

Elise reads it. 'He writes that… "Mr Briggs has returned from Deal and reports that Mr Jonas is not known there and Miss Friezland has not been seen there either." Well, that's not surprising. He finishes by saying if he doesn't hear from Mr Eugene Jonas by the end of this week, "he will have to assume that the gentleman is leading us all a merry dance and will act accordingly".' Elise sighs. 'Whatever accordingly might be.'

She can't be bothered with Mr Gutteridge. What concerns her is why Neva and Mr Dênou should be returning so abruptly to London.

The garden gate bell rings again. Cassie goes to open it and finds there a footman sent by the Duke of Boswell to collect a ring. Cassie asks him to wait. She goes to her bedchamber and comes down with a sealed note addressed to the duke. She hands it to the footman.

'And the ring, Miss Lamb?'

'I will give it back the minute the marquess asks me in person.'

The footman leaves.

'I suspect,' says Elise, 'that the duke and Lady Tillingham are behind this sabotage. What did you write?'

'It's none of your business.'

'Cassie, you didn't!' says Elise.

'Auntie, it doesn't matter. We won't be getting married. The duke thinks me a whore – why disappoint him?'

The kitchen smells of coffee and freshly baked bread. There is butter and marrow jam, and just when they've sat down, George comes in with a newspaper.

'Have you seen this?' he asks. Cassie and Elise look at him blankly. 'It's Lord Wardell. He's dead.'

Elise can't think why the death of this unpleasant aristocrat should matter to them. 'Oh – of course,' she says at last. 'Lord Wardell was Mr Dênou's uncle. I suppose that's the reason they're coming home today.'

'This is a big scandal,' says George. He looks up from the newspaper at the two solemn faces staring at him.

'How did he die?' asks Cassie.

Elise has a feeling Neva and perhaps Henri will turn up this evening and she wants the house to look its best, even though it's somewhat bare of furniture. She lights all the candles in the long drawing room and puts one of her cakes on the table along with a decanter of wine. At about seven o'clock they hear a carriage pulling up. The door opens and there is Neva. Perhaps it's the light, thinks Elise, but the sight of her takes her breath away. She looks ravishing. She looks content. Elise and Cassie are speechless. It's only a moment, hardly noticeable, before they embrace her and ask her a hundred questions. Cassie pours the wine and Neva talks a little about the wedding and a lot about Henri.

'Did you have any luck searching the church registers?' asks Cassie.

'I started out with good intentions and I could have spent the entire summer looking and then... and then...'

'And then you and Mr Dênou made your own entry in the marriage register,' says Elise, smiling at her. 'It's all right, Neva. After everything Mr Gutteridge has said, I don't feel we have any hope of Victor's will being upheld.'

'I'm sorry, Auntie.'

'Don't be. I'm not.'

Only now does Neva see all that was bright and primrose yellow in Cassie has turned muddy since she's been away.

'Cassie, something's wrong, isn't it? You're not ill, are you?'

And out comes Cassie's woeful story.

'And the duke sent a footman this morning to collect the ring and I wrote his grace a note.'

'I hope you told him it's none of his business,' says Neva.

'I did!' And all three women burst out laughing.

But Neva is even more concerned about Cassie when she says she's tired and will go to bed. Neva can't remember her ever complaining about tiredness; usually Cassie is the one who can talk into the small hours. Neva follows her upstairs.

'I'm quite well, really,' says Cassie. 'I'm sorry – I'm a rain cloud on your happiness and I don't want to be. I'm so pleased you're home and that you're married to Mr Dênou. I'm just tired, that's all. It's a difficult situation and Mr Gutteridge hasn't helped.'

This is the second time the solicitor has been mentioned and Neva goes downstairs to find Elise.

'He wrote, he called, he wrote and wrote,' says Elise.

'Where are the letters?' asks Neva.

Elise shows them to her. 'And this one arrived this morning.'

Neva reads them all. 'This has to stop,' she says. 'I'm going to see him tomorrow.'

'As yourself or as Eugene Jonas?'

'As Neva.'

'I think that's wise,' says Elise. 'Victor's plan was never going to work.'

Henri wonders if he has left it too late to go to the Friezland house. He had told Neva he would stay the night in Berkeley Square but the thought of not being with her hurts. He takes a cab and arrives to find the house dark. Silhouetted against the velvet sky it resembles a fantastical galleon that has set sail without him into the sea of dreams. He will walk back across London Bridge, he thinks, he's not sleepy. But the garden gate opens.

'I knew you would come,' she says, taking him into the kitchen. 'Would you like something to eat or drink?'

'No,' he says and she leads him to her bedchamber.

He's only ever seen the kitchen and the long drawing room. Neva's room with its porthole window reminds him uneasily of a ship's cabin. In the darkness, with the rain on the water and the sound of the tall ships' rigging jingling on the river, the scent of lilies of the valley comes to him; the perfume of Mrs O'Donnell. Neva instinctively knows where he's gone.

'It's the river,' she says softly. 'The ships are safe and the dead have yet to ask the question.'

'What is the question?'

'Why give me an ounce of light in return for an infinity of darkness?' She holds him as the wind and rain gust against the window pane. He is inside her, feels the tide flowing through her and in their quiet ecstasy she says softly, 'That's how stars are made.'

Without a word of explanation she's asleep. He lies, hearing her breathe, waiting for the light. It's dawn when he too falls asleep.

50

London is full of nothing but carriages. Horses and vehicles of all shapes and sizes filled with people wanting to be somewhere else. Consequently, everyone is stuck in the good intentions of their arrivals and the fury of their anticipated lateness. Neva at least has time to think. She was up early and has sent a message to Mr Gutteridge informing him Mr Jonas will call at his chambers at half-past ten. She will be back, she thinks, by the time Henri rises.

In the darkness of the carriage she sees Eugene Jonas sitting opposite her. 'It's time,' she says, 'it's time.' To the cabby she calls, 'I'll get out here and walk.'

'You sure, madam? If you fell down in this traffic, you would be as good as crushed.'

She walks on the shaded side of the street and catches a glimpse of Eugene in the shadows of the Temple colonnade as she approaches Mr Gutteridge's chambers. Out in the sunshine, she knows exactly what she's going to do.

The chambers are on the ground floor. The heavy door with the solicitor's name written in gold is pushed back and she only needs to open the inner door. It takes a moment for her eyes to adjust to the gloom. It is cool inside. She imagines it's always cold here.

The clerk gets up from his desk.

'Good morning. You must be Mr Briggs.' Mr Briggs bows. 'I wish to see Mr Gutteridge. I'm Neva Dênou.'

'Mr Gutteridge has an appointment at half-past ten,' says Mr Briggs. He hesitates, not certain he heard her name correctly. 'But I'll tell him you're here.'

She hears him whisper, 'I think it's Miss Friezland to see you, sir.' And he shows Neva in.

'This is a pleasant surprise, Neva,' says Mr Gutteridge, rising from his seat but not leaving the fortress that is his desk. 'I'm expecting Mr Jonas shortly, but how can I help you?'

Neva smiles as she sees the prints on the wall: Hogarth's *A Rake's Progress*. She notices Mr Gutteridge glance at the clock on the mantelpiece. One of Papa's she thinks. She says, 'I won't take up much of your time, Mr Gutteridge, and if Mr Jonas arrives that would be a bonus.'

'I thought you were staying in Deal,' says Mr Gutteridge.

'I wasn't,' says Neva.

'That will be all, Briggs,' says Mr Gutteridge. 'And close the door. But tell me immediately when Mr Jonas arrives.'

Neva moves to look more closely at the prints and reflected in the glass she can see the solicitor waving Mr Briggs away. The door closes with a sharp, decisive click.

'Where were you if not in Deal?'

She turns to Mr Gutteridge.

'I was in Hastings.'

Mr Gutteridge is confused. 'I hope,' he says hesitantly, 'that you have given more thought to my proposal.'

'There was no need, sir. I made it quite clear when I said "no" that I meant "no". But I want to ask you, Mr Gutteridge, what makes you feel you have a right to interfere as much as you do in our family affairs?'

Mr Gutteridge is taken aback.

'You came to tell Cassie it was quite impossible for her to marry the Marquess of Smedmore. Without any evidence or knowledge of what has taken place between Cassie and the marquess, you took the side of the duke.'

The solicitor tries to interrupt but she raises her hand.

'I was young when Papa told me this: sometimes it's hard to know whose side you are on, the prosecutor's or the defendant's.'

'This is out of order, Miss Friezland,' says the solicitor sharply, in the tone of voice that had cowed many clients. 'I think we have nothing more to say to each other this morning.'

'Sir, I don't care what you think,' says Neva. 'It's more important what *I* think. I think you have caused Elise and Cassie no end of worry. Whether it's because you feel injured by my refusal to accept your offer of marriage, I don't know, but what it shows me is that you possess a profound lack of wisdom and have no understanding of the human heart.

'My father had a deep respect for you and wanted to avoid compromising you by consulting you about his estate.'

'You have said enough,' says Mr Gutteridge.

'I haven't finished,' says Neva. 'But your reaction reminds me of your chess-playing skills. You look at the immediate problem. I thought by now you would have worked out why my father made that decision. But you haven't. Have you still no idea why my father didn't want you to administer his estate?'

Mr Gutteridge clears his throat and adjusts his spectacles. He rings the bell on his desk.

'Yes, sir?' says Mr Briggs, opening the door.

Mr Gutteridge changes tack. 'Neva, you are upset – Briggs,

some refreshments, perhaps some tea?' He stands. 'But Neva, I must ask you to wait outside and this conversation can continue when Mr Jonas has left.'

Neva doesn't move but says, 'I would prefer a whisky, if you are offering me anything, and a cheroot.'

Mr Gutteridge is truly shocked. 'Thank you, Briggs.' When the door is closed once more, he says, 'Gentlemen drink whisky and smoke cheroots, not ladies.'

'I know that,' says Neva. 'I know that all too well. The question is, why do I like whisky and cheroots?'

'Because Victor encouraged you?' he says weakly.

'When you and I played chess, you always protected your queen to the detriment of the other pieces on the board and I took you every time – mostly with my knight. You never learned to let your queen go. Have you still not worked it out? Let me help you. Most women of our time – unless they are exceedingly wealthy – have very few avenues open to them. But if a woman has been born with a unique gift, there are no opportunities for her to broaden her education or be anything other than a decorative piece of frippery. The role of a woman is marked out from birth: if she is born into the aristocracy, her golden hour comes when she finds a husband, when her role in life will be to have children, preferably sons. If that doesn't kill her then she must support her husband through all his follies and make him believe he's clever.

'Papa was an immigrant from Saint Petersburg. He saw what the English were like, he knew their capacity for cruelty. The luckiest day of my life was when he found me. Papa gave me Eugene Jonas. Master Jonas protected Neva. Master Jonas could go to lectures, Master Jonas could go to gentlemen's clubs. Papa was aware that if he left his estate to me and Elise, it wouldn't be hard for Aubrey Friezland to make sure we never received a penny of it. Aubrey's plan is to have me committed to an asylum for the insane. To prevent such a move, Papa left the bulk of his estate to Eugene Jonas.

'In August I married an exceptional man. A man I have been in love with since I was sixteen. He understands me and it is his belief in me and his love for me that gives me the courage to say this to you.'

Neva takes from her reticule the blue spectacles and puts them down on the solicitor's desk. 'Mr Gutteridge, I give you Eugene Jonas. Do with him what you will. I'm fed up with hiding.'

Mr Gutteridge sits down heavily and his chair lets out a puff of air, the sound of a long drawn-out sigh.

'I made the weather predictions, no one else,' says Neva. 'I am married to Henri Dênou. Do your worst. I know the will won't stand. What does it matter? I would be found out sooner or later. I was Eugene Jonas. I am the Weather Woman.'

51

Henri had lain in bed thinking of their arrival at Berkeley Square; his aunt's delight in seeing them, her obvious relief to be free of Lord Wardell. But Henri saw that within this world of calling cards and invitations, where Neva and he would be expected to give dinner parties and conform to social niceties, the treasure he held in his arms would be gone.

His father had possessed great wealth and Henri's early childhood had been surrounded by opulence. He had watched his uncle thoughtlessly squander a fortune, had experienced his cruelty and witnessed his callous disregard for his many servants. Henri wanted none of it.

The house, his own house, had struck him last night as completely inappropriate. The innocence and joy he had found with Neva would be corrupted. What had she said about teasets and teaspoons? Berkeley Square was full of them. No, he wanted more than anything a happy, unconventional marriage of *liberté, égalité, fraternité*. When Sir John asked Henri before he had left last night if he would consider renting the house to them, he had said he would think about it.

By the time he fell asleep, he had decided he and Neva should look for a new home in London, one more suitable to the life they aspired to lead.

He wakes shortly after Neva has gone. It's still early, the house is quiet and, unsure of its layout, he makes his way downstairs into the passage leading to the kitchen. The sunlight shines on a scene that could have come from a painting. Two people sitting opposite each other, drinking tea. Henri instinctively feels that he should go back upstairs but Jetsam comes hurtling down and skids into the kitchen. The man is already at the door to the garden. He stops when he sees Henri.

'I came last night, rather late,' says Henri, apologetically.

Jetsam runs this way and that before Elise lets him out.

Elise stands and says, 'Mr Dênou, I can't tell you how pleased I am to welcome you to our family. This is Mr Cutter, George Cutter.'

Henri bows.

'How do you do, sir,' says George.

Elise puts out another cup and saucer.

'I'd better get on,' says George and he disappears. Jetsam trots after him.

'I suppose Neva will be moving to your house in Berkeley Square today,' says Elise.

'Do you think it would suit her?'

'It's not for me to say. But she's grown up without airs and graces.'

'A house at that address comes with social obligations which hold little appeal for me. We have our house in Sussex but we want to live in London too.'

George returns and shows Henri around the house. Before he goes out, Henri asks Elise how she would feel if he and Neva lived there with her. 'Neva predicts this winter is going to be a bad one. The house needs a lot of work to make it sound. If you are in agreement, I could have the house enlarged a little to accommodate us. You must think about it, Mrs Friezland, for it will mean change.'

'I don't need to, Mr Dênou,' says Elise. 'Nothing would make me happier. But if Victor's will doesn't stand, you will be spending your money for Aubrey's benefit, not ours.'

'Do you know how first I made my money?'

'No,' says Elise.

'It was due to Neva. When she returned my pebble to me, she enclosed a list of predictions. I gambled on them and won a substantial amount which I then invested wisely. I have enough to pay for the work without noticing it. I am in a very privileged position thanks to my extraordinarily clever wife.'

'What will she say?'

He smiles and says with confidence, 'I know exactly what she'll say.'

Elise follows him to the garden gate. 'Mr Dênou, the Weather Woman – the automaton – was stolen from the workshop and Mr Gutteridge blames George. It's causing him so much worry. It's cowardly of me, I know, but would you tell Neva about the burglary? I couldn't bring myself to last night. She's gone to see Mr Gutteridge this morning. I hope she'll tell him the truth about Victor's will – about Eugene Jonas. And, Mr Dênou, if you are to live here, may I call you Henri?'

'I would be honoured if you would. May I call you *Tante Elise*?'

Henri takes a waterferry to Temple Stairs. He and Jetsam walk through the Lincoln's Inn gardens and stop opposite Mr Gutteridge's chambers, Jetsam sitting still by his side for once, both anticipating Neva's appearance.

Neva walks out of the chambers and stands on the steps, her head high. She looks around her and is surprised and yet not surprised to see them.

'I thought you wouldn't have eaten,' says Henri, 'and you might want someone to talk to.'

She takes his arm and says, 'You make me very happy.'

'"The necessity of pursuing happiness is the foundation of liberty," so said the philosopher John Locke.'

'A very wise man,' says Neva. 'Oh, let us always pursue happiness.'

'And may we always have liberty.'

They set off in the direction of London Bridge and find a coffee shop where they sit in a corner.

Neva gathers his hands in hers. 'Last night...' she says, and bites her lower lip.

He leans forward. 'Last night I lay in bed thinking how much I like your house by the river. It is a home, which the house in Berkeley Square is not. It's too grand, too formal. It's not right for you or me. What was it you said about teaspoons?' A look of relief crosses her face. 'Sir John asked if I might consider renting the house to him. What do you think of the idea?'

'Where would we live? In Sussex?'

'We need a home in London too. How would you feel about us living in the house your papa built?'

To the surprise of the other customers, Neva stands up and throws her arms round Henri. 'Yes,' she says, 'oh, yes!'

'We would live with *Tante Elise* and Mr Cutter. *En famille.*'

'George?' says Neva. 'He has his own place...' She stops and laughs. 'Of course – he's been staying at the house with Auntie, hasn't he?'

'I believe he has been doing so since you left for Hastings. But *Tante Elise* told me Mr Gutteridge has accused Mr Cutter of negligence.'

'Negligent of what?' asks Neva.

'Of the automaton. It was stolen while you were away.'

Neva sits down again and is quiet.

'What are you thinking?'

'About when Papa built the Weather Woman and we began giving performances. I sat beside her, looking at the audience while secretly moving the pedals. After you'd gone away, it seemed to me her glass eyes had a jealous look to them. I began to loathe that automaton. I imagine it's Aubrey who took it, in which case they deserve one another. But I'm also thinking I should go back and give Mr Gutteridge another bruising piece of my mind. I can hardly remember life without George Cutter. No one could have been more steadfast. What right has Mr Gutteridge to appoint himself head of our family? I told him as much and I told him more.'

'I think you underestimate what he feels for you. But I suspect his greatest love was your papa, though he'd never acknowledge it.'

'He's not a man who would care much for the pursuit of happiness,' says Neva.

Neva is momentarily lost in a daydream and they are both silent until Henri says, 'I thought we should see Mrs Dent about your talk. Perhaps you could give it in early December. We'll invite everyone who is interested in meteorology and the sciences. I spoke to Sir John last night and he has agreed, if you wish, to publish your predictions. He was most intrigued – he always wondered how the Weather Woman was so accurate.'

Neva has taken off her gloves and is pulling at the skin on her finger. She looks up and says, 'People will laugh. It will damage your reputation.'

'They won't. It won't. I will be at your side and if you stumble...'

She smiles. It's the smile that Henri will have painted, a

cheeky smile that lights up her face. She says, 'I won't stumble. Though I fell once.'

'You did?' he says.

'I fell in love with you.'

'Do you know when?'

'Yes. I know the precise moment. It was when I was sixteen and you gave me your pebble. Do you know when you fell for me?'

'Twice. When I saw you that night at Mrs Dent's and you stared at your slippers. But I truly fell and hurt myself badly the evening I spent with Eugene Jonas.'

'Oh – do you miss him?'

'No, because you are you, because he is a part of you. But not all of you.'

She leans across and kisses him.

'You'll shock the customers,' he says.

She kisses him again and says, 'I have found in you the liberty to be myself, all myself, and not be half-hidden in gentlemen's clothes or behind an automaton. That is liberty.'

52

The day being fine, Mr Ratchet walks to Lincoln's Inn with Old Bones. He's in the mood to enjoy the late summer sunshine. He may well have passed Henri and Neva, but if he has, he hasn't seen them, for at Puddle Dock Stairs he catches sight of a group of boys and girls dressed in rags which if sewn together would have made a shirt just large enough for one of them to wear. He remembers when he was a lad their age, before he possessed shoes, mudlarking for coal, for metal, for any treasure that might translate into bread. By the steps that lead down to the shore is a boy of about twelve with another lad who can be no older than six. He's been crying.

'On account, sir,' says the older boy, 'of a nail that has gone through his foot and he has just pulled out.' He shows Mr Ratchet the offending object. The little lad's face is smeared with a mixture of mud, tears and snot. Mr Ratchet takes a handkerchief from his pocket, puts in it six shillings and ties it up. He hands it to the older boy, who is astounded by the amount of money.

The moneylender's white handkerchief is now grey with

the river mud. 'Listen to me: you are to take the little fellow home. Do you know where he lives?'

'He's my brother, sir.'

'Do you live with anyone?'

'Our mother. Father died of coughing.'

'Go home and get a doctor to look at your brother's foot.' The older boy glances at his comrades on the shore. 'Don't worry about them.'

Mr Ratchet watches the two mudlarks as they go and is instantly surrounded by mud-caked children. He hands each of them a sixpence. They look at him open-mouthed then run away.

'That was my life, Old Bones,' he says. He thinks the river mud is probably still ingrained in him from the days when he, with one leg shorter than the other, tried to support himself and his widowed mother by mudlarking.

At Mr Gutteridge's chambers he finds Mr Briggs looking anxious, though, given the darkness of the place, it's hard to be sure.

'I'm here to see Mr Gutteridge,' says Mr Ratchet.

Mr Briggs is about to say that the solicitor is busy when the door to his chambers abruptly opens.

'Mr Ratchet,' says Mr Gutteridge. 'What a pleasure it is to see you, sir. Do you feel like a walk?' And before Mr Ratchet can reply, Mr Gutteridge has put on his stovepipe hat and his overcoat, and there is nothing for Mr Ratchet to do but follow him out into the sunshine. They set off to Gray's Inn.

'It's the gardens I like,' says Mr Gutteridge as they reach the iron gates that lead to the tree lined gravel walks.

The gardens were designed in what Mr Ratchet considers a very dry way with few flowers and two mulberry trees.

'Sir Francis Bacon bought the wrong kind of mulberry tree, not the ones for silk. Did you know that?' says Mr Gutteridge, not expecting an answer.

They sit down and only then does the solicitor say, 'I have been a perfect fool,' as if they have had a long conversation and this is the summary of it. 'What have I achieved? You, Mr Ratchet, have a dog.'

'I do,' says Mr Ratchet, 'and my dog means the world to me, more than a human being ever could. Perhaps you should get a dog, Mr Gutteridge.'

'I don't think so,' says Mr Gutteridge. 'Neva Friezland has married Henri Dênou. Do you know him?' Again he doesn't wait for a reply. 'I proposed to her – Neva Friezland, that is. She turned me down.'

'You would have been most ill-suited,' says Mr Ratchet. 'In my life I've only once met someone who is not of this world, not of our time, and that someone is Miss Friezland. Personally, I never believed in all that machinery Victor went in for. I long thought it was she who could tell the weather. You can't hold onto someone like that; hold on too tight and they disappear.'

'Where did you go to school, Mr Ratchet?' asks Mr Gutteridge.

'I went to the school of the mudlarks, Mr Gutteridge,' says Mr Ratchet. 'I made pennies from the treasure the Thames threw up. One day a gentleman called me over. He said he'd been watching me, he saw I had one leg shorter than the other and yet I seemed to be the gang leader. He had taken out a wager with a colleague who'd said a lad like me would never amount to anything. The gentleman bought me my first pair of shoes and a suit of clothes and I went to work in his office where they did accountancy. In less than two years I was his assistant, and worked my way up from there. I stayed in that company until the day he died. Poverty makes criminals of us; opportunity in the form of shoes is the only way to walk out of it.'

'And here am I,' says Mr Gutteridge, 'with all the benefits

of education and of inheritance, but I haven't half your wisdom.'

They sit together, quietly watching the barristers come out to take the air. Mr Gutteridge says at last, 'What did you come to see me about?'

Mr Ratchet hands him the marriage certificate. 'This proves my sister was married to Lieutenant Robert Letchmore before she married Victor Friezland. Bob Letchmore brought it to me. And he told me his son – *his son* – Aubrey is looking for Eugene Jonas.'

'Indeed,' says Mr Gutteridge, thoughtfully. 'What a muddle. I never thought of myself as a muddler but today I know I am one. Thank you, Mr Ratchet, you have been most helpful. I have made my decision.'

'I haven't said a thing,' says Mr Ratchet, 'except get a dog.' He watches the solicitor walk away. 'Come on, Old Bones,' says Mr Ratchet. 'Let's go and find Mary. I have a proposition for her.'

53

October to November 1813

Cassie has still heard nothing from Bos. Henri has written to him and, receiving no reply, made enquiries of the Duke of Boswell. His grace would only say his son was away and not expected back until November. Henri admits to being baffled. Cassie returns the engagement ring with a letter saying that Bos is free to marry whoever he wants and takes to her bed.

Elise thinks Cassie is pregnant.

'I've never known her monthlies to be late,' says Elise to Neva when they're alone. 'You've always been irregular, but not Cassie.'

Neva tries to get some sense out of Cassie. She asks her carefully if it's possible that she could be pregnant.

'No,' she says.

'Are you sure?' asks Neva.

'No... yes. I kept my clothes on.'

Exasperated, Neva asks bluntly, 'Have you been to bed with Bos or not?'

'No. Just kisses and...' She stops.

'It's the "and" I'm asking about.'

Cassie responds with a downpour of weeping.

'Was it enjoyable?' Neva asks.

'Yes,' says Cassie between sobs. 'Yes.'

The house is thrown into turmoil and into this walks Mrs Dent who everyone has forgotten was invited for supper. She arrives with a colourful bouquet of flowers for Neva and is full of congratulations.

Fortunately, there's much to show her for the work on the house is well under way. Meanwhile Elise lays the table and Mr Cutter lights the fire in the long drawing room.

Mrs Dent declares the improvements are much to her satisfaction. 'But where is Cassie?' she asks.

Elise explains and Mrs Dent marches upstairs to find her.

'Do you know Cassie is with child?' she says when she comes down. 'She's having twin boys.'

Henri laughs.

'You may well laugh, Mr Dênou,' says Mrs Dent. 'I have second sight when it comes to women and babies. I'm never wrong, am I, Elise?'

'Then tell us, what has kept the marquess away?' asks Neva.

'That is what I intend to find out,' says Mrs Dent. 'The duke – the old goat – was quite smitten by Cassie when she was presenting the Weather Woman. I suspect he hasn't realised she is the lady his son wants to marry.'

Neva is taking the plates through to the kitchen when she hears Elise say, 'It will be a scandal if the marquess doesn't marry Cassie — which I fear might be the outcome.'

'I wouldn't be so certain,' says Mrs Dent.

'Whatever happens we'll take care of her.'

'That's my girl. You're a lucky woman, Elise. You have a charming son-in-law and the love of a good man.'

'What do you mean?'

'George Cutter has eyes for you, I'd say.'

'Perhaps he does, Cora, but I couldn't think of it.'

'Don't give up on life, Elise.'

'You never found anyone else.'

'No, but I didn't have such a fine figure of a man admiring me.'

Neva wonders why she hasn't noticed this. Perhaps because she is so wrapped up in Henri. But when she thinks about it she can see George helped Elise out of her melancholy. George is as much a part of their lives as the house itself.

A note from Mrs Dent arrives the next day. Measles, she writes. First little Lady Camille, who had been very ill, then just when they were to return to London, her nanny came down with it and then the marquess. Now Lady Tillingham is said to be seriously unwell.

A week later Henri hears Bos is back in London. The news that he has returned and hasn't called on them breaks Cassie's heart.

'He didn't love me,' she says quietly to Neva and for the first time takes off the necklace he gave her.

She begins to look unwell and a doctor is called. He confirms she is having twins and must rest.

'Please don't let Henri tell Bos,' she says to Neva. 'I don't want him to know.'

Henri finds his friend in White's, looking thinner and more miserable than he has ever seen him.

'Measles is wretched,' says Bos. 'I was very ill, blind for a time too, and there were no letters from Cassie until I returned home to a very blunt message saying our engagement was off.'

'Did it not occur to you that the Bishop may have had something to do with this?' says Henri. 'Cassie never received any letters from you and your father sent a footman with a request to return the ring .'

'The devil he did!' says Bos. 'I wrote every day when I could —' he stops and runs his hand through his hair. 'Oh lord — what a fool I've been.'

'Yes,' says Henri, then softens. 'But aren't we all when it comes to love?'

Bos springs from his seat. 'I must see her — I want to explain.'

'Tomorrow, eleven o'clock,' says Henri.

Cassie has spent the morning dressing, concerned her pregnancy is showing, and it matters little how often Neva tells her it isn't

'A dark gown,' Cassie says, having changed three times.

Finally she is satisfied. Neva kisses her and she and Henri leave to buy furnishings for the Sussex house.

Cassie, left alone, walks up and down the long drawing room. As the clock chimes eleven, her nerves fail. She goes outside, too restless to be indoors.

What if he doesn't come? What then? She remembers something Neva said earlier. Growing inside her are twenty fingers and twenty toes. It hardly seems possible. She stares out at the river. Two hearts, she thinks. How strange.

Elise shows Bos into the garden. He stops when he sees Cassie. Whether it is the light from the river, or the light in Cassie, she looks lovely.

'Cassie,' he says, quietly.

She turns to him, her face pale.

'I am so sorry,' he says. 'I'm stupid, I didn't think — I only received one letter from you, returning the ring, and I thought you didn't want anything more to do with me. Especially after that day when . . . I should have waited until we were married. I felt ashamed that I was carried away. I should have been more reserved. When I didn't hear from you I thought my love-making repulsed you as it did Kitty and . . .'

Cassie feels her strength come back to her. 'I love you,' she says.

It starts to rain and oblivious of the weather they stand by the river gazing at one another, until Cassie suggests they go inside.

Elise has made tea and biscuits. They talk of nothing. Cassie feels shy and Bos feels awkward and they both are full of the words they need to say to each other.

'Cassie,' says Elise. 'Why don't you show the marquess around the house?'

Henri and Neva arrive home after the theatre. Neva finds Elise and George playing cards in the kitchen.

'Well,' says Neva, 'what happened?'

Elise smiles. 'I don't know the outcome yet. Queen of Spades.'

'I can see that,' says George.

'What do you mean?' asks Neva

'I think Cassie took to her bed.'

'Oh no,' says Neva.

'I won that hand.' Elise puts down her cards.

'I'll go up and —'

'I wouldn't,' says Elise.

'What are Bos's hat and coat doing here?' says Henri, coming into the kitchen.

'Waiting for their owner to come down and retrieve them,' says Elise.

Three weeks later, the duke attends the wedding of his son to Miss Cassandra Lamb and gives his blessing to the marriage. What objection can he possibly have, now Mrs Dent has told him he is to be the grandfather of twin boys? That news has settled any disagreement between father and son. The Bishop is still in bed with measles when the marriage takes place.

Neva has never been good with change. Henri knows this. She tells him she feels as if she's an artichoke. Leaf by leaf, people, things, rooms, even she herself is changing. She is being stripped bare, her soul exposed. And there is a panic in her that wasn't there before. This new world she finds herself in is so different from what she's known. Where, she wonders, has her courage gone?

'What if I can't stand up and be the Weather Woman? I've been hidden for so long. And now even my breasts are bigger.'

'You look delicious,' says Henri. 'They are the sweetest breasts I've ever known.'

'Henri, what if we have a child and it's strange like me?' She has just finished dressing and Henri is sitting, waiting for her. They are expected to go with Elise to dine at Mrs Dent's house in Harley Street to discuss Neva's first performance and Henri's carriage is waiting outside.

'I can't go,' she says. 'I can't do this.' She bites her bottom lip then stands up and pulls off her gown. 'I need you to make me.' And now he has her in his arms. When Neva's words fail, her body talks and in their frantic love-making Henri understands what she's saying though he doesn't know if she does.

'It's all right,' he whispers. 'It's all right, my love.'

It's a cold, sunny morning when Mr Ratchet arrives with Old Bones, having crossed the river by ferry.

'You are to wait,' he says to the waterman who helps him up onto the bank. He stands in the garden looking at the scaffolding now cocooning the house. 'My word, Old Bones, what a hive of activity.'

Jetsam emerges from the workshop, followed by Henri. Seeing Old Bones, Jetsam's tail disappears between his legs and he flops to the ground.

Mr Ratchet bows. 'Good day, sir. I am Ratchet and you, if I am not mistaken, are Mr Dênou, Neva's husband.'

'I have that privilege, sir,' says Henri, bowing. 'Pleased to meet you, Mr Ratchet. I'm afraid Neva and Mrs Friezland are out.'

'I know they are, sir. I spied them from my shop window in Cheapside and hurried to the water. Mr Dabbs often ferries me here and there. I don't trust many of the ferrymen. I don't trust Mr Dabbs either but he's a good waterman. Now, sir, I came here this morning in hope of having a word with you. What I have to say is grave.

'Mary, that is Mary Letchmore, my half-sister, lives with me now as my housekeeper. Surprisingly, she is a remarkable cook. She has one child, Aubrey. His name will be familiar to you and not only in the context of Victor Friezland's will. He was also your uncle Lord Wardell's companion, so to speak. Aubrey, was, I believe, in no small part responsible for his lordship swallowing – or not swallowing – the fish. Aubrey has come to my home, shouting abuse at me and his mother, but that is by the by. The questions I've been battling with are these: is he just a harmless madman? Or is he dangerous? I have come to the conclusion, sir, that he is a serious threat. Not to me or to his mother, but to Eugene Jonas as the only person who understands the mysteries of the Weather Woman. After that, he is going to murder the usurper. Without the usurper, Aubrey thinks, all this...' Mr Ratchet waves his stick at the house, 'would be his. Do you know who, in his insanity, he calls the usurper?'

'I think I know,' says Henri.

'The usurper is Neva, Mr Dênou. Aubrey is a strong, wiry man and his insanity has only made him stronger. He said Lord Wardell is instructing him what to do. My advice, sir, is take Neva out of London for a while.'

Henri helps Mr Ratchet climb awkwardly into the ferry. 'Don't delay, sir,' he shouts as the ferry sets off across the Thames. Henri watches as it disappears into the river traffic, with Old Bones in the prow, barking at the ships.

* * *

Henri doesn't tell Neva about Mr Ratchet's visit. But her fear of change gives him the perfect excuse to suggest they leave London. The renovations to the house in Sussex are completed and Elizabeth has spared Morton to run the house and hire staff. The butler writes that he is confident that everything is in order.

'Come with us, *Tante Elise*,' says Henri. 'You and Mr Cutter would be most welcome.'

'I thank you,' says George, 'but someone has to oversee the building work here. It must be shipshape for the winter.'

Elise too would rather stay.

Three days before they're due to leave Henri returns home and as he lets himself in through the garden gate he has the uncomfortable feeling he is being watched. He wonders if he should warn Mr Cutter about Aubrey Friezland. He is contemplating this as he enters the house but it goes out of his mind when he hears Neva in the kitchen with Elise.

'Auntie, I don't think I will have children.'

'What makes you say such a silly thing?' says Elise. 'Don't you want a child?'

Henri moves further away. He doesn't want to hear this. But he stops when Neva says, 'I didn't think I did, but now… anyway, perhaps I'm too old.'

'Come here, you noodle. You're not too old for a hug.'

Neva and Henri leave on a wet Thursday and it is only after they have passed Tunbridge Wells that the sun comes out and Henri says, 'I've invited Bos and Cassie to stay.'

As with all surprises Neva's reaction makes him laugh. Her face lights up and she leans over and kisses him. 'Thank you,' she says.

The Queen Anne house is almost unrecognisable, the garden tamed, the grass cut, and if a house of bricks and mortar can look pleased with itself, this house most definitely does. In the late afternoon light it seems to be waiting for them to give their approval.

'This is how it must have looked to the sea captain before the dice was thrown,' says Neva.

Jetsam is up on the seat, whining to be let out of the carriage, while Morton stands outside with the staff to greet them. Whatever formal welcome Morton had in mind is quickly undone by Jetsam. He leaps out of the carriage and bounds up, his tail like a windmill, and doesn't stop until everyone is in fits of giggles.

Inside, the house is magnificent, as if it's standing up straighter. They go round every room, inspecting the furnishings and agree they suit the rooms well. Neva had wanted the drawing room to be full of comfy chairs and a Chesterfield sofa. A fire is roaring in the grate and it is just as she'd wished.

That night, as they sit down for supper, Morton says, 'I took the precaution of bringing in a horse, sir.'

'A horse?' says Henri.

'Very wise,' says Neva. 'That's always a good precaution.'

'It is?' says Henri when Morton has gone. 'A precaution against what?'

'Ghosts and bad luck.'

'Well, that's good to know,' says Henri.

After breakfast the following morning Neva is standing in the hall, the mellow autumn sun shining through the tall windows. The house feels different from when she and Henri camped there alone. Now there are servants and she must run the place. The trouble is, she doesn't know how to do that and she wishes Auntie was there; she would know.

For the first time she realises the difference between Henri and herself: he is used to all this, she is not. Henri is not there for her to ask what she should do, because after breakfast, he left to see about the land that is to be rented out.

Morton appears. 'Madam, we should discuss the arrangements for the visit of the marquess and marchioness.'

For a moment Neva wonders who on earth these grand people are. 'Of course,' she says. She takes a deep breath. 'I don't know how to run a house like this.' Neva wonders if the confession makes her look foolish. Morton's face is inscrutable. She adds, 'My papa didn't agree with having servants.'

'That must have made life hard for Mrs Friezland.'

Neva hadn't thought of it that way. 'Yes, I suppose it did,' she says.

'Madam,' says Morton, 'I think I understand, the house is more formal than you expected. But I can assure you it doesn't need to be.'

'It doesn't?' She's relieved to hear that. She finds herself ushered into the morning room.

'Perhaps we should start with which bedchamber you wish your guests to stay in,' says Morton.

With Morton in charge, the day begins to take on an order all of its own.

Neva says, 'There should be toys for the little girl.'

Morton makes a note.

'Do we need a housekeeper?' Neva asks, as she looks at the menus for the coming days.

'If it would suit you, madam, I can manage more than adequately.'

Neva nods. She likes this quiet, efficient man.

'No housekeeper,' says Morton.

'No housekeeper,' says Neva, smiling.

'Toys though,' says Morton.

'Yes, toys and pillows — there are too few on the beds.'

By teatime Neva feels the house is manageable after all.

★★★

Cassie and Bos arrive a day later with Camille and her nanny. Neva runs out to greet them and Cassie is looking so happy that Neva, who isn't given to weeping, bursts into tears.

'You are radiant,' she says.

'I can't wait to see round this house of yours,' says Cassie, taking her arm.

'This is the drawing room,' says Neva, opening the door. 'The wallpaper is from China.' She laughs to hear herself saying it.

The fire is lit and tea is served.

'Mama,' calls Camille, 'there's a rocking horse in my bedchamber.'

'"Mama"?' says Neva when Camille and her nanny have gone to explore further.

'I had nothing to do with it,' says Cassie. 'Camille called me that as soon as Bos and I were married.' She puts her hand on her belly. 'Isn't it extraordinary? I think I must have become pregnant the very first time. I honestly didn't think…'

Neva smiles. 'Because you kept your clothes on.'

'Come here,' says Cassie and takes Neva's hand.

'What's that?' says Neva.

'One of them is kicking. Now,' says Cassie, 'what are you going to wear for your lecture? I want you to be sensational.'

'I thought, if it wouldn't tire you, we could go to Brighton for the day,' says Neva. 'Henri knows of a dressmaker there.'

That night when they all sit down for supper, Neva thinks it's easy to believe they had always lived this way. The conversation is entertaining and Neva loves listening to Cassie talk about the freedom she felt when she presented the Weather Woman.

In bed that night, Neva says, 'I once said…'

Henri looks at her quizzically.

'I once said I didn't want a child. But I think I do.'

'In that case, we have to keep on…'

And Neva laughs. 'So we do.'

The next day Henri shows Bos round the gardens. His friend's smile is back and he is the old Bos, the one Henri first knew.

'Isn't Cassie wonderful?' Bos says. 'Camille adores her.'

'You look completely different,' says Henri.

'Yes, I'm outrageously happy.' He stops and says, 'What happened with Kitty was so awful, it haunted me.'

'You mean her dying?'

'More the manner of her death. I can't bear the thought of anything happening to Cassie, and twins are always difficult. I have the best doctor in London looking after her. He tells me there's no need to worry.'

'You're sure it's twins?' asks Henri.

'Yes – two heartbeats. I'm terrified, if I'm honest. I couldn't live without Cassie. When I was ill I stupidly convinced myself it would be the same with Cassie as it was with Kitty, once we were married. We'd made love obviously, but with clothes on and… oh, Henri, it's not the same at all. She loves me, all of me, and wants me as I want her. I told Cassie about my relationship with Kitty, that she thought my love-making was disgusting. I feared Cassie might think the same. I even said perhaps we should wait until after the twins were born before we made love again. She said, nonsense, it shows they are being born into love. I never knew love-making could be so…'

'Wondrous,' says Henri.

'Yes. I don't think anyone should marry unless this part of loving works. The rest is easy. And you?'

'What do you think?' says Henry smiling.

'That you, like me, are a lucky man. Neva grows more beautiful every time I see her. Is she really going to stand up and openly be the Weather Woman?'

'Yes,' says Henri. 'I believe she can do it.'

★ ★ ★

Neva feels calmer having Cassie with her again.

'You haven't lost me,' says Cassie. 'You never will.'

'So much has altered.'

'For the better.'

'Henri thinks we need servants at Papa's house, as well as here.'

'What would Uncle Victor say?' says Cassie, laughing. 'But did he ever sweep, scrub and clean the house?'

'He did,' says Neva.

'He didn't! And you aren't good at housework. You never were and Auntie could do with some help now.'

'Before you and Bos were married I overheard Mrs Dent telling Auntie that George had eyes for her.'

'I think George has been in love with Auntie since the beginning of time.'

This puzzles Neva. Why had she never noticed?

They are silent for a moment before Cassie says, changing the subject, 'I do think Auntie needs more help — perhaps some changes are to be embraced.'

Cassie and Neva go to Brighton in Bos's carriage, a wedding present from the duke. 'I know it's outrageously grand,' says Cassie. 'If the duke could have had the words "Expecting Twin Boys" painted on the outside, instead of the Smedmore coat of arms he would've.'

The dressmaker who made Neva's wedding gown is most impressed with Cassie's designs. 'This is daring indeed, Lady Smedmore, and I predict will be much copied.'

'It must be ravishing,' says Cassie, 'and show off Mrs Dênou's sweet figure to advantage.'

Measurements are taken and Cassie and Neva spend a happy morning choosing fabric. Afterwards they have tea and shop for ribbons and lace, until Cassie is tired.

'Who would have thought that you would be a marchioness?' says Neva, as they are driven home amid a pile of boxes.

'Who would have thought you would be a *comtesse*?' says Cassie and falls asleep.

One afternoon when Bos and Henri have gone fishing, Cassie and Neva are playing cards.

'How are you coping without Eugene Jonas?' asks Cassie.

'I can't think about it,' says Neva. 'I'm anxious about giving my talk. I'm sure I'll be laughed at. Even Henri thinks some might find what I have to say so incredible they will leave.'

'I think no one will.'

'Mama,' says Camille, coming in with Jetsam who is covered in mud, 'look what I found. Nanny says I can't keep it.' Cassie looks at what Camille has in her tiny hands. 'It's a frog,' Camille adds helpfully.

Cassie lifts the little girl onto her lap. 'Now tell me,' she says, 'if a giant came along and said, "I like the look of this little girl and I want to keep her," do you think Father and I wouldn't be heartbroken?'

Camille sighs. 'Yes, I'm a giant to the frog. Come on, Jetsam,' she says and they go off to put the frog back.

'She needs a pet of some kind,' says Cassie.

It arrives most unexpectedly.

Lady Calthrop, whose estate is not far away, turns up a day or two later just as they have sat down to dine. She demands to see the owner of the house and Morton reluctantly announces her. Lady Calthrop has with her a basket; what's in the basket is unclear except it wriggles.

Jetsam disappears under the table as Neva stands up to greet her. 'Your dog, madam, polluted my bitch in her first season,' says Lady Calthrop. 'She's a pedigree.' She puts the basket on the floor. 'She gave birth to these. They're yours.'

Camille is down from the table and has opened the

basket. There are two sweet-looking puppies, both with the undeniable look of Jetsam to them.

'This one,' says Camille, picking up the smaller of the two. 'Please, Father, it's much better than a frog.'

'Yes, but only the one,' says Bos firmly.

Lady Calthrop turns to leave.

'Stay, please stay,' says Neva. 'All your colours are hidden in clouds of ill-temper but behind them is such a softness of pinks and reds.'

Everyone is quiet. Lady Calthrop looks at Neva astonished then smiles. 'I like you,' she says. 'A straight talker, which is rare. Yes, I will have a glass of wine.'

Introductions are made and before Lady Calthrop leaves she tells Neva and Henri they must meet more local people, and it's good to see the old sea captain's house restored. She graciously accepts Jetsam's apology.

Camille goes sleepily upstairs with one of the puppies. Morton takes the other one to the kitchen. In the morning he has a word with Henri.

'I wonder, sir,' he says, 'if I could have the puppy. I will, of course, have to ask her ladyship, but if...'

'Morton, she's yours,' says Henri.

And for a man given to perfecting a solemn poker face, Morton's expression tells Henri all he needs to know.

'Happiness is unfathomable,' says Neva. 'Its colours are richer than that of the sunrise. Perhaps it can only ever be understood as a memory.'

'Or as a constant pursuit,' suggests Henri.

Neva thinks it's extraordinary she's married and often, when she wakes early, she lies watching Henri sleep, waiting for his eyes to open and for him to wrap her in his arms. Each day, she says 'Thank you.' To whom, she doesn't know.

54

November 1813

It's early morning, on 14th November. After a misty night, a fog has settled, lazy on the Thames, thicker at the shoreline, climbing up into the streets. The church bells have rung four, the day has yet to be lived and in his ferry, among the ghosts of the drowned and the murdered, sits Mr Magnus Dabbs, a waterman by trade and an unofficial dealer in the dead.

Mr Dabbs considers himself a wealthy man. Every Sunday he has a fine joint of roast beef, accompanied by Yorkshire pudding, served on a china plate, set on a starched, white linen tablecloth. He has a fine wife to lend the appearance of respectability. The local constable and the nightwatchman are often to be found at Mr Dabbs's house enjoying his generous hospitality. His guests marvel at the way he carves the beef into wafer-thin slices. Neither his wife nor his guests suspect anything untoward.

He keeps his cellar locked and the key on a chain about his person. 'Like Bluebeard,' he jokes. 'It's the one door in the house, my little darling,' as he calls his wife, 'is not allowed to open.' For alongside his fine wine there is often to be found a fine body.

Mr Dabbs knows each surgeon in the anatomy department of every teaching hospital in London. He knows exactly how much they are willing to pay for a good body, a body that can be carved finer than his Sunday joint. If it's a clean, wholesome body, it can be sold again and again and, if lucky, again.

This week he has picked up a young gentleman of about twenty-six with dark hair and nondescript features.

The landlady of a tumble-down boarding-house near Smithfield Market thinks the young gentleman might have been a clerk with gambling debts. What Mr Dabbs likes about this body is that he apparently has no name or at least none that appears to belong to him. He had taken rooms for a fortnight under the number 6K1. On Sunday the landlady had heard him drunk and cursing. On Monday she hadn't heard him at all. On Tuesday, having not seen him come in or go out, she feared the worst. With a trembling hand she opened the door of his room, only to find him dead, eyes wide open, foam at the mouth. Not wanting trouble, she called on Mr Dabbs. At three in the morning, when most people are sleeping and the streets are quiet, Mr Dabbs arrived with his cart. He asked to be left alone with the body and went through the gentleman's clothes. There he found a gaming slip. In his hand was a letter to his sweetheart.

Mr Dabbs offers a full professional service, guaranteeing not to leave a trace of the dead man. He gave two shillings and sixpence to the landlady in consideration of calling him out. The landlady has since treated herself to a pork pie and a tumbler of gin.

Mr Dabbs took the body on his cart through the back streets to his house by the river, entering through the outside door to the cellar to save the inconvenience of going through his spotlessly clean hall. He stripped the body of its clothes, putting aside those he considered good enough to keep. The small items he burned.

He has boxes of clothes, all neatly labelled. The dead, in his humble opinion, need order. If you dress a corpse in finery, the surgeons believe they are getting a superior specimen. Clothes are what defines a man in death as they do in life.

Four days have passed and seemingly no one has sung a song of sorrow for this young clerk, one of London's many lost and lonely. But Mr Dabbs would like to get rid of the body before it deteriorates. There's an inn near Barts Hospital where he drinks. When he has a good corpse he wears a red spotted handkerchief in his breast pocket. A surgeon will pay well for a sorry young man such as the one he has in his cellar.

He's sitting down with a pint of Fuller's ale and is studying his fingernails. They bother him a lot. He likes to keep them clean, has a special bar of tar soap with which he scrubs the smell of the dead off him. He's thinking he should've cut them shorter when someone sits down beside him, a little too close. Someone else sits on the other side of him, also a little too close.

He lifts his head to see on one side a face he never wished to see again, and on the other a face he could never forget.

'Mr Gutteridge,' he says, 'what an unwelcome surprise. And Mr Briggs too. You want your money, I imagine. I can get it to you, sir.'

Mr Gutteridge says, 'Four years ago, Mr Dabbs, I made sure that the hanging rope did not find your neck.'

'I was innocent, sir – I was found not guilty.'

'Is my hat black, Mr Dabbs?'

'It is, Mr Gutteridge.'

'Then I say you were guilty as charged and it was only due to my skill and that of your barrister that we extricated your neck from the noose. And yet, you seem to think it right not to pay us.'

'I can get you your money by the morning, Mr Gutteridge.'

'I hear you are a dealer in the dead,' says Mr Briggs. 'I suppose we could regard that as a positive career change.'

'I'm an honourable man leading an honest—'

Mr Briggs interrupts him. 'Be quiet, Dabbs, and listen.'

'This is what you must do,' says Mr Gutteridge. 'I want you to supply the body of a young gentleman. He will be found well dressed and wearing these blue spectacles, and these documents will be in his breast pocket.' He places the spectacles and the documents on the table and keeps his hand over them. 'What I don't want, Mr Dabbs, is the cadaver ending up on the dissecting table. I repeat: it must be recovered with these spectacles and these documents. I hope I make myself quite clear. If it is quickly discovered by the watch then you will have repaid your debt to me. But if I find you have used force in the demise of said cadaver, I will not hesitate to have you rearrested.'

The ferryman swallows hard. 'It takes old Father Thames a while to show his wares,' he says, 'and sometimes the mud claims them or the eels nibble them.'

'Not this one,' says Mr Gutteridge.

Mr Magnus Dabbs is marking time. The cadaver is tied by a rope to his boat. It's the kind of night the dealer in the dead likes; he won't be noticed, as long as he keeps close to the bank. The tide will be out by dawn and all being well this body should be discovered. He has been careful to dress it smart, the documents are in the breast pocket of the frock coat in an oilcloth pouch. He has bent the wires of the spectacles so they cling over the ears.

Just below the new Blackfriars Bridge he slides the body

into the treacly, receding waters of the Thames. Then, quiet as a ghost, Mr Dabbs rows away from the corpse and goes to report a dead body in the river to the nightwatchman.

In Lincoln's Inn, Mr Gutteridge is fast asleep, his conscience clear, his mind at rest.

55

That night, in the house in the lane off Tooley Street, George Cutter isn't thinking about the scaffolding erected that morning so the roof could be mended. His mind is on other matters. All he can think about is Elise. Ten nights ago she had knocked on the door of his bedchamber. He hadn't made love for such a long time and he was ashamed that it was over almost before it had begun. She hadn't said a word and in the morning it was as if it never happened.

George thinks she's regretting it. He wishes he had been better; perhaps then things might have turned out differently.

He'd thought about writing her a letter, telling her not to worry, but it's out of character. He longs for her to knock at his door again. The builders have finished her new bedchamber on the ground floor. A wrought iron bed has been set up with a new feather mattress. George has been sleeping upstairs in Victor's study.

In the nights he was unable to sleep he busied himself decorating Elise's bedchamber. Tomorrow he will show her what he's done. He now knows what happened between them was a mistake. Her silence tells him as much. Perhaps he should leave, find work elsewhere. But the thought is too terrible to contemplate. He can't forget how lovely she felt. Her skin was as soft as velvet to the touch.

He sits up at the sound of his door opening.

Elise hasn't been sleeping well either. She shouldn't have gone to George like that. She feels ashamed of herself and since then they have hardly spoken. Tomorrow she will explain, tell him she's sorry. It was a moment of madness, that was it. He was nothing like Victor, but then no one ever would be. Two lost people. How deep the scars of grief, of loneliness are. No, he isn't Victor, and neither is she George's lost wife. Outside it's raining and still she can't sleep.

She jumps. There's a loud thud and a bang as if something or someone has fallen over. She feels the whole house hold its breath. She has always dreaded a break-in. Long ago, when all the talk in the neighbourhood had been about Neva, Victor had taught her how to fire a pistol, in case any fool did break in.

'But I'll be shaking with fear,' she'd said.

'You cannot predict how you'll be until the time comes – if it ever does,' said Victor.

Now she is steely calm. She takes the two pistols from their case in the drawer of the table by her bed. By the light of the fire, she checks they are both loaded. In bare feet she quietly opens her chamber door. It is pitch black but she knows every floorboard, every creak of the house, which steps to avoid, where to stand on tiptoe.

'Where is he?'

She hears Aubrey before she sees him. Now she is in the passage leading to the kitchen and her heart is thumping because George is tied to a chair.

'Where is he? Where is Eugene Jonas?' says Aubrey and

slaps George across the face. 'You'd better tell me if you want your tomorrows. Where is he?'

Elise catches a glint of the knife. He is waving it wildly, dangerously close to George's face.

Up to this point Elise isn't sure if she can fire a pistol but now she knows she can.

There is a madness about Aubrey. 'Shut it,' he says. 'Shut it,' he says again to himself.

Elise lifts a pistol. She waits until Aubrey walks away from George and kicks over a chair, then she takes aim. Don't think, she tells herself, and in that split second Aubrey sees her and she fires the pistol. She lets the pistol drop and lifts the other.

There is a long, smoke-filled silence. Then a scream and a clatter as his knife falls.

'You fucking whore, you hit me!'

He's about to pick up the knife and Elise says, 'If you move any closer, Aubrey, I will kill you.'

Aubrey backs away towards the kitchen door. He rattles the handle and it gives.

'I'll be back,' he shouts. 'I'll be back for him. Shut it. Shut it. I'll find him, I'll find Eugene Jonas.' And he's gone.

It's still raining. Elise closes and locks the kitchen door then unties George.

'Are you hurt?' she says, taking the gag from his mouth.

'No. You?'

'No,' says Elise. George opens the back door. 'Where are you going?'

'To make sure everything is secure.'

She starts to say, 'But you're only wearing your nightshirt...' but he's already out through the door.

He's soaked when he comes back.

'You're drenched and your face...' She stops.

'You were so brave,' says George.

'No, I—'

'You were,' says George. 'And you're shaking.'

'So are you,' says Elise.

'Come on, let's get warm.'

He takes her into the new bedchamber and goes to find another nightshirt.

'George,' she says, when he comes back, 'who decorated this room?'

'I did.'

'It's a work of art.'

He has painted a panoramic view of the river with different types of sailing ships, galleons with their sails billowing, a frigate, and a man-o'-war, flags flying. Floating above them, like a cloud, is...

'That's me,' she says.

'Yes.'

'And the man in the fishing boat is you?'

He nods.

'I can paint it over and...' He stops. 'I wanted to write you a letter and I couldn't. So this is my love poem to you. I will leave when Henri and Neva return.'

'Come here,' she says. 'It's me that got into a muddle. It isn't a year yet since Victor died. I wanted you, then I felt guilty. Where are you going?'

'To get some brandy.'

They lie on the new bed and he takes her hand.

'Tonight,' she says, 'when I saw Aubrey had you tied up, I thought my heart might stop. I couldn't consider a world without you, George. Some might say I was fond of you, I might even have said you were a good friend, but what I didn't know until tonight is that I love you.'

George holds her tight. 'I've loved you, Elise, such a long time. I felt a fool, being caught off guard tonight, but you see I thought it was you coming to me.'

In the morning his side of the bed is empty, and Elise lies there thinking she's no longer ashamed. His loving was so sweet and healing. We belong to the living, she thinks, to the light.

It's a cold morning and George comes in with a tray. He is wearing her dressing gown and his nightcap. Elise bursts out laughing and realises that in all her life no one has ever brought her breakfast in bed.

George smiles.

Elise sits up. 'You have a black eye.'

'It doesn't matter.' He kisses her. 'I have your heart.'

'That you do.'

They get dressed and carry on with the day. It's like any other day and in the evening, over supper, Elise says, 'We don't have to make a fuss of this.' George stops eating. Elise laughs. 'We can make as much fuss as you fancy when the bedchamber door's closed.'

'That's a relief,' he says. 'I'm just getting the hang of it again and I wouldn't want it to stop.'

'Neither would I. But I don't want to get married.'

'No,' says George. 'I think if you've done it well once, that's enough.'

And that night they lie in bed together as they always will.

Two days later, Elise is in the long drawing room, waiting for the furniture to be returned. By the end of the day the house will be its old self again but smarter.

A familiar double ring at the garden gate tells her who it is. She sighs.

George shows Mr Gutteridge into the drawing room. He looks more pleased with himself than she has ever seen him.

He rocks back and forth on the balls of his feet and says, 'Elise, I'm sorry to call on you so early but I wanted to tell you as soon as possible, before you read it in the papers. Mr Eugene Jonas has been found in the river, dead.'

56

The death of Eugene Jonas is a mystery to Neva. How such a thing has come to pass she doesn't like to ask but there is a great relief in knowing that her made-up friend has found freedom to walk the clouds unencumbered by gravity. Elise wrote that Mr Gutteridge had more than redeemed himself, dealing with the necessary paperwork and the burial without bothering her once. The two solicitors, Mr Gutteridge and Mr Seaton, had attended the funeral. The word 'burial' seems to Neva to be as final as any word could possibly be especially when set beside 'funeral'.

Shortly after, a letter from Mr Gutteridge arrives for Henri informing him that Victor Friezland's will has been upheld by the courts. Mr Briggs obtained a sworn affidavit from Mr Robert Letchmore stating that Aubrey is his rightful son and this, combined with a certificate of the marriage of Mr Letchmore and Miss Mary Kydd, had put an end to Aubrey Letchmore's claims on Victor Friezland's estate. Furthermore, Mr Ratchet's wise investments of Mr Friezland's monies have meant the estate is fully able to meet the terms of the will regarding Mrs Dênou, and Mr Seaton has assured him the sum of £5,000 will be paid annually into Henri's bank account.

'I suppose that's his way of saying "checkmate",' says Neva.

'The money is yours, not mine, and when we are back in London, we'll open a bank account for you at Coutts.'

'But I trust you,' says Neva.

'But I believe women should have control of their own finances.'

It had been Henri's idea not to return to London until the day before Neva's lecture. He can see that any sooner and Neva will become anxious. If they're honest, neither of them have much desire to return.

'We could hibernate here,' suggests Neva, but they both know it isn't possible.

The carriage is called for early on 11th December. The surprise is Morton's request to be allowed to stay on to take care of the house, and for his position to be permanent. His reason is the puppy and a fondness for the new mistress.

It's early evening when they arrive at the Friezland house. Neva has been quiet for most of the journey and Henri thinks she is dreading seeing the changes. This, he always knew, was going to be hard.

'We're home,' he says, and takes her hand to help her down from the carriage.

For a moment she is bewildered by the alterations to her father's house and the presence of the two servants who come to greet them.

All Neva can do is spin her amber pebble through her fingers as she looks round the long drawing room. The furniture is back and the house has undergone a transformation. It's decidedly warmer than she has ever known it to be at this time of year.

'Shall we see upstairs?' says Henri gently and takes her

hand. 'I think the house feels the same – and the changes are for the better.' He opens the door to their new bedchamber, which has a window leading to a balcony. Next to it is their drawing room where a fire has been lit. He looks at her. 'What is it?'

She says nothing but goes to her old bedchamber, and is glad to find it is still the same as she left it. 'All these changes,' she says. 'You don't think the house will fall down?'

She begins to undress and he doesn't ask her what she's doing. Neva has unlaced the front of her gown and he closes the door.

'The house is not the same,' she says.

'I know,' he says, 'but you'll...'

She kisses the words out of him as he unbuttons his waistcoat. All she knows is she needs him, only he will make sense of her fears. At that moment they are overwhelming.

Henri lies on her small bed, his limbs floating. He had never imagined finding a lover like Neva; with the freedom to love, to be loved, his need echoed back to him.

'I'm frightened of this winter, that's all,' she says.

This is the day Neva has waited for, when she will stand in front of an audience and be seen as the Weather Woman. All she must do is hold fast to the knowledge that what she does is extraordinary.

At five o'clock she arrives at the house in Harley Street. It is a hive of activity; the staff are still arranging the flowers and lighting the candelabra. One footman carries a tray of glasses, others plates of fancies. How many times did I wait here before going onto the stage with Papa? How many times did I sit at the table, hoping no one would notice the movement of my feet? Tonight is going to be different.

Mrs Dent comes bustling down the stairs, wearing a

dressing gown with her hair in curling rags. 'Neva, are you feeling well?' she says by way of a greeting. 'You look pale.'

'I'm quite well, thank you, Mrs Dent.'

'No, no,' says Mrs Dent to a footman with a tray. 'Plates to your left, to your left. Where is Mr Dênou?'

'He'll be here later. Have Mr and Mrs James arrived?'

'Yes. They said they were to be sent up to the room you're changing in. Are you sure you don't want Annie to help you? Where are you going with that table?' says Mrs Dent to another footman.

Neva laughs.

'This is what happens when all the tickets have been sold. I could have sold them twice over, they've gone so fast. The excitement, my dear, knows no bounds.' She looks at Neva again and is about to say something more and stops.

Neva goes up the stairs, passing several footmen coming down. She knows which room she has been given and waiting there is Mr James, who has laid out his scissors and brushes. Rose has hung up the gown Neva is to wear.

'I've never seen anything like this,' Rose says. 'It will cause a sensation. What do they say nowadays? "It's going to be all the..."?'

'"All the rage",' says Neva.

She sits down and Mr James wraps a cloth round her. 'What's it to be, sir?'

'I want you to dress my hair as you did when I first became Eugene Jonas.'

'Won't that give the game away?'

'I don't believe it will,' says Neva. 'Those who do have an inkling will have the wisdom not to say anything for it will reflect badly on them for being taken in. This is in loving memory of Eugene Jonas, without his blue spectacles and with a much more feminine cut to his garments. I had a dressmaker in Brighton make the gown.'

'We should lock the door,' says Rose.

'A wise precaution, my love,' says Mr James, his scissors snipping.

While her hair is being cut, Neva asks about life downriver and what they've done to make sure they're safe in the freezing weather to come.

Then it's time to dress. First the chemise over which her corset is laced, pushing up her breasts. Over this goes a beautiful waistcoat embroidered with gold and yellow threads. Black silk trousers stop just above her ankles revealing pointed red suede slippers. Finally, an elegant velvet gown in the blue of Eugene's spectacles and fastened by one enticing button. It falls open at the front when she moves and shows off the trousers and the waistcoat. Round Neva's neck Mr James ties a crisp white linen cravat which cascades into the waistcoat and is held in place by a pin. He makes sure her hair is artistically tangled. Only then do he and Rose stand back and examine their handiwork. They are both satisfied and the whole enterprise has taken them until seven o'clock.

'I believe Beau Brummell only takes two hours to get dressed every morning,' says Neva. 'I'm sure he would be impressed by how long we've taken.'

'You look breathtaking,' says Rose. 'Who designed the gown?'

'Cassie, who else.'

Mr James unlocks the door and he and Rose escort Neva down the back staircase to an anteroom lit by candles. There are mirrors all round the chamber and her reflection spins into an infinity of images. Beyond is the stage in the double drawing room.

'Do you want us to wait with you?' asks Rose.

'No,' says Neva.

She has waited here many times with Papa and she can see him in her mind's eye.

'This,' she says to him, *is the same audience that came to see a machine, your machine, Papa. They longed to believe a wooden woman could predict the weather. They would rather have worshipped at that altar than see the truth of me, a young girl of flesh and blood who knew the secrets of the skies. I doubt they'll listen now. I can already hear the laughter when I tell them the weather possesses an innate intelligence.'*

'No,' says Victor, *'tell them a story – that's what they want, something they can understand.'*

'That the winds enjoy blowing ships off course, that Zeus relishes the power of storms, that Poseidon, the king of the waves, will never relinquish his hold on the sea.'

'Yes, talk to them in narrative, make the incomprehensible understandable.'

'I will tell them frost marvels at the poetry of its own beauty in the hawthorn bush. You are right – there has to be a beginning, a middle and an end. I will start with the future, a future which belongs to those who understand the weather system, not just small pieces of it but as a whole. The middle part will be that we earthbound creatures have an effect on the delicate balance of the skies. Will it shake their lazy thoughts? No, Papa, it won't.'

'And the end?'

High above her, Eugene Jonas is cloud walking, his mind free of the ticking clocks, of society's preconceptions, free of a religion that turns thought into a logical landscape of illogical beliefs.

Most probably the audience will think her mad and comfort themselves with this proof of her insanity.

'Oh, Papa, can I do this?'

But he is gone.

On the stage the cellist has begun to play.

Henri arrives at a quarter past seven and finds the house is filling up. There are guests on the stairs, guests in the double drawing room where he joins Bos and Cassie and Elise and George. On the far side of the room he sees his aunt with his cousins and their husbands. And there, of course, is Sir Edward Fairbrother with his cronies. Henri has a sinking feeling they will relish making a mockery of this.

'Have you seen her yet?' asks Cassie.

'I'm going to find her now,' says Henri.

'Did she tell you what she's wearing?'

'No,' says Henri, who hasn't given it a thought. He assumes she will be wearing an evening gown like all the ladies here tonight.

In the crush on the main staircase he hears one of them say she has only come to see who the dashing Frenchman has married. 'She's quite mad, you know.'

He overhears a gentleman say, 'How will she prove she can tell the weather? Surely we can all go around saying it's going to rain and at some time in the day we will be right.'

His companion says, 'But you never saw the Weather Woman. Oh, my dear, you missed out so terribly.'

A curtain hangs over the door of the antechamber. A footman says helpfully it's so no one can take a peep.

Assuring him he is Mrs Dênou's husband, Henri draws it back and opens the door. Neva is waiting anxiously for him.

'*Mon dieu,*' he says. 'You look as you did when I first saw Eugene Jonas. My love, what madness that I didn't know he was you.'

'What do you think?'

'I think you look utterly sensational. If you were only to walk out and say "Good evening", it would be enough to take London by storm.'

'Truly?'

'Truly. The gown is fabulously original. You are fabulously original.'

On the stage, Mrs Dent is asking for quiet.

'Kiss me,' says Neva.

Henri kisses her and says, 'I'm so very proud of you. Do you have your pebble?'

Neva is biting her bottom lip. 'Yes,' she says.

Henri leaves her and goes to stand at the back of the room where once, long ago, he watched a fearless girl ask Lord Wardell who he thought he was.

The lights are dimmed, and the oil lamps turned up on the stage. Mrs Dent stands in front of the curtain and rings a little bell.

'My lords, ladies and gentlemen, please settle down,' she says. 'Many of you came here in the past to see the late Victor Friezland present his extraordinary invention, the Weather Woman. I know there were those who wondered how it worked and how the Weather Woman was always so accurate in her predictions – down to the hour. Those who followed her and knew this to be a mystery worthy of solving will be surprised. Those who believed the predictions were made by a machine might find an element of disappointment in what they are about to see. I long suspected the truth. In all the time she worked with her father, Victor Friezland, not one of her predictions fell short of the mark, and tonight I present to you the real Weather Woman, Madame Neva Dênou.'

The curtain is pulled back and the audience gasp as Neva walks towards the footlights and stands there, elegant, defiant.

'My lords, ladies and gentlemen, I have waited nearly all my adult life to be here tonight, not hidden behind a table or appearing as a ghost. Tonight, I have nothing to hide behind. I have been hidden, I have hidden and now I will hide no more. I will not be ashamed that there is no science or meteorology to explain what I can do. I care little if I am the only person who is capable of doing it. One person is more than enough. So, let's begin. First, can we open the windows?

Don't be alarmed, it will only be for a moment.' Two footmen step forward and in harmony the windows rise. 'It is, as you know, a cold night,' says Neva. 'In twenty minutes there will be a light shower of snow. It will continue until ten o'clock in the morning and will have melted away by dinner time. To all of those here who like accuracy, may I suggest you set your watches now.'

The footmen close the windows to the rustle of pocket watches being taken from waistcoats. Then all is quiet.

She begins. The audience are spellbound. She holds them as lightly as the pebble that dances through her fingers. She starts with hearing the ice singing when she was a child, describing how she sees the clouds.

She goes on to make her predictions.

'This winter will be one of great extremes. On 27th December – this month – at two o'clock in the afternoon a fog will arrive in London. It will be the first fog in which man has had a hand. The soot being pumped from every chimney into the clouds will help make this fog the worst in living memory. By the evening it will be so dense the city itself will become a stranger to its inhabitants and it will be accompanied by one of the greatest frosts we have known. The fog will last for five days lifting just as the snow comes and it will snow without stopping for forty-eight hours and this after nearly four weeks of continuous frost. The wind will blow north to north-easterly. On Sunday, 30th January, after a day of thaw, an immense mass of ice will float from the upper part of the river and the thaw will last for two days, as ice moves and blocks the Thames between London Bridge and Blackfriars. The following day the river will freeze on the turn of the tide. On Tuesday, 1st February, the floating mass of ice will solidify and the river will become frozen until 5th February. I'm sure some people will swear the ice is safe to walk on until 6th February, but I can promise you the ice will thaw on that day.'

She stops and asks the time. A gentleman says twenty minutes has passed. The footmen open the windows and the audience can see it has begun to snow.

Neva takes questions and gives predictions for the dates requested, until finally Mrs Dent rings her bell. Neva stands, head held high, certain that she is going to be booed. There is the sound of chairs scraping across the floor and people are standing. She realises the deafening noise is that of applause.

Victor is smiling proudly at her from the side of the stage. *'You did it,'* he says.

57

December 1813 to February 1814

The curtain falls but Neva doesn't move until she hears the antechamber door behind her being thrown open. She turns and there is Henri. She goes to him and he lifts her off her feet.

'My darling, you astonished them.'

'They're not laughing?'

'No, they're not. They're talking about my brilliant wife.' He holds her in his arms. 'No laughter, no ridicule, just respect. Now shall we go and meet your admirers?'

This is the first time she has had supper at one of Mrs Dent's soirees. Papa had always insisted they should go home straight away. The dining room is painted dark blue and everything in it is refined. It shows that under Mrs Dent's garish clothes there is a lady of immense sophistication. The guests all stand as Neva and Henri enter and she is seated at the head of the table, surrounded by the eccentric gentlemen her father used to dine with.

When supper is underway, Lady Warren asks, 'Tell me, why were you hidden behind such bizarre contraptions? Surely people should have known about you?'

'I agree,' says a man of science. 'It's not as if we weren't interested. I asked Mr Friezland many times how the predictions were so accurate, but he was adamant it was his machine. If we had known you were the real diamond, his machine would have been seen as nothing more than clever fairground entertainment.'

Sir Edward Fairbrother taps the side of his glass. 'I wish to say that I found Mrs Dênou's talk truly fascinating. I'm sure my esteemed colleagues would agree.'

There are cries of 'Hear, hear' from round the table.

Neva and Henri, with Elise and George, arrive home at half-past twelve. One of the maids is still up to help Neva undress and bring a tray of hot chocolate and pastries to their drawing room. Tonight they will sleep in their new bedchamber.

Neva sits down across from Henri and studies him. 'What are you thinking? You have been thinking about something on and off all evening and there is a smudge in your colours.'

'Would you like a game of chess?' asks Henri, ignoring the question. He puts the chessboard between them and they play in silence. He has taken her bishop when he says, 'I was thinking about my uncle Wardell, and that he was the reason I didn't recognise you when you were Eugene Jonas.' She looks up at him but he is concentrating on his next move.

'I was nine when I went to live with Lord Wardell and he wasted no time in sending me to boarding school. When I was sixteen I returned to his house and saw he was looking at me differently. He used to take me to a molly house for his amusement. I felt safer there than I did at home.' Henri gives a short, bitter laugh. 'He told me time and again I was like him.'

Neva puts her hand to his face. 'You're not like him.'

'I know that,' he says, taking her hand and kissing the palm.

'When I was Eugene, women fell in love with me but I

didn't fall for them,' says Neva. 'I was drunk that evening we went to Brooks's. I had never been drunk and when you put me in the cab I know I confused you by kissing you. I thought next time I saw you I would explain, except there was no next time and I felt ashamed of what I'd done. I didn't tell anyone, I didn't tell myself. This is the weather of passion: sometimes it blows one way, sometimes another, sometimes it blows us off course, sometimes it doesn't. More often than not it fogs up our souls.'

'It fogged up mine,' says Henri. 'Though boy-girl girl-boy I would always have loved you. Checkmate.'

And she is in his arms, the chess pieces scattered on the floor along with her dressing gown.

Neva is still fast asleep, but Henri is up and lighter in his thoughts. He dresses, sits on the edge of the bed and strokes Neva's face. She rolls over and says softly, 'I couldn't live if you weren't here in this air that I breathe.'

'I feel the same about you, my love,' says Henri.

Elise has breakfast laid out and the papers are on the kitchen table.

'They're calling her sensational,' she says.

'I'll take them up with a breakfast tray,' says Henri.

'Wait,' says Elise. 'You haven't seen the building work.' She calls for George.

'Would you mind if we inspected the house later?' says Henri.

'Not at all, but we have something to tell you,' says George. He and Elise relate what happened the night Aubrey broke in.

Henri wishes he'd made George aware of Mr Ratchet's warning. 'I would rather we didn't tell Neva, not now.'

And any potential danger lurking outside the gate is forgotten.

It is a quiet Christmas. So much has happened in one year and without Cassie it feels strange to Elise and Neva. Although no one will say it, a year ago Victor was still with them on this day. It also marks a year since Henri nearly drowned.

Christmas might have passed completely uncelebrated, if Mrs Dent hadn't arrived on Christmas night, accompanied by two footmen carrying a smoked salmon, two roasted pheasants, roast potatoes, parsnips, and red cabbage and apple. Elise has given the maids the day off and she and Mrs Dent lay out the sugared plums and mince pies.

'Before we eat,' says Mrs Dent, lifting her glass of champagne, 'I want to raise a glass to Victor who would be immensely proud of Neva, and I think not surprised she is married to Henri.'

'Victor,' they say and drink to him. Elise surreptitiously wipes away a tear.

Henri stands and says, 'I would like to remember all those who drowned on the *Sea Wind*. And especially Mrs O'Donnell, a courageous woman.'

Mrs Dent, the mistress of entertainment, changes the mood. After the finest of Christmas suppers, she says, 'Who will play the piano?' And to everyone's surprise it is Henri who says he will give it a try. It turns out he knows even more sea shanties than George and there is much dancing and laughter.

'Well, girl,' says Mrs Dent to Elise as she is leaving, 'you know Victor would be so very pleased to see you this happy.' She kisses Elise then all the colour and gaiety that is Mrs Dent vanishes in a golden carriage like Christmas itself.

On the morning of 27th December, the anniversary of Victor's death, Neva is looking out over the river from the window of her new drawing room. Already there are islands of ice floating up and down with the tide, growing bigger by the hour, and the fog lies low, like a thief silently waiting.

Then it creeps up the ships into the tall rigging, spills into the streets, rises over and around the houses and up into the sky to snuff out the light. Neva thinks of all the hundreds of years that the Thames, a ribbon of water, has wound its way through this ever-expanding city. It seems that her life has come full circle. This winter there will be a frost fair just like the one she went to as a child. She can recall fragments but even they may be clouded by the stories she has been told. What does it matter, they are hers. She sees herself, kneeling on the ice, looking down at the frozen fish, listening to the ice singing.

Underneath her memories, she is worrying that the ice is a harbinger of tragedy. This is folly, she thinks, and not to be indulged. She is no longer a child. The chess-playing bear, the Punch and Judy man are long gone. She knows when the ice will arrive and also the hour of its going. There's no need for anyone to be near the frost fair. Yet still out of the corner of her eye, she sees the chess-playing bear.

By that evening the garden has gone, the fog has swallowed the house and there are muffled cries as watermen collide with one another on the river. In the street people are ringing bells and shouting to make way. Late at night there are people out on the water, calling for help.

Henri can't sleep. He stands at the window, looking out at the wall of fog, rather wishing he was in Berkeley Square, anywhere away from the noise on the river. Out of the fog appear the faces of the drowned sea captain and sailors. When their hollow eyes fade away, Mrs O'Donnell taps on the window to be let in. And he is haunted again by the thought that he hadn't been able to save her.

Jack Frost, Neva thinks, has taken up his throne. This is the sound of his tambourine, this is the noise of his drum, these are the cries that accompany his arrival. He has brought with him Death, wearing his cloak of consequence. This year he has brought his mistress, Frostiana.

On the second day a thick gloom has settled over everything. The frost has frozen the fog on windowpanes, forming strange coral shapes from an unknown sea. By the third day London has been silenced except for the eerie sound of ice moving in the ebbs and flows of the sluggish river and the occasional explosion when it careens into Blackfriars or London Bridge, making Neva jump.

Now there is silence in the street, silence on the river. The weather is every bit as bad as Neva had predicted, and is a challenge even for a house as well prepared as theirs. Candles must be burned night and day. Every morning the fires are stacked. George fears if they go out it will be hard to rekindle them.

Icicles form on the roof of the workshop and to Neva the house seems under a strange spell as if time has stopped, is waiting. On the fourth day, one of the maids comes running into the long drawing room hysterical, saying a man is walking in the sky.

Henri, Neva and George go out and on top of the garden gate is indeed the figure of a man, his shape contorted by the fog. When he raises his hat it looks as if he's taken off his head. He holds up a lantern that gives no more light than a candle through the thickness of the fog and in the muffled silence there is the beating of a drum. Then it's gone and the figure calls, 'Good evening.' Neva feels this could be disputed.

No one likes to think how high the death toll must be for those who are ill, those who are poor and whose houses are too cold. Jack Frost is merciless.

At night the noise of the ice grows louder and when the tide changes it sounds like artillery fire as huge blocks of ice smash into the bridges. There is genuine fear that London

Bridge may fall down and will at least sustain considerable damage from the battering of the tides.

On the fifth day the fog is gone but before there is a moment to celebrate, the snow starts, one innocent flake on top of another, until, thick and fast, it comes for two days. The drifts are so high they barricade the garden gate and on the river there are mountains of snow. In the greyish light London looks different, a city given over to the fairy world. Buildings take on strange shapes and the snow grows ever higher on the ice islands and freezes at night.

The mail coaches have given up. Communications to and from London have come to a halt. On 28th January there is a respite, a thaw. The streets turn to slush and the talk is that the bad weather is over. Neva knows the fog is just a prelude to the symphony of snow and more frost to come.

A letter arrives, proving the mail is getting through again. It's addressed to Henri. The chairman of the Royal Society congratulates him on his wife's extraordinary gift and her powers of prediction. This gentleman has never in his life witnessed such accuracy and a date is proposed for Mrs Dênou to address the Society.

30th January and Neva wakes, knowing the river is freezing. It has done it without anyone seeing in the middle of the night, on the turn of the tide, with plates of ice welded together by frost. London holds its breath, waiting to see if the surface is solid enough for a frost fair.

Henri and Neva go out. They're approaching London Bridge when they are overtaken by children. A circus is moving along Tooley Street with whistles, drums and a hurdy-gurdy man with a monkey wrapped in a fur. The procession is making its way to the river. Among the carnival folk Neva notices a man dressed like her first father, Andre, carrying a banner proclaiming he is the one-armed wrestling champion.

She and Henri stand on London Bridge and watch nervous young men place their feet on the ice, wondering if it's strong enough to carry their weight.

The next day booths and tents with flags flying are set up either side of a man-made street on the ice called the City Road. Thousands of Londoners descend to be entertained and robbed.

Cassie and Bos come with Camille to spend three days at the Friezland house and show Camille the wonders of the frost fair. Elise and Neva are pleased to see them and Neva tries not to show how worried she is.

'Don't be a noodle,' says Cassie when Neva does confide in her. 'There's nothing to worry about. I won't go on the ice if you say it's unsafe. But think, if it never came again and Camille had missed seeing this.'

'Cassie, admit it, you want to see it even more than Camille does.'

'You're most probably right,' says Cassie, laughing.

'But is it wise, when you're six months pregnant?'

'Please don't say that to Bos. The only thing that sends him into paroxysms of worry is the thought of anything happening to me. You would think I was the only woman ever to expect a baby.'

Neva says nothing and reassures herself. There is no need to be concerned.

When they do go to the frost fair the next day, Neva thinks it is wonderful to see how thrilled the little girl is at the sight of the booths and how excited she is when an elephant crosses the river. Elise takes her to see the toys for sale. Bos and Henri play skittles. Cassie and Neva want to go on the swing-boats and Bos pays the man double not to go too fast. The sun is setting and it begins to snow again, as if nature is cleaning up the mess man made that day, dusting down the river and making it beautiful once more.

The next morning Camille is heartbroken to find she has lost the Lapland doll Elise bought her. Neva feels a rising sense of panic that will not go away. To pacify Camille they go to find the doll-seller. A whole sheep is being roasted or rather burned, wine is free-flowing and Neva sees the one-armed wrestling champion is challenging every man to have a go. It is a day of such happiness that Neva refuses to hear the nagging voice of concern, quietly telling her she's missing something, something is wrong, something is waiting.

Lazy, that's what Aubrey thinks. They have all become lazy. Not him, not him. He knows what he's going to do. He waited to see if the usurper was right and on the 27th the great fog had rolled in. The predictions had been published in a newspaper and the reporter wrote that they were made by the Weather Woman. The usurper. There is only one Weather Woman and that's his, the one his father, Victor Friezland, made. He has her and he has a plan. He is ready, biding his time. He has saved up his money and rented a booth, a red and white striped tent. He misses Wardell but the carnival people are his friends. He likes them. They think he's funny. He has a pistol and knows soon no one will be laughing, not the usurper nor the whore, the whore who shot him. He's been out there watching, in the fog, in the snow, on the ice. He's seen them all, seen the whore fussing over the little girl crying for her doll. Enjoy your day, he thinks, it will be your last. He knows this time there will be no gap between expectation and execution. Yes, the usurper and the whore have grown lazy.

58

February 1814

The ice is melting.

Neva wakes on Saturday, 5th February, and knows that this morning it's unsafe for the frost fair to continue. The wind has shifted to the south and opening the shutters she can see the weather deceives. A light falling of snow hides the truth that, underneath, the ice is singing a farewell song. It is the song from her childhood.

Something inside her flutters, a fledgling bird. Has she imagined it? If she is pregnant, which she might be, then surely it's too soon to feel movement? Yet there it is again. No, she hasn't imagined it and she wonders if Eugene Jonas is determined to find another way to be near her. Is he a ghost? Is that what she accidentally called down all those years ago, a boneless spirit waiting to be given a skeleton?

She goes back to bed. 'Couldn't we stay here and make love and leave this day unattended?' she says, cuddling up to Henri. She takes his hand and puts it on her belly. He is awake now, alert, hardly daring to breath. She looks into his face. 'Is it a baby,' she asks, 'or is it the ghost of Eugene Jonas?'

'It's a baby,' he says. 'Our child.'

'But Cassie says the baby only moves after...' She stops. 'You knew?'

'I thought I might be wrong, and I should wait.'

'So, I'm not imagining this?'

'No,' he says, laughing, and gathers her to him.

'Perhaps all babies are ghosts until they take their first breath and forget whose ghosts they are.'

That morning at breakfast she says firmly that no one should be tempted to go to the frost fair.

Camille looks at her with huge violet eyes. 'Aunt Neva, couldn't we just go and find my doll?'

'No,' says Neva softly.

Last night they had all walked to London Bridge to look at the river in the moonlight. It was as picturesque as if it belonged to the land of fairies. Camille had been much taken by the notion.

'Is my doll lost forever?' she asks now.

'I'm sure we can find another doll,' says Cassie.

Camille rests her head on her hands and says, 'I hope she found a home with the frost fairies.'

'That's the spirit,' says Bos.

Cassie decides they should visit the menagerie in Bond Street. Bos says if it's all the same, he'd rather stay there. Elise has no interest in going as she can't abide seeing animals in cages.

Neva isn't sure if she wants to go either but Henri says, 'It will do you good to be away from the river and the noise of the ice. It will clear your head and you can tell Cassie your news.'

After the late breakfast, it's around one o'clock when Neva, Cassie and Camille set off in the marquess's carriage.

'What are you going to do, Bos?' asks Henri.

'Read by the fire. And you?' Bos looks at Henri and says, 'You look like the cat that got the cream or whatever the saying is.'

'Neva's with child. I felt it move this morning.'

'That's wonderful!'

'It is.' And there is a smile on his face as he and George go to see what damage the snow and ice have done to the workshop roof.

Elise, finding the house calm and having little to do, takes her shawl and basket. She has no intention of going to the frost fair, though she thinks another look wouldn't do any harm. After all, she doubts she will ever see one again. And she would like to get the little girl a present. Near London Bridge she had noticed the woman who had sold her the original doll. Elise slips out unnoticed. She'll be back in no time at all.

Henri and George have been busy all afternoon on the workshop roof. It's coming up to a quarter to five and the light is going when Jetsam starts barking. George goes to the gate and finds Mr Ratchet and Old Bones there. There's something about the moneylender's silhouette in the gloom that strikes Henri as wrong. He is off the roof in an instant.

Mr Ratchet is a man not given to being flustered but there is no doubt he is flustered now. 'Mr Dênou,' he says, raising his hat. 'I don't want to worry you and Mr Cutter but Old Bones and me came to make sure Neva and Mrs Friezland are safe at home.'

Henri says Neva has gone to Bond Street with Cassie and Camille, and Elise is probably in the kitchen. George goes to see.

'What's happened, Mr Ratchet?'

'I've been told there's a man on the ice who has this day set up a booth,' says Mr Ratchet. 'He was seen earlier having a fight with a woman, then he told everyone that he had the whore and now he wanted the usurper. He's wearing carnival clothes and has a banner that says "The One and Only…"

"Weather Woman," says Henri.

Mr Ratchet nods as George comes back. Even in this light, Henri can see he is as pale as a ghost.

'No one's seen her since about half-past one.'

'Me and Old Bones believe Aubrey has her,' says Mr Ratchet.

'Where?' says George, his voice rising in panic.

'On the ice at the frost fair.'

When the *Sea Wind* was sinking, Henri remembers, a sense of calm overcame him as he confronted what looked like his inevitable fate. Now, putting on his greatcoat, he feels that same irrational calm.

Henri finds Bos still reading by the fire. 'Elise is missing,' says Henri.

'Missing? Surely she'll be back at any minute?'

'I fear Aubrey Friezland has taken her. And he wants Neva too.'

'Oh Lord,' says Bos, springing to his feet.

'Listen to me,' says Henri. 'When Cassie and Neva return you are not to let Neva come looking for us. It will make matters worse. And I want you to have a doctor waiting here.'

'But…' Bos stops. On Henri's face is a look Bos hasn't seen since he watched him play cribbage for high stakes at Mrs Leach's, the night they met. 'Of course,' he says.

Jetsam is charging this way and that. Henri takes him by the collar and tells the two worried maids that on no account is he to be let out.

It is now raining hard. Henri, George and Mr Ratchet make their way towards London Bridge. They are going against the crowd and it is slow work, though Old Bones's pugnacious presence is helpful. Everyone is coming off the ice and the talk is all about the thaw and how sad it is the ice couldn't have stayed a bit longer. On London Bridge they lean over the balustrade and look down at booths that have been abandoned and the debris of a thousand people who have found their wonder world melting away.

'There,' says George, pointing.

It's hard to see but there is one booth that looks newly set up.

'Are you sure?' asks Henri.

'I'm sure,' says George.

Their best hope is the steps at the side of the bridge. People are pouring off the ice now and Henri, George and Mr Ratchet have to push against the surge. Henri looks up when he hears shouts from a crowd of apprentices on the bridge. 'Get off, get off, you madman! The ice is melting!'

Henri can now clearly see the new red and white striped booth and Aubrey, his face white against the approaching night. He is dressed in a garish carnival costume and dancing a mad jig. He is shouting that he is waiting for the usurper.

'Dabbs!' Mr Ratchet has spotted the ferryman.

Mr Dabbs has been doing a roaring trade on these steps, charging tuppence to fourpence, depending how well dressed his customers are, for the privilege of going onto the ice. But now the water round the steps has turned to slush.

'Mr Ratchet, you and the other gentlemen should get back, the ice is going,' says Mr Dabbs.

There isn't much time, Henri knows this. 'There is a woman out there in that booth,' he says to the ferryman. 'A madman has kidnapped her and we need your ferry and those planks of wood.'

'It doesn't matter if he's kidnapped the Queen of bloody England,' says Mr Dabbs. 'There's little to be done. That, sir, is a dead man dancing.' He points at Aubrey.

'I want you to keep everyone back,' says Henri. 'I'll pay

for any damage to your boat. We'll need your help – and I'll make it worth your while.'

A group of young men, most of them drunk, come up behind them. They are determined to go on the ice. Mr Ratchet and Old Bones turn on them and they find themselves quickly heading up the stairs.

Mr Dabbs sighs. 'All right,' he says. 'It's your funeral.'

Henri takes off his hat and greatcoat. The cold is shocking, his mind is clear. It's still raining as he steps onto the ice.

'I have the whore,' shouts Aubrey. 'I have the whore but I will let her go if you bring me the usurper.'

The ice is moving. Henri can feel it under his feet. He is on board a different type of vessel in this frozen ocean.

Aubrey sees him, recognises Wardell's nephew. 'I have no beef with you. Go back.'

Cold rage and the memory of his failure to rescue Mrs O'Donnell propel Henri further across the ice. It's hard to see where he is going. He passes abandoned tents and banners, upended tables and cups and saucers left behind in the sudden exodus. Only one flag flies across the sky, the words *THE WEATHER WOMAN* occasionally catching the light.

'Get back,' shouts Aubrey again. 'Come any closer and I'll kill you.' Henri can now see he has a pistol. He's drunk, Henri thinks. Or drugged. And then he's gone.

Henri didn't see where Aubrey went but he's reached the booth and as he pulls back the flap he expects to hear a shot. Elise is sitting on a bale of straw, her face caked with white powder. She starts to say something but Henri raises his finger to his lips. A fire burns in a brazier and this light illuminates the small space. Henri can see Aubrey's not in there.

Behind Elise, Victor's wooden Weather Woman, in a Madonna-blue gown and red slippers, is perched on a chair balanced on a makeshift altar of straw bales. Her face has been painted blue and on her head is a gold paper crown.

Henri unties Elise. 'Can you walk?'

'Yes, I think so,' she says.

Henri sees a pole supporting the Weather Woman. He takes it and the wooden doll slumps forwards.

'Keep behind me,' he says.

Aubrey is waiting outside the booth, the pistol in his shaking hand. One swing of the pole and Henri has batted it from his grasp. It slides across the ice. With three punches he has Aubrey down and unconscious.

'Apologies, *Tante Elise*,' says Henri, lifting a startled Elise over his shoulder. 'Stay still.' There are cheers from the apprentices on the bridge. The spectacle has attracted quite a crowd.

Aubrey has come to and is scrabbling across the ice, desperate to find the pistol.

The ice feels thinner to Henri. The tide is battering at it, the water longing to own its kingdom once more. Behind him Aubrey shouts, 'And down we all go.' There is a shot and the ice near Henri's feet splits with a high-pitched shriek.

Henri doesn't rush. Carefully, very carefully, he feels his way. Now he is on an island of ice, not far from George who is on the ferry boat. He has pushed out a plank as far as it will go and he and Mr Dabbs have secured it as best they can.

'Hurry,' shouts Mr Dabbs, 'it won't hold.'

Henri puts Elise down. The ice island moves in an alarming way and he holds her tight until they find their equilibrium and the ice rights itself. The plank just reaches them. 'You must run, *Tante Elise*, and don't stop.'

She looks terrified. 'You can do it,' shouts George.

'Go,' says Henri, his voice a command.

Elise doesn't hesitate. But after two steps she slips, and the plank breaks free. She's half in and half out of the freezing water but George is there.

'I have her,' he calls.

'Jump, sir,' yells Mr Dabbs to Henri.

But the island of ice is hurtling out into midstream. It's taking all his strength to keep his balance. Any sudden movement and he will be in the water. The river is regaining its tide and he is being pulled towards Blackfriars Bridge. He must think quickly. A lighter that has come free of its moorings bangs against him and as he jumps into it, he realises he's no safer than he was before – a small mountain of ice is careering towards him. Blackfriars Bridge looms over him and all is disappearing into darkness.

Mr Ratchet has limped up the steps with surprising speed, shouting for a hackney carriage. George is soaked, carrying a stunned Elise who is trembling with cold. She hasn't said a word and he is fearful she might not survive this.

Mr Ratchet helps her into the carriage and as George gets in he says, 'Old Bones and I'll go and look for Mr Dênou.' He tells the driver, 'The Friezland house, off Tooley Street – and hurry.'

And Mr Ratchet slams the carriage door.

'Well, Old Bones,' he says as the carriage rattles off towards the bridge, 'have we lost Mr Dênou?' He sighs. 'Better go and settle up with Dabbs.'

George puts his arms round Elise. 'Don't you die on me,' he says. Elise's teeth are chattering and he holds her to him. He thinks he's never been this cold. Halfway across the bridge the carriage comes to a halt, the driver shouting. From the window George glimpses flames lighting up the ice. With a jolt the carriage sets off again. 'Not far now,' he says to Elise.

Mr Dabbs and Mr Ratchet watch Aubrey dancing with a large wooden doll on the ice outside his booth. Up and down, up and down, he dances. Those on the bridge encourage the madman in his frenzied jig. Mr Dabbs thinks, what a waste, two serviceable bodies going tonight. The water is rising and he, Mr Ratchet and Old Bones retreat up the steps while not taking their eyes off Aubrey Friezland.

Aubrey has knocked over the brazier. The red and white striped booth is on fire and he and the doll are still dancing but the ice he's on moves with great speed upriver, whirling round and round as the flames burn higher. Only at the last does he scream for help then he is lost in the sound of artillery fire as the ice explodes against Blackfriars Bridge.

59

Neva knows the moment she, Cassie and Camille arrive home that something is wrong. She can hear Jetsam howling pitifully before she opens the door. She finds Bos in the kitchen. He looks older than he did this morning.

He says, with forced cheerfulness, 'Camille, run up to your room. Agnes will go with you.'

The maid takes the little girl's hand.

'But I want to show you my doll, Father,' says Camille. 'We met Grandfather and he gave it to me.'

This startling news would at any other time have been the main topic of conversation. But Bos says, 'Later, little one.'

Camille goes with Agnes. Neva looks at Bos and feels the floor melting beneath her.

'Where is he? Where's Henri?' she says and in the dimness of the kitchen she sees the mangled chess-playing bear sitting at the table.

George comes in. He looks completely washed out. 'Neva,' he says and stops before saying, 'Neva, Elise went missing. We didn't realise until about five o'clock. The doctor is with her now. She's very poorly but he thinks she'll get over it in time.'

Cassie lets out a little cry and goes to Elise.

'Sit down,' says George gently to Neva who is digging her nails into the table to balance herself.

'Tell me what has happened,' she says.

George takes a shaky breath. 'We – that is Henri, Mr Ratchet and Old Bones and I went to find Elise. Aubrey Friezland had her prisoner… in his booth at the frost fair. He'd beaten her up… quite badly…' His words trail off. There are no words for what he has to say to Neva.

'Where is Henri?' she says again.

There is silence. Some silences are too deep, this one is unfathomable. In her mind's eye she sees again the Punch and Judy man floating off down the river.

She says carefully, as if speaking a foreign language, a language stripped of hope, 'George – where is he?'

Tears trickle down the Bosun's face as he tells her.

'Did you see him – actually see him go into Blackfriars Bridge?'

Everything is a question. There are no answers. Or no answers she wants to hear.

'I saw him going that way, yes.' He pauses. 'A mountain of ice was bearing down on him. But it was hard to see in the dark.'

Neva knows that's not what she asked.

George wipes his face with the back of his hand. 'The ice hit the bridge. It sounded as if a cannon had been fired.'

Neva thinks they're all moving slowly, as if they're underwater. Perhaps they are. 'I'm going to find him,' she says. She knows she has to get out of the kitchen, do something.

'No,' says Bos, firmly. 'That's not what Henri wanted and it's not what you're going to do.'

'Mr Ratchet went to look for him with Old Bones,' says

George. 'We're waiting for him to...' He stops then starts again. 'If Henri isn't in the water, he'll come home and he'll want you here to greet him.'

Henri can't be dead, she thinks. It's not possible. But she's familiar enough with the river and its ways to know it is more than probable. She thought the ice had been waiting for her, not Henri. Never Henri.

The kitchen is lit by only three candles. It falls into darkness and no one seems to have the energy to light more. Perhaps the truth is better hidden. There is nothing more to say, there is nothing more that Neva wants to say. She sits staring at the kitchen door. She can't see Elise as that would mean accepting what George has told her and she can't do that.

It's after nine o'clock when Mr Ratchet and Old Bones arrive, both looking frozen. The news isn't good. From what he's heard, Mr Ratchet believes Aubrey drowned. It's also being said the other man didn't stand a chance. The lighter he'd climbed into broke up the second it hit the bridge and became no more than kindling.

The news swirls round the room but doesn't settle on Neva. She sits stroking Jetsam, who's stopped whining. 'No,' she says. 'He's not dead. He cannot be dead.'

About five minutes later there's a knock on the door. The maid, fearful of more bad news, tentatively opens it and Jetsam springs up, slips through it and is gone. The maid cries out.

Neva too is up. She runs out of the kitchen door calling for Jetsam and nearly bumps into a lad of about nine, looking up at her anxiously. The boy is out of breath.

He says, 'I've been in a dither of a pickle trying to find this house. Up and down the street I've been which isn't good on account of I'm supposed to be here faster, my Pa boasting that my legs are sprung right for running. My Pa is the one-armed wrestling champion,' he adds proudly.

'And the reason you are supposed to be here faster?' asks Neva. A kernel of hope grows in her heart.

The lad takes a gulp of air. 'It's to stop the lady who is going to have a baby from getting a shock because the man on the bridge is all right.' He looks up, quite pleased with himself. 'I meant to say the man on the bridge is right behind us.'

Neva is out in Tooley Street. A crowd of people is coming towards her, all dressed in carnival costumes, and Jetsam is jumping up at the chess-playing bear. It seems suddenly to Neva that the street is empty, that there is no one there apart from the chess-playing bear, no longer mangled, but walking towards her calling her name. The bear has the face of Henri. She puts her hands to his cheeks. He is made of flesh and blood. He puts his arms round her and rocks her.

He says, 'My love,' and it's Henri's voice.

Is she speaking? She thinks she is. She's trying to say, 'I thought I had lost you, I thought you were drowned.'

Following them into the kitchen for a reason Neva can make no sense of is her father, Andre Tarshin. She's not sure if this chess-playing bear is real or is what her mind so longs for, that she has created it from the fabric of wishes. She is falling. She is falling.

Neva wakes up on the couch in the long drawing room. A fire is roaring and the doctor is saying she fainted and not to worry as the baby has a good heartbeat.

'Where's Henri?' she says, hardly daring to breathe.

'He's gone to change,' says the doctor. She sits up, regrets it and has to lie down again. 'It was clever of the wrestling champion to put him into the bear costume. He would have been in a worse way if he hadn't got warm before coming home.'

Henri is in the long drawing room, looking much more

himself. He gathers her into his arms. Try as she might she can't stop the tears. She thinks they belong to an ancient river of fear and so powerful are those waters that they shake her soul.

Neva is slowly convincing herself that Henri is here with her.

She remembers what she hasn't asked. 'How is Auntie?'

'The doctor is with her again,' says Henri. 'She will survive, but she's very badly shaken, and she sprained her ankle.'

Are there borders in time, Neva wonders, where you walk from one possibility into another? If she searched the kitchen, she would find it, for this kitchen she's now walking into isn't the one she was in, when she first came home that day. There is food on the table, more candles have been lit and Cassie is taking a tray to Elise.

Henri says, 'Let me,' and Neva goes with him into Elise's bedchamber. George is sitting beside Elise, holding her hand. Her face is swollen and her eyes are closed.

'Look, Elise,' says George, 'look who's here.' He stands up so Henri can sit next to her. 'She won't open her eyes.'

'You were very brave, *Tante Elise*,' says Henri.

Elise's eyes flutter open at the sound of his voice. 'Henri,' she says, 'I feared you were dead. And I couldn't bear it, I truly couldn't.'

'Neither could I bear losing you,' says Henri.

Neva, who has been in this room only briefly, looks up and for the first time notices the painted ships. In the flickering candlelight they appear to be moving. And there is Auntie floating above them, holding a cup and saucer.

'Who painted this?' she says.

'It was George,' says Elise.

'George is in love with you, isn't he?'

'I'm a lucky woman. I know it seems too soon after... Do you mind, Neva?'

'No, Auntie. Cassie thinks George has been in love with you for a long time.'

'Since I first tasted her cooking,' he says and sits down and kisses her hand.

Elise smiles. 'We're two pebbles from the same beach,' she says, sleepily.

Henri and Neva return to the kitchen where Mr Ratchet is telling Bos it is a miracle Henri survived. 'I had him down for a watery grave – but Old Bones thought he might prevail.'

Bos pours him a glass of excellent burgundy and Cassie offers him a slice of pie.

'I want to know how you were rescued, Mr Dênou,' says Mr Ratchet.

'So do I,' says Cassie, sitting down heavily and folding her hands protectively across her belly.

'I was lucky,' says Henri. 'I made a leap for one of the piers. It was pitch black until Aubrey obligingly set his booth alight. Then I saw a rope and the way to the top of the bridge where the one-armed wrestler was waiting for me. It was he who lowered the rope. I was unbelievably cold and saved, in a way, by a bear costume.'

He and Neva are standing and he is holding Neva close.

The evening, she thinks, feels unreal and perhaps it is, as unreal as the frost fair. By some miracle they have been washed into a new, hopeful day the waters of the Thames have given them as a gift.

That night Neva lies in Henri's arms listening to his heartbeat.

'You know what all this shows,' he says.

'That you are an extraordinarily brave man.'

'No, it shows your predictions were accurate to the day, to the hour. You, my love, are a force of nature, the weather in you electric.'

★ ★ ★

Outside the ice is thundering into the bridges as the tide changes and in her dream Neva sees the child kneeling on the ice, whispering to the river. What is she saying? What is she asking?

The river answers her as only a river can.

'I will keep flowing, my tides will come and go, the relics of lovers' footsteps will be hidden in the silt of my ancient beds.

'I, the keeper of secrets, of treasure, of bones, of the wished for, of the drowned, of the murdered, my past and future merging in my ebbs and flows, in the darkness of my sullied, silted waters that once ran blue and clear.

'I will wait, wait and wait for the ice to return once more, to hold me still again in her frozen embrace.

'I will never be satisfied with the shortness of her stay or the tragedy of our melting.

'I am surprised at my own submission to her icy touch, and that I, the oldest and most powerful river, should find his tides majestically transformed, his surface solid enough to bear the weight of a child's wish.'

Acknowledgements

Every book is a strange journey in its own way. I had no plan for this one, only the beginning in my head and a rough synopsis that I didn't stick to. The novel grew organically and consequently I got lost and spent a lot of time up blind alleys and battling my way out of them.

First I must thank my daughter Freya Corry for her editorial input in the early chapters. She kept me up to the mark when it came to describing the workings of the Weather Woman, for which I am immensely grateful.

I find it helpful to hear how my words sound and so I thank the patient people I've read endlessly to – Rodrigo Canete, Jane Fior, Georgie Adams and my wonderful sister Lucy Gardner in Melbourne. Week after week she listened to chapter after chapter during long phone calls. Her eagerness to know what happened next kept me going.

A huge thank you to my dog-walker Becky Congreve who this book is dedicated to. I have a magical, one-eyed, miniature Yorkie called Sparrow who has the personality of a diva. She loves nothing better than to be in the middle of a pack of dogs on a long walk with her best beloved Becky.

Many, many thanks to Rosie de Courcy who had to wait quite some time for this book. She has been a brilliant editor. All books require a great deal of work and time but what they need as well is a good publishing house. I've been very lucky finding that in Head of Zeus. I hope these acknowledgements lead the reader to realise that writing is not a solitary activity but involves many people other than the author: a great editor, a cover designer, a sales team and more. All with the push and enthusiasm to get the book into the shops.

A big shout-out to my agent Catherine Clark who I adore, and to Jacky Bateman who came to work on this book when I'd got myself into a right muddle and as always proved to be indispensable to the end.

My grateful thanks to Adam Mars-Jones who – unbelievably – reads my manuscripts and gives insightful guidance. If my historical facts are accurate it's due to his encyclopaedic brain.

I must acknowledge the London Library, which is full of the most extraordinary books. There I found White's Club's Betting Books and a slim volume that proved to be a source of information on all the English frost fairs. At the London Library I find books that touch the period of history I'm researching; to me they smell of a time long gone.

Writing a book is like pushing a heavy wheelbarrow full of ideas and words up a mountain. Days are lost in another world. In the end, dear reader, the success of this book rests with you.

Sally Gardner
Hastings, June 2022

About the Author

Sally Gardner gained a first-class degree at a leading London art college and became a successful theatre costume designer before illustrating and writing books. Her debut novel *I, Coriander* won the Nestlé Gold Award and she is also a Costa and Carnegie prize-winner. Her books have been translated all over the world and have sold over two million copies.